# Wish Upon A STUD Series

elise sax

*Wish Upon A Stud Series* is a work of fiction. Names, characters, places, and incidents are the products of the author's imagination or are used fictitiously. Any resemblance to actual events, locales, or persons, living or dead, is entirely coincidental.


Published in the United States by Elise Sax

Cover design: Natasha Brown
Formatted by: Jesse Kimmel-Freeman

Printed in the United States of America

elisesax.com
elisesax@gmail.com
http://elisesax.com/mailing-list.php
https://www.facebook.com/ei.sax.9
@theelisesax

ISBN-10: 1508676909
ISBN–13: 978-1508676904

Wish Upon A Stud Series #1

# Going DOWN

elise sax

# *Going* DOWN

(Wish Upon A Stud – Book 1)

elise sax

*For my Street Team. You know who you are. And you're fabulous. Thank you.*

# CHAPTER 1

I clutch my lucky silver dollar firmly in my hand. I don't want to give it up, but this wish is really important, and I can't leave it up to chance.

I'm down to my last two hundred bucks. I'm a month behind in my rent, and I'm in pain from giving myself my own bikini wax in order to save money. Nothing can get between me and this wish coming true.

The wishing fountain is in the center of town, right next to my apartment. In fact, I can see it from my bedroom window, but this is the first time that I'm trying it out. I've been saving up my wish for when I'm desperate. And boy, am I desperate.

It's the ugliest fountain I've ever seen, bone dry with just a few coins, dirt, and a used condom at its bottom. But it's famous for its wishes. I'm not crazy to believe in it. It has a long history as a wishing fountain. It's been on the news. Katie Couric. Oprah.

I focus on my wish, pull my arm back, and release the coin.

Please let me get this role.

Please let me ace this audition.

With my wish out into the universe, I shut my eyes and throw the silver dollar into the fountain. It lands on the cracked plaster, making a loud clanking sound in the town square.

A breeze blows, which I take as a good sign. I swear I feel different, like I'm infused with good luck. I sure need some good luck. I open my eyes, half expecting an angel to appear, or at the very least, a leprechaun.

But I'm on my own. The sleepy little town of Esperanza isn't exactly bustling with people on its busiest day, and today it's particularly dead.

I step down from the fountain and go on my way. I don't have to go far. Just across the street to the diner, which is located on the bottom floor of my apartment building.

Built in the 1950's, the building is no-frills and covered in pink stucco. There are twelve units and four flights. I'm on the top floor, next to the landlord.

This location has its good points and its drawbacks. I get woken up every morning with the smell of fresh coffee brewing from the diner downstairs, which is a good point. However, I'm also tempted to eat a slice of Mack's homemade cherry pie to go along with it, which is a drawback.

And that's the other plus and drawback: Mack.

I open the door to the diner, making the bell ring. The diner is enjoying a lull in the day, that time between breakfast and lunch where everyone is busy at work or at home. Mack is wiping off a table but looks up when I enter.

"Sit anywhere," he says.

I take a seat by the window. Without having to order, Mack fills my mug with coffee. He looks like he does every day. He's a scruffy, thirty-something guy with perfect bone structure, thick dark hair, and blue eyes that will laser beam right through any woman directly to her uterus.

"I got pie," he says.

"I don't want pie. I'm an actress. Actresses don't eat pie."

"You're an actress?"

"You know that I'm an actress. So no more out of you."

At least I'm trying to be an actress. I've never actually gotten a job, but I've taken three classes, and a casting agent, who I met while shopping at The Gap, told me at the pocket tee table that I have what it takes to become a star.

"How about a sandwich?" Mack asks.

"I have to be skinny."

"You are skinny. You've got no ass, no boobs, and your collarbones are sticking out."

"I do too have boobs." It's true. I do have boobs. I'm a 36C, which is huge on my small, five-foot-two frame. I don't know what he's talking about. Is he blind?

Mack takes a step back and studies me. Most specifically, he studies my chest. He cocks his head to the side and squints, as if he's having a really hard time finding my cleavage.

It's not hard to find. I'm wearing a tank top and a push up bra. I'm the queen of cleavage. I'm cleavage and nothing else. I could signal ships at sea with my breasts.

He shrugs. "Yeah, maybe you do have boobs. But last time I looked, you don't have an ass."

"What the hell do you know? You don't understand what Hollywood wants. I need to be skinny."

"Okay. Okay. How about a salad?"

"No! Salad will bloat me."

"So, you'll fart. Problem solved."

"Mack, you don't understand. Being an actress is very demanding."

He plops down on the chair across from me and leans forward. His eyes are big and they suddenly turn dark and focus entirely on me. My heart does a little hiccup, which I try to ignore, but Mack always has this effect on me. If he was on the menu, he would be the house special. Delicious and probably very bad for my health.

"I'm not going to leave here without feeding you," he says. "I'm sure Meryl Streep eats."

"Nobody cares about Meryl Streep. They care about Angelina Jolie, and she doesn't eat."

At least I don't think so. I mean, she's awfully skinny. No bloat there.

"What the hell do you mean nobody cares about Meryl Streep? Deer Hunter? Sophie's Choice?" he says, counting on his fingers.

"Tomb Raider, Mr. & Mrs. Smith," I counter, sticking my fingers in his face. Mack shakes his head.

"Even skinny Angelina Jolie eats," he says, obviously annoyed with me.

"No, she doesn't."

"If I have to shove the food down your throat, that's what I'm going to do."

"That's charming, Mack. Violence against women. Not your most attractive quality."

Mack grins and raises an eyebrow. He drags his chair on the linoleum floor and puts it down next to me. He sits down so close that his knees graze my legs. I clamp my mouth closed, in case he really is going to shove food down my throat. But I'm not exactly scared. First of all, I'm hungry. Hungrier than Angelina Jolie. Second of all, Mack's chest is stretching the fabric of his t-shirt, making my hormones do the Take Me Mambo.

His hair is so thick and gorgeous. I'm sorely tempted to run my fingers through it, but I hold myself back. I hate that I'm so attracted to him. He's a gruff, contemptuous man. A confirmed bachelor, who I'm sure doesn't even like women. I mean, he's never been nice to me.

However, he smells nice. And even though his wardrobe is stuck in the Grunge period, he definitely takes care of himself, and his jeans fit perfectly in all the right places.

He scoots even closer. His cheek is almost touching mine. There's a zing of electricity between us, which feels fabulous, and if

I'm not mistaken, is coming directly from him.

He touches my forearm, letting his fingers trail up and down in a sensual, seductive way.

"Angelina Jolie has nothing on you, Marion," he says, his voice low in his throat, deep and gravelly, like he's choking with desire.

At least, that's how I want to look at it. He probably just has phlegm.

Meanwhile, my tongue has swollen, and I think I might be having a coronary. "Okay. Pie à la mode. Two scoops of vanilla, and be quick about it," I hear myself say.

I'm immediately racked with guilt. I'm positive Angelina Jolie doesn't eat cherry pie and ice cream. But I have no choice. Since I don't drink or do drugs, pie is my only recourse against an overwhelming desire to jump Mack's bones.

"That's my girl." Mack pats my arm and hops up, dragging his chair back to the other side of the table and tucking it under. He trots to the counter to fetch me my pie. I catch myself staring at his ass as he walks, and I pinch myself. It's a psychological training technique I picked up when my mother tried to stop smoking. Every time I'm attracted to Mack, I hurt myself.

"I'm not your girl," I say to his back.

"Oh, yes, you are."

# CHAPTER 2

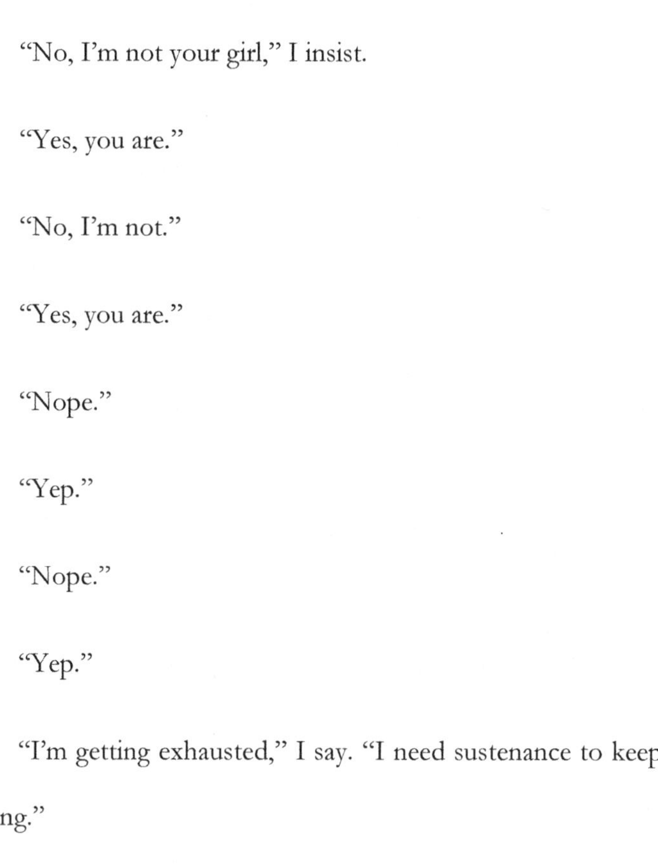

"No, I'm not your girl," I insist.

"Yes, you are."

"No, I'm not."

"Yes, you are."

"Nope."

"Yep."

"Nope."

"Yep."

"I'm getting exhausted," I say. "I need sustenance to keep me going."

Mack plops two scoops of ice cream onto a slice of cherry pie and brings it over to me.

"Did you remember to warm up the pie?" I ask.

"Hey, Mona Lisa didn't tell Da Vinci how to paint. So, you don't tell me how to serve pie."

But I know he's warmed the pie because the ice cream is already melting on top of it. I put a big forkful in my mouth and let the sugar calm my nerves.

"How long have you been coming in here?" Mack hovers over me as I stuff my face.

"Two years," I say with my mouth full. "Ever since I moved into the building."

"Two years. We're neighbors, and I feed you every single day. That means you're my girl."

We lock eyes. He's got a magical thing going on with his eyeballs where he's speaking to me through them. It's like some kind of Vulcan mind meld thing but instead of Dr. Spock, it's sexy diner owner psychic communication. I take another bite of pie without breaking our eye contact. I can't break away. He's got me in his tractor beam of hotness.

But here's the thing: After two years, he's never made a move. Never jumped my bones. Never taken me into his arms and stuck his tongue down my throat.

"So, we're friends?" I ask.

"I wouldn't go that far."

Of course he wouldn't. He's been feeding me for two years, but we've also been fighting during that whole time. We don't agree on anything.

I eat the last of my pie. "Yep, that would be a stretch."

"Are you done? I'm locking up early today."

"You're what?" Mack never locks up early. He's always in the diner. He's my go-to for breakfast, lunch, dinner, Thanksgiving, and the occasional midnight snack when I can't sleep.

Not that he's in the diner at midnight. After diner hours, I have to pound on his apartment door to get him to feed me, which isn't hard because he lives on the fourth floor right next door to me. He's my landlord, and so far, he hasn't made a stink about me being behind in the rent.

"Locking up early. I got places to be."

"Places?"

I wonder if he has a date. I don't think he's gone out with anyone since I've known him, which is odd, considering he looks like Channing Tatum and owns his own building.

"You know. Places," Mack says.

"Sure. Places."

He yanks at my chair. "So, you gotta get up if you've finished stuffing your face."

"What do you mean stuffing my face? I didn't stuff my face. You stuffed my face!"

What nerve. I stand up and wag my finger at him. He's tall, and I only come up to mid-level on his chest, but I'm spitting mad with a fabulous manicure, and I figure I can probably scratch his eyes out before he has a chance to retaliate.

But he's saved by the bell. The door opens with a ding, and Raine Harper walks in. She waves a picnic basket at us.

"Sorry I'm late," she says. "What a day!"

Raine stops in her tracks. She stares at Mack and me and seems to give my finger, which is poised right under Mack's nose as if I'm going to pick it, extra attention.

"You guys will never change," she says, rolling her eyes. "You're like Tom & Jerry, but horny."

"What are you talking about?" Mack growls. "You're talking Greek. No sense at all. I'll get your order."

I think I'm hallucinating because Mack turns a deep shade of red, which is totally out of character for him. Nothing fazes him, normally. He grabs Raine's basket and storms into the kitchen with his head down.

"What's with him?" I ask Raine.

"Like you don't know." She plops down onto a chair and rests her elbows on the table, her chin in her hands. "You've got that man so tied up in knots, he's six inches shorter."

I sit down next to her. "You think so?" I ask her, hopefully.

"You should put him out of his misery and jump his bones. He probably has a major case of blue balls."

I gasp. "So, he's not seeing anybody?"

"Come on, Marion. He only has eyes for you. Is there pie around?"

"I'll get you a slice," I say. "Don't stop talking."

I grab a plate and fork from behind the counter and scoop her up a slice of pie, even though Mack hates it when I go behind the counter. But Raine stops talking, and her head slips off her hands and lands on the table with a loud thud.

For a minute, I think she's had some kind of stroke or heart attack and is slumped on the table, dead. But she moans, signaling that she's still alive. It's not a pain kind of moan; it's more of an I-hate-life kind of moan.

"Eat the pie. Quick. It'll help," I say, putting the plate next to her mouth. I find that food is the best medicine for just about everything.

"I'm not hungry. I'm never eating again. I have to lose

forty pounds by next Wednesday." She moans even louder against the table. She's slumped over in total defeat.

I try to think of a diet that can melt forty pounds of fat in less than a week, but I can't think of one. No carbs can only go so far.

"Why do you have to lose forty pounds?"

"By next Wednesday."

"Why do you have to lose forty pounds by next Wednesday?"

"That's when Wade Gates is coming back to town," she moans again. Her face is in profile, and she's talking out of one side of her mouth. Her arms are hanging down under the table, and her hair is flopped over. She hasn't taken a bite of the pie, and I'm sorely tempted to eat it for her.

Wade Gates is the best-looking man to ever come out of Esperanza. And the richest. He's a big corporate attorney for one of the Silicon Valley monster companies. He grew up next to Raine's family's ranch by the lake, and Raine has had a crush on him since she learned to walk.

"You don't need to lose any weight for him. You're beautiful." I'm not lying. She's beautiful. Piercing green eyes, thick black hair, flawless skin, and a button nose. But she's also chubby, and Wade goes for the stick-thin model types. He's a total jerk. He's not an annoying jerk like Mack. He's just a plain old jerk. Mean.

"No, I'm not beautiful. I'm drooling on the table."

"You're drooling on my table. There's a whole puddle of it next to your face," Mack growls. He's returned from the kitchen, carrying Raine's basket, and it's filled with burgers and fries and other lunch food. I can smell it, and it's giving me a hankering to eat something more than just pie.

Raine's family owns several vacation properties at the lake, and Raine handles most of the catering and deliveries. Some vacationers request Mack's food, and I don't blame them. Raine is an excellent cook, but Mack is the best at everything diner food.

"Sorry," she says, sitting up and wiping off the table with a napkin. "I was just contemplating burying myself alive."

"That sounds like a lot of work. The ground around here is clay. Very hard to dig," Mack says.

"Shut up," I hiss. "Don't you see that Raine's in crisis? You're such an oaf." I punch him in the shoulder for emphasis.

"Don't worry, Raine," I continue. "I'll come by next week and do your hair and give you a manicure. You'll look amazing."

"Wade's a jerk, anyway," Mack says.

Raine hops up, and the chair falls back onto the floor. She's fighting mad. I half expect steam to come out of her nose. Nobody bad-mouths Wade Gates in front of Raine. She's got it bad.

She stomps her foot and grabs the basket out of Mack's hands. "What the hell do you know? You're a jerk. You've got blue balls!"

She throws open the front door, knocking the bell off its perch to land with a clang onto the floor, and storms out. I catch Mack adjusting his pants. His face is red, again, and I wonder just how blue his balls really are, and if he really has eyes only for me.

Mack reattaches the bell onto the door. "That was pleasant," he says. "But it won't upset my day."

"It won't?" I ask. If it were me, I'd be pretty upset if someone yelled about my blue balls in the middle of the diner.

"Nope, because I'm going fishing."

"Oh…" So that's where he's going. Mack has his own fishing boat. He's talked about it, but I've never actually seen it. He's a fanatic fisherman. Half of his place is devoted to fishing gear. I like fish sticks and the occasional tuna sandwich, but I don't see the attraction of getting seasick while I wait to hook some poor, unsuspecting fish through its mouth.

I shudder. Blech. The thought of it makes me nauseated.

"Oh my God!" I yell, suddenly remembering my audition. "I'm going to be late! I need to get dressed in a hurry."

I push Mack out of the way and make a beeline for the back door of the diner. "Hold on. I'm coming with you," Mack calls out.

I keep walking. I hear him close up the diner and jog

toward me. We walk out the back door together, and he turns to lock it. "Can't be too careful," he says.

I think you can be too careful. Esperanza isn't exactly a hub of criminality. I think we've had one murder, and that happened in 1863. Since then, most people keep their doors unlocked.

We walk through the tiny hallway toward the elevator. The building is quiet. I'm Mack's only resident while he renovates. He doesn't seem to be in a hurry to finish, and he's doing all the work himself, renovating from the bottom up.

"After you," he says, letting me enter the elevator first. I push number four, and the door closes with an ominous creak.

"One of these days, this elevator is going to die, and I think it's sooner rather than later," I say.

"I'll bet you a million dollars this elevator outlives us all. It's built to last. Not like stuff is built nowadays. There's no place safer than right here."

The elevator is small, and Mack stands very close to me. I

can feel the heat bouncing off of him, or maybe it's just that we're in an enclosed space without any air conditioning.

Nope. It's definitely him.

Mack traces my cheek with his finger and tucks a strand of hair behind my ear. "It was in your face," he croaks.

I nod. Time freezes. He leans over until our faces are almost touching, and I'm sure that he's going to kiss me. I'm torn between excitement and panic. If we finally do something about this attraction, what will happen if it all goes kablooey? All of my relationships go kablooey sooner or later. It's sort of a sure thing.

If that happens with Mack, where will I get my coffee? Where will I find another landlord who won't mind if I'm behind in my rent?

And what will I do without my daily dose of Mack?

# CHAPTER 3

No need to worry about a failed relationship with Mack, because there isn't going to be any kind of relationship with him. Before anything can happen between us, we arrive at the fourth floor, and the elevator doors open with a loud groan.

"You're so wrong about this elevator," I say, stepping out.

"Could be. I'm wrong about a lot of things. Good luck on your audition." He steps out and heads down the hall to his apartment.

"Oh!" I cry. "You never say good luck to an actress. You say break a leg. I need to break a leg."

"Sorry," he says, unlocking his door. "I hope you break your leg."

"I don't think that's exactly what you're supposed to say."

I stand by my front door, too scared to open it. Suddenly, I'm wracked with self-doubt. My self-confidence level has plummeted to new lows. What was I thinking? I can't be an actress. I don't know anything about acting.

Actors train for years. They do theater before they do television or films. They starve for their craft. I'm not starving. I just ate pie.

Besides, I've got nothing to wear to the audition.

"What's wrong?" he says, looking at me. "Go on in. What are you waiting for?"

"What do I wear? I've got nothing to wear. Actresses wear clothes. I mean, they usually wear clothes. I don't have clothes. I can't go like this!" I shout, pulling at my tank top. "I'll never get this audition. I've lost. I'm a big, fat failure. What was I thinking?"

Mack turns toward me. "Relax. Relax. You have the no-sleeve black dress that goes just above the knees. You can wear that with your black sandals with the three-inch heels."

"You think so? You don't think that's too funeral-like?"

"Well, if you don't like that, you can wear your flowery minidress with your gold flats. Or you can go the slacks route and wear your pleated in the front white slacks with your tan pumps."

I've been holding my breath, and I take in a healing gulp of air. "Yes, that's right. Of course. Those are good choices. Which of those do you think I should wear?"

"I think you should go summery. Flowery minidress. Gold flats."

I clutch my chest and take a deep breath. "Okay. Phew."

"And whatever you got going on there," he says gesturing to my push up bra chest. "Keep it. It works."

Mack goes into his apartment, and I enter mine. My place is big and bright, with the view of the square. I love it, even though it's furnished with garage sale chic.

I head right for the flowery dress in my closet and put it on. I slip on my flats and douse myself with perfume. I fly out of the apartment just as Mack comes out of his.

He's carrying his tackle box and fishing rod. He didn't

change his clothes except for his hat, which is covered in hooks and lures.

"What are you going for here? The American geek award?" I ask, uncharitably.

"Why? You think I got a shot?"

"You could be the poster boy for geeks everywhere."

"Ouch. You're brutal for an actress. It's a good thing you're not really an actress."

I stumble backward, as if he's hit me right in the solar plexus.

"I am too an actress," I say, which of course, isn't totally accurate, but I'm desperate. I have to be something. And right now, that's an actress.

"No, you're not."

Mack pushes the button for the elevator, and I slap his hand away.

"No," I say. "I'm not sharing an elevator with you. You

take the stairs."

"You know I can't do that." Strictly speaking, there are no stairs. The staircase was ripped out and is being renovated. The only way to get down, besides the elevator, is to use the fire escape or jump out a window.

"You could jump out a window," I say.

"You want me to jump out a window?"

"Yep. That's a good idea. Jump out a window."

I elbow him out of the way and leap for the elevator as the doors creak open. I push the button for the first floor, but Mack throws his arm inside and blocks the doors from closing.

"Fine," I say, crossing my arms in front of me. "But stand on your side of the elevator. I want to be as far away from you as possible."

He steps inside and pushes the button again. "It's a thirty-second trip, Marion. I don't think I stink that bad."

I'm halfway tempted to apologize to him. I'm not normally a bitch. But I've got a lot riding on this audition, and I'm nervous as hell. The least he could do is support me. I mean, besides not kicking me out of my apartment for nonpayment of rent.

The doors close halfway and then stop. "What the—"

"I'll get it," Mack says. He puts the tackle box down on the floor and leans his fishing rod against the wall. He struggles to pull the doors together, making the muscles on his arms and shoulders bulge. I bite my lower lip. "Just a little sticky. I'll oil the doors later," he says.

The elevator groans back to life and begins to descend. Mack picks up his box and grabs the fishing rod with his other hand. He shakes his head. "Jump out a window," he mumbles under his breath.

I'm about to shoot back a real zinger when the elevator lurches to a stop, throwing me off my feet to fall against Mack. We're stuck between floors.

"You owe me a million dollars," I tell him.

Then, I panic.

# CHAPTER 4

I push the buttons, frantically. I try all of them, gently at first, and then I'm slamming my fists against the panel.

"It's not working!" I scream, punching the panel for all I'm worth.

"Calm down, Bruce Banner. Let me look at that."

Mack clamps his hands on my shoulders and moves me to the other side of the elevator. He turns around and pushes every button.

"I already did that. Why are you doing what I did already? Is that your only strategy?" I say, my voice hitched up a couple octaves.

"Don't worry. I've got a ton of strategies up my sleeve."

"You're wearing short sleeves."

He ignores me and unclips a tool from his belt. It's one of those all-purpose things that turns into a million kinds of tools. It's like a New Age Swiss Army knife. He opens it to a fancy kind of screwdriver and uses it to unscrew the panel.

"Here we go," he says, looking at the wiry innards of the control panel.

I push him out of the way to see what he's seeing. "What? What? What do you see?"

"I don't see anything with you blocking the control panel, Marion," he says to the back of my head.

"Sorry." I step to the side and urge him to stick his tool back into the maze of wires. "What is it? Can you fix it?"

"Well…" He scratches his head. "I've never actually fixed an elevator before."

"Oh my God. I'm going to die! I'm going to die trapped in an elevator with you! And I'm not going to make it to my audition!"

Mack pushes the wires back into the control panel and

screws on the cover. Calmly, he pushes the buttons, again. Nothing. Nada. We're stuck.

"Do the alarm," I say. "Push the alarm button."

"The elevator doesn't exactly have an alarm."

"What do you mean, doesn't exactly have an alarm?"

"It doesn't have an alarm."

My panic reproduces itself like an amoeba that you study in tenth grade biology class. The panic doubles and triples in size until my body is too small of a place to hold it, and it needs to burst out of me.

"I'm going to die! I'm going to die! I'm going to die in a broken, old, ugly elevator!" I scream. I grab fistfuls of Mack's shirt and pull him toward me. "I'm going to die!"

He raises an eyebrow and seems to think a minute about the odds of us dying. It's irritating as all get out that he's so calm in the face of our terrible demise. I open my mouth to scream, again, but he stops me cold.

Like a magic trick, his strong arms are suddenly wrapped

around my middle, pulling me close and lifting me slightly off the ground. He's massive, even bigger in the small space.

"You're really big," I note.

"Oh, you have no idea," he says.

To prove it, his hands slip under my ass, and he lifts me. He pushes me against his ever-growing bulge, which threatens to bust through his button-fly. I worry that there won't be enough room in the elevator for the three of us: Mack, me, and his giant penis.

He takes a step forward until my back is against the wall, and he goes in for the kill.

I mean, he kisses me.

Which is a killer.

It's the deadliest, takes your breath away, hot damn kiss that's ever existed since lips were invented.

I'm suddenly very grateful for lips. What a fabulous topper for the mouth. I've never fully appreciated lips before Mack Ryan presses his against mine in a broken elevator between the third and fourth floors.

He doesn't play around. No tentative peck. No timid nibbling. My mouth opens to him, as if he's Ali Baba and he's said the magic words. His tongue searches for mine, and once he finds it, he demands more.

He's very demanding. With one hand cupping my ass, his other hand travels to my breast. I discover I like it when a man's demanding. In fact, I want more demanding.

I demand it.

My hands curve behind Mack's neck, pulling him even closer. My fingers thread through the thick hair that pokes out from underneath his fishing cap. He's all kind of good. I knew he was fine, but I didn't know how fine. Even his neck is sexy. It's long and muscled. I want to kiss and suck and lick his neck.

If his neck is this good, I reason, the rest of him is probably off the charts. I need to inspect his everything to verify my assumption. I want to do all kinds of things to him. Different things. For the first time in my life, I'm hankering to bite a man's ass.

Oh, yeah.

For a moment, I think I hear Barry White singing. Somehow, the R&B crooner has joined us in the elevator, and his deep voice is spurring me on to get naked in a hurry. It doesn't seem odd at all to me that Barry White would appear out of nowhere to give a free concert while I kiss the man I've been crushing on for two years.

But it's not Barry White, I realize. It's Mack. And he's not singing. He's crooning. There's no other word for it. Officially, I guess it would be called moaning, but his voice is impossibly deep and smooth, and it's so filled with arousal that it beckons me to glide my hands down his back and tuck them inside his jeans.

His lips don't stop. It's the never-ending kiss. A few seconds more, and I'm sure the friction will ignite us into flames. But what a way to go… Dying in a ball of flames, brought on by the most talented pair of lips I've ever come across.

It gets me to thinking. Lips. Tongue. Lips. Tongue. The possibilities are endless with two simple body parts.

Oh, God.

His hands are everywhere. Talented fingers explore my body while he kisses me in a familiar, seductive rhythm.

I'm aroused from my head to my toes. My blood is pumping to my hoohah, like it's going for gold in the Olympics. I'm also wet. Very, very wet. I've peed in my pants kind of wet. If I wasn't ovulating before, I sure am now. I've probably got three eggs pushing each other out of the way to see which of them can make it down my fallopian tubes first.

With the thought of eggs and fallopian tubes, I sober up. At least, I sober up enough to take my hands out of his pants, break off the kiss, and push him away. I'm still pretty drunk with arousal, though. It's all I can do to not take a running leap at his midsection.

"You kissed me," I say, breathless.

"Did I?" he asks. His chest rises and falls with heavy breathing. His fisherman's hat has slipped over one eye, and he rights it on his head, taking a second to wipe his forehead with the back of his hand. His lips are red and swollen, and his eyes are predator dark.

"Why did you kiss me?" I demand.

His eyes travel up my body, pausing briefly at my chest. "You were panicking. I thought I would calm you down."

"I wasn't panicking," I lie. "And you certainly didn't calm me down!"

"You're right. You weren't calm. I like that."

"Oh, geez." I slap my cheek to wake myself out my hormonal stupor. "Shut up!" I yell.

"I didn't say anything."

"Not you. My body. It needs to shut up," I explain.

"Sorry, I can't help you with that," he says with a grin. "I only know how to make your body talk."

"Gross," I say and bite my lower lip. I notice that his jeans are still ready to explode, and his eyes are big as saucers. Flying saucer big.

He's definitely attracted to me, or maybe it's just the trapped with a woman in an enclosed space that's got him hot and bothered. But I don't want to be kissed merely to stop from freaking out. In fact, it pisses me off.

I'm about to work up the courage to tell him my lips are off limits forever, when the elevator lurches back to life. It creaks and groans, and for a glorious half a second I think we're going down to the bottom floor, where I'll be freed and will make it to my audition on time and become rich and famous or at least employed.

But nope.

It's only a hiccup. A death rattle. A momentary last gasp from an otherwise dead machine.

"No!" I yell. "Keep going! Keep going!" I hop up and down, trying to get it to start again. "Help me out here," I urge Mack. I continue to jump up and down, but he doesn't join me. The elevator sways from side to side, but it doesn't budge. I keep jumping, but we're as stuck as ever.

"You might want to stop doing that," he says.

"We have to do something! You could at least help me."

He puts his hand on my shoulder. "I really think you should stop."

I give it everything I got, jumping up as high as I can to fall as hard as possible to give the elevator a shock into starting. "I think I've almost got it going," I say, optimistically.

Mack leans over and looks me in the eyes. "Please stop. If you don't stop, we have a good chance of plummeting to our deaths."

"Deaths?"

I stop jumping. Even if he's wrong, I'm out of breath. I drop to the floor and curl into the fetal position. I close my eyes and pant, like I'm a dog.

"What are you doing down there?" he asks.

"There's more oxygen down here."

"Are you claustrophobic?"

"Only in small, enclosed spaces."

Mack sits down cross-legged next to me. He takes my

hand and rubs my palm with his thumb. "We're going to be fine," he says. He's so calm and strong that I almost believe him. "There's plenty of oxygen. It's not exactly airtight, if you know what I mean."

I take a deep breath. "Okay. What if I have to pee?"

"We'll cross that bridge when we come to it. Let's focus on getting help. Take out your cellphone and call 911."

Suddenly it's easier to breathe. My cellphone. Of course. Why didn't I think about that before? Esperanza's fire department will get us out of here.

"Where's your cellphone?" he asks.

"In my purse."

"Where's your purse?"

Where's my purse?

I look around the elevator. There's Mack. There's me. There's a tackle box. There's a fishing rod. No purse. I must have left it in my apartment when I was rushing to leave for the audition.

"You're full of shit," I say. "There's not a lot of oxygen in here."

Mack grips my hand tight. "Don't worry. Not a problem."

"You're using that word wrong. I don't think you know what 'problem' means."

He grins. "I know what 'problem' means."

"You're looking at me like you think I'm a problem."

"That's not how I'm looking at you."

"You're not?"

"Nope."

We lock eyes, and I realize he's not looking at me like that. He's looking at me in a whole different way. Like a bulimic eyeing a bag of M&Ms.

His thumb travels from my palm to the inside of my wrist. My skin erupts in goosebumps, and I gasp. We sit like that for a while, both of us watching his thumb on my wrist with rapt attention.

"I didn't kiss you to calm you down," he says. "I've wanted to do that for a long time."

"Really? For how long?" I turn my other hand palm up so he can caress that wrist, too. He does.

"Two years."

We've only known each other for two years. That's when I moved in, which wasn't that long after he moved to town and opened the diner.

"That's a long time to want to do something without doing it," I say.

"Tell me about it."

"I'm glad you finally did it."

Mack tugs my arm, and I sit up. He pulls me onto his lap. He smells like sex and expensive cologne. "You smell better than you think," I note.

"It's probably a good idea if you work on your compliments. You start well, but then you slide off target."

"Do I? Maybe you should show me how it's done."

Mack takes off his hat and tosses it into the corner. His lips brush my neck. "You're the sexiest woman I've ever met," he whispers. He continues with long, languid strokes of his lips on my neck, and then he sucks ever so gently on my earlobe.

"Oh," I moan. "Yes, that's a good compliment."

"You drive me mad each time I see you. Mad to kiss you, possess you, to be inside you."

"That's another good one."

My head tips back, as his lips make their way to the front of my neck. He trails light kisses down, down, down…

"Sure, you're a pain in the ass, and you're flighty, and you can't figure out what you want to be in this world," he continues. "But I don't mind all that."

I pull back and fall off his lap. "You slid off target," I say. "You were doing great before that. You should probably take back everything you said, starting with me being a pain in the ass."

Mack pushes up from the floor and helps me up, too.

"Nope. Sorry. Can't do that. It would be false advertising."

I put my hands on my hips. "Are you playing with me?"

"Yes, and I'm not done yet."

"I hate being played with."

"Well, I love playing with you. I'm planning on playing a whole lot more, once we get out of here."

"Are we getting out of here?"

Mack scans the elevator, looking at the buttons, the door, and the ceiling. "It would have been easier if you had your cellphone with you," he says.

A bell goes off in my brain, signaling a stroke of genius. "Your cellphone," I announce, slapping his shoulder. "You can call for help on your cellphone!"

"I don't have a cellphone."

"What do you mean you don't have a cellphone? Everyone has a cellphone. Stop playing with me."

"I don't have internet, either," he says, studying the

elevator doors. "Come and help me."

He sticks his fingers into the crack between the doors and pulls. I do the same, pulling in the other direction. "How can you not have a cellphone?" I ask, pulling at the door with all my strength. "And no internet?"

He ignores me, focusing on opening the doors. When we manage to get the doors halfway open, I wedge my body between them, ready to be the first one out of the elevator. But there's no exit. The doors open to reveal a concrete wall.

"No!" I yell, pounding my fists against the wall.

"Get back here." Mack pulls at my hips, but I'm wedged between the doors. The pressure is terrible, and now I'm not only trapped in an elevator, but I'm going to be crushed to death between its doors.

"Why don't you have a cellphone!" I scream.

"Take a deep breath." He sounds like a drill sergeant, loud, deep, and bossy.

I take a breath just as Mack yanks me quick and hard. I fly

back, free of the doors and slam into him. He takes my weight easily and keeps me upright. I look down at my body and count all my limbs to make sure I haven't lost anything important.

"Sonofabitch!" I yell.

"What? Are you hurt?" He turns me around and pats me down, looking for injuries. I stick two fingers in front of his face.

"Yes. I've broken two fingernails. Two!"

"I thought you were hurt."

"I am hurt. I paid fifteen dollars for this manicure."

Mack stares at me without blinking. His jaw clenches, and his face gets red. It looks like he's going to explode. And he does.

# CHAPTER 5

Mack screams at the top of his lungs, as if he's being murdered. He's a booming baritone, and he's got impressive lungs. He basically sounds like a foghorn. A foghorn in a six-foot-tall, heavily-muscled frame.

I slap my hands over my ears. "It's okay," I yell over his yelling. "I can get another manicure. I mean, if you loan me fifteen dollars I can get another manicure. I'll look as good as new."

"Come on," he says, taking a break from his screaming. "Join me. Maybe somebody walking by will hear us."

It's Old School cellphone. Nobody's in the building, but he's right that there's a good chance somebody's walking by. I'm not sure that they'll hear us from inside the elevator, but like Mack said, it's not exactly airtight.

He starts hollering again, and this time, I join him. We sound like a couple in a horror movie, getting hacked to death by an immortal psychopath. We scream as long as our voices hold out.

After we finally stop, we stand and wait for a sign that someone has heard us. But there's no Good Samaritan running into the building, no police sirens, no nothing.

"You were pretty convincing. Maybe you really are an actress," Mack tells me.

I slump against the wall and slide down until I'm sitting on the floor. "I'm not an actress."

"You can be an actress if you want to."

"Don't patronize me."

"I'm serious."

I'm supposed to feel better. Mack's saying all the right things. He believes I can be an actress. He's opening the door to my dreams.

My dreams.

I struggle to see acting as my dream, but I can't. Do I have a dream, beyond paying my rent? Does Mack really see me as an actress or as something else? Perhaps he can tell me who I am and what I should be in life. Maybe he has all the answers.

But I don't dare ask him.

Besides, he's too busy staring at the ceiling.

"What are you looking at?"

He takes his fishing rod and jams it with all his strength at the trapdoor in the ceiling. The door doesn't budge, but the rod breaks in two.

He holds the pieces in his hands and stares at them, as if it's all a mistake and they're going to regenerate into a whole fishing rod by the will of his mind. "Shit!" he yells. "Shit! Shit! Shit!"

"I'm sorry. I know what it's like," I say, showing him my broken fingernails again.

"Are you comparing your fifteen-dollar manicure to my fishing rod?"

His voice is cold. Angry.

"Well, my manicure is prettier than your rod."

"My rod cost me over a thousand dollars. A thousand. I'll do the math for you, Marion. That's sixty-six of your manicures."

"That's a lot of manicures in a stick with a hook attached to it."

Mack shuts his eyes tight.

"Are you sleeping?" I ask.

"No. I'm picturing your boobs so I don't get upset."

"Oh. Okay."

He stays that way for a while. At one point, he covers his face with his hand and sighs, pitifully.

"We're dead, aren't we?" I ask. "This is it. We're done for. Goners."

He drops the pieces of his fishing rod on the floor and grabs the tackle box. He slams it against the trapdoor, which is either bolted closed or so old that dirt and rust have sealed it tight. The box makes a horrible racket on impact, and I think it's is going to fall apart, but it holds strong. The trapdoor, however, has met its match and cracks opens with a loud noise.

Mack has managed to bend back a portion of the metal door, but it's not totally open. Still, it's our first bit of success since we got trapped. I hop up and peer into the gap in the ceiling. It's just like the movies… a cable reaching up into a long shaft.

"Are you going up there?" I ask Mack.

"Yep." He puts the tackle box on the floor, underneath the trapdoor, and he steps on it in order to better reach the ceiling. He pounds against the door until it bends further, opening up wider. It's like opening a can without an opener. He's got it open a little, but it's not wide enough.

"You can't fit through that," I say.

"I'll fit."

"No you won't."

"Yes, I will."

"No, you won't," I say, shaking my head. I take off my shoes because I know where this is heading. I'm going to have to be the one to climb through the door.

"Yes, I will."

"Fine. Go ahead and try," I say.

Mack clamps his hand on the ceiling ledge and pulls himself up. My whole life I've never been able to do a single pull-up, but he pulls himself up like it's nothing at all. His biceps bulge with the effort, but otherwise it's easy peasy for him to haul his big body up there.

But it's not easy peasy for him to fit through the small opening. He gets his head through and then one shoulder, and then he's stuck.

"You're stuck," I say.

"I'm not stuck." He's trying to pull himself through, but he's not moving.

"You're really stuck."

"I'm not stuck."

"You're going to need the jaws of life to get you out of

there. If you had a cellphone, we could call 911."

"I'm not stuck." He punches the trapdoor with his free hand several times. It opens a little more, but not enough to climb through. He groans as he pushes and pulls, trying to unjam himself from the door.

"You're stuck."

He swings his legs to try and dislodge his body from the trapdoor, but he's not going anywhere. "Sonofabitch!" he growls.

"I told you that you were stuck."

"I'm not—" He begins but stops himself. He's so stuck.

"Don't worry. I'll save you!" I announce.

"No! Don't save me, Marion. I'll get myself out," he says with more than a hint of panic in his voice.

"No way. I'm not going to have you die in here and leave me alone with a corpse. I'm going to save you, no matter what."

I leap in the air and grab onto his legs. I hold on for dear life, my arms wrapped around his thighs and my face smooshed up against his butt. "This is awkward," I say, just as Mack finally breaks free with the force of our combined weight, and we fall to the floor together.

We lie in a heap and catch our breaths. "I wasn't stuck," he says.

"You were totally stuck. I saved you."

Our limbs are intertwined. My dress is hitched up to my hips, and my left leg is wrapped around Mack's torso. Our faces are nearly touching, and I can smell his breath. Bacon and eggs, if I'm not mistaken.

"I think you're going to miss your audition," he says.

"I'm never going to be an actress. I should have had pancakes with my pie."

"You can be whatever you want to be."

He means it. He's dead serious. Mack has faith in me, which is a first in my life.

"No one's said that to me since Mrs. Fletcher in third grade," I say.

"Smart woman, that Mrs. Fletcher."

Tears sting my eyes, and I wipe at them with my hand. Being able to be what I want in life isn't the only issue, but I can't talk to Mack about it. He would never understand that I'm aimless, that I don't know what direction to take. He owns his own diner and apartment building. He knows what he wants in life and has taken every step to make it happen.

My tears graduate to weeping. Mack kisses my tears away as they fall onto my cheeks. "Don't worry. We'll get out of here. Eventually somebody's going to come by for a cup of coffee,"

"No they won't. You're closed. You went fishing."

His mouth sets into a tight line. "True."

He caresses my leg, from ankle to hip. The air molecules shift and buckle, changing from confidences and friendship to seduction and something much deeper. Serious.

Is this the normal evolution from friendship and attraction? Was this detour in our relationship inevitable, and should I go with the flow? Or is this wrong, wrong, wrong? Is it a terrible mistake to get cozy with a man I've been fighting with for two years? Is this unnatural, immoral, and just plain weird? Is this going to end in disaster, where feelings are hurt, hearts are broken, and I'm left without a place to eat really good pie?

I have so many questions that I don't know where to begin.

"When's the last time this carpet was cleaned?" I ask. My guess is never. It smells horrible, like rotten eggs and ashtrays.

Mack doesn't seem to care about the carpet. He's ogling my body parts, and his hand has traveled the distance to the space between my legs. I feel a finger tug at my panties, and then Mack's safely in the DMZ, that no man's land between the thighs and the just-been-waxed that makes my eyes roll back in my head and makes me put my hand over his to guide him further.

Sex in a broken elevator. Talk about some crazy-ass foreplay.

But I don't care. Gone is the worry about carpet-carrying diseases. Gone is the claustrophobia. Gone are the concerns about friends becoming lovers. Gone, even, is the certainty that if I don't get to a bathroom on the double, I'm going to pee in my pants.

That's all because of Mack's hand. His magical, warm, hand with one finger slipping inside me and the other rubbing me in just the right way. How does he know exactly how to drive me mad?

Somebody moans. I'm pretty sure it's me, but I can't be totally certain because it doesn't sound quite human. My body's rocking to the rhythm of his hand. I'm so close to an orgasm. I've gone from zero to sixty in ten seconds. "You can kiss me now," I suggest.

Mack's mouth captures mine with a wild ferocity. He possesses me totally. One arm circles the back of my head and pulls me even closer. I'm spinning around and around, and I'm about to take off to the stratosphere.

That's when the screaming starts.

# CHAPTER 6

"Hello! Can you hear us? Don't worry! We're going to get you out!"

I hear the shouts as if I'm in a dream. "No, don't go out. Stay right where you are," I mutter against Mack's mouth.

He stops kissing me, and his hand stops moving, and he pulls back to listen.

"No. No. No. No," I moan. "I was so close."

"It'll just be a second! Hang in there!" The shouts are saying.

"Okay!" Mack shouts back. In a second, his hand is gone, he's extricated himself from my embrace, and he's hopped up and helping me up, as well. He pulls at my dress, which is up around my waist.

I'm disoriented. I'm not entirely sure what's going on. I'm still highly aroused, but I feel abandoned, rejected. I have a strong desire to suck my thumb.

"You okay?" Mack asks. "You look sort of used."

"I wish."

"Your hair," he says, pointing.

My hands fly to my head. It's a rat's nest on one side, and flat on the other. "Oh."

There's squealing and clunking and knocking. Men's voices discussing elevator mechanics reach us. Then, the lights flicker, and the elevator creaks back to life. We descend for a few seconds, and then we stop. I'm just about to bemoan getting stuck again, when the doors open, pulled apart by two hunky Esperanza firefighters.

They're not alone. The whole fire department is there, along with two police officers, the mayor, and Raine. They look at us and the inside of the elevator, and they don't say a word.

All except Raine. She talks.

"What did you two do in there? It looks like World War

Three. Broken everything, and… Oh."

It's written all over their faces that what we've just done and almost done is written all over our faces. And my hair. Probably my hair is a dead giveaway.

"Thank you so much," I say, acting cool as a cucumber. "That was… and we were… the thing just… and anyway…"

Raine takes a step forward and grabs my arm. "Come on, Shakespeare. Let's clean you up."

She yanks at my arm, and I stumble out of the elevator, stubbing my toe.

"My shoes—" I begin to say.

"Keep walking," Raine whispers.

All heads turn as we pass. I look down at the ground to avoid eye contact. Raine digs a large key ring out of her jeans pocket and searches through the keys. Finding the right one, she unlocks the back door of Mack's diner.

"I can't believe he gave you a key," I say. Mack is highly territorial, and the diner is his prized possession.

"Sometimes I need to fetch some of our guests diner food at odd hours. Mack lets me use his kitchen in case of emergency."

Raine's job is a lot of work. She's at the beck and call of a whole slew of tourists and long-term renters. It's a family business, but she takes a lot of responsibility for the nuts and bolts of its day-to-day running. It gets me thinking.

"Here we are," she says, opening the diner's bathroom door.

"None too soon." I go right to a stall and sit down on the toilet. "I didn't think I was going to make it. I thought I was going to leave a big puddle on the elevator floor. Although that might have cleaned the elevator a bit."

"Speaking of dirty," Raine begins. "You guys finally decided to get down and dirty while you were trapped?"

I flush and leave the stall. I turn on the water to wash my hands but am stopped by my reflection in the mirror. "Oh God."

It's not just my hair. My lipstick has vanished, and it's been replaced with a passion rash. Mack has kissed the skin off me. I look like I took a ride on the freeway, face first. My dress is one big wrinkle, too.

"And it's ripped up the back," Raine tells me.

I turn around. My dress is ripped up to the top of my thong, revealing all kinds of cheek. No wonder they watched me walk away.

"I have sweats, a t-shirt, and flip flops in the car. I'll go get them for you. In the meantime, here's my brush," Raine says.

While she's gone, I wet the brush and run it through my hair. Then, I wash the rest of the makeup off my face. After I put on her sweats and t-shirt, I look human, again.

"They say the elevator is almost safe. They've got a whole team on it," Raine tells me, after I'm dressed. "Mack is serving pie and coffee to the firemen, the cops, and the mayor. So, before we go out there, tell me what happened. I figure you must be pregnant, now."

"I'm not pregnant."

"Maybe a little pregnant? Like half pregnant?"

"I'm not half pregnant. Not anywhere close to pregnant. Mack and I are just friends, and probably not even that."

Raine studies my face, as if my nose has slipped off-center or something. "Is that what the kids are calling it these days? 'Friends'?"

I try to decide how much lying I should do. Raine is a good friend. I've known her since kindergarten, and she was there for me when my mom died three years ago. She's extremely hard working and sensible. Who better to tell my problems to? Who better to work my life out for me?

"I might have a little crush."

"I knew that already, Marion."

"Okay. Okay. We might have kissed."

Raine points at my lips. "You think? They're swollen to twice their normal size."

"Fine. We almost did it. We were close. Oh wow, was I almost close."

"Oh my God!" Raine yells, skipping around in a circle in

the bathroom. "I knew it. I knew it. You guys are perfect for each other. I think you should name your first son Mark and your first daughter Mavis. Then, it would be Mack, Marion, Mark, and Mavis. How cute is that?"

I flinch. "I don't think it's that cute, Raine. Besides, we didn't discuss life after the elevator, you know? It'll probably just go back to normal. He'll give me coffee in the morning, and I'll avoid him when rent is due."

"You could get married by the lake. I'll cater."

"And we fight all the time."

"That's called sexual tension. That's good. I would cut off my left arm to have some sexual tension with Wade."

Wade is where Raine goes off the sensible rails. She's been gaga for him for so long that she doesn't see what a grade-A jerk he is. And I can't tell her. She's not ready for that information.

"I know you would," I say, putting my arm around her shoulders.

It's time to leave the bathroom—past time—but I'm too

chicken to go out into the diner and face Mack, post almost-coitus. Maybe he'll look different outside of the elevator. Maybe our little interlude was just a moment of insanity, brought on by our imprisonment.

"Raine, I missed my audition," I say, staring down at my broken fingernails. I'm embarrassed to ask her for a favor, but nothing ventured, nothing gained. Right? "And I sort of need a job."

"Audition for what?"

"I was going to be an actress."

"Was?"

"I'm back to not knowing what I want and aimlessly wasting my youth."

"Well, that's good for me," Raine says, smiling. "I'm short of staff and could use your help. I wouldn't even have to train you because you know how our business works. Do you remember how to make apple crumble and hospital corners?"

I've worked for Raine's family on and off my whole life.

I've been a maid, a cook, and a bottle washer. I even did the books for a week, before I screwed them up so bad they had to bring in a forensic accountant to fix the mess I made.

"I do," I say.

"Perfect."

Raine invites me to start right away, to get updated on this season's crop of guests and the schedule. I'm thrilled to go with her and to get away from Mack for the rest of the day. Mack confuses me. But Raine and her family make me feel secure, like everything is supposed to be just as it is.

So, that's how I have enough courage to finally leave the bathroom. Raine holds my hand as I open the bathroom door.

The diner is crowded, but the town's first responders and the mayor are filing out, probably going back to work. They're careful not to say anything about seeing my butt through my ripped dress or my almost-had-an-orgasm hair. But they wave to me as they leave, and I can read their minds. And it's not pretty.

Mack is clearing the tables but stops when he sees me. We

lock eyes, sending shockwaves to my lady parts. Wow. I mean, wow.

Maybe Raine is right. Maybe I am a little pregnant. Just his look could probably do the trick.

"I'm taking your girlfriend to work with me," Raine announces, as we walk through the diner.

"Not girlfriend," I say. My face is hot, most likely bright red. "She didn't mean girlfriend, Mack. I don't know why she said that. No idea at all."

I push on Raine's back to make her walk quicker. We're close to the front door. I'm so anxious to be away from Mack's sex stare that I'm tempted to take a running leap at the exit.

Just as we get to the door, he steps in front of us, blocking our path. "No," he says.

"No?" Raine and I repeat in unison.

"We have unfinished business, Marion. I'm not letting you run away."

# CHAPTER 7

"I'm not running away," I say, affronted. Who does he think he is, saying I'm running away? Sure, I'm running away, but how dare he think I'm running away? "Why would I run away from you? You don't scare me. Do you think you scare me? Big bad Mack Ryan, scaring little Marion MacAlister? I don't think so."

I punctuate my words by poking him in the chest. It's hard as a rock. It's like a super chest. The manliest of manly chests. I've never actually seen him without a shirt. Could his naked chest be as good as I think it is?

"Mack, let Marion run away just for today," Raine says. "Just for five hours or so."

"I'm not running away. I have a job," I say.

"Congratulations," he says, giving me the sex stare again.

"But you can start tomorrow. Today, we have unfinished business." He steps forward, getting deep into my personal space. Heat and testosterone are bouncing off him like a trampoline at an amusement park. My heart starts to pound. I drop Raine's hand.

"Oh, my," I breathe.

"This is so good," Raine says, looking from Mack to me and back again. She steps around Mack and goes right out the door without looking back or saying another word.

"Traitor!" I yell after her. She's abandoned me without having the decency to look back even once.

I take two steps backward, out of Mack's reach. "Hey," I say, stomping my foot. "Why'd you do that? I need that job."

"The job will be there tomorrow. Raine loves you. She'll hold the job a few hours for you."

He makes up the space between us and takes my hand. I pull it back, as if I'm burned.

"Don't you think this is weird?" I ask.

"No."

"Not at all?"

"No." His voice is impossibly deep. He's looking down at me from up high. Tall. Strong. I step back until I crash into a chair, toppling it over.

"Nervous?" he asks.

"Terrified."

He nods. A man in overalls enters the diner, and waves at Mack. "I just wanted you to know that Joe is on his way to San Fernando to get a part. Then, we should finish up the work on the elevator. It should be right as rain tomorrow morning."

"Tomorrow morning?" I ask. How will I get to my apartment?

"That's fine," Mack tells the man. "We're going to be gone until then, anyway."

"We are?" I ask.

"Yep. We're going fishing, remember?"

"I don't remember that."

"Remember the fishing rod that you broke? Remember the tackle box? Those signify fishing."

"They signify that you're fishing, not me. I don't do boats. I don't do fish."

Mack yanks my hand, making my body slam against his. He wraps his arms around me and holds me close. "Today you do. Today you do it all."

I almost swallow my tongue.

"What do you mean I broke your fishing rod?" I croak.

*

Mack parks his SUV in front of the 7-Eleven. "Are we getting Slurpees?" I ask. "If I knew that Slurpees were part of fishing, I would have been an avid fisherman my whole life."

"I wasn't planning on getting a Slurpee. But if you want one, it's my treat."

"Oh, you know I want one."

Mack owns an all-electric SUV. It's fancy, with lots of

doodads and widgets. It's very different from Mack's normal style of worn jeans and undershirts. I wonder if there's more than meets the eye in regards to Mack Ryan. We've been sort of friends for two years, but maybe I don't know a thing about him.

We get out of the car, and Mack locks it with a beep. "I didn't know you were a fan of Slurpees," I say.

"I'm not. Not since I was nine years old. I've graduated to more robust drinks."

We walk into Esperanza's only 7-Eleven. I haven't been in here for months. When I was a kid, my friends and I used to hang out here every day after school. So I've got the layout memorized. Slurpees and sodas to the right. Condoms to the left, directly in front of the cashier, because everybody tries to steal them. Beer, beer, and more beer straight ahead in the refrigerated section.

I head straight for the Slurpee machines. "Blue raspberry isn't working today, Steve?" I call out to the cashier.

"Nah, been out for two days. But the Cherry Explosion is just as good," he calls back.

I have my doubts that the Cherry Explosion is anywhere near as good as blue raspberry. Just drinking something blue makes me happy. There's no blue in the Cherry Explosion. Oh, well. I mix the Cherry Explosion with the Coke flavor in the biggest cup they have. Since Mack is paying, I go for the candy straw and slip it through the top. Yum.

I meet Mack at the counter. He's got beef jerky, Doritos, and a bottle of iced tea piled high. "So, what is it today, Mack?" Steve asks him. "Are you picking your own numbers, or are you going for the random pick?"

"I don't know. Let me think a second."

"You play the lottery?" I ask. I don't know why I'm so surprised, but Mack never struck me as the lottery kind of guy. I rarely play the lottery. It's not that I don't think I can win, even though I'm pretty sure I can't win, but most of the time I forget to play. Besides, aren't you more likely to get hit by lightning twice in the same spot than win the lottery?

Winning the lottery sounds fabulous. I could get a new manicure and maybe even a car! Hit by lightning odds or not, I'm hit with a strong desire to play. I must play.

"I want to play," I say. "Please! Please! I want to play, too."

Mack seems to think about it a minute. I guess playing the lottery with someone is kind of like a commitment. I've heard stories of winners suing each other over the winnings. But since lightning doesn't strike twice in the same place, I don't see why Mack would hesitate.

Still, I really want to play the lottery. And I want to play with Mack. I don't know why. Maybe it's a moment of lunacy.

"Please," I say, looking up at him. I can tell the moment he melts or makes a decision. His whole face changes. I really don't know what's going on in his brain, but he comes out on my side.

"Fine. We'll split it. You pick out half of the numbers, and I'll pick the other half. Where's your fifty cents?"

I don't have fifty cents. My purse is in my apartment, and there's not much more than fifty cents in my wallet, in any case. I'm flat broke, and I'm pretty sure Mack is aware of that.

"Can I borrow fifty cents?"

"I don't know. Are you good for it?"

"Probably not, unless I win the lottery and then I can pay you back your fifty cents."

"Okay. Sounds like a deal. What's your first number?" He holds a pen poised over a lottery card, which is covered in little number bubbles.

I think hard, as if I'm taking the SATs or balancing my checkbook. What number to pick? What number to pick?

"Thirteen. My birthdate," I say, finally.

"Lucky number thirteen," he says, filling in the number thirteen bubble. "Okay. April, right?"

"Why? Are you planning on getting me a present?"

"Not if you win the lottery, because then you'll be rich enough to buy your own present," he says, smiling. "I guess if we're going the birthday route, I'll pick number two."

"November, right?"

"Close. May."

"Oh, an Aquarius. I don't think I'm compatible with Aquarius. That explains so much."

Mack nods. "Yes, it would explain so much, if I was an Aquarius, but I'm a Taurus. Next number. Your choice."

"Twenty-four. That's how old my mother was when she had me."

"Twenty-four for the 'aw, sweet' number. If we're going that route, I pick thirty-six," he says, filling in the bubble.

"Your mother was thirty-six when she had you?"

"Nope. If I'm not mistaken, that's a measurement on someone I've taken an interest in." He gestures at my chest with his pen. Thirty-six is my bra size. I cover my chest with my arms.

"I don't want to know how you know that. There's a certain creepy stalker quality to the fact that you know that bit of information."

Mack smiles and does a dancing thing with his eyebrows. Steve snickers behind the counter.

"You mind your own beeswax, Steve," I bark. "And forget that number."

Steve snorts. "Fine. I'm going to clean out the hot dog tray. Let me know when you're ready to pay." He walks over to the hot dogs, singing, "Thirty-six. Thirty-six" over and over.

"Geez," I mutter.

"Your turn," Mack reminds me.

"Fine. One. To mark your measurement," I say, pointing at his crotch.

"One foot? Yep, sounds about right." He's smiling ear to ear and eagerly colors in the number one bubble.

"I meant one inch!" I yell.

"Too late. One foot. So accurate. I wonder how you knew. Anyway, time for the last number. The bonus number. I think the only bonus number could be three."

"Why is three the only possible bonus number?"

Mack leans his hip against the counter. He searches my

face for something, and I blush in response.

"Well, when we get hitched, that makes two, and our first child will be the bonus. Three," he says, holding three fingers in the air.

# CHAPTER 8

Time stands still. I forget how to breathe. I forget how to swallow. So, my eyes are stinging, and there's drool coming out of my mouth. I stick my finger in my ear and wiggle it around, because I'm sure I'm hearing things.

Mack finishes filling out the lottery card and calls Steve over. He pays for everything and picks up the bag of supplies. I finally get control over my mouth again. I wipe the drool off on my sleeve and take a sip of the Slurpee and a bite of the candy straw.

He puts his hand on the small of my back, and we walk out to his car. He opens the car door for me, but I slam it shut again and slug his arm.

"What do you mean, hitched? Where did that come from?" I demand.

Mack rubs the place on his arm where I punched him. “Isn’t it the natural progression of all this?”

“Of all what?”

“This.” He pushes me up against the car. His hands reach behind my thighs, and he lifts me up, fitting himself between my legs.

“People will see,” I say.

“There’s only one person I care about.”

Mack brushes his lips against my neck, making my skin come alive. I’ve never reacted so strongly to a man. Either he’s the most adept kisser in existence, or he really does it for me.

Off the charts chemistry.

Or could it be soulmates?

“No,” I say, turning my head away from him. The “no” word is all it takes. Mack doesn’t second guess me. He stops immediately and puts me down, gently.

“Sorry,” he says.

"Too fast. It's all too fast." I talk down to the ground because I can't bear to make eye contact. I can't bear to see the emotion in his face. And I don't know how strong I can be when I'm faced with his desire. He has a certain effect on me that's disconcerting. Scary.

*

We pull out of the parking lot and drive toward the lake. The silence grows heavy between us. I'm torn between needing to explain myself and being a big chicken. I'm just about to come out on the side of being a big chicken when Mack breaks the silence.

"Was it the hitched part or the three part that freaked you out?"

"It was all the parts. This is going too fast. Just this morning, we were fighting over what I was going to eat for breakfast. Now you're talking about getting married and having a family." At the word "family," I choke.

Choke like I have a chicken bone stuck in my throat. Choke like an entire chicken is wedged in there. But I don't have anything stuck. It's just commitment that's got me gasping for air. I hack and sputter. Mack pounds on my back a couple of times.

Finally, a sip of my Slurpee calms me down.

"Okay. My bad," Mack says. "So, how about we make a deal?"

"What kind of deal?"

"We won't talk about you know what and the thing that shall not be named."

"Deal!" I shout. Phew. What a relief. My stress level plummets, and I breathe a lot easier. The overwhelmed feeling I've had for hours leaves me, and finally I can enjoy being with Mack.

"I'm not finished," he adds, making my stomach lurch. "We won't talk about any of it. However, if we happen to win the lottery tonight, we get married in the morning."

I explode with laughter. I roar with it. It's the best belly laugh I've had in years.

"If we win the lottery? We have more of a chance of getting hit by lightning twice in one spot," I giggle.

"So it's a deal?" He puts a hand out, and I shake it.

"Deal."

*

"This is a fishing boat?"

"I can fish from it."

It's not a fishing boat. I've seen my share of fishing boats, living my whole life in a small town by a lake. The lake is lousy with fish, and the lake is lousy with fishing boats.

But this is something altogether different. It's longer, for one thing, two stories, and it's flat on top. There's a complicated barbecue thing going on the upper deck. It looks like a…

"It looks like a house," I say.

Mack is holding my hand, and he gives it a little squeeze. "That's because it's a houseboat," he says.

"A houseboat," I repeat. "Like a yacht?"

"Nothing like a yacht. Totally different animal. Much more comfortable and perfect to glide around the lake, which is what we're going to do right now."

"Gliding sounds okay. Gliding doesn't sound like unbearable seasickness."

"Nobody gets seasick on Bessie's Castle." He points at the back of the boat where "Bessie's Castle" is written in big black letters.

"Who's Bessie?" I ask, horrified at how jealous I sound.

"My golden retriever. She died when I was sixteen. The love of my life."

I study him, trying to figure out if he's pulling my leg. "You named your boat for a dog?"

He nods. "The love of my life."

"I'm impressed, Mack. I love dogs, too."

"Come on," he says. "Let me impress you, again."

He helps me onto the boat, and we climb the stairs to the top deck. It really is like a house. Nicer than any house I've ever lived in. An outside kitchen takes up most of the deck. A huge stainless steel barbecue takes up most of the kitchen. Cushioned benches wind around the top deck, giving guests a bird's eye view of the cooking.

"All this for a Slim Jim and Doritos?" I ask.

"Those are for après l'amour. I'm making you a dinner to explode your taste buds."

"I'm not sure exploding taste buds is a good thing."

"Well, you know what I mean."

"What do you mean après l'amour?" I don't speak French, but I get the impression he's being presumptuous. "How do you know there's going to be an après or a l'amour in the first place?"

The sun is going down, and Mack is standing way too close to me. He's not standing at an I'm-going-to-make-dinner distance. He's at more like an are-you-going-to-be-on-top-or-shall-I distance. Totally inappropriate.

Inappropriate in a good way, of course. He smells great, like he has access to a pheromone machine. I take a step closer to him.

It may be my imagination, but I could swear he's gotten better looking. He's blown past Tatum Channing, and he's full on Chris Hemsworth, now.

And he's looking at me.

I mean, really looking at me. I wonder if he's thinking about what he's going to prepare for dinner, but I'm pretty sure he's thinking about something entirely different.

I'm thinking about something different, too.

"Remember when I said it's going too fast?" I ask.

"It's branded on my brain, like mad cow disease. What about it?"

"I lied."

# CHAPTER 9

I wrap my arms around his neck and jump. I'm a sex vixen. I'm fifty shades of grey, but I've flipped the roles. I'm the predator and he's the prey. I'm the red hot mama in charge, and he's going to submit.

I'm also heavier than I look, and he's caught off guard. He stumbles backward, swinging his grocery bag to try and catch his balance. But there's this momentum thing happening, and we just keep going.

Ah, physics. You're a horrible bitch.

We do a little dance: Stumble backward. Stumble backward. Teeter. Totter. Stumble backward. Stumble backward. Teeter. Totter.

But then the stumble backward crashes into the teeter

totter, and we hit the boat's railing with surprising force and go right overboard.

Do you ever have dates like this?

We hit the water with a loud splash. We've fallen three stories, after all. Higher than Greg Louganis. And we land—the both of us—flat on Mack's back.

We sink deep into the water, but I'm a good swimmer. I dislodge myself from Mack's neck and kick my way up to the surface, accidentally knocking my foot against his groin. I think I hear him scream, but it's underwater and the sound is muffled.

I make it to the top and gasp for air. It takes Mack significantly longer to come up from the deep, and I'm almost ready to dive down to find him when he breaks the surface.

"Are you okay?" I ask.

He puts a finger up in the air in the international gesture for "wait a minute."

"You're blue," I note.

He puts his finger up again.

"I don't think you're breathing," I say.

He shakes his head.

"Do you need CPR?"

He shakes his head, again.

"That's good because I don't actually know CPR, but you're awfully blue. Should I pound on your chest?"

He furrows his brow. "I'm fine," he gasps, finally. "My testicles are tucked away next to my appendix now, but I'm fine."

I feel guilty about kicking him. I hope the damage isn't permanent. I was planning on using that part of his anatomy.

"At least the fall wasn't too bad," I say, trying to look on the bright side.

"Thankfully, something broke your fall."

"Yes… Oh," I say remembering that he broke my fall. "Well, I guess we should get back on board."

I climb the ladder without looking back. I've sort of ruined the mood. Will we go back to being friends or has emasculating him with my super-strong leg put pie and his easygoing attitude toward my rent in jeopardy?

I step onto the lowest deck. I'm soaked through, and Raine's sweatpants now weigh a ton. Mack climbs up after me, and I'm relieved to see he's no longer blue. "Do you have a bathroom?" I ask.

He takes my hand and shows me to a very nice bedroom. There's a king-sized bed with a blue and white comforter. The walls are paneled in wood, and the floor is wood, also. We're dripping all over it.

"Nice," I say. The room is decorated entirely in bachelor chic, but it's nice and tidy. And new.

At first, I don't notice that Mack is stripping off his shirt. He tosses it into the corner of the room and unbuttons his pants. He's got muscles everywhere. Since he's always in his diner, I can only imagine his muscles are genetic. Like his blue eyes. "You probably have no problem with jar lids," I say, staring at his biceps.

"The bathroom's in there," he says, pointing to a door.

I nod, but I'm rooted to the spot. I'm not moving, and I'm not blinking, for that matter. Mack kicks off his jeans, and then it's just his boxer briefs and his muscly everything.

And me.

The air grows thick with tension and anticipation. I swear I can hear his heart beating.

"You all right?" I ask, gesturing toward his manly parts.

"I don't know. Let's see if it still works."

He takes two steps forward and put his hands on the hem of my shirt and lifts it up. My arms follow, and he pulls my shirt over my head, throwing it onto the heap of his clothes. His fingers work their way under my elastic waistband and pull at my sweatpants until they fall to the floor.

I shut my eyes tight and take a few deep breaths.

"Meditating?" Mack asks.

"I'm trying to remain calm so I don't cause any more damage."

"You were pretty assertive before. Surprisingly strong for your size."

"Like King Kong, you mean," I say with my eyes still shut. I feel his breath on my neck. It's all I can do not to do a Gabby Douglas straddle jump all over him.

"Like King Kong," he agrees.

His hands slowly travel from my back—where he deftly unhooks my bra—to my front, where he cups my breasts in his large, hot hands. My head falls back, and my mouth drops open.

"This is going to happen," he says, sounding almost surprised. I gurgle in response. His hands have rendered me speechless. Tamed.

I have to hand it to him. Most men would have given up on our date after being almost drowned and having their balls kicked in. Not to mention everything else that's happened today. But Mack is more determined than most. Lesser men would have left well enough alone. But Mack is focused on getting the show on the road right to Broadway. And by "Broadway," I mean my vagina.

He lifts me in his arms, carrying me like a child, and places me gently on his bed. He strips off his boxers, quickly.

And there he is in all his glory.

Lots and lots of glory.

“Oh, my,” I breathe.

He lies down on top of me, his body cradled between my legs. I’m still wearing my thong, and I struggle to remove it. But Mack is quicker than I am. He grabs some material and pulls, making it fall to pieces.

He holds his weight on his forearm and kisses me, his lips traveling lower until he’s laving my nipple with his tongue. His hand’s down between us, working to drive me crazy.

There is a time and a place for making love, but this ain’t it. I’m ready to do the big nasty, and if I don’t do it soon, I’m going to explode. My hand wraps around his manhood, and I guide him inside me.

Mack makes an inhuman noise, as we fit together perfectly. Pure arousal. “Holy hell,” he says.

"Hell doesn't have anything to do with it." At least I hope it doesn't. I mean, I'm feeling pretty wicked.

With the foreplay out of the way—thank God—he begins to rock his hips. In. Out. In. Out. The nursery rhyme Home Again Home Again Jiggity Jig plays in my head. Mack inside me feels like home, like this is how it's supposed to be.

My knees lift to his hips, and I clutch the bars of the headboard above me. I'm hypnotized by his slow, steady rhythm, and my body meets him for every thrust. As his pace increases, faster and harder, I claw at his back, raking a trail from his butt to his shoulders.

Once again, Mack Ryan has got me right on the edge of ecstasy. In the back of my head I worry that some repairman or firefighter is going to burst into the room and blow this whole gig for me just as I'm about to have the biggest orgasm of my life, but my worries are unfounded. Nobody's coming but me. In a couple of minutes, my eyes roll back in my head and my body seizes in the miracle of the good old climax.

Mack is not far behind me. He collapses next to me, his

breathing labored. "That's a relief," he says. "I was worried."

"Worried?"

"Well, we're sort of a disaster together, but it turns out not where it counts." He turns on his side and grabs my ass, pulling me close to him. "Where it counts, we're the Fourth of July."

"Christmas," I add.

"Ferris Bueller's Day Off."

"Ice cream birthday cake."

"TV marathon."

"Shoe sale."

"You," he says, effectively ending that part of the conversation. I touch the bridge of his nose. It's straight, like the rest of the planes and angles of his face. Like a Greek statue come to life.

He's uncommonly handsome. Striking. I can handle him being good-looking. I've been involved with several hunka hunka burnin' loves. But it's the romance that's got me frazzled. It's the way he's looking at me. If I'm not mistaken, he's got the love look.

It's either that or acid reflux, but I've been with him most of the day, and he hasn't eaten a thing.

"Me?" I ask. "As good as Ferris Bueller's Day Off?"

"Yep," he says. His voice is yummy and a dead ringer for Cary Grant's, minus the accent. "I guess I shouldn't have worried."

"Well, it's been rough going between us."

"That's behind us, now."

Gulp. Behind us means we're well on our way to our future. I'm not sure it's wise for me to be thinking about a future as a couple when I'm in the dark about what my future should be as a single.

"What if this thing doesn't work out beyond the whole mind-blowing sex part?" I ask.

"It will."

"What if it doesn't?"

"It will, but if it doesn't, we'll handle it."

"But who will I talk to if it doesn't?" My voice cracks, and my eyes burn with unshed tears.

"What do you mean?"

"I talk to you about—well—everything. If this doesn't work out, I won't have you to talk to, and I'll need to. Do you understand?"

It doesn't matter if he understands, because for the first time I understand. I understand that Mack is my best friend, the person I go to when I'm sad or happy, the person I run to when I want to share news about my life.

Maybe he's not the only one with the love look. Maybe I have the love look, too.

Maybe I've been a couple since the moment I walked into Mack's diner two years ago. Being a couple might just be how I figure myself out as a single.

Mack tucks a strand of my hair behind my ear and kisses me ever so softly. There's so much in his kiss: Passion. Tenderness. Ownership. And there's something else… A promise.

I reciprocate, promising it all right back to him, and he accepts it with the trust that only a man in love can give.

# CHAPTER 10

My definition of a perfect evening has always been watching television in bed while eating chips and/or peanut M&Ms and reading a hot romance at the same time.

Boy, have I been wrong all these years. My new definition of a perfect evening is what's happening right this second. Mack has his head between my legs, and he's doing something with his tongue.

Something wonderful.

I squirm against him. "There! There! Yes!" I call out. He's very good at this. Like he should teach classes.

"Do. Not. Stop," I order. Poor guy. He's been doing this for a while, and I'm slightly concerned his tongue will get injured—repetitive stress injury—but he seems unconcerned. Like he could go all night.

Oh, God. I hope he can go all night.

Despite his cardio fitness, I reach my end a minute later. My body crosses a bridge of heightened arousal until I peak in an uncontrollable seizure. I cry out, "Mack!", levitating off the bed for a second and then floating back down with my heart slowed to an unnatural rhythm.

"The little death," the French call it. Died and gone to heaven is more like it.

Despite dying, Mack doesn't stop. He takes his tongue on the road all over my body, kissing and tasting and biting his way to every nook and cranny. His hands are everywhere, too. I must have been Mother Theresa in my past life to deserve this, I figure. If this isn't Nirvana, I can't imagine what is.

With every inch of me kissed and loved, he cradles my body in his large arms and kisses my face. I'm spent. Totally relaxed. I'm a limp noodle. But his noodle isn't limp at all. Nope. He's got a very stiff noodle, and I get the impression he has all kinds of plans for his stiff noodle.

He holds me as if I'm the most valuable thing on the planet. And he holds me like I'm his. "I should have done this the first time you walked into my diner two years ago," he says.

"That might have been odd, us naked with you on top of me, especially since I walked in that day during the lunch rush."

"No, you didn't. You came in at three. It was dead." He sucks on my earlobe, and I caress his shoulders.

"No, you're wrong. The place was packed. I had to sit at the counter," I say.

Mack stops sucking on my earlobe and moves off of me. He sits on his knees at the edge of the bed. "It was three o'clock. You were the only one in the place. The fry cook was even on his break."

I sit up and cover myself with the comforter. "Your memory's faulty. It was packed. It took you forever to wait on me. I think I ordered the special."

"My memory is perfectly fine," he growls. "You came in at three. You ordered chili cheese fries, paid in quarters and dimes, and you didn't tip me."

"You own the place. Customers aren't supposed to tip the owner."

"I'm just pointing out the facts."

"It sounds like you think I'm cheap," I yell. Duh. Of course he thinks I'm cheap. I'm really cheap. I'm like Scrooge, but cheaper.

"I didn't say that." His face twitches. "I just wanted to prove that I remember that day."

"I knew this wouldn't work," I say. I wrap myself in the comforter and roll off the bed. I walk toward the bathroom and stand in the doorway wearing my best pissed off expression. "You insist on being right all the time. But you're never right. Never. You make me so mad!"

I stomp my foot and then stomp it a second time to really make my point.

Mack is angry, too. He runs his fingers through his hair, and his noodle looks cooked. He stands up in all his nakedness and marches toward the pile of clothes. I figure he's going to get dressed and take me home, that our little romantic experiment is over. But he removes his wallet.

"Are you going to pay me?" I ask, affronted and hopeful at the same time.

"You came into my diner two years ago," he says. "It was August 12. A Sunday. I had finished with the after-church crowd, and I was tired and out of butter. I gave my fry cook a couple of hours off and told him to go to the grocery store."

"Are you one of those photographic memory people?"

"Don't interrupt," he says, wagging his finger at me. "You came into the diner. You were wearing a flowery skirt and a t-shirt with "I hated flies until I opened one" written on it. With the sun shining through the windows behind you, I could see right through your skirt. You were wearing Hello Kitty panties. Pink."

"This is getting specific."

"You made a crack about the diner being empty and how long would you have to wait to get a table. I told you to sit anywhere. You proceeded to sit at every table in the place."

"Proceeded? Big word."

"I yelled at you to stop it, and you said, 'You told me to sit anywhere.' I said, 'I don't serve smart mouths'. You said you were hungry. I pointed at the door, but you wouldn't go. It went on for a while. Finally, you said, 'If I promise never to be a smart mouth again, will you feed me?' You wrote your promise down on a napkin, and I fed you."

Mack opens his wallet and takes out a soggy, folded piece of paper. He carefully unfolds it, I see that it's not paper. It's a napkin. He hands it to me.

In my handwriting is a note. I can barely make it out, but I manage. "I promise not to be a smart mouth to the jerkface diner guy so that he will feed me," I read.

"You kept this?" I ask, astonished.

Mack takes the napkin back and lays it out carefully on the nightstand, I suppose to dry out.. "Of course, I did. I fell in love with you the first moment I met you."

My mouth turns dry, and I have difficulty swallowing. "You fell in love with me because I insulted you on a napkin?" I croak.

"Either that or it was your Hello Kitty panties that got me. It's a toss up."

I let the comforter drop to the ground, and I walk over to him. "You win," I say. "Your memory is better than mine."

"I won the moment you came into my life, Marion." His eyes are huge and dark. The blue has turned almost black.

"I think you deserve a happy ending," I say.

"Being with you is my happy ending."

"Don't be so literal, jerkface diner guy," I say and drop to my knees. Turnaround is fair play, after all.

*

"You have to turn down the grill. You're going to burn the steaks," I tell Mack. We've finally made it upstairs after hours of rolling in the hay. With everything we've done, we could add another volume to the Kama Sutra.

But we're tired—I think we've run out of bodily fluids—and starving. My stomach is rumbling louder than Mack's is growling.

"You're telling me how to cook?" he growls, holding steak prongs in a threatening manner. I'm dressed in a pair of his boxers and an undershirt. He's dressed the same. His hair is a tangle, and his lips are chapped.

The upper deck of his boathouse is dark except for the lights of the barbecue, and we have a breathtaking view of the night sky with all its stars. The kitchen is stocked with food and drinks, and the cushioned seats are more than comfortable. Mack insisted that he cook for me, and I didn't refuse, but he's sure to burn the steaks.

"Yes, I'm telling you how to cook when you're going to burn the steaks. You have to turn down the heat," I say, maneuvering to reach the BBQ controls.

"Woman, don't touch my grill. There's no community property where grills are concerned." He towers over me. He's imposing and drop dead gorgeous.

"You don't scare me," I say. Not really scared. But wary. I step back from his grill. I don't mind burned steaks.

"Steaks have to be cooked on high to seal in the juices," he explains. He's also made a salad and a sauce to go over the steaks.

"Your ability to cook is almost sexier than that thing you do with your tongue," I say, taking a seat.

"Your tongue isn't half bad, either."

He turns on the radio and smooth jazz comes out. Mack gives me his hand, and I take it, standing. He slips one hand around my waist and begins to dance me around the deck. He's an amazing dancer. As smooth as the jazz.

"What's that sound?" he asks.

"I think it's Marvin Gaye."

"No, not the music. Listen."

There's a faint sound. "Heavy breathing? Do you have another woman onboard?"

"No. I don't do that until the second date."

He dances me to the railing. We see and hear a woman running along the shores of the lake. She's dressed in layers of sweats and hoodies, even though it's a hot summer's night. I recognize her, immediately.

"Raine? What the hell are you doing?" I call as she gets closer.

"Must—lose—forty—pounds," she struggles to call back while running. She sounds like a locomotive.

"We might need to call the paramedics," I whisper to Mack. "You're beautiful just as you are! Stop running. It's two in the morning!" I yell at Raine.

"I'm not going to stop running until I'm a size six!" she yells back and runs out of our line of sight.

"Women are nutjobs," Mack says.

The music on the radio changes to Luther Vandross. "Women are not nutjobs," I say. "Women are wonderful. Raine is perfectly sane. Men just make women slightly unbalanced because men are jerks."

"You think running in the middle of the night to lose forty pounds in a week is only slightly unbalanced?"

"Yes," I lie. "It's not her fault. It's the wiener Wade's fault. Why do men want to sleep with a bone?"

"I don't want to sleep with a bone," he says, smiling. He gives my backside a squeeze.

I stop dancing and push away from him. "What does that mean? Are you calling me fat?"

"Uh—"

"I'm not a bone, but I'm not fat!"

Mack's mouth is open, and he looks like I just told him his favorite golden retriever was dead again. "I didn't mean—I wasn't trying—oh, hell," he says.

I hear Raine approaching on her latest lap. "Mack says I'm fat!" I call out as she gets close to the boat.

"Remember I'm catering your wedding!" she calls back.

"Wedding? There's no wedding!" I shout. "Nobody's

getting married here!"

"I'll give you a choice of beef or fish!" she huffs and puffs. "Nobody wants chicken at a wedding."

On the radio, Luther Vandross's song ends, and the DJ comes on to announce the time as 2:30 AM. "And for that lucky someone in Esperanza who picked the right lottery numbers, today, congratulations," he says. "Sixty-five million dollars. Spend it, wisely, lucky person. I know a certain DJ you could spend it on! Just kidding. But here's those lottery numbers, in case you missed it: 1—2—13…"

"Christ," Mack says. "Do you know what this means?"

"… 24—36…" the DJ continues.

"Yes," I say, pointing at the grill, which is billowing out smoke. "You burned the steaks."

The End

Wish Upon A Stud Series #2
Man
CANDY
elise sax

# *Man* CANDY

(Wish Upon A Stud – Book 2)

elise sax

# CHAPTER 1

Wade Gates is mine. His gorgeous, perfect, hotter-than-hot everything is all for me. I've waited my entire life—ever since I fell in love with him when he lent me his glue stick on the first day of preschool—but now I'm through waiting.

I've pined and dreamed and hoped and prayed. I've hinted and suggested and plotted, and during one particularly humiliating drunken evening, begged. But that's all over now.

Twenty years later, he's going to give me his proverbial glue stick, and give it to me good. Better than good. Perfect, if I'm not mistaken about Wade's potential. And not just perfect. Forever.

Wade's forever, perfect glue stick.

Mine.

All right. Sure, I admit that Wade doesn't know he's mine. He has no idea, in fact. It's not just that he's playing hard to get. It's more like he doesn't know I exist. Yes, he grew up next door to me in a house on the lake. Yes, we went to school together all the way through high school.

But I was invisible all that time. Fat girl invisibility. It's an official disease. You can look it up on WebMD. Symptoms include the inability to get help in a store.

Normally, I'm perfectly happy with how I look. But Wade Gates only has eyes for model-thin women. He likes Keira Knightley, and I'm more like… well, nothing like Keira Knightley.

But I'm determined to make him see me. After years away, he's coming back to visit our town, Esperanza, and it's now or never, as far as I'm concerned.

I'm thinking all these things as I take another lap, running around the lake late at night. It's T-minus six days until Wade lands back in Esperanza, and I'm sweating calories as fast as I can.

I hate running. I'd rather have a root canal than run. I'd

rather take a math class than run.

Just as I've spent the past few years successfully avoiding root canals and math, I've never actually run before. I mean, not unless you count that one time at the Walmart after-Christmas sale, but I don't count that because I only ran a few steps before I was trampled by sadistic discount shoppers, hell-bent on hundred-dollar flat screens.

But tonight I've been running for thirty minutes straight. Thirty minutes of one foot after another, pounding the hard sand of the lake's shoreline. Thirty minutes of hell.

I ran out of oxygen twenty-five minutes ago. I'm pretty sure I'm going to have brain damage. I've got a stitch in my side, and since I'm not wearing a sports bra, I think I've permanently injured my boobs.

No wonder I'm not skinny. Who would voluntarily do this to themselves?

I would.

All for the love of Wade Gates.

"On your right," a man announces behind me.

I turn to see him, just as he catches up to me. In the dark, I can only make out his outline, but he's big, in great shape, and he's not wearing a shirt.

"Are you okay?" he asks me.

"Just keep moving, bub," I gasp and sputter.

"You might want to rest. You're breathing pretty hard."

"Nothing to see here," I pant, waving him along. "I just need to alter my pace. I've been running full out for too long."

"Are you running? I thought you were walking."

"Ha. Ha. Funny," I say with the last bit of air left in my lungs. I've reached the end of my breathing ability. "Gah!" I sputter, and then my legs refuse to go any further. Stopped dead in my tracks, my knees lock, and I fall over. Flat on my face.

*

I'm spinning around and around. What is this? Astronaut training? In the distance, I see the fountain in the middle of the town square. I spin my way to it and finally stop spinning to land on my butt.

The fountain is over a hundred years old, and it's bone dry. It's never had water in it, as far as I know. A coin appears in my hand. I'm desperate to throw it into the fountain, but I can't stand up. I can't even move my legs.

If I don't throw the coin into the fountain, however, my wish will never come true, and I need it to come true. I can't be happy unless my wish comes true.

Wait a minute. The coin, the fountain, my wish… it's all familiar to me. I've been here before. In fact, I've already made my wish.

"Are you coming around? There you are."

I hear the voice as if it's coming from inside a toilet bowl. Far away with a flushing sound. I will my eyes to open. It takes a few attempts, but they finally flutter open.

"Good morning," he says.

I'm lying on my back in the sand. I realize the flushing sound is actually the gentle waves of the lake. I have a perfect view of the star-filled sky and the shirtless man, who is holding up my legs, I'm guessing to make the blood flow back to my brain.

"Who are you?" I ask. "Let go of my legs."

"Dirk."

"You're not wearing a shirt."

"It's hot," he explains. I notice he hasn't let go of my legs. "How many shirts are you wearing? Six?"

He's close. I'm wearing four layers. "I'm in training."

"For what? Your funeral?"

"What do you know? Let go of my legs."

He drops my legs, and I struggle to stand. He tries to help me, but I shrug him off. "I'm fine," I say.

And then everything goes black.

# CHAPTER 2

I don't know how long I'm unconscious, but I come to on a couch, staring up at Dirk the Shirtless Man. He doesn't look real. Much too good-looking. And he looks familiar, too.

I rub my eyes. "I'm seeing things," I say.

"You passed out. Here. Drink some water." He slips his hand under my neck and lifts my shoulders slightly off the couch. With his other hand he gently puts a glass of a water up to my lips. I take a sip. "Slowly. You're pretty dehydrated."

I steal a look at him while I drink. He has dark blond hair and big brown eyes. His eyelashes are twice as long as mine. His nose is slightly bigger than perfect, but otherwise, he's got the whole proportion and symmetry thing down. Like a Greek God.

"Where am I?" I ask.

"In my cabin. Well, not really my cabin. I'm renting it for a couple of weeks."

I sit up. The cabin is decorated in Turkish rugs, samovars, and a large poster of a belly dancer. Bizarre for a California cabin in the foothills of the Sierra Nevada, but I know why it's decorated that way.

"This is my cabin," I say. "I mean, my family's cabin. The Harper family. I'm Raine Harper. You're renting it from me. From us. Oh, my head," I moan, lying back down. My head feels like it's in a vice.

"You're dehydrated. That's why your head hurts. I like your cabin, by the way."

I nod but keep my eyes closed. My family has lived on the lake for a hundred and fifty years. We have seven properties, which we rent out as vacation rentals and for special occasions. I'm the caterer and errand boy for our family business, which keeps me busy about thirteen hours a day.

Something occurs to me, and I open one eye. "How did I

get here?"

"That would be me," he says, putting the glass up to my lips, again.

I take a couple of sips and push it away. "But how?"

"I carried you," he says, matter-of-factly.

"With your arms?"

"With my arms."

"With your two arms, you carried me from the lake into the cabin?"

"Why is that so hard to understand?" He sits down on the coffee table next to the sofa and takes a sip of water from my glass. A lump forms in my throat, and I try to swallow.

I hold back my desire to touch his biceps.

"Nobody has ever carried me before. Not since I learned to walk." Just how many calories did I burn from a thirty-minute run? How many pounds did I lose to allow a man to carry me such a long distance?

I pat my stomach to see how much it's shrunk. But it's still there, just as soft and lumpy as always. If someone pokes me, I'll giggle like the Pillsbury Doughboy.

So, I'm still the same, but I'm not entirely dressed.

"Where are my clothes?" I ask, alarmed.

"On your body."

"Not all of my clothes!"

Shirtless Guy touches my knee and leaves his hand there. A zing goes up from my knee to my hoochie mama, and I have a small orgasm. Or a seizure. I'm not a doctor so I'm not totally sure.

"I just took off a few layers. You were overheated and dehydrated. I was trying to help."

"What? Did you say something?" I mutter. I'm entirely focused on his hand on my knee. His magic hand.

"I said that I just took off a couple of layers. You're not

naked. You know, you're lucky you're okay. Why were you doing that to yourself?"

I snap out of my catatonic state and slap his hand off of my knee. I don't like any criticism about my strategy to hook Wade Gates. "I told you. I'm in training. What's your name, again?"

"Dirk."

He's so familiar. His face. His body. His name.

I wag my finger at him. "Dirk," I say. "You're going to laugh at me, but has anyone ever told you that you look exactly like Dirk Adams?"

He doesn't blink. He combs his perfect hair with his perfect fingers.

I jump up off the couch. "Oh my God! Oh my God!" I yell, pointing at him. "You're Dirk Adams! You're Dirk Adams!"

I take two steps backward and knock into one of the samovars, sending it crashing to the floor. I scream really loud, like I'm being murdered.

Dirk Adams rolls his eyes. I've seen every movie he's starred in, but I've never seen him roll his eyes before. I scream again.

He stands and waves his hands for me to shut up. My mouth slams shut in embarrassment. I didn't realize I was screaming until he pointed it out. My face grows hot. I must be beet red.

"Totally normal reaction," he says, smiling. "Happens all the time."

"Dirk Adams touched my knee," I tell him, as if I'm giving TMZ an exclusive. "Dirk Adams carried me."

He nods. "Yes, I know. I was there."

"Dirk Adams took off my clothes," I continue. "My clothes!" I point at him and hop up and down. "Dirk Adams isn't wearing a shirt!"

Dirk runs into the bedroom and comes out a few seconds later, slipping a t-shirt over his head. The thin piece of cotton covering his upper body calms me slightly. At least, I'm no longer screaming.

He gestures toward the sofa. "Please," he says, calmly.

I take a seat, and he sits back down on the coffee table. Our legs are almost touching. I bite my lower lip to stop the scream I feel building in my throat.

"What are you doing here?" I whisper.

"I'm on vacation," he says.

"But this is my cabin. I would know if you were here," I whisper.

"And now you know."

"But why wasn't I told before? I'm in charge of the food." I'm still whispering like an idiot, but it's either that or I'm going to start screaming again. It's some sort of psychosis that a person develops when they're in close proximity to the biggest movie star on the planet.

"I guess you were kept in the dark because they didn't realize how calmly you would handle my presence here," he says.

"Oh," I nod. "Maybe."

"And I like to cook. I cook for myself. Are you hungry?"

"Yes," I say without thinking. He slaps his thighs and bounces up. I watch him walk away toward the kitchen. He looks exactly like he does in the movies. Tall, heavily muscled, with an ass you can crack walnuts on.

"Are you coming?" he asks, turning his head.

# CHAPTER 3

Am I coming? Hell, yeah. I would follow him anywhere. He's Dirk Adams!

"Yes!" I announce and take two steps. "I mean, no! I can't eat. I'm in training."

He ignores me and keeps on walking. The kitchen is small and practical with the Turkish theme my mother insisted on giving the whole cabin. My family is pretty eccentric, to use the politically correct word for batshit crazy. My mom gives every cabin her own touch, either an international theme or something New Agey.

Dirk Adams pulls a frying pan out of a drawer and puts it on the stove. He takes a dozen eggs out of the refrigerator and cracks six open into a bowl. He takes a handful of mushrooms and dices them on the cutting board and throws them in the frying pan with a half stick of butter.

"I'm in training," I squeak.

He's still ignoring me. He pours in the eggs and after a minute, a hunk of cheese. While it's cooking, he slices a loaf of sourdough and washes up some grapes. He folds over the omelet, turns off the stove, and slides the omelet onto a plate. He puts it all on the kitchen table, hands me a fork and sits down.

"Come on," he says. "Sit. Eat."

"But—" I start, but I sit, anyway. Even though I'm in training, how can I refuse Dirk Adams?

He hands me a slice of bread and cuts half of the omelet and put it on my plate. Dirk eats with gusto, taking a bite of egg, quickly followed by some bread. It all looks delicious, but my head is filled with visions of Wade in his custom-made suit ignoring me, and I can't make myself eat.

Dirk doesn't like to take no for an answer, at least not at mealtimes. He pushes my plate closer to me. "Eat," he says with his mouth full.

I look at my piece of bread. "How many carbs are in a slice of sourdough?"

"Who gives a shit?"

"I'm in training!" I yell, pounding the table. "It's also the middle of the night. You're not supposed to eat after six."

He finishes his omelet and pops another slice of bread in his mouth. My stomach growls. Training sucks. I hate training.

I love bread.

My fork is still in my hand. I poke the omelet tentatively and finally cut a piece and put it in my mouth. Delicious. I eye the bread while I take another bite of the eggs. Dirk picks up the slice of bread I've been eyeing and hands it to me.

Dirk Adams is feeding me.

It takes me about three minutes to finish my omelet, eat four slices of bread, and a handful of grapes. I look down at my empty plate and say goodbye to my future with Wade Gates.

"You look like someone shot your puppy," Dirk says.

"I was in training," I say, my voice cracking with emotion.

"Take it from me, training is not supposed to make you pass out or starve to death."

He has kind eyes. They're not just pretty. There's something behind them. Intelligence. Caring.

My head drops onto the table. "The sun's going to come up soon," I cry. "That means I'm down to five days. I can never become Keira Knightley in five days."

"Keira Knightley?"

"She's skinny. And I'm—I'm—fat!" I break down in sobs, and my nose drips on the table. Dirk hands me a napkin.

"Okay. Enough of this. You're not fat," he growls.

"Yes I am. I'm way fatter than Keira Knightley. I'm way fatter than you!"

"I'm six-foot-four and two-hundred-twenty pounds. I think you have a ways to go before you're as big as I am. Why do you need to lose weight within five days?"

"That's when Wade comes back."

Dirk laughs. One loud guffaw. "A man. Of course. I should have known. You're killing yourself over some guy?"

I lift my head off the table and sit up straight. "Not some guy. Wade Gates."

"Your boyfriend?"

"Yes, but he doesn't know he's my boyfriend, yet."

Dirk smiles. "Why do you want a jerk who doesn't want you just the way you are?"

"He's not a jerk. He's perfect."

"So perfect that he doesn't want you?"

"Yes," I say, louder than intended. "He's perfect, and I'm not."

"Oh, geez."

"It's true." My voice hitches, and I will myself not to cry in front of a movie superstar.

"Nobody's perfect."

I blow my nose on a napkin. "You're not supposed to say that. Don't you know anything? You're supposed to tell me that I'm perfect. Come on, make me feel better."

He rolls his eyes. "My father used to be in the car business," he says.

"I know." I know pretty much everything about Dirk Adams. Who doesn't? He was voted Sexiest Man Alive five years in a row. He's H.O.T.

"Okay," he continues. "Well, my dad used to tell me that there's an 'ass for every seat.' In other words, no matter even if it's a purple car with orange interior, somebody out there is going to want that car. You may not be perfect—and nobody's perfect—but there's an ass out there for you. I guarantee it."

Could he be right? There's an ass out there for me? I'm just a purple car in a silver car world?

"But the only ass I want is Wade Gates," I say. "I mean, I want his ass."

Dirk clears the table and washes the dishes. I rub my eyes to make sure I'm seeing what I think I'm seeing. My family has rented out cabins and houses to a lot of rich people, and most of them are slobs. It wouldn't dawn on them to clean up after themselves. That's what servants are for.

But not Dirk Adams. He washes his own dishes.

Once the kitchen's clean, he throws a bag of popcorn into the microwave and takes two beers out of the refrigerator.

"Let's go sit on the couch. The living room is a hell of a lot more comfortable."

"Don't you want me to leave?" I ask. "You kind of saved my life, but I'm fine now, and you must want to get some sleep."

"I'm a night owl." He takes the popcorn and the beers and

walks to the living room. I follow him and sit next to him on the couch.

Oh my God. Dirk Adams and Raine Harper are sitting together on a couch. I hear the Twilight Zone music playing in my head. I can't wait to post about this on Facebook.

"So what's so special about Wade Gates' ass?" he asks.

"I've loved him since preschool." In my mind's eye, I see little Wade Gates walk into Mrs. Chinster's class, his crayon box in one hand, and his blankey in his other. Even then, he was something special. "And I walked right up to him and said, 'Hello, let's be best friends,' and I took his hand."

"And you were inseparable ever since?"

"Well, not exactly," I say.

Dirk hands me a bottle of beer and swigs from his own. "How much of not exactly are you talking about?"

I bite my lip. I don't know how much to tell him. I've gotten a lot of crap from people about my love for Wade Gates.

But Dirk is so understanding. His whole thing about an ass for every seat was very insightful.

"Well, he bit my hand and went to play with Lucy Ferris, the prettiest girl in class," I admit.

Dirk spits out his mouthful of beer, spraying it across the room. He's laughing uncontrollably, spilling even more beer from his bottle, as he convulses with laughter.

"It's not funny!" I yell. "I had to get two stitches." I show him the tiny scar above my thumb, and he laughs even louder.

"Typical," I say, upset that he's laughing at my relationship with Wade. I put my bottle down on the coffee table and cross my arms in front of me.

"Okay. Okay." He catches his breath and taps my leg. "Sorry. I'm sure he got better from there. Did you guys go out in high school? Homecoming dance? The prom?"

"Not exactly."

"Did you flirt? Share an ice cream cone?"

I pick up my beer and take a swig. My face is hot. Embarrassed.

"Does he know your name?" Dirk continues. "If you walked down the street, would he know who you are?"

"Yes!" I shout, snapping my fingers. "I tutored him for senior French, and he grew up on the lake, a couple houses away from mine. He would definitely recognize me."

"Good. That's something. So you guys grew up together."

"Well, our families are pretty different," I explain. "Mine's certifiable and his are certified accountants."

"So, no summer barbecues together?"

"But I love him!"

"So tell him," Dirk says, reasonably.

"Don't be an idiot. I can't just tell him. I'm not ready. I have to be thin first." I take a handful of Dirk's popcorn and shove it in my mouth.

Dirk grabs some, too, and we eat half of the bag before I get a stroke of genius. "I know! I know!" I yell. "You can train me. You're always training for one movie or another. You were a beast in Speed Freak III. I only need to be one-tenth of a beast."

"You can't become a beast in five days, even one-tenth of a beast. Besides, you're fine. Guys like a little junk in the trunk. Men don't want to sleep with a bone. It's gross."

He's so full of shit.

"You're so full of shit," I say. "You've slept with every bone in Hollywood. You're the king of bones. You wouldn't know junk in the trunk if you were hit in the head with it."

Yes, I realize I'm yelling at an American treasure. But I have no choice. He's so full of shit. Besides, not only do I have junk in my trunk, but I have it in every other part of my body, as well. He's full of shit, and I'm full of junk.

"Point is, he'll love you the way you are," he says.

"Look who's been drinking the Oprah Kool-Aid."

Dirk drops the popcorn bag on the coffee table and put his bottle down. He wipes his hands on his shorts and turns toward me. I giggle. It's a lot sitting next to him. It's like spotting a four-leaf clover. Special.

"All right. So you're not his typical type," he says. "There are other ways to catch a man."

"You mean roofies?"

"Uh, well, no, I didn't mean roofies." He gives me a double take, and I smile reassuringly.

"Threesomes?" I ask. "'cause I'm not going there. It's bad enough to be naked in front of one person."

"Nothing quite that drastic. I was thinking more of sharing an interest with him, showing up at the same place. Fitting in. That sort of thing."

"That's a good idea," I say.

"What interests do you share?"

"Well, he's a big corporate lawyer in Silicon Valley, and I'm a caterer at the lake in Esperanza."

Dirk nods. "So, nothing there. How about hobbies?"

"I think he plays tennis. That's way too much running for me. I cook, obviously. I don't think he cooks." I think hard. What does Wade like to do? "Deep sea diving!"

"Great. So you have that in common."

"Oh, no. I couldn't do that. Bad ears," I say, pointing to my ears. "And I'm not a big fan of water. But I hear he's quite accomplished. He went to the Great Barrier Reef. He posted pics on Instagram." Dirk furrows his eyebrows. "Don't look at me like that. I'm not stalking him," I say. "I just like to see what he's up to."

He's grinning at me like a madman. I'm cracking him up, and I'm not sure I should be happy about that.

"Maybe you just need to up the sex appeal. You need to show him some more va-va-voom," he says. "Walk for me."

"Excuse me?"

"Walk," he says, pushing me off the couch. "Show me your walk."

He leans back on the couch, kicks off his shoes, and puts his feet up on the coffee table. He's relaxed, but he's expecting me to put on a show. I can't walk. I can barely stand. But he's waiting, and I figure since he's been so nice to me, I might as well give it a try.

"Should I swing my hips?" I ask.

"Just think of Marilyn Monroe and walk across the room. Men are suckers for a woman with a good walk."

I stand at one end of the small room and take a deep breath. I try to remember how Marilyn Monroe walked. I sneak a glance at Dirk. "I can't believe I'm walking for Dirk Adams," I say.

"One foot in front of the other," he says, gesturing with his hand like a symphony conductor.

I put my hands on my waist to steady myself. I take a step

and wiggle my hips as much as I can. "I'm doing pretty well," I announce, surprised at myself as I make it halfway across the room.

"Keep going. Give it all you got. More. More!" Dirk yells.

I should feel ridiculous, but I'm feeling pretty sexy. I'm channeling Marilyn Monroe. I'm wiggling and walking. Walking and wiggling.

I make it just past the coffee table when my wiggle goes too far for my walking, and my back locks in a muscle spasm that drops me to my knees in pain.

Dirk jumps off the couch and makes a beeline for me. He kneels down and sticks his face in mine. "Are you all right?"

"Back," I croak. "Back. Ow. Back."

I'm on all fours, and I can't move at all. "I can't see Wade like this," I wail.

"Oh my God. You were done in by Marilyn Monroe."

*

Here's why I think I'm either dead or hallucinating. I'm lying on my stomach on Dirk Adams' bed, and his hands are working their way all over my body.

"I wish I had my camera," I say into his pillow that smells like him and is driving me crazy. "This would be the best selfie ever."

"Feeling better?" he asks.

"I can assure you that even if I were feeling pain, I would be feeling no pain right now."

He works the back spasm out of me, and when he's done, covers me with his blanket and lies down next to me, facing me.

"I'm in bed with Dirk Adams," I say, giggling.

"I think I've figured out how to get Wade," he says. It takes me a second to recall who Wade is. Dirk is awfully close. "Perception is reality. Even if Wade is attracted to bonier females, you can up your attractive quotient by upping your demand."

"You lost me."

"You need to make him jealous. You need to show him that other men want you. One man in particular."

"Who? Who?" His idea sounds like it has potential, but who could I find to want me who would make Wade jealous? Wade is the best-looking and most successful man our town has ever known.

"What do you mean, who?" Dirk asks. "You're looking at him."

# CHAPTER 4

I'm never late to work. Never. I'm the responsible member of my family.

"You're late," my brother Lennon says as I walk through the kitchen door. "Dad's pissed. He had to do your breakfast run instead of go fishing."

I have twelve siblings, but Lennon and I are the only ones still living with our parents. I'm number twelve in the family lineup, and he's lucky number thirteen. The others are spread out around the lake. Nobody has ventured far away. My parents may be loons, but they have a magnetic quality that's kept us close.

"He didn't make the renters his famous Eggspectacular. Did he?" I ask Lennon. "Please say he didn't."

"It was either that or his Velveeta fondue, which isn't

exactly appropriate for breakfast."

Dad only knows how to cook two dishes. I shudder at the thought of my father's Velveeta fondue. I ate it every Wednesday for dinner for almost a whole year when I was seven years old, when my mother was busy taking a Reiki class. While she was learning alternative massage, her husband was packing her children's arteries with cheese product.

Now my twelve siblings and I are pretty anti-Velveeta fondue.

Lennon grabs a wrench off the counter and burrows under the kitchen sink. Every member of my family has a role in our family business. Lennon's the plumber. He has his work cut out for him. Not only do we have properties all around the lake, the family house is a pioneer-era sprawling building. Three stories. There's even a tower. It needs constant maintenance and upkeep.

I check out the list of guests and renters. I have a big shopping list to deal with and several lunches to prepare. There's not a lot of time to get things done, but I'm dog-tired. I put a pot a coffee on and sit at the kitchen table.

The door bursts open, and my mother and three oldest sisters storm in. I call them the triumvirate of terror. They and my mother rule the family with an iron will and an abundance of hippy logic. They're convinced they're living in Woodstock circa 1969. Each of them has gray hair that falls to below their shoulders. More than one kid has mistaken them for witches.

My mother throws her hemp shopping bag on the table and takes a look at me. "Your aura is off," she says, pointing at me, punching the air with her finger, as if she's testing my aura for durability.

"I'm tired," I explain.

My sisters, Serenity, Willow, and Moonbeam circle me, studying me.

"I'm sensing a disruption in Raine," Moonbeam tells the others, as she rifles through my hair.

"Maybe because you're sticking your armpit in my face,

and you don't believe in using real deodorant or shaving," I say, swatting her hands away.

"I've seen this before," Serenity says. "Might be rabies."

"I don't have rabies," I growl. I get up and pour myself a cup of coffee.

"It's not rabies," Willow says. "It's something worse. Halitosis."

"Halitosis is not worse than rabies," I say. "Halitosis means bad breath."

Willow nods. "I know," she says.

Lennon pops his head out from under the sink. "She doesn't have rabies. She got laid."

My sisters laugh. The idea that I have a sex life is a laugh riot.

I slam my coffee cup on the counter, making half of it spill. "Why is that funny?" I demand. "Is it so crazy to think that someone would want to make love to me?"

They're still laughing. The idea of my sex life is like an Adam Sandler movie to them, but funny.

Of course, Lennon is flat out wrong. I didn't get laid. Nobody made love to me or even offered. No kiss. No cuddling. No flirtation. But that doesn't mean it's impossible.

My mother catches her breath and pats my shoulder. "Your aura isn't reading sex, Raine," she explains, as if I'm confusing a fork with a spoon.

"I'm telling you, it's rabies," Moonbeam says.

It's not easy having hippy sisters who are thirty years older than I am. They think they're my mother, and they believe way too much in the power of the colonic. It's just a matter of time before they chase me around the house with a hose. I need to nip this whole aura thing in the bud before they Niagara Falls my ass.

"Look at her hair. That's sex hair," Lennon says, wielding his wrench for emphasis. The four of them argue about my aura and the sex or non-sex aspects of my hair. It gets pretty heated for a group of pacifists. The only thing they can agree on is my halitosis.

I try to tune them out and drink the rest of my coffee. If I don't start making sandwiches, the Goldstein family across the lake is going to be foodless on their picnic. I cut thick slices of homemade brioche and take a chicken I roasted yesterday out of the refrigerator.

"Rabies!"

"I'm telling you, she got nailed! Boned! She took a ride on the screwed express!" Lennon shouts over my sisters' assertions that I have a terrible disease. Meanwhile, my mother is still poking the air at my invisible aura.

There's a knock at the door, which shuts everybody up. My family has a well-known open door policy, so a knock raises suspicions. Who would knock on the Harper family's door?

"The cops?" Willow mouths.

"Should we hide?" Serenity whispers.

Lennon raises his wrench high, like it's a weapon.

I wipe my hands on a towel and answer the door. "Yes?" I ask.

"Muffin!"

It's not an exaggeration to say the air molecules in the room warp and twist into something totally different, proving the theory of an alternate universes. If I turned into bubble gum, my family wouldn't be as surprised as they are by our guest.

"Muffin?" my mother asks. "Who's muffin?"

I have no idea who Muffin is, but movie star superstar Dirk Adams seems to know, because he's standing on the threshold, and he shouted it with absolute certainty—if I'm not mistaken—right at me.

He's blindingly handsome in the daylight, tall, built, and dressed in worn jeans and a tight t-shirt. He's clean-shaven, but his hair is slightly too long. Thick blond hair that's been blown off target by a windy day. Big brown eyes that are focused entirely on me.

I stumble back a step, and he catches me in his arms, embracing me, as if I'm his long lost lover.

Lennon is the first one to snap out of our communal shock. "Holy shit! It's—It's—It's—" he waves at Dirk and hops up and down.

"A man!" Moonbeam finishes for him, clapping her hands.

Here's the thing. I'm not a monster. I'm twenty-three years old and have had my share of boyfriends. Not Madonna's share of boyfriends, but a normal share of boyfriends. But my family doesn't know that, because I've never brought any of my boyfriends home to meet them. No sane man would stay with me after seeing my father's all-squirrel Polka band.

Dirk hugs me, my face smooshed against his chest. He smells so good that I could eat him. I'm not entirely sure why he's here, but I have a sneaking suspicion it's about something he told me in the wee hours of the morning. Something about making

Wade jealous.

I didn't take him seriously, but here he is hugging me. So, I guess he's all in.

"It's not a man!" shouts my brother. "It's Jake Storm!" Jake Storm is the name of Dirk's character in his Space Ho series. Space Ho has made more money than Star Wars and Avatar, combined.

Lennon tears Dirk and me apart and pumps Dirk's hand, like he's trying to bring up water. "Jake Storm! Jake Storm! I can't believe I'm meeting you in person! I mean, you're real, man. You're real!"

"This is Mr. Adams," my mom corrects him. "He's staying at the Turkish cabin."

My sisters nod together like the witches in Macbeth. "The Turkish cabin," they say in unison, as if that says it all.

Dirk wraps his arm around my shoulders. "I just came to pick up Raine for the day," he announces.

"You what?" I ask.

"I'm not going to spend any precious time away from my Muffin," he says.

It's amazing that he gets paid thirty-million a picture, because this is the worst bit of acting I've ever witnessed. Still, my family seems convinced, even if they're shocked, and I'm giggling like a schoolgirl.

"Oh, dude, that scene in Speed Freak II: Freakier where you jump off the cliff, land on the car, jack it, drive off the bridge into the water, down the waterfall, steer to shore, and go right on driving until you hit downtown Los Angeles.... Dude, that was epic!" Lennon says. His face is lit up with excitement. He's a kid on Christmas morning, faced with a new bike, a puppy, and a PlayStation.

"Are you in the theater arts?" my mother asks. She and the triumvirate of terror don't believe in movies or television.

"He's a god, Mom. A god," Lennon informs her.

"Vishnu's a god," she corrects him. "This is Mr. Adams."

I will the strength to push Dirk away. His touch is way too distracting. I can't think clearly when he gives me skin contact. "I have to prepare the Goldsteins' picnic," I say. "I don't have time for whatever this is."

"I'll put the picnic together," Dirk offers. "You can go get cleaned up and get dressed."

My hand flies to my hair. I forgot that I haven't brushed it since yesterday. And I'm wearing yesterday's clothes. I take him up on his offer to make lunch. "The bread's there. So is the chicken. Just make it simple and delicious, okay?"

I run out of the kitchen and up the stairs. I live in the tower on the top floor. It's enough out of the way to afford me some privacy, and I have a spectacular view of the lake and each evening's sunset.

I hop in the shower and wash off the night's run and let the hot water loosen up my back. Dirk did a good job massaging it, but it's still a little sore. I squeeze a dollop of wickedly priced anticellulite cream into my hand and smear it all over my body.

"Shrink. Shrink. Shrink," I urge my body. I'm down to five days until Wade arrives. I know what I'm going to wear when I see him. I have the dress in my closet, waiting for the moment. Sure, it's a size too small, but I'm trying to be optimistic.

Cellulite cream, training, and a movie star to make Wade jealous are all stacked on my side in my effort to snag the love of my life. I also have the wish I made at the fountain two days ago. I can't forget about that. I used an entire roll of quarters to make sure the wish would have a shot.

I stood at Esperanza's famous centenarian fountain and ripped open the quarters, squidged my face, focused on my wish—please let Wade love me. Please, please, please—and threw the ten dollars' worth of quarters into the dry fountain. They bounced and ricocheted, cracking the old plaster.

I watched them roll around the bottom of the fountain until they were stopped by years of debris. "Huh," I said. "That's all it takes?" I didn't feel any different, but what could it hurt? The fountain is famous. People come from all over to make wishes in it.

As I stood there, a young woman in round-rimmed glasses approached me, I guess attracted by the noise of the coins. "Interesting," she said. "Is this a form of charity, or are you engaging in the pagan ritual of using a fountain or a well or likewise containers of water to make a wish?"

"Charity," I lied.

"Interesting."

"I've seen you around," I said. "At the university, right?"

"I'm Marie." She held out her hand for me to shake. "PhD candidate in chemical engineering."

"That's right. Wow, you're young for a PhD student."

"I started college when I was thirteen." Her hair was pulled back in a ponytail. She was wearing jeans and a man's t-shirt and flip-flops. She was way too pretty to be a genius, but she was dressed a lot like Einstein. It dawned on me that I could use a genius chemist right about then.

"I'm Raine," I said. "I catered a lunch for the engineering department. Chemistry, huh? I've been doing an experiment in chemistry."

"With the coins?"

"Well sort of. I'm trying to figure out if where there's no chemical attraction, one can be built or appear—you know, where it wasn't before."

Marie pushed her glasses up on her nose and seemed to think about my experiment. "Interesting. A spontaneous chemical reaction between two hitherto indifferent forces. Between what objects?"

"Humans."

"Interesting. Interesting."

"So, is it possible?" I asked.

"Everything's possible."

"How about making it happen? Can you do that with your

chemical engineering?"

"Hmm…"

I might have twisted her arm, but the scientist in her couldn't resist studying my dilemma. So, I have science on my side, too. We have an appointment today right after I deliver the picnic to the Goldsteins.

Am I crazy to feel optimistic? Is this how Patton felt right before the Battle of the Bulge?

I step out of the shower and wrap one towel around my body and one around my head. I wipe the mirror and study my reflection.

Sigh.

I look the same.

"Why? Why!" I yell at my reflection.

"Is that the way to talk to a beautiful woman?" At first, I think the mirror is talking to me, but then I realize Dirk Adams has invaded my mirror. His reflection is right next to mine. I spin around, and there he is, standing in the doorway of my bathroom. I must have forgotten to close the door.

"I'm in a towel!" I yell, horrified, waving my hands to block his view.

And then my towel slips.

# CHAPTER 5

I stand frozen in place, staring down at the towel, which is pooled at my ankles. Seconds turn into minutes, and I'm just staring at the towel. I can't believe I'm standing naked in my bathroom with Dirk Adams looking at me.

I'm naked. I'm mortified. I urge myself to bend down and get the towel, but I've forgotten how to move my limbs. I've got some kind of disconnect happening between my brain and my limbs.

"Would you like me to get that?" he asks.

I shut my eyes. Maybe if I can't see him, he can't seem me. I hear him approach, and my skin comes alive as he bends down and picks up the towel, and his hair grazes my body ever so slightly.

"Lift your arms," he says, his voice impossibly low and

smooth. I lift my arms and crack open my eyes, looking up to meet his gaze. His brown eyes have turned black as night. He looks a lot like his alter ego Jake Storm right now. Like he's going to blow something up or steal my car.

Gently, he wraps the towel around me and rests his hands on my chest where the towel comes together. I gurgle and cough. First my limbs and now my power of speech. I'm falling apart.

"I may be having a stroke," I finally manage to say.

Dirk flinches and seems to wake up. He runs his hand through his hair and looks around. Anywhere but here, I think. He turns around and bolts out of the bathroom, letting my towel fall back to the floor. This time my limbs work, and I quickly grab it around me and shut the door.

I take deep, healing breaths, but it's not enough. I still feel like I've been hit by a truck. I lie on the bathroom floor and try to calm down. Really, Dirk has no idea of the power he has over women. He needs to register himself as a lethal weapon.

I get dressed in jeans and a blue top. "I'm coming out," I

announce. "I'm not naked."

Dirk is sitting on my bed, rifling through my high school yearbook. "This is Wade?" he asks, showing me his photo on the senior page. I nod. "'Susan, have a nice summer, your science partner, Wade Gates,'" he reads. "Who's Susan?"

I look at the photo of Wade. His thoughtful blue eyes stare back at me. I drew red hearts all around his picture right after graduation. Mistaking my name hurt my feelings at the time—especially since there wasn't even a Susan in our class to confuse me with—but I'm just happy to have his autograph. I touch it and smile.

"Oh, you've got it really bad," Dirk says.

"I thought I made that clear," I say. "I have it really bad. Really, really bad."

He closes the yearbook. "Okay. We'll make it happen."

The Twilight Zone music is still playing in my head. "Why are you here?" I ask.

"I'm going to help you. Operation Jealousy. He'll finally see you because I'll worship you, and you'll pretend you don't care about him."

"This sounds like an episode of The Brady Bunch."

"In which you're Jan."

"Typical. I've always wanted to be Marsha," I say and sit down next to him. "Why are you doing this? You don't even know me."

"Maybe I don't have anything better to do."

"You're Dirk Adams. Everything you do is something better to do."

"I'm not really Dirk Adams."

"Huh?" I ask.

"I'm Adam Dirkson."

"Adam Dirkson," I say, tasting the name on my lips. "Are you sure?"

Dirk takes his wallet out of his pocket and hands me his driver's license. "That's an old one from before they made me change my name."

It's definitely him. Younger, but unmistakable. His hair is blond and wavy, and his smile is brilliant as always, but with something more. Eternal potential with no pressure or worries.

"Adam Dirkson," I read. "Six-foot-four. Two-hundred-twenty pounds. Yep. It's you."

I return his license. He glances at it and puts it back in his wallet. I don't know why he's confiding in me. I search his face for a clue, but I get nothing. Just sexy movie star face.

"Okay. I'll be your Jan Brady," I say. "But I don't really understand how this is going to work."

"Just follow along. We'll set the foundation now so it rings true when Mr. Perfect comes to town in five days."

I don't want to pretend I have a boyfriend in front of my family, but he has a point about making this work. The illusion has to be complete.

"Okay."

*

We practically have to fight our way out of the house. Lennon called my other six brothers, and they ambush Dirk in the kitchen. Dirk insists on holding my hand to make the boyfriend thing believable. I guess as an actor, he's all "method". He doesn't fall out of character once.

"Dude, that scene where you jumped off the cliff onto the car, jacked the car, drove off the bridge into the water, went over the waterfall, steered to shore, and drove all the way to downtown Los Angeles. That was epic!" my oldest brother, Gandhi says.

I roll my eyes and try to grab the picnic basket, but I'm blocked by a wall of testosterone. "Arm wrestle me, man," Lennon orders Dirk. "Come on, let's see what you got."

"Yeah!" my other brothers shout. Suddenly they've turned into the World Wrestling Summer Slam, and my mother's kitchen is the center ring. Meanwhile, my sisters and mother are nowhere to be found, leaving me and Dirk against the band of mouth breathers.

"We have to go," I say, trying to get to the basket, again. I still can't get past my brothers. "Out of my way," I grunt, pushing at them. No luck. They're immovable.

Then, just like the Red Sea with Dirk as Moses, they part. Dirk's muscle-bound arm paves the way for me to walk past my brothers and get the basket.

"How about another time?" he asks my brothers. "The little lady says we have to be on our way."

The little lady. The little lady?

"No problem, man," Gandhi says, slapping his back. "We'll wrestle tonight, when you come back for the party."

"Party?" I ask. "What party? No, no party. Dirk, you don't have to go to any party."

"We'll arm wrestle and wrestle for real," Gandhi says,

ignoring me.

"Fight club!" Lennon shouts, and my other six brothers cheer on this fabulous idea.

"No! No fight club!" I yell. "You don't have to do the fight club," I tell Dirk. "Or the wrestling. Or the party. In fact, you never have to come back here again. Never."

I direct the last part to my brothers.

"A party sounds like fun," Dirk says, and he's greeted by another round of my brothers' cheers.

Lennon slaps his back. "Of course we're going to have a party. My sister's dating Dirk Adams!"

My head begins to throb. How am I going to pretend that a movie star is my boyfriend in front of my whole family? I grab the basket in one hand, and I drag Dirk out the door. Once outside, I gasp fresh air, and he takes the basket from me to carry.

"That went well," he says.

"Maybe I can get us out of the party," I say, biting a fingernail. "There must be a way. Maybe I could set fire to the house."

"Fire to the house?"

"No, you're right. They would just move the party outside. What we need is a major earthquake or a tsunami."

He gives my hand a squeeze. "Okay, girlfriend. Which way are you taking me?"

# CHAPTER 6

It's a thirty-minute walk to the house where the Goldstein family is staying. We could get there in a fraction of the time if we took a boat, but I prefer dry land. It's another beautiful summer's day in Esperanza. The lake is filled with boaters, either fishing or just relaxing and enjoying the day.

The Goldsteins are going to be among them. They're renting our speedboat for the afternoon. The shoreline is quiet, except for the occasional group of teenagers, who're sunbathing and swimming. I enjoy people watching. It's one of my favorite things about my job. But most of the time I work alone. I like the solitude, and it's disorienting having Dirk with me.

"You don't have to hold my hand," I say. "Nobody can see. You can give it a rest."

"I'm a consummate actor, Raine. I don't break the illusion for anything." He gives my hand a squeeze. I'm almost getting used to the skin contact. My urge to scream has left altogether, and I only giggle occasionally, now.

"I love it here," he says. "Beautiful. Peaceful. No paparazzi."

"Paparazzi? They wouldn't know where to find us. Nobody knows where to find us. We are the last secret in America."

"I hope it stays that way. I'd like to spend a lot more time here."

"But you have to fly to Iceland at the end of the week to start shooting Speed Freaks IV."

Dirk looks at me and grins. "You know more about me than I do."

"Subscription to People magazine. I'm not stalking you. Honest."

"If I had a dollar for every time somebody said that to me, I'd be a very rich man."

"You are a very rich man."

*

I'm late, again. The Goldstein family set me back a full hour. Normally I hand off the food to the guests, and then I'm gone, letting them enjoy their vacation. I do the shopping, I bring the groceries, and then I'm all like the wind. The invisible woman.

But being escorted by America's treasure is slowing me down. No, not slowing me down. Making me come to a full stop. Period.

"Does that happen every time?" I ask Dirk as we walk into town.

"Every time. Every stinkin' time."

"I think you may have impregnated Mrs. Goldstein."

"I think Mrs. Goldstein may have impregnated me," he

counters.

It was a free-for-all when we arrived. Mr. Goldstein recognized Dirk first. He ran out to us before we even got to the house. Just like my brothers, he wanted to arm wrestle Dirk, and Dirk complied. With the whole family looking on in the kitchen, Dirk threw Mr. Goldstein's arm down on the table within two seconds or less.

"You didn't have to sprain the man's hand," I tell Dirk. "He's a pianist. How's he going to play the piano?"

"Look, I've learned not to let the fan win the arm wrestling. It disappoints them. They want me to win. They want me to be Jake Storm. Me spraining his arm just fulfills his fantasy."

"It's a shame you couldn't fulfill Mrs. Goldstein's fantasy."

"Mrs. Goldstein is a freak. I wasn't about to fulfill her fancy. There aren't enough antibiotics in the world to do that."

The University of Esperanza is a beautiful Adobe-style group of buildings, laid out a lot like Stanford, in long rows with a center plaza for students to mingle in.

"Are you in college?" Dirk asks.

"Oh God no. High school was bad enough. I'm not the academic type. We're here to hedge my bets."

"Huh?"

"I'm getting science on my side. Wade isn't going to stand a chance."

"You're not going to try and clone me, are you? They tried that before, and it hurt."

I stop walking. "You shouldn't joke about things like that. A lot of people would like to see you cloned."

He lets go of my hand and wraps his arm around my waist, pulling me close. "What are you doing?" I ask.

"My hand was getting sweaty. And I like it better this way, anyway. "

Dirk Adams is a mystery to me. I don't know if he's bored

and just playing with me, or if he's really into this act, but one thing's for certain, it sure feels good to have his arm wrapped around my waist.

*

It takes us a while to find Marie's lab. It turns out it's a windowless cavern, full of mysterious machinery. There are four scientists working hard, so focused on their work that they don't even look up when we enter. Marie is in the back, hunched over a pad of paper and furiously marking down rows of equations.

Math. Blech.

"Hi, Marie," I say. "Sorry we're late."

She looks up and pushes her glasses up on her nose. She's blank-faced, disorientated, and it's obvious she has no idea who I am.

"Remember me? The fountain? The chemistry experiment?"

Marie slaps her forehead as she remembers. "Oh, yeah. I'm

ready for you. I've asked around, and I think I have something that'll work. Is this your boyfriend? It looks like you already have an active chemical attraction going."

I laugh. "You think that he's my—" I start and become hysterical. I snort and clutch onto my side, as I laugh harder. "He's Dirk Adams. He's not my boyfriend," I say, finally.

"Nice to meet you, Mr. Adams," Marie says. There isn't a glimmer of recognition in her eyes. She has no idea who he is.

"We really are boyfriend and girlfriend," Dirk says, winking at her.

"That's what I thought. There's some definite mating posturing going on, not to mention flushing of the skin, showing that you are in a constant state of arousal."

"Of course I'm in a constant state of arousal," I say. "He's Dirk Adams. But he's not my boyfriend." Sheesh. She's supposed to be some kind of genius, but she can't figure this out? "You can tell her the truth, Dirk. She's part of team Raine."

Dirk shrugs. "I don't know what she's talking about," he says, his voice deadpan, and his face unreadable.

"Well, he's not the target of my experiment," I tell Marie. "There's no mating posturing going on with my target. You understand? This is urgent."

"Right. So, here's what we came up with." Marie opens door of her desk and pulls out a small metal cylinder.

"Deodorant?" I ask.

"Close," she says. "Pheromones. A mixture of several animals, reputed to work very efficiently. Highly potent. All I ask is that you carefully note the amount of sprays that you apply and the time of day and the outcome."

She hands me the container, and I take it, greedily. For the first time since I found out that Wade was coming back into town, I'm optimistic that I'll make him fall in love with me and we'll live happily ever after. Science is on my side. I know this will work.

# CHAPTER 7

"It occurs to me that we haven't eaten today," Dirk says. After the university, he helped me make a grocery run, and I delivered supplies to a few of our renters. But this time, I had the presence of mind to hide him behind the bushes, so three deliveries only took fifteen minutes.

"Really? I forgot to eat?" I ask. I'm not known for skipping meals. I once ate an entire pizza while I had the stomach flu. "Do you think it's the spray Marie gave me?" I hold up the silver cylinder.

"You haven't tried it, yet."

I'm dying to try Marie's secret sauce. It's my ace in the hole. Dirk seems pretty confident that the jealousy ruse is going to work, but I like having some cold, hard science on my side.

"Maybe I should spray some on me to try it out, now." I take the silver cylinder out of my pocket. It's about the size of a deodorant bottle but metallic, smooth and cool to the touch.

Dirk snatches it out of my hand. "Nuh uh," he says. "Too dangerous. Wait until the moment's right. Okay?"

He gives me back my chemical weapon, and I slip it into my back pocket. My stomach growls. "I guess I'm hungry," I say.

"Good. I'll cook."

We walk to his cabin, together. I'm relieved to have someplace to go besides my house. At this point, I imagine my family is in full gear, preparing for the party. With my family and their families and friends attending, it's going to be a monster. A nightmare.

"I hate parties," I say.

"Me, too."

"I usually hide in the corner. If I go, I mean."

"Me, too."

I search his face to see if he's lying. I'm spending a lot of time with him, and I'm getting used to him. He's almost like a real person, now. He has a good sense of humor, but there's a deep, serious side to him, too. I still don't understand why he's spending time with me, but I figure there's more to him than meets the eye. More to him than just a charismatic superstar.

"How's that possible?" I ask. "I've seen pictures of you at Hollywood parties."

He unlocks the cabin door and opens it. "After you," he says, careful not to reveal too much about himself.

*

Dirk seems happiest in the kitchen. Relaxed. He's good with his hands, chopping like a pro. It's a pleasure to watch him, not only because he's beautiful, but because he seems more like an artist than merely cooking lunch. He loves it.

"Let's eat in the living room," he says when he's done

cooking. We put our plates on the coffee table and sit cross-legged on the floor, facing each other.

"This looks wonderful," I say. Dirk's prepared big, juicy T-bones, some kind of potato dish, and a tossed salad.

"I don't want to hear a thing out of you about your training," he warns, pointing his fork at me. "This is a clean meal. All healthy. So eat up."

I take him at his word and cut a large piece of steak. "God, that's good," I moan.

"Nothing better than a steak. Nothing."

"Except these potatoes!" I say, spearing one with my fork. "What are these called?"

"They're my invention. Hemingway's potatoes. He used to live off something like them when he was a starving writer in Paris."

"I love Hemingway," I say.

"Me too."

We eat and talk about Hemingway and Paris. I've never been anywhere, but Dirk's been everywhere. "I've taken a few French cooking classes. I'm an ace with sauces," I say.

"So, you'll cook for me next time."

Next time? "You don't have to… I mean, I know you're doing the whole jealousy thing, but I don't want to take up your vacation."

"I'm not going to miss a chance at a home-cooked French meal," he says, smiling. I smile back. His lips glisten with the oil from Hemingway's potatoes. He sticks his tongue out slightly and licks his lips clean. My mouth drops open, and I look away. Looking at the sun can make you blind.

"Are you done?" I croak. I pick up my plate, and move to take his. He doesn't say anything, and I look up for my answer. Instead, I find him studying me. His eyes travel from my lips, all around my face, and settle on my eyes.

"Do I have something on my face?" I ask.

He smiles. "You're a beautiful woman, Raine," he says.

"Are you practicing for the Brady Bunch jealousy thing?"

"I'm done."

"What?"

"With my lunch. I'm done. You can take it, if you want."

"Oh," I say. My forehead has erupted in sweat, and I wipe it with a napkin. I take the plates and cutlery and walk to the kitchen. Putting them in the sink, I grip the counter and take a deep breath.

Dirk touches my shoulder, but I don't dare turn around. "Don't worry, I'll do the dishes," I say.

"Let's leave it until later. I have something more enjoyable for us to do now."

# CHAPTER 8

Oh, shit. What does he mean, "enjoyable?" I can't do enjoyable with Dirk Adams. It would probably kill me. Although, I would die smiling, right?

I turn around, slowly. "Enjoyable?" I ask.

"I think so. Don't make fun of me. I'm kind of a dork." He holds up a Scrabble box.

"Are you kidding? Is that what you mean by enjoyable?"

"I know, but I'm an addict." His face drops, and he lowers the box. Embarrassed.

"No," I say, touching his arm. "I'm the western Sierra Nevada champion. I can triple score your ass into next week."

"You're on."

*

"Autochthonous is too a word," I insist. We've been playing for two hours. Dirk is a fearsome competitor. I thought he had me with a triple word score, but I've got him, now. I lean back against the couch and stretch.

"Prove it."

"It was the 2004 winning word at the National Spelling Bee," I say.

He furrows his eyebrows.

"It's true," I insist.

"Western Sierra Nevada Scrabble champion strikes again?" he asks, smiling.

"I'm sorry. It's impossible to beat me. I'm a freak with a Scrabble board."

Dirk leans forward and gently touches my cheek. He focuses on the spot where his fingertips meet my skin, and he exhales. Sighs.

I crash into a million pieces. All the king's horses and all the king's men would never be able to put me back together, again. I'm done in. I close my eyes and try to think of anything else besides Dirk's fingers on me.

"An eyelash," he says, removing his fingers and leaning back. "Time to make a wish."

He hands me my eyelash and urges me to throw it over my left shoulder. "But I already made a wish with a roll of quarters," I say.

"I thought you were a fan of hedging your bets."

He's right. I am. I pinch the eyelash off his fingertip and toss it over my shoulder. But I don't make a wish. I've forgotten what to wish for.

"Do you hear that?" he asks.

At first, I think it's my heart beating out of my chest. The boom boom of the bass is making my teeth rattle, however, and there's only one thing that does that.

"It's my brother's band," I say. "I guess the party's started."

We put away the Scrabble pieces, and Dirk helps me up. He interlaces his fingers with mine and kisses my hand. "Thanks for a good game," he says.

Holy crap. Lips. Hand. Hot.

"We don't have to go to the party, you know," I say. "They're probably already sloshed and won't notice if we don't show up. They'll just convince themselves they spent the evening with Jake Storm and be happy as can be."

Dirk grins. For the first time, I notice a tiny dimple on his right cheek.

"I promised them Jake Storm, and I'm going to give them Jake Storm," he says. "Besides, it might be fun."

*

"Having fun yet?" I ask Dirk, yelling to be heard over the noise of the party. He grunts in response. Three of my brothers and my father are wrestling him at the same time. They've pushed aside the living room furniture, and they waylaid him the second we walked through the door.

I can barely see him in the middle of the pile of bodies. I only catch glimpses of an arm or leg, but mostly it's my family trying to murder him.

"Maybe you should attack him one at a time," I suggest.

"Storm! Storm! Storm!" the party guests shout, cheering on Dirk as they surround the melee in the living room. It's most likely the last thing Dirk will ever hear because he's not long for this world. At the very least, he's going to have one hell of a concussion. I tried to nix the whole wrestling idea when we arrived, but nobody paid attention to me. Not my father. Not my brothers. Not Dirk.

They went after each other like rams, but in this case, one ram against four. I'm thinking about calling the cops on my own family, and trying to remember the quickest route to the emergency room, when my oldest brother Gandhi flies up in the air, flipping once and landing—fortunately for him—on the couch, which is shoved up against the wall.

For a moment, I get a clear view of Dirk. He roars in triumph, flexing his muscles before his remaining attackers go back for the kill.

"Holy shitballs," I say.

"I hope they don't break the coffee table," my mother says behind me. "It was my grandmother's."

"What about Dirk? Aren't you worried they're going to break him?"

"Well—" she begins, but stops when my brother Lennon flies out from the center of the room to land two inches away from the coffee table. Dirk roars again, much to the delight of the cheering crowd. It's down to Dirk against my father and my brother Harmony.

My father's strong as an ox, but he's in his seventies. My brother Harmony, however, is a beast. He's a former UFC fighter, and he keeps in shape.

"It looks like your boyfriend is doing fine," my mother says.

I turn around. "He's not really my boyfriend," I say. "He's just helping me with a project."

"To make Wade Gates jealous?" she asks.

I gasp. "How did you know?"

"I gave birth to you. I've lived with you for twenty-three years. And Wade is going to stay at the Greek cabin for a couple of weeks while his house gets renovated."

"He is?"

"He's a jerk."

"He's not a jerk," I say, stomping my foot. "You don't like him because he's a Republican."

"Please," she says, putting out her hand, palm forward. "Don't say that word in my house. Anyway, Wade is in the past. Here on out, it's all about Jake Storm."

She gestures behind me, and I turn back just in time to see Dirk lay out my father and brother. He lifts his arms up in victory, making the muscles on his upper body flex. He does his signature roar, making the crowd go wild. Then, as the people rush to congratulate him, he gives a hand to my father and helps him up.

"He's not my boyfriend, Mom. He's Dirk Adams. Don't you understand?"

She taps me under my chin. "I understand better than you, Raine. You're nowhere near understanding."

The crowd clears enough for me to reach Dirk. I inspect his face and arms for permanent damage. Besides a few scrapes and bruises, he's fine. "Your shirt's ripped," I say.

"Oh," he says, looking down. He rips off the remains of his shirt and tosses it to a fan.

"You can't go around like that," I say.

"Why not? Why don't you let your boyfriend be?" my father asks. His nose is bleeding, and he's got a doozy of a shiner, but he's deliriously happy.

"It's indecent, that's why!"

"I go without a shirt all the time," my brother Harmony says. He's happy, too, but he's holding an ice pack over his hand.

"You're not Dirk Adams," I explain. "Simple." It's very hard to think straight and function normally when Dirk is half-naked. I keep closing my eyes to dull the effect he has on me.

"You got an extra shirt, man?" Dirk asks Harmony.

"You can take one of Lennon's. His room is on the second floor. I'll show you."

"After you go to the hospital to set your hand," my mother says.

"Aw Mom, it's just a broken hand. Do I hafta leave?" He's

thirty years old, but he regresses when he's around my mother.

"You broke you hand?" I ask.

"Yeah, on my face," Dirk says, smiling. I count his teeth. Yep, all there.

"People with faces like yours don't get in fist fights," I say. "Would you treat the Mona Lisa this badly?"

"Are you comparing me to the Mona Lisa?"

"You know what I mean. Come on, let's get you a shirt."

With the floor show over, the party transforms to more or less normal with the band playing and drunk people dancing and getting more drunk.

I take one of Lennon's t-shirts from his chest of drawers, and Dirk puts it on. Then, I sneak him out the back and we walk toward the shoreline. It's a huge relief to be away from the people and the noise.

"That's better," I say.

"Listen," he says.

"The bass? I know. It's making my chest hurt."

"No, listen. It's coming from next door."

I try to tune out the hard rock pounding and the general noise level of the party guests. Sure enough, there's something more.

"Jazz!"

"Duke Ellington," Dirk says and takes me in his arms. "I hope you like to dance."

I love to dance. Not the shake my hips and pretend I'm a robot kind of dancing. This dancing, in the arms of a beautiful man who's in complete control, who leads, effortlessly.

"Dancing on the beach," I comment. I give myself a little pinch to make sure I'm not dreaming.

"Under the stars," Dirk adds. I look up. It's a gorgeous night. Magical. I rest my head on his chest and let him dance me on the sand.

"Maybe Wade will dance with you like this," he says.

"Who?" I mumble.

"The man you love."

"Yes, the man I love." I step closer to him, and he holds me tighter. It's a sensual pleasure: the soft jazz, the warm summer night, the sand under my feet, and Dirk's arms around me, our bodies pressed together, as we sway to the music.

He lets go of my hand and puts two fingers under my chin and tilts my head up. "There's so much you can do with the one you love," he says.

I'm about to agree, when he kisses me. One minute he's fighting off four men at once like a beast, and the next minute, he's kissing a woman with a velvet soft touch. His lips sweep mine in a vicious tease that makes my blood boil and my insides melt.

I'm liquid heat, instantaneously wet, my every pore dilated, every nerve strung tight in arousal. I'm both transported and rooted deep to the spot. I'm all things under his kiss.

It's a fucking awesome kiss.

So gentle. So sweet. I almost doubt that we're touching. I barely taste his warm breath. Perhaps I'm dreaming all this, I think. But then he deepens the kiss, his mouth possessing mine with a ferocious need. I have needs, too. I squeeze him tight and kiss him for all I'm worth.

I hear a cheering section of my own in my head. Go, Raine! Go, Raine! Go, Raine!

I search out his tongue with mine and caress it, play with it. I'm dizzy, and the world is spinning around, as if I'm on the teacups ride at Disneyland. I'm spinning so fast, I'm pretty sure I'm going to take off.

Take off. Get off.

One more second of tongue interaction, and I'm going to blow sky high.

But there isn't one more second of tongue interaction.

We're interrupted by footsteps on the beach and drunk talk. And then I see him.

"Wade!" I yell into Dirk's open mouth.

# CHAPTER 9

I push Dirk away with superhuman strength, sending him flying backward to land on his ass. "It's Wade," I hiss. "Five days early. I'm not ready."

"Why'd you stop kissing me?"

He has a point. We were set up perfectly to make Wade jealous. What have I done? "I'm sorry. I'm sorry," I hiss. "I blew the plan."

Wade's coming closer up the shore, and I got nothing. All my scheming and wishing is going to land me a big, fat goose egg.

But I do have something left up my sleeve! Or in this case, in my back pocket. I take Marie's super sauce out my pants pocket. I wave the metal cylinder at Dirk and give him a thumb's up.

I've got about three seconds to spare before Wade comes in reach, and I fling the cover off the container and spray the whole thing all over me. In my hair. Down my shirt. Down my pants. Every square inch of me is doused. I'm not leaving anything to chance.

"What the hell is that smell?" I hear Wade say, just as the fumes hit me, making my throat burn and my eyes tear up.

"Wade, welcome home!" I try to say, but what really comes out of my irritated trachea, past my swollen tongue, is, "Bade, momome mome!"

I'm blinded and I feel like there's an elephant on my chest. "Elp," I say to no one in particular.

"What the hell is that smell!" Wade yells.

"Elp," I repeat with the last bit of air able to pass through my throat. With the initial shock of the pain behind me, I start to panic. I go from zero to sixty in the panic department in no time flat.

I flap my arms and run around in circles, as if I'm preparing to fly. "Elp. Elp," I say over and over. But as far as I can tell, Wade and his companions are running in the opposite direction. The direction away from the stench.

I can't freak out about Wade running away from me because I'm too busy freaking out about the noxious fumes that are killing me, and if I'm not mistaken, are getting stronger.

"I'm bwind," I cry. "I canp wee."

"Hold on. I'm coming," I hear Dirk say. "We need to get you in the water."

"Elp."

"Yes. I'm here."

He gets to me just as I hear a loud growl. And then another loud growl.

"Was wat woo?"

"No, that wasn't me," Dirk says. The growls get louder

and then there's a galloping sound that I've never heard before. Not the sound of a person. And bigger than a horse.

"Oh my wod," I say.

"Bear! Bear!" Dirk shouts.

I try to think about what I've been told about surviving a bear attack. Mostly, I remember that it's pretty hard to survive a bear attack.

Dirk takes my hand and tugs. "Run! Run! Bear!"

Bears run really fast, and we've already established that I don't. So, needless to say, I'm seeing my life flash before my blind eyes. There's a little of my childhood, but it's mostly images of playing Scrabble with Dirk, and our mind-blowing kiss.

"The water! Get under the water!" he shouts. We run into the dark lake, and I dive, swimming as far and fast I can. Either the water or my adrenaline is counteracting the effects of Marie's chemical attraction spray. My eyes have stopped stinging, and I no longer feel that an elephant is sitting on my chest.

I go up for air for a split second and dive back down. I keep swimming like that underwater for a long time until Dirk grabs my leg, effectively stopping me.

"It was the scent," he whispers. "It attracted the bear."

"And turned off Wade," I whisper back. "I can't catch a break."

But at least I'm alive, and I can breathe. Dirk and I tread water while we make sure that the bear is really gone. The lights of my parents' house serve as a beacon in the night. Through the kitchen window, I can see my mother doing the dishes. Meanwhile, my father and brothers are outside running around.

"I think the coast is clear," I whisper.

"Hold on a second," he says, just as a shot rings out and then more running around.

I'm tired of treading water. So, I flip onto my back and float. I'm an excellent floater.

"How are you feeling?" Dirk asks.

"Better. But I'm disappointed. I thought science was on my side."

"It was Chernobyl all over again," he agrees.

"I should have just stuck with the Brady Brunch plan."

"Tomorrow's another day."

"Who are you kidding, Annie?" I ask. "Wade's never going to love me, now. He'll always think of me as the woman who smells worse than raw sewage. No, that ship has sailed. Speaking of ships, do you think it's safe to go back to shore?"

"I think so." He puts his hands on my shoulders and pulls me, as he does the backstroke. It's not a bad way to travel.

When we make it to land, however, we realize the party may be over, but the bear has decided to stay. My brothers have it cornered, but there's a lot of yelling going on, and I don't see how this is going to end without somebody getting hurt.

There's no way past the bear, but I figure I have a good shot at the house, if I go around the other side. Unfortunately, the wind is blowing from behind me, and even though I can't smell it, anymore, whatever the chemists put in the special sauce is making the bear really angry.

It claws at the ground and charges right at me. I crouch down on the ground and cover my head with my hands. But Dirk doesn't crouch or hide or run away. He charges the bear, like a locomotive express train.

He hits the bear in its side, sending it into a barrel roll and making the bear supremely pissed. It rights itself and rounds back on Dirk. I don't know who's growling louder, Dirk or the bear.

Dirk leaps onto it and wraps his arms around the bear's neck, holding on for dear life. In other words, he gives it a bear hug. But I don't know how long he can hold on. The bear is growling and snapping his teeth and trying to claw Dirk.

"Can a guy get a little help, here?" Dirk calls out.

"Oh, sorry," I say and walk toward him.

"Not you! You stay there. I meant your brothers. Help me

out!" he shouts.

*

So, now I've seen everything. And by everything, I mean a man fighting a bear.

Before my brothers could help Dirk, the bear had enough. It got free from Dirk and ran as fast as it could out into the woods, away from the lake.

"I can't wait to tell my grandchildren about this," Lennon says at the kitchen table, after all the excitement.

"You're twenty-one years old," my mother reminds him.

"You know what I mean. Dude," he says to Dirk, fist bumping him. "That was more epic than any movie you've been in. You fought a fucking bear."

I'm inspecting Dirk for wounds. Miraculously, besides a pretty decent case of shock, he's in one piece. I make him a hot totty and force him to drink it. Then, I take him upstairs, have him change his clothes, and I put him to bed in one of my brothers' former bedrooms. Even though it's a warm night, I put extra blankets on the bed to keep him from getting too chilled.

"Your turn," he says.

"Okay. Sweet dreams."

I turn off the light and walk into the hallway. Lennon is there. "Was that awesome or what?" he says. "I totally approve of your boyfriend."

I bite my lip. Lennon's going to be very disappointed to find out that the bear-fighting boyfriend isn't real.

"Thanks."

"So much better than that jerk."

My ears prick up. "What jerk? You mean Wade?"

"Yeah, that's the one. We were talking about your new boyfriend, and all of a sudden, he said that he needed to see you tomorrow for lunch at Lou's Café."

"See me?"

"Yep."

"For lunch?"

Lennon nods. "At noon."

Holy shit. The jealousy plan worked. I'm Jan Brady.

# CHAPTER 10

"It doesn't fit."

"It fits."

"No, it doesn't."

"Yes, it does."

"Hey, I like tight dresses probably more than most men, but—how should I put this?—you're falling out of it, and you're zipped only about halfway in back."

"It fits," I say through clenched teeth.

"If you don't want an honest opinion, why did you invite me to your room to see it on you?"

"I didn't invite you in," I remind him. "You invited

yourself. But I don't need you anymore. Your plan worked."

Dirk is sitting on my bed, and he looks deflated. Wounded. I've wounded him more than a bear could. I bite my lip. I don't want to hurt him. So much so that I'll even take fashion advice from him.

"Okay. Okay. So tell me what to wear," I say.

"Don't ask me. I like you best naked."

"What? What did you say?"

"You heard me."

"Very funny." I've lived my whole life avoiding being naked. If I could wear clothes in the shower, I would. I'm not amused that Dirk is reminding me that he got to see the full monty, up close and personal.

"Who's joking?" he says.

I try to read him, but I come up blank. "I have a yellow dress that fits," I say, walking around him to get to my closet. But as I pass him, he puts his arm out and stops me.

"I wasn't joking," he said. "Don't go."

"What do you mean don't go? I have a dress that fits."

"I don't want you to go."

"But this is what we've been working for. I got the date with Wade. My first date with him."

I'm trying to understand what he's saying. There's an undercurrent that I can't seem to grasp. What could he want from me? He's Dirk Adams. I'm nobody.

I remove his hand and walk around him.

*

I'm nervous, but not nearly as nervous as I thought I would be. Wade Gates wants to have lunch with me. The idea is preposterous, yet here I am at Lou's Café, and there Wade is, sitting at a center table, waiting for me.

Despite its name, Lou's is our small town's offering of a

semi-fancy restaurant. With its French décor and real linen tablecloths, it's the only restaurant in Esperanza that requires reservations.

The idea that Wade reserved a table for lunch with me tickles me. But it doesn't tickle me as much as I thought it would. I suck in my stomach and walk toward his table. He's just as handsome as ever. Not as handsome as Dirk, but it's not fair to compare anyone to Dirk.

Wade looks me up and down and smiles. Suddenly, I have a strong desire to run away. Be careful what you wish for, you just might get it, I think to myself.

"Hello, Raine," he says, giving me a soft hug.

"Hi, Wade. Thank you for inviting me."

"My pleasure."

We sit down, and I open the menu that's resting on my plate. Before I have a chance to read it, Wade rips it out of my hand. "Oh, no," he says. "I do the ordering." He snaps his fingers.

"Hey, we don't have all day, you know," he shouts at the waiter. All heads turn in our direction.

"We'll have the chicken breast, no oil with asparagus," he tells the waiter. "I keep trim, and the lady I'm sure would like to lose a few pounds."

I stop breathing. I literally cease to take in air. My lungs, heart, and just about every organ in my body has stopped functioning.

Wade's smiling at me, but suddenly I don't like his smile. I don't like his face.

"You're probably wondering why I asked you here," he says.

Not really. Not anymore. But I nod.

"I have to tell you Raine, I was a little stunned to find out you're with Dirk Adams. Talk about the Odd Couple!"

I pick up my butter knife and clutch it in my hand. I wonder if it's sharp enough to go through his head.

"You probably know I'm a corporate attorney for a large firm in Palo Alto. I'm on the partner track, too." He winks and points his finger at me as if it's a gun, and he shoots.

Yada. Yada. Blah. Blah.

"Someone like Dirk could benefit by having someone like me at his side," he continues, calling him Dirk like he knows him. "A win-win. You know how it goes. Well, actually you probably don't. Errand girls aren't up on the ways of the financial world. Am I wrong? You never did go to college, right?"

Where's a charging bear when you need one?

He takes out his cell phone. "So, let me just plug in his contact information," he says. "I'm ready. Shoot."

Oh, how I want to shoot. What a jerk.

"You are such a jerk," I say.

"Excuse me?"

"A jerk. A big, fat stinking jerk."

I stand up and throw my napkin on the table. I move to leave, but he grabs my arm. "That's a laugh calling me a big, fat stinking jerk. You're the big, fat queen of Esperanza. A big, fat loser."

At this moment, I feel exactly like a big, fat loser. Why have I spent so much energy loving a jerk, who would never love me and never even see the value in me? He probably doesn't even know how to play Scrabble.

"Let go of my arm," I say, but he holds on tight. I try to pull my arm free, but he's got me, and he's not letting go.

The back of my neck prickles, and I turn my head to see my own personal bear charge the table.

# CHAPTER 11

The thing about Dirk is he's sexy as hell, but dangerous too. Women want to sleep with him; men want to be him; and everyone is slightly afraid he's going to kill them. I've known him a couple of days and have been witness to incredible kindness, but I've also seen him wrestle a bear.

But I've never seen him scarier than he is right this second, focused entirely on Wade's hand latched around my arm.

There really should be theme music as he marches to the table. One of those big drums playing, at least.

"Take your hand off of her," Dirk says. His voice is impossibly low. Commanding. "Now."

Nobody in the restaurant is eating. The waiters stop serving. We're all waiting to see what Jake Storm is going to do next. "You want my butter knife?" I ask him.

"Nah, I got this," he says.

Wade's hand flies off my arm. At least he's intelligent enough to do that. But then he proves just how stupid he really is. "Dirk, so glad to see you, man," he says, standing. "I've got some business opportunities to discuss with you. Let's work on your judgment together. Obviously, this is a case of bad judgment. Am I right?" He points at me with his thumb, as if he's hitchhiking.

"Do you have something fundamentally wrong with your brain?" Dirk asks Wade.

"He's a jerk," I say. "I think that's the official medical term."

"I'd ask you to apologize, but you're such an idiot, it doesn't matter," Dirk tells him.

"What?" Wade asks, nonplussed. He's honestly surprised that his business strategy has turned bust.

"But that doesn't mean I'm not going to beat your ass,"

Dirk growls.

I love it when he growls.

"You might want to stand back," he tells me. "You all might want to stand back," he tells the restaurant patrons.

"I don't want you to get arrested," I say.

"Don't worry. With jerks like these, they're the ones to throw the first punch."

He's right. Wade's so scared, he tries to sucker punch Dirk.

Oh, poor, dumb jerky Wade. Obviously, he doesn't know Dirk fought a bear and won.

It's over almost before it begins. Dirk lands a punch across Wade's jaw with a loud crack, which sends Wade falling on the table, crashing everything to the floor. Dirk hands a wad of bills to the restaurant manager and apologizes.

Then, he takes my hand, and we walk out of Lou's.

"Where are we going?" I ask.

"We're going to get naked."

"Oh, good."

Dirk's car is parked at the curb. It's a two-minute drive to the cabin, but it seems like forever. "Wade is going to be sipping a lot of milkshakes," I say.

"I hope you're not upset that I put the kibosh on that relationship."

"Of course not," I say. "I mean, if I knew what kibosh meant."

"I can't wait to make love to you," he says, turning onto the dirt road, leading to the cabin. "I'm going to worship your body, worship you like you deserve."

"Really?" I ask. "'cause I can't wait to fuck your brains out. I'm dying to have your girthy cock inside me. On top, on the bottom, from behind, we're going to do it all. I'm going to come all over your face, and I'm going to swallow you down. I hope you took your vitamins this morning."

It's a really good speech. The best I've ever given. And I mean every word of it.

Dirk's face is red and his eyes are big black saucers. He's staring me down with his mouth open.

"I'm so wet," I say.

He growls like he's going to attack a bear. He hops out of the car, and he's right there when I get out. He pushes me against the car door and slams his body against mine.

I lift my knee to his hip, and he grinds against me. His mouth comes down hard on mine, his tongue darting and caressing. I pull at his shirt, and he takes it off over his head, breaking our kiss. I pounce, claiming his lips, again.

His hands travel to my breasts, kneading them and driving me mad with desire. I moan against his mouth and clutch at his back, letting my fingernails rake down it.

He inhales through his teeth. "This is going to be good,"

he says. He lifts me up with his hands under my ass, pulling me against him, and he walks us to the house.

Unable to open the door while carrying me, he gives it a swift kick, breaking it off at the top hinge. "Oh, my," I breathe. It's like being ravaged by Conan the Barbarian but with access to running water.

Once inside, he lays me down on the couch. "I love the living room," he growls, looking down at me. He lifts one of my legs and trails his hand up to the inside of my thigh and beyond.

"Take off the panties," he orders.

Slowly, I hitch up my dress over my hips. I slide two fingers inside my panties and tug at them, shimmying slowly until I'm naked. For the first time in my life, I don't care that I have a Pillsbury Doughboy tummy. I don't give a damn what my thighs look like.

All I know is that Dirk is looking at me like I'm the most desirable woman on the planet, and that's exactly how I feel. He kicks off his shoes and takes off his pants over his throbbing, engorged cock.

While I watch, I caress myself slowly and slip one finger inside me. "I want you so bad, but if I have to wait, I'm going to pleasure myself," I moan.

"Jesus."

He parts my legs and kneels between them on the couch. He takes my hand, forcing me to remove my finger. "I'm going to pleasure you," he says. "I've been dying to do this since I first met you. Last night I had to jack off just to get to sleep."

Scrabble is great, but talking dirty while a gorgeous man goes down on me is possibly the greatest thing ever. What am I talking about? Of course it's the greatest thing ever. Duh.

My head falls back, and I rock against Dirk's mouth. His clever, generous mouth. He's in no hurry to get done with this part of the foreplay. He grabs my ass and lifts me up, licking and kissing my liquid heat. It's almost too much to bear. I touch his head, running my fingers through his hair. He groans, as I rock faster, my body preparing to come. My blood rushes through my veins, my heart pounds, becomes shallow and ragged.

"Yes!" I scream. I'm not a screamer, normally, but how can I refrain from screaming now? I'm on the edge of something wonderful and completely out of my control. "Yes! Yes! Yes!"

I spasm over and over. I come hard, making my body levitate off the couch. And then I fall back down to earth, half-comatose and thoroughly used.

"That's a good start," Dirk says, wiping his mouth on the back of his hand. He shoves the coffee table against a wall.

"Oh, my," I say.

"Just wanted to make some room." He sits on the couch and lifts me up. "Move your legs," he tells me.

I separate them as he slowly lowers me onto his lap. I guide his manhood inside me, as I sit on him, making him utter an inhuman sound. Then, it's off to the races. I put my hands on his shoulders, and I ride him hard. He helps by lifting me up and down, squeezing my hips.

Is there anything better than a big man?

We go on forever. He has amazing staying power. But just before he comes, he lifts me off him and places me on the floor on all fours. He kneels behind me and slips inside me with one thrust. As he pounds into me, he touches my clit with his hand, massaging me and making me crazy aroused.

"Come!" I shout. "Come!"

He does.

We collapse in a heap on the Turkish rug. He kisses me and brushes my hair out of my face. "There you are," he says, smiling. "My beautiful Raine."

"My beautiful Dirk."

"You have the hottest pussy. Like fire."

And so it begins, again. We can't get enough. We're screwing machines. Up against the fireplace. Upstairs on the bed. In the shower. Back downstairs again and into the kitchen. Wherever we go, we break things. There isn't a samovar left standing. The picture of the belly dancer has been torn in two, hit with an old encyclopedia, thrown during the throes of passion. My bad.

"Food," he says. Oh, yeah. I didn't eat lunch. "Get on the table. I'm going to eat off you."

"No. You get on the table. I'm going to eat off you."

He clears the table with a sweep of his arm, sending plates, napkins, and a box of cereal flying across the room. He lies down on the table while I search the fridge and the pantry.

"How about a sandwich?" I ask.

I squirt his belly with some mayo, and I wrap his manhood in two slices of bread. "Very creative. Very artistic," he says.

"And dessert," I say, holding up a jar of Nutella.

I wouldn't say we're eating a balanced meal, but there's definite variety. After we eat, I lick him clean. He stands up, knocking the food onto the floor.

"Who's the cleaning lady in your family?" he asks.

"That would be Moonbeam. She loves order and cleanliness." We look around. The cabin looks like it's been the victim of a break-in.

"She's going to love what I've done to the place."

"What we've done to the place," I correct him.

We've spent the day screwing around, and now the sun is setting. We put on robes and walk past the broken door to the outside in order to enjoy the sunset. "Let's pretend there's jazz playing," he says, taking me into his arms and spinning me around.

He holds me close, swaying me to the imagined music. A day spent in frenetic sex winds down to a moment of tenderness and intimacy. Dirk nuzzles my neck and whispers sweet nothings: "My angel." "My sweet beauty." And then he takes a deep breath.

"I love you, Raine. I've only just met you, but I don't ever want to be away from you."

"Me, too," I say, smiling.

"Say my name."

"Adam."

I feel safe, secure, and taken care off. I'm also sure that I've met my soul mate, as odd as it is to have a movie star superstar be my soul mate.

"I'm one-hundred-ninety pounds," I say happily and rest my head on his chest. We dance on the shore for a long time, long after the sun goes down. Just as we're about to go inside, a woman approaches the cabin.

"Marie? Is that you?" I ask.

"Oh, phew there you are," she says, pushing her round-rimmed glasses up on the bridge of her nose. "I was worried. It wasn't easy finding you. I just need to tell you that under no circumstances use the spray I gave you, okay?"

"Uh, sure."

"There are some side effects I didn't know about. Trust me, you don't want to use it. There's a FDA EPA CDC issue."

"I'll make sure she doesn't use it," Dirk says.

"Oh, good. In any case, it doesn't seem like you need any more chemical attraction. So no harm no foul!" she says, waving goodbye.

"FDA, EPA, CDC issue?" I ask Dirk. "That doesn't sound like no harm, no foul. Am I glowing in the dark? Has my nose fallen off?"

He studies me a moment. "A little glowing, but that's to be expected."

And he kisses me, again.

The End

Wish Upon A Stud Series #3
Hot
WIRED
elise sax

# *Hot* WIRED

(Wish Upon A Stud – Book 3)

elise sax

*For Melissa Foster, otherwise known as Superwoman.*

# CHAPTER 1

I straighten my tan suit, arrange my round rimmed glasses firmly on my nose, and take a seat on the bar stool.

"What'll you have?" the bartender demands.

"Well, between you and me, this is my first time in a bar," I say.

"Congratulations. What'll you have?"

"I'm an academic. I mean, was an academic. That means school."

"Thanks for the definition. What'll you have?"

"It's awfully dark in here. Is that normal?"

"It's so nobody sees your shame. What'll you have?"

"I've never actually consumed alcohol before. I'm trying new things out," I announce to her. She's about my age but a lot prettier, and she's dressed like Beyoncé. I try to maintain eye contact, but I'm distracted by her ample cleavage. She's got a lot of everything… hair, makeup boobs.

"I'm thrilled for you. What'll you have?" she demands a little louder.

"What do people who go to bars usually get?" I ask. "I want to be just like them. I'm going to be a bar kind of person. I'm not going to care about science or studying or reasonable hygiene."

"Then you're in the right place," she says. "You can have what's on tap or tequila shots. Your choice."

"What's a tap?"

*

"I'm feeling awfully warm," I say unbuttoning the top two buttons of my shirt. "Is that normal?"

"Tequila makes everything normal," the bartender says.

"Now, you need to get out from behind the bar, or I'm going to have to kick you out."

I look around at my surroundings. "How did I get back here?"

"You sang *I Gotta Be Me* and when you finished, you climbed onto the bar and rolled over onto the other side. But now, you gotta get out from behind it. This is my territory, and I don't share."

I believe her. She doesn't look like the sharing kind.

"Of course. I'm sorry," I say. I hitch my skirt up and try to lift my leg up onto the bar. But it's no use. I've never been very flexible, and I can't get my foot up there. I've no idea how I climbed over it in the first place because my leg won't reach at all.

"Oh, no!" I shout. "I'm trapped! I'll never get out!"

"Oh, my God. Why me?" the bartender moans. She puts her hands on my waist and pulls. "Come on." She guides me to a table and shoves me into a chair.

"You have the biggest breasts I've ever seen," I note. "Huge. Do they give you back trouble? Do you find it difficult to balance?"

"I have a bat behind the bar. If you don't shut up, I'm going to triple play your ass right to the hospital."

"You can call me Marie," I say, trying to pat her arm, but I'm seeing double. I wind up slapping the table.

"I was going to be Dr. Marie Foster, but Dr. Farrington said I'm a cheater," I tell her. "I'm not a cheater, big boob lady!" My voice booms louder than the soft rock coming out of the bar's speakers.

"Okay, look, if you insist on talking to me, call me Layla," she says.

"Layla," I say, giggling. "Funny name."

"It's better than Big Boob Lady."

"I didn't plagiarize my Ph.D. dissertation, Layla," I tell her, truthfully. "'Fluid Dynamics in Momentum Transfer of Chemical

Species' is all mine. The other guy plagiarized *me*! But they didn't believe me. They kicked me out. Can you believe that?"

"Rough."

"Rough," I agree. "Rough! I should be a chemical engineer! Now, I'm just a drunk bar addict. Just like all of these other people."

I gesture toward the room. It's small, and I wonder how it compares to other bars. Are they larger or smaller? Are they all this dirty?

The other patrons are either drinking on their own, their attention focused purely on their drinks, or they sit at tables in twos. An older couple sits in silence at one table. A young couple is arguing at another table. In the corner, a young man and an older man are deep in conversation.

I focus on them. They're both well-dressed. Custom-made suits. Fitted. They obviously have money, and by the looks of them, they're talking about business. Successful. Suddenly, I need to ask them how they became successful.

Because I'm a big, fat failure. My whole life is ruined.

I get up and walk over to them. I tug on the young man's jacket sleeve. He turns toward me, and I take a step backward in surprise. He grabs my arm just in time before I fall flat on my back. "Whoa, you're hot damn sexy," I blurt out.

"I think you've had too much to drink," he says, looking up at me with a snooty, I-can-hold-my-liquor expression on his face.

"You're right. I didn't know one shot of tequila could pack such a wallop." I punctuate my words by poking him in the chest with my index finger.

"You got this drunk off of one shot of tequila?"

"Yes. Well, half of one. I knocked the rest over when I was finishing my song."

"I think we're done here, Jarrod," the older man says, standing up. He's even snootier than the younger one.

"Wait," I say. "I didn't get to ask you yet why you're not a big, fat failure."

The older man ignores me and shakes Jarrod's hand. "I'm sorry this couldn't have worked out differently. I thought we had a great future. But you know what they say about business."

Jarrod nods and I can tell he's pissed. His jaw's working overtime, and I debate with myself whether to warn him about TMJ problems and the wear and tear from grinding his teeth. But I bite my lip. I don't think it's the moment to discuss dental issues.

The older man walks out of the bar, and I sit down next to Jarrod. It's not that I want to spend time with him, but the room is still spinning, and I sort of fall onto the seat.

"Are you old enough to be drinking?" he asks sensibly.

"I'm twenty-one. So, I'm exactly old enough to be drinking. Are you old enough to be drinking?"

His mouth turns up slightly in a grin. "I've been old enough for a while now. I like your glasses." He's leaning forward, which forces me to lean back. The close proximity is making me uncomfortably warm.

"I like my glasses, too. I can't see without them, and that would be unfortunate, considering my current company." I wink at him. Holy shit, am I flirting? Is this what flirting is? Am I doing it right?

Jarrod's smile broadens. He has thick, dark hair, which is perfectly cut. It perfectly frames his perfect face and makes his perfect blue eyes pop. His suit fits him, perfectly, over his perfect body. Long and lean with a broad chest and strong hands. Big, strong hands. Perfect.

He's got a lot of perfect happening.

"So, tell me how you made it. How did you get to be successful? Why aren't you a big, fat failure?" I ask.

I plop my elbow on the table and rest my chin in my hand. My face is only inches from Jarrod's, and I can see his dark blue eyes better up close. "Did I tell you you're hot damn sexy?" I snap my fingers, remembering. "Oh, yeah, I did. Let's move on to the big, fat failure topic of conversation."

He arches an eyebrow again and leans in even closer. The heat is bouncing off of him like a nuclear blast, and I mop my forehead with a cocktail napkin.

"How do you know I'm not a big, fat failure?" he asks. His voice is impossibly deep, rich, and silky like really good chocolate cake.

Geez. I'd do just about anything to hear his voice again.

"Your suit," I croak, pointing at his chest.

Jarrod looks down at himself. "You're right. This isn't a big, fat failure suit."

I point to my suit. "This is a big, fat failure suit. The biggest, baddest, failurest suit ever made."

"That's a lot to put on one poor suit."

I point my finger in the air, as if my suit is hovering over us. "It deserves it! I wore it today to defend my Ph.D. dissertation, and they threw me out on my ear! I mean, literally on my ear!" I shout, showing him my bruised ear.

I slap my hand over my mouth. "I didn't mean to speak so loudly," I whisper. "The tequila is doing weird things to me."

Jarrod nods. "Tequila does that to people. Maybe you shouldn't drink."

"I never drink. I mean, I never used to drink, but now I'm going to drink every day. Because I'm going to do the opposite of everything I've ever done in my entire life. And you know why? I'll tell you why. Because I'm a big, fat failure. That's why. Because I've done everything right so far in my life, and guess what it's netted me. Guess. Guess! You don't have to guess. I'll tell you what it's netted me. Nothing. It's netted me nothing. And today was the worst day of my life. Did I tell you you're hot damn sexy?"

Jarrod nods. "Three times. You're not so bad yourself. Despite the suit. So, I think you should take me home."

"You do? I live within walking distance. I don't need a ride."

"I wasn't offering to drive you home," he says. He stands and pulls me up by my arm. "I'm suggesting that you take me home and we do the big nasty."

My elbow slips, and my head falls onto the table with a loud thump. I pick myself up and straighten my glasses. "You're suggesting what?"

"We're going to do the big nasty. I want to rock your world." Rocking my world sounds like a good idea, especially when it's said with his chocolate-cake voice.

"I've never actually had my world rocked," I admit. Honestly, I don't even know what rocking a world entails. Is it painful?

"Good. You said you're doing everything the opposite of what you usually do. This is a good start."

He's got X-ray eyes. They're looking right through my face, down, down, down my body into my uterus and making me ovulate. I gulp.

"Okay."

# CHAPTER 2

The minute we walk outside into the fresh air, I sober up completely. The sun is setting, casting a beautiful red and orange glow in the evening sky. With my clear head, come enormous self-doubt and a couple rounds of second-guessing.

What am I doing? Somehow, I picked up a man in a bar. I sneak a glance at him, looking through the corner of my eye. He's even sexier than he was in the dark bar.

He's about six foot three, built like a Calvin Klein underwear model, with drop dead gorgeous looks. He's Adonis on his very best day. Adonis's best day, that is. Jarrod doesn't need a best day. He's all kinds of hot on all kinds of days. I'd bet money on it.

But even hot guys can be serial killers. This is what my

hundred and fifty IQ is screaming at me, standing next to him outside on the sidewalk. I'm about to tell him that there'll be no big nasty tonight or ever. I'm a responsible, wise woman of the scientific community. At least, I was a member of the scientific community before I was kicked out on my ear.

Jarrod doesn't give me a chance to back out. He slips his large hand into mine and begins to walk me down the street. His hand is warm and dry, and at his touch, my insides turn into hormone-laden jelly.

He smells good, too. Like expensive cologne, dollar bills, and all kinds of dirty, nasty sex. I bite my lower lip. I feel a moan threaten to come out of my mouth, and I want to save myself that embarrassment.

But there's no denying that Jarrod has a definite effect on me. A horny kind of I'm-going-to-jump-your-bones effect.

Perhaps it's just that I need a little attention, a little love in the wake of the worst rejection of my life. My life's ambitions were dashed during the worst day ever. Maybe this is some kind of crazy rebound situation.

"Is this the way to your home?" Jarrod asks after we walk about a block.

"Uh huh," I gurgle.

"How much further?"

"What? Oh, actually my place is in the opposite direction."

Jarrod raises his eyebrow. "Nervous?"

Nervous? Damn straight I'm nervous. I don't know what I'm doing. "No, I'm not nervous. I'm a woman of the world. A woman who goes to bars, drinks, and picks up men."

"Sounds appealing," he says, grinning. "Classy."

Our eyes lock. Jarrod's face drops. He goes from amused to confused in a split second. I'm feeling the same way. His pupils are dilated, and I half wonder if he has a concussion. But I've learned enough about biology to understand what his physical reaction means. I bet my pupils are going all Incredible Hulk in my eyeballs, too.

My arms sprout goose bumps, and my melted insides bubble and swirl, making me even dizzier.

"Oh, my," I moan.

"Maybe this isn't a good idea," he says, wisely.

"You're righ—" I begin, but he's captured my mouth with his.

So much for bad ideas. It doesn't matter if we're doing the right thing or not, because good, bad, or indifferent, we're never going to stop kissing. Our lips have made contact, and it's going to take an act of Congress and a really strong crowbar to separate us.

To prove my point, the sun continues to set while we continue to kiss. As it becomes darker, our kiss intensifies. Deeper and deeper, our tongues dart against each other, sending shock waves of electricity through my body.

He steps closer until our pelvises are grinding against each other. His arms wrap around me, and his hands trail down my back to cup my butt. I'm pretty sure I can get pregnant this way. My uterus is doing a happy dance, and I bet dollars to doughnuts he's got the world's strongest swimming sperm.

I'm not worrying about getting pregnant, though. I'm not worrying about much. My eyes have rolled back into my head, and my brain is flying up into the clouds. Meanwhile, my hands are roving all over Jarrod's chest and then, much to my surprise, down lower.

I'm melty and goopy and liquidy and mushy, but Jarrod is all kinds of hard. His arms, his chest, and his rather large doodah is hard as a rock. This adds proof in my mind about his Olympic-worthy sperm.

"Doodah," I moan against his mouth.

Jarrod stops kissing me. He leans his forehead against mine and breathes deeply. "What?"

"Nothing. Slip of the tongue."

"You can say that again."

His breathing sounds like a locomotive. I'm more than my share of proud that I'm the cause of his hot and heavy breathing. Such power! I may be a big, fat failure, but an over-the-top sexy man is halfway on his way to a stroke just from a kiss from my lips. Hot damn!

Perhaps I'm not a total failure, after all. With my surge of newfound optimism, my doubts about taking home a stranger vanish. I feel positively Amazonian. I'm Wonder Woman in a cheap suit and round-rimmed glasses.

Without another word, Jarrod takes my hand, and we walk down the street toward my apartment.

# CHAPTER 3

"This is your apartment?"

I grab a dirty T-shirt off the couch and stuff it behind a cushion. "Yes."

"Someone actually lives here?"

"Of course someone actually lives here. I live here! What's wrong with my apartment?" I scan my apartment, trying to see it through Jarrod's eyes. It's a small studio. A double bed is pushed up against the wall with a poster of Einstein as its headboard. The kitchenette is clean and tidy, but the table and two chairs next to it are covered in dirty cereal bowls and coffee mugs.

Most of the studio is filled up by my desk, a giant wood plank perched on cinder blocks. The desk is piled high with papers and reference books. Somewhere in the mess is my laptop. There's nothing out of the ordinary. It's a typical apartment of any Ph.D. student.

"It's just that it doesn't seem like an actual apartment. It looks like a broom closet," Jarrod says.

"I don't know what you're talking about. I don't even own a broom."

Jarrod walks the two steps to my desk and picks up a reference book. "Chemical species? Kind of heavy reading."

"Are you interested in chemical engineering? I can suggest some great books, if you want."

"That's okay. I'm more of a James Patterson kind of guy."

He takes a seat at the foot of my bed, and he pats the place next to him. I bite my lower lip. Is the foreplay over? Are we going to get right down to it now? I will my feet to walk over to him, but they don't obey. I'm frozen in place.

"When you said you've never done the big nasty, what exactly did that mean?" Jarrod asks. "Does that mean you've never…?"

"I've had sexual intercourse. But it was the normal kind. You know, with a boyfriend, somebody I knew for long time. He was a scientist in artificial intelligence."

"I see. So… it's just dawned on me that I don't know your name."

"Oh, I'm sorry. My name's Marie. Marie Foster."

"Marie, why don't you come sit down next to me? I promise I won't bite, unless you want me to."

I wonder if doing the big nasty usually includes biting. Perhaps there's a whole laundry list of things that men and women do that I never knew about. Maybe I should have researched this whole lifestyle before jumping into it.

I decide to take a seat next to Jarrod. He's oozing so much sexy appeal that I'm sure that I can taste his pheromones on my tongue.

Yum.

"Marie," he says.

"Yes. I'm named for Marie Curie, the physicist. My father was a big fan. He's a scientist, too."

"Didn't Marie Curie die from her experiments?"

"Yes. From radiation poisoning. Dad admired that. Devotion to her field of study."

Jarrod nods. "I gather that you're a scientist, too. What's your field of study? Should I worry about radiation poisoning?"

"I was working on a Ph.D. in fluid dynamics in momentum transfer of chemical species."

"That's a mouthful."

"But I'm not doing that anymore. That's the old me. Now I'm somebody totally different. I've turned over a new leaf. No more mouthfuls for me."

Jarrod grins. "Maybe just one more mouthful."

Now that Jarrod has asked personal questions, I feel that

I'm allowed to ask him about himself. We know each other's names, but not much more than that.

"And you're Jarrod?"

"Jarrod Wright Sinclair, the third."

"That's a mouthful," I say, smiling.

Jarrod's face is so close to mine that we're almost touching. His eyes are the most glorious shade of blue. Dark. There's a lot of intelligence behind them.

"Indeed. I am a mouthful," he whispers. My arms sprout goose bumps, and I shudder.

"Do you want a cup of coffee? Aren't I supposed to offer you a drink?" I ask.

"You can offer me a drink afterward."

I swallow with difficulty. Afterward implies that a great event is about to happen. I'm at once nervous, apprehensive, and impatient to begin.

"What do you do for a living, Jarrod Wright Sinclair the third?"

"I'm a billionaire."

"Billion? Wow. That's a lot of dollars."

"Yes, it is. Keeps me busy."

Jarrod traces my jaw line with his finger, and my mouth drops open with a sigh. His finger moves from my jaw to my lips, caressing them ever so lightly.

"I mean," I croak. "You have to count really high to get to a billion."

"I'm not afraid of heights."

Obviously, I am. I have fourteen dollars in my bank account. You don't have to count very high for that.

"You're an extremely sexy woman, Marie. Do you know that?"

"You're the first person to tell me. But I'm reasonably sure that you have enough experience with these things that you're correct. In any case, right now I'm feeling sexy as hell."

"Good. For what we are about to do, it's a lot better if you're feeling sexy. But if you weren't, I'd get you there. My promise to you."

"Is there usually this much talking while doing the big nasty?" I ask.

"We haven't started yet."

"Oh. Then, let's start. Just holler out if I'm doing it wrong."

I hop up and leap on him, throwing him backward on the bed. He makes an *oomph* noise, but I'm reasonably sure I haven't injured him. I rip open his shirt, sending buttons flying all over my studio. One bounces off my glasses, and I'm thankful for severe nearsightedness. Otherwise the button would've knocked my eye out.

Jarrod looks down at his now naked chest. "You ripped

my shirt," he says, shocked.

"You're a billionaire. What do you care?"

"You have a point."

He shrugs out of the rest of his shirt and his jacket. He fumbles with the buttons on my blouse, but he's having a hard time because I'm determined to get his pants open, and my arms keep blocking his path.

It becomes a competition to see who can get the other one naked first. But I have a head start, and faced with his semi-nakedness, I've got a head full of determination to see the rest of him. He doesn't stand a chance.

# CHAPTER 4

It's a frenzy. We're like Cirque du Soleil performers but naked, without music, and no discernible talent. We tumble around on the bed like acrobats, throwing off each other's clothes.

Finally, I'm wearing only my glasses, and Jarrod's wearing only a twenty-thousand dollar watch and a twenty-thousand watt smile. He's lying on the bed, diagonally, and I am straddling him, my legs around his hard belly and his erection teasing my backside.

My goal reached, a sudden tranquility washes over me. I'm content to take a moment and study this beautiful man. There isn't an ounce of fat anywhere on him. Every muscle is defined. He's probably never eaten a Cheeto in his life.

His limbs are long and strong. His chest is hairy with a line that goes down through my legs toward his happy place. I imagine this is what Adonis would look like naked. Jarrod is, quite simply, breathtakingly beautiful.

He is so gorgeous that I wonder what he's doing with me. I'm not gorgeous. There's no way I can compete on the beauty scale with him. I'm just me. Normal. I'm hit with a wave of embarrassment, and I cover my breasts with my hands.

"Please don't do that," Jarrod says. "You're so lovely. I'm enjoying looking at you."

Gently, he takes my hands into his and pulls them down to my sides. He replaces my hands on my breasts with his. His hands are warm and dry, and his touch makes me crazy with desire. His thumbs gently caress my nipples, transforming them into erect peaks.

Our eyes meet. It's almost as if he can see right through me. Is this the big nasty? It doesn't feel like cheap, anonymous sex. Jarrod doesn't feel like a stranger that I've picked up in a bar. I can't believe that my body would react this way if that was true.

In a swift motion, Jarrod pulls my top half down onto him

and flips me so that his body is on top of mine. Through some kind of natural instinct, my legs separate and my knees lift up so that I can cradle him inside me.

He leans his weight on one arm and slips his other hand down my belly and between my legs. "Holy hell," he groans.

"I'm sorry I'm so wet," I say.

He responds by kissing me. This time he's tender, gentle. Even loving. I get lost in his embrace. My mouth is his mouth. My lips are his lips. My tongue is his tongue. We're one person, and it seems completely natural that we should be.

As he kisses me, he strokes me in a slow, regular rhythm. My hips undulate against his hand. My hands travel down his body and clutch his hips. I reach for his erection, but he moves out of the way, stops kissing me, and inches down the bed until his mouth takes the place of his fingers.

This is new for me. My ex-boyfriend never did this to me. Why on earth didn't he ever do this to me? Maybe he didn't know it existed. Maybe he was concerned about his technique. I feel like calling him and yelling at him for never doing this to me.

Because it's so good. It's better than good. It's the best.

My head tips back, and my mouth drops open. Somebody moans. It must be me because Jarrod's mouth is busy, but it sounds nothing like me. The voice is deeper and animalistic.

My eyes close, and the blood rushes in my ears. I know that I'm on a bridge to somewhere. It's pure ecstasy, and I don't want to get off. But I do. I crash in a wild orgasm, and my body levitates off the bed.

My heart, which was pounding a moment ago, slows to an inhumanly slow beat. If I weren't so completely relaxed, I would be worried that I was in a coma. I curl up on my side and fall fast asleep.

But I only sleep a moment. I hear Jarrod scoot next to me. I can feel his eyes on me. I can sense his desire. He wants to get on that bridge, too.

"Open your eyes, beautiful," he says.

I obey, but I see nothing. I'm completely blinded. I panic. Has the world's biggest orgasm taken my sight? Am I being punished twice in one day? The first for a crime I didn't commit and the second for defying gravity by the power of sheer pleasure?

"I'm blind!" I scream.

"Shh," Jarrod says.

"But I can't see!"

"Shh," he repeats. He gently removes my glasses from my face. Like a miracle, I can see just fine. "All fogged up," he says, showing me my glasses. He cleans them on a sheet and puts them back on my face. "There. All better."

"That's the danger of having sex with my glasses on," I say.

"You want to try it without your glasses?"

"No way. I won't be able to see you if I do that and I'm not going to miss one second of seeing you."

"You want to see something, do you? I have something for you to see." He guides my hand to his erection. He's enormous, rock hard, and ready to burst. "Can you help a guy out?"

"Of course! What do you want me to do?"

He doesn't answer. Instead, he pulls a condom wrapper out of his pants, which lie in a heap on the bed. He turns me on my back and climbs over me, careful to hold his weight on his forearms. He guides himself deep inside me and lifts my legs to rest on his shoulders.

"That's what I want you to do," he says, smiling.

I gurgle in response. He feels so good inside of me. I've never actually felt anything quite so good. I can't imagine it could get any better than this, but he surprises me when he pulls out a little and pushes back in, and it feels even better. He maintains a slow rhythm until sweat beads on his forehead, and he shuts his eyes tight.

I'm flying overhead in ecstasy, somewhere. Probably heaven.

I feel him contract inside of me and then release. My body shudders, releasing a small orgasm along with his. He collapses on me, and I lower my legs to wrap them around his back. I'm exhausted, but sublimely happy. Right before I fall asleep, I note that I'm blind, again. But I don't care.

*

I go blind three more times during the night. After the second time, Jarrod accepts my offer of mint chocolate chip ice cream. I have a full pint in the freezer, which I was saving to celebrate my Ph.D. Now I'm celebrating something else. But I don't exactly know what it is.

"This apartment is growing on me," Jarrod says, scooping up a spoonful of ice cream and licking it clean. He's naked, and it's all I can do not to lick him clean.

"Maybe I can get a job at the bar to pay for it. I know all about beer on tap now," I say.

"You don't want to be a scientist anymore?"

"I can't. Not with the charge of plagiarism hanging over my head."

Jarrod drops his spoon into the carton of ice cream. He lifts me onto his lap and caresses my breast. "I have a hard time believing you plagiarized something, Marie."

"I didn't."

His fingers roam down my belly and lower still, making me squirm. "Then you'll fight it. Simple."

"They're sure of their proof. It will take years to fight them, and even if I win, it will destroy my reputation."

"Okay, then. First things first."

He lifts me again and sits me onto his arousal. I go blind a fourth time.

*

I wake up at six in the morning, as if it's a normal day. But it's not normal. I have to tell my father that I'm a big, fat failure.

My goals have been dashed. And I have no idea what I'm going to do next. On the bright side, I'm feeling relaxed, as if I've had sex with a gorgeous, generous lover. And I have.

I assume he's left the apartment. I mean, isn't that what men do after the big nasty? I don't have any experience with one-night stands, but a little deduction makes me believe that they're only for one night.

That's why I'm surprised when I turn on my side to see Jarrod sitting on the edge of the bed. He's dressed as much as he can be since I ripped off a big chunk of his clothes. His slacks are back on, but he is shirtless under his suit jacket. His hair is a mess, but weirdly that just makes him look sexier. Wow, he sure looks good in daylight.

"Hi," I say.

"Hi." He smiles. He has a beautiful smile. Perfect teeth. A billion-dollar smile. In a flash, I realize I don't want him to leave, and I chastise myself for feeling this way. Remember, Marie, you're a new woman, I think to myself. I'm turning over new leaf. Women who pick up men in bars want them to leave the next morning. It's easier that way. Simpler.

But he's not just beautiful. He's also nice. And he's looking at me like I'm beautiful. He's looking at me like he likes me. Am I delusional? Am I seeing something in his expression that isn't there?

He gently pushes aside a stray strand of hair that has fallen over my face, and he tucks it behind my ear. "Thank you, Marie. It was a great night. Perfect. I'll never forget it."

My stomach lurches. I feel sick. Sad. This is the big goodbye. It's nice that he's being so kind and thoughtful. But there's no doubt it's a goodbye. I feel tears sting my eyes, and I will them not to fall.

"I enjoyed it, too," I say. Talk about understatement of the year. I'm basically ruined for any other man. I'll never pick up another man in a bar who comes close. Nobody will ever come close. I might as well become a nun. Come to think of it, that might be my only choice for employment at this point.

"Good. You're going to think I'm crazy for what I'm about to ask you, but I'm asking you to keep an open mind. Can you do that?"

"I think so?" I say it like it's a question.

"Good. Good." Jarrod runs his fingers through his hair, making it stand up on end. He looks nervous, totally out of character, as much as I know him after one night of hot, sweaty sex.

"Okay. Here goes," he says and hands me a small, blue box with a white ribbon and black lettering on top.

*Tiffany & Co.*, I read.

# CHAPTER 5

"You're giving me jewelry?" I ask.

"Open it."

I do. Inside the Tiffany box is a smaller ring box. I've seen them before, but I've never opened one. I can't imagine why he's giving me this.

"Open it," he urges.

I look up at him. Something inside me tells me not to open it. Opening it probably means, *complicated.* Handing it back to him is probably the simpler, wiser choice.

I open it. Inside, is a magnificent diamond ring. It's huge. Jennifer Lopez would blush if she got a ring this big. I close the box and hand it back to Jarrod.

"It's beautiful. I'm sure whoever you give this to will love it," I say.

Jarrod clears his throat. "That's just the thing. I'm giving it to you."

"Why?"

"It's traditional when a man asks a woman to marry him."

"That's true. So why are you giving me the ring?"

"Because I'm asking you to marry me."

*

I sit up in bed and wrap myself in a sheet. It's time to think clearly, and obviously I can't do that when I'm naked.

"I'm sorry, Jarrod. I don't think I heard you correctly. Funny, I thought I heard you ask me to marry you."

"I know it sounds funny. But if you hear me out, you'll agree that it's the wisest course of action."

"Why? Are you pregnant?" I ask. "Don't answer that. I need coffee. I can't talk about this without coffee. I also have to pee."

I close the bathroom door and sit down to pee. What have I gotten myself into? Obviously, Jarrod is a lunatic. Sure, he's a gorgeous, rich lunatic. But this is my fault for picking up a strange man in a bar. What was I thinking? Have I gone crazy, too?

I put on jeans and a T-shirt and brush my teeth. I hardly recognize myself in the mirror. I look—well—used. My hair is matted, and I have mascara smeared across my cheek. It was a wild night. I don't bother to wash my face, because I'm dying for a cup of coffee. I must clear my head.

I open the door, hoping that Jarrod has left. But he's still here. I fill the coffee maker with coffee, pour water into it, and turn the switch on. Jarrod begins to say something, but I stop him, putting my hand up, palm forward, in his face. "Not until it brews," I say.

We stand in my kitchenette and wait for the coffee maker

to stop gurgling. I take a mug from the cabinet and pour a cup of coffee. I sip it, looking down so I don't have to see Jarrod's gorgeous eyes. I drink about a quarter of a cup, before he takes it from me and sips it, himself.

"Better?" he asks.

"Better."

"I'm not a lunatic. If I don't get married within two weeks, I lose my company."

"This sounds far-fetched. I need more coffee." I take the mug from him and fill it back up.

"I know. I'm the CEO, but it's my grandfather's company. What he says goes. If I don't get married by my thirty-second birthday in two weeks, I'm blackballed from the company. I don't want that to happen. The company is my baby. The company is my life."

I understand why he doesn't want to be blackballed. I'm blackballed, and it hurts. I know what it's like to have your life's work slipped out from under you. To have all your dreams, wishes, and goals dashed to the ground.

"I think I've seen this plot in a movie," I say.

"You have. That's where my grandfather got the idea. He hates that I'm the end of the Sinclair line. He wants me to breed and breed right. Marriage. And he wants to see the babies and the wife before he dies."

"You have a grandfather who's alive?" I ask. I only have my father. My mother died when I was a baby. Everyone else in my family died before I was born.

"I have a grandfather and a grandmother. Both still alive. My parents died in a car crash when I was twelve."

I think about Jarrod being twelve years old. He must've been a beautiful boy. Smart. It must have hurt him to lose his parents at that age. "I'm sorry," I say.

"Listen, Marie. You're at a crossroads. I'm sure you'll get the Ph.D. thing worked out eventually, but right now you're in a bind. So am I. I think we can help each other out. Besides, we get along like a house on fire. Literally, you set my house on fire." He counts on his fingers. "We get along. We're attracted to each other. The sex is great. A lot of marriages start with a lot less. What do you say?"

What do I say? I say he's crazy. I say, how dare he pick me to marry him just because I'm desperate? I say, I don't need to get married to a man in order to survive or do well in life. I say, I'm an intelligent, independent, more than able woman.

"Show me the ring, again," I say.

He takes the box out of his pants pocket and pops it open. "Do you want bigger? I can get you bigger, if you want."

"I don't think diamonds come any bigger than that. Show me your chest, again."

He unbuttons his jacket and lets it fall to the floor. He should be naked all the time. He should be on a giant billboard in Times Square in his birthday suit. My eyes are drawn to the dark line that goes from his belly down into his pants. I bite my lower lip.

"Put the ring on my finger," I say. "If it fits, it's a deal."

# CHAPTER 6

I'm in a very large Mercedes. I accidentally turn on the seat warmer, and my ass is on fire. I'm wearing a long wool skirt and a cotton blouse. Jarrod chose my outfit from my closet, saying it was the most acceptable attire I had for meeting his family.

Besides the clothes on my back and my purse, I have a small suitcase filled with my clothes in the trunk of his car. Jarrod tells me someone will pack up the rest of my belongings and close my apartment for me. This is how billionaires do things. In other words, they don't do things. They have other people do things for them.

Jarrod drives like a bat out of hell out of Esperanza. The little town has been my home for the past six years, and I'm sad to say goodbye. I thought it would be my home for years to come while I did research at the university.

Now we're driving up to the Bay Area. Jarrod's family has some kind of castle or compound or wherever billionaires live in Marin County. It's a four-hour drive, but I think Jarrod wants to make it in two.

He plays classic rock on the radio, and he's humming along. I study his profile. He's better than any Greek sculpture. I kind of want to jump his bones while he's driving, but at the same time, I'm freaking out about what I just agreed to do.

Fortunately or unfortunately, Jarrod's grandfather picked a ring that's exactly my size. I look down at my hand. The ring fits perfectly. I can't help myself from sneaking looks at it every couple of minutes. It's shiny and massive and makes me look like a hand model. It dawns on me that I could sell this ring and have enough money to live on for years.

But a deal's a deal.

We don't say a word to each other during the whole trip, but just as we turn into a long driveway and a Great Gatsby-esqe mansion appears, Jarrod shudders. "It's going to be just fine," he says. "They'll love you."

He doesn't sound convinced.

*

A butler answers the door and lets us in. He calls Jarrod "master," and Jarrod calls him Thomas.

"Does someone actually live here?" I ask.

"Of course someone actually lives here. What do you mean?"

"It looks more like a train station than a house."

"It's not a train station," Jarrod insists. "And two people live here. Two people plus twenty servants."

"This is why revolutions are fought," I whisper to him.

"This is just the beginning, Marie. You have no idea."

The mansion puts Hearst Castle to shame. It's like Downton Abbey but bigger and ten times glitzier. "Do you live here, too?"

"God no. I have a place in Silicon Valley, near the company."

Thomas escorts us through the mansion to a large library. Inside, an old man sits at the desk, reading a book. Jarrod's grandfather, obviously. I can tell that he's old, but he's still a very handsome man. He's a promise of great genes, and a guarantee that Jarrod's future will be all kinds of hunky.

Jarrod's grandfather looks up when we enter the room. He checks me out and arches an eyebrow. Curious. Confused.

"Grandfather, I'd like you to meet my fiancée. Marie Foster, may I present my grandfather, Jarrod Wright Sinclair the first."

The First's face lights up. His eyes are bright, and his mouth is set in a killer smile. There's no question he's delighted to see me. He hops up from his chair and bounds over. He takes me in his arms and gives me a warm hug.

"Not only a fiancée," Jarrod's grandfather announces with glee. "But she's smart, not like those models you usually hang around with."

I don't expect anyone to confuse me with models, but his statement hurts my feelings. I smooth out my skirt and push my glasses up on my nose. Do I look smart? Something tells me that smart means not particularly attractive.

Jarrod rubs the small of my back, as if he's trying to make me feel better. He does. My hurt feelings vanish.

"Marie is very smart, grandfather," he says. "A Ph.D. student in chemical engineering no less."

Without saying another word to us, the grandfather calls in an assistant and begins planning the wedding. I overhear some details about flowers, the cake, and the San Francisco Philharmonic. But mostly I hear an ominous buzzing in my ears, the kind people get right before they suffer a cataclysmic stroke.

I flail my hand in the air and Jarrod catches it, grabbing me firmly. "Come on," he says. "He doesn't need us for this. Time to meet my grandmother."

We walk hand-in-hand outside behind the mansion. We walk along an Olympic-size pool toward an English garden, full of topiaries and a rather extensive maze.

"Grandmother's always puttering around her garden," Jarrod explains. "It's her pride and joy. So if you want to get in good with her, think up a compliment for her gardening skills."

"I don't need to think up a compliment. This is the most amazing garden I've ever seen. This is like Versailles, but a hell of a lot more impressive."

An old woman pops out from behind a well-manicured bush. "Wise girl!" she shouts, scaring the hell out of me, and making me jump a foot into the air.

"I like her already, Jarrod," she gushes. "Which surprises me to no end, as you can imagine."

"No, grandmother, I can't imagine," he says, obviously affronted. "Why would you be surprised?"

She doesn't answer him. She takes hold of my arm, slipping her hand around it and tugs me in the direction of the house. "Where on earth did he find you, my dear?" she asks. "You're not his normal type of female, which is a good thing, I should add."

I don't know if I should tell her he found me in a bar. I don't know if I should tell her the truth, that we had a one-night stand, and he's marrying me in order to save his company. And that I'm marrying him because I'm a disgraced former-scientist with no life skills beyond high-level chemical engineering lab work. Normally, honesty is the best policy, but in this case, honesty is probably not what his grandmother wants to hear.

I shrug. "You know," I say, as if people meet up in all kinds of places all the time, and the details are really not all that important.

"No, I don't, my dear. But perhaps you'll tell me, eventually. You can also tell me why you're not wearing a shirt, Jarrod. For now, how about we all have a drink? Stinking rich people love to drink, my dear. It distracts us from our guilt for having so much money."

*

Jarrod takes the martini from my hand. "Perhaps you should stick to iced tea," he says. He has a point. My first bout with drinking led to all kinds of trouble.

Jarrod's grandfather joins us at our table by the pool. Jarrod's grandmother is working on her third martini, while I'm sipping my iced tea. I notice that Jarrod's also drinking iced tea. I figure he wants to keep on his toes as much as he wants me to keep on mine.

"I like your hips!" his grandfather exclaims, as he takes a seat.

"Excuse me?" I ask.

"Your hips! You've got breeder's hips. How many grandchildren are you planning on giving me? The more the better. How about six?"

The buzzing in my ears returns. I take a big gulp of the

iced tea.

"We're thinking four children, grandfather," Jarrod says.

My head snaps in his direction, and I spill the iced tea all over myself.

"We are?" I shriek.

Jarrod's grandmother instructs him to show me to the blue room. Evidently, there's a change of clothes waiting for me, there. My clothes are covered in iced tea and panic.

Four kids. Four kids? Four kids!

Jarrod holds my hand, as we walk up the giant wood staircase to the second floor. Wherever we go, he holds my hand. I think he's trying to prevent me from running away. Smart man. Every fiber of my being is telling me to run out the door as fast as I can, but I don't know where to run. I've nowhere to go.

Besides, his hand feels awfully good. And he's had a puppy dog expression on his face ever since we drove up the driveway to his grandparents' mansion. He needs this. And he's scared, too.

But four kids?

The blue room is blue. It's about forty-two times the size of my studio apartment. It has a massive four-poster, king-sized bed against one wall and a full set of living room furniture. Two couches. Assorted armchairs. Artwork everywhere. It's a man's room. Lots of dark wood and hunting themes on the walls.

Jarrod shows me to the walk-in closet. It looks like the men's department at Neiman Marcus, not that I've ever been to Neiman Marcus.

"I've got a couple of women's outfits here, somewhere," he says.

"Wait a minute. Is this your room?"

"Was. Was my room. I'm a grown man, now. But my grandparents insist on maintaining a bedroom in their house for me. Silly, I know." He shrugs. He wipes his brow on his jacket sleeve. "I guess I should change my clothes, too. What do you think?"

"I think it's a pity for you to ever get dressed. I also think I need to sit down and breathe for a minute."

As the words exit my mouth, I drop to the floor, like I'm the wicked witch of the West, and Dorothy has just melted me. I'm surprised when Jarrod does the same. We sit cross-legged on the floor of his over-the-top closet and stare at each other.

"You don't have to do this, you know," I say.

Jarrod arches an eyebrow and grins. "I know. I want to, though."

"So you can keep your company."

"It's more than just a company, Marie," he says, his face deadly serious.

"I understand. I understand about life's work. I used to have that."

"Are you sure you want to do this?" he asks.

"No. Yes. I don't know. Yes."

"Are you doing some kind of multiple-choice thing?" he asks.

"I don't know."

I fall back on the floor and lie down in the fetal position. It feels so good to lie down and rest. I realize I haven't gotten a lot of sleep. Jarrod lies down next to me. His face is an inch from mine, and I can feel his warmth. He still smells so good. I wonder what kind of cologne he uses. Probably Eau de Sexy, and it probably costs more than most people make in a year.

"Thank you, Marie," he says. He kisses me ever so lightly on the lips, and I fall fast asleep.

*

When I wake, our limbs are intertwined and my head is resting on his chest. I feel at home, strangely enough. Comfortable.

But what am I doing? Why am I letting events carry me? I don't believe in destiny. I believe we're the masters of our own lives. And for sure, I don't believe in love at first sight.

Love? Who's talking about love? Who put that notion in my head?

Jarrod stirs. He puts a finger under my chin and tips my head up. "Good morning, sunshine," he says.

"Actually, it's afternoon now."

"Yes, of course. How could I've been so foolish? Very unscientific of me. Do you want to take a shower before you change?"

"A shower sounds heavenly."

*

It isn't really a shower. Showers have one head. This has—well, I lose count at eight. Jarrod turns it on for me, because I can't figure out how it works. Water shoots from everywhere.

I bite my lower lip. "I'm not sure about this."

"Scared? You? A woman who picks up men in bars?" He shakes his head, like he's disappointed.

"I'm not scared. It's just that I can't swim."

"I have lifeguard training. I'll save you."

He takes off his jacket and drapes it over a chair. Then, much to my surprise, he unbuttons his pants and let them slip to the floor.

"What are you doing?" I ask.

"The same thing you're doing. Taking a shower."

"But I'm taking a shower," I say.

"Yes. I thought we already went over that."

He is so naked.

Jarrod isn't like other men. When he's naked, he's really naked. His body goes well above and beyond just ordinary men's body parts. He's the candy aisle at the grocery store.

He's perfectly proportioned. Perfectly defined. Is this only attraction I'm feeling? No. Jarrod is objectively, scientifically, hotter than hot.

"Oh," I breathe.

He takes a couple of steps toward me and gets right to work, unbuttoning my blouse.

"Are you sure we should do this?" I ask. "I mean, we barely know each other."

"I think it's a little late for false modesty, Marie," he says.

Finished with my blouse, he unzips my skirt and lets it fall to the floor. "Your grandparents are downstairs. That's only about a half a mile away. Aren't you worried they're going to come in and see us?"

"They walk slowly. And it's more like a mile away."

He unhooks my bra with two fingers and takes it off my body, throwing it to the other side of the bathroom. "You don't have to do this to try and convince me to marry you," I say. "I'm wearing the ring. It fits. You don't have to take a pity shower with me."

"I don't take pity showers, Marie," he says. "I'm not a man

of mercy. I'm a man who does exactly what he wants. And there's nothing more that I want right this second than to get in that shower with a naked Marie."

I try to swallow. "You weren't lying about the lifeguard training, were you?"

"Nope. You have nothing to fear. I've got you."

He turns me around and walks behind me toward the shower. His body is up against my back, and the evidence of his desire pushes against me. I've never taken a shower with a man. I've never been with a man like Jarrod. We step into the shower and the water feels amazing. It hits us from every angle.

"All showers should be like this," I say.

"No joke. It's the water softener. Makes it very sensual."

His hands slip around me and cup my breasts. I shut my eyes, overwhelmed at the sensation. "Woman, you could become a habit," he says. I lean my head back against his chest, and guide his hands down lower.

I'm getting excited, fast. My insides are throbbing. Sex twice in two days? I feel like a slut but in a good way. Sex with a fiancé is kosher, after all. It's written somewhere, but I can't recall where. I can't recall anything. I can't even recall my name. Jarrod has his tongue in my ear, and I think I might have brain damage.

I writhe against him. My hand touches his manhood behind me. Wrapping my hand around his thickness, I massage him. Up and down. Up and down. He grows even larger under my touch.

He groans and juts his pelvis forward. "Just a minute," he says.

I drop my hand and turn around. "What?"

"One second." He hops out of the shower and rifles through some drawers. Finding what he's looking for, he holds it up in the air. A condom. "Eureka."

"Oh. You don't want to start on the four kids immediately?"

Jarrod stops at the threshold of the shower. "Why, do you want to start right now?"

"No!"

"Right, then."

He hops back in and grabs me by my hips, turning me around. He nuzzles my neck, as he pushes me up against the wall. He bends me over, and without further ado, enters me from behind in one thrust, tip to root.

Sex in the shower is good. Clean and dirty at the same time. Jarrod fills me, and I welcome him, pushing back as he thrusts forward. This isn't about making love, though. It's about getting the job done. It's a navy shower instead of a long bath. Quick and to the point but completely satisfying.

So, it doesn't take long for us to both find satisfaction. I come suddenly, my body convulsing in pleasure. Jarrod comes soon after. He slips out of me, and I turn around to face him. We kiss until the water runs cold, and that takes a very, very long time.

# CHAPTER 7

I'm not an expert on sex and relationships. If it has nothing to do with engineering or math, I probably know nothing about it. But my instincts are telling me that I'm no longer doing the big nasty with Jarrod.

Our big nasty sex has evolved to serious relationship sex. Not that I know about serious relationships. But I feel different. Jarrod looks at me differently. And after a world record amount of orgasms, our super long cuddling sessions spell one thing.

Not that I'm going to spell it. But it has four letters. And it begins with an L.

It's one thing in my mind to marry a billionaire stranger because I'm having a nervous breakdown, an identity crisis, and my life is getting worked out in luxury along with great sex. But it's a whole different thing to marry a man who I'm having feelings for. The kind of feelings that go with a four-letter word.

We turn down a dirt road. The Mercedes rolls over rocks and kicks up dust. My father's goat barn and pigsty are up, just ahead.

"Don't ask if someone lives here," I order Jarrod. "My father lives here. It will be hard for you to accept it. But he has decided to live a certain kind of life that requires eccentric behavior."

Jarrod turns his head toward me and raises an eyebrow. "What kind of eccentric are you talking about? Reciting limericks kind of eccentric? Or sleeping with animals eccentric?"

"Sleeping with animals. But nothing inappropriate."

"Of course not."

Jarrod parks the car near the pigsty and I lead him toward the goat barn. Three goats run out of it, heading straight for Jarrod. They chew on his suit jacket, and he tries to push them away.

"Nina, Pinta, Santa Maria, where are you going? We must continue our studies on Russian literature." My father peeks his head out of the barn and looks around. It takes a minute for him to recognize me.

"Marie, is that you?" he asks.

"Yes, Father. I've come for a visit to introduce you to a friend."

"A friend? Interesting. I don't see the purpose in that, but perhaps you're doing some kind of experiment or study?"

"Something like that, sir," Jarrod says, offering his hand to shake.

My father looks down at Jarrod's hand as if it's a strange creature. "Interesting," my father repeats.

"Father, invite us in so that we can sit and talk."

"Indeed. Indeed. Come in and sit. You can see my advances in communication with barn animals."

We follow him inside. "Communication with barn animals?" Jarrod mouths to me. The inside is filthy, just like one would assume a goat barn would look like.

"I'm making great strides in my research, Marie," my father says, sitting on a stool. I sit on a broken crate, and Jarrod remains standing.

"That's wonderful, father."

"And you? How's your fluid dynamics going?"

I swallow. I don't want to lie to my father. I've never lied to him before. But I'm ashamed that my Ph.D. was declined, and that I've been kicked out of the scientific world in disgrace.

"Oh, you know," I say.

My father nods, vigorously. "Yes, I do," he says, as if we just had a long conversation about my research.

"Mr. Foster," Jarrod says, leaning down to face my father and speaking in his yummy, deep chocolate cake voice. "I've come here today to ask you for permission for your daughter's hand in marriage."

I face-palm, slapping myself, loudly. "Are you kidding?" I ask Jarrod. "My father won't understand that. Nobody would understand that. That's archaic. Just because he lives in a goat barn, doesn't mean he thinks I'm a goat to be traded off to some man. You don't need his permission. You only need my permission. What's wrong with you? I'm not a commodity, you know. Even though I pick up men in bars and do tequila shots and have sex with strangers and have no prospects for employment or prospects to make an impact on the planet doesn't mean you can treat me like I'm not even human."

I slap my leg and jump up, stomping my foot on the dirt floor. I harrumph, loudly and storm out of the goat barn.

I march around my father's property. I'm so angry that I could spit. What was I thinking, agreeing to marry a man I didn't know? We're from two different worlds. Jarrod comes from a family that makes the one percent look downright poor, and I come from a family of one, who studies communication with barn animals, and wouldn't know a 401(k) from Special K.

I make it around the property once and by the time I get back to the pigsty, I've decided that I'm not going to have a nervous breakdown any longer. I'm going to clear my name in the scientific world all on my own without a man, without a ring, and without a home. Worst-case scenario, I'll move in with my father. I've nothing against goats except for the smell, and I'm sure a little Febreze will clear that right up.

With my mind made up, I step calmly back into the goat barn. I'm surprised to find Jarrod and my father laughing together.

"And the software developer shouted, *kowabunga*, and jumped into the barrel of optic fiber, and we had to throw out the entire batch," Jarrod announces, joyfully.

My father erupts in laughter, as if this is the funniest thing he's ever heard. When his laughter finally dies down, he pats Jarrod on the back. "You're a good man, Jarrod. You're devoted to your science, and I respect that. Normally CEOs are all about the dollar sign, but I can tell you're about the science."

"It's true. I am."

"And you'll love my daughter?"

"I think I will. Yes, I think I will."

A feather could knock me down. I'm speechless. I don't know what to think. I'm disoriented, confused, and I have a strong desire to jump on Jarrod, wrap my legs around him, and swallow his tongue. But I hold myself back. I try to remain calm.

My father notices me and wags his finger at me. "You made a good choice," he tells me. "He likes goats, too."

# CHAPTER 8

I'm getting married. I've spent the past week going to parties and dinners, meeting the rich and famous and accepting their congratulations and best wishes on my upcoming marriage.

I have a new wardrobe, new hair color, and eyelash extensions that drive me crazy. Jarrod and I have been staying in his blue room until the wedding takes place in the backyard of his grandparents' mansion.

Every day, I almost talk to Jarrod about canceling the wedding. Every evening, when I'm alone with him in the blue room, I change my mind. I mean, marriage can't be that bad. A lot of people get married. Of course, those people probably don't get married to a man who's only doing it to keep his company.

So whatever feelings I'm feeling for Jarrod, the reasons

behind the wedding hang over my head. In fact, as a whole team of young women in high heels and red lipstick get me dressed for my wedding, I'm writing a pro-con list.

Pro: his penis. Jarrod has the most beautiful penis on the planet, and he does marvelous things with it. It's always happy to see me, and I get the impression that I bring out the best in it.

Con: sexual attraction doesn't equate to lifelong companionship, devotion, or monogamy. Our so-called relationship is based purely on sex.

Pro: sex with Jarrod is really, really good.

Pro: I mean, really good sex.

Con: getting married is a distraction from my work. I should be spending my time trying to clear my name in the scientific world.

Pro: there's no reason I can't clear my name while married to a gorgeous billionaire, having fabulous sex with his beautiful penis.

Con: I might L-word him. This is scary. I can't even say the word.

Con: he might not L-word me. And I think I want him to L-word me. And I shouldn't want that because I'm an intelligent, independent woman who doesn't need to be L-worded by anyone.

Pro: even if he doesn't L-word me, he makes me feel great when I'm with him. Sometimes, I catch him looking at me, and it's not the look of someone who doesn't care. I think he might care. Maybe he cares. I hope he cares.

Con: I don't want to have to wonder if he cares.

Pro: he likes goats. My father likes that he likes goats.

Pro: I'm wearing the biggest honkin' diamond ring. The Hope Diamond can kiss my ass with this ring.

Con: this is crazy. I barely know the guy. I'm probably having a nervous breakdown. I need antipsychotic drugs, quickly. Somebody tell me to stop. Somebody tell me to take off this couture dress and wipe off my professionally done makeup. But leave the ring. I don't want to take off the ring.

The wedding planner takes the pro-con list from me and rips it in half. "Oh, no," she says. "Oh, no. No. No. No. No!"

She wags her finger in my face and scowls. "Brides are not allowed pro-con lists, my dear," she says. "Trust me. Elizabeth Taylor made them, and look where she wound up."

"Who's Elizabeth Taylor?" I ask.

"Funny. That's my girl. You look beautiful. All ready?"

The team of dressers help me to my feet. They steam out the back of my dress and fluff the train so it covers a large section of the room. They point me toward a full-size mirror, but someone totally different stares back at me. She's beautiful, like someone on reality TV.

"Who's that?" I ask, pointing at the mirror.

The wedding planner speaks into a Bluetooth headset. "All set?" she asks someone on the other line. I guess the answer is yes, because they take me by the arms and pull me into the next room.

I hear classical music playing. It must be at least a twelve-piece orchestra. I've been to the symphony once when I got free tickets from the university. Other than that, I have no experience with live music. But now, the live music is all about me.

They're playing me in.

The wedding planner hands me a large bouquet of white flowers. "All systems go. Go. Go. Go. Cue the bride, now," she says into the headset. For a minute, I have no idea what she's talking about. Then, she points at me, and someone pushes me from behind.

The large doors open, and I'm faced with a room of about three hundred people. They turn, look at me and stand at attention.

I realize, dimly, that they're standing for me. The music plays the Wedding March, and I feel another push from behind. My feet start walking, even though I don't remember telling them to move.

It's a long flower-covered path to the altar. The music's playing and the people are watching me. It's the first time in my life that I'm the center of attention like this, and I don't like it one bit. I manage to get halfway to the altar when I'm gripped by a nervous stomach that threatens to make me hurl all over the rich and famous.

I stop in my tracks. I can't take another step. I know that if I do, I'm going to throw up all over the dress, and I don't know if it will wash out. I close my eyes and take deep breaths, willing my stomach to calm down. In the distance, I can hear the wedding planner tell her Bluetooth to go. But I'm not going. I've lost all ability to go.

# CHAPTER 9

Seconds pass, followed by minutes. A warm, strong hand touches my back. I open my eyes to see Jarrod. He's dressed in a tuxedo with tails. He looks like Cary Grant.

"You're okay," he tells me, but it comes out more like a question than a statement. I try to answer, but my mouth is dry and my tongue is swollen. I might be having anaphylactic shock. Is it possible to be allergic to couture?

"You don't have to do this if you don't want to," he whispers.

His eyes are big and thoughtful. I can tell that he's afraid. Afraid of losing his company or afraid of being humiliated in front of three hundred guests? Or maybe just afraid that I'll reject him? No, the last option is impossible. He looks like Cary Grant in his tuxedo.

He looks like the best opportunity I'll ever get.

"I can do it," I say, finally. "Just help me to the altar."

He holds my hand, just like he always does, and I'm instantly relaxed. Gone are the three hundred strangers staring at me. Gone is the symphony orchestra. Gone are the eyelash extensions. It's just him and me, and I can handle that.

At the altar, the pastor says a lot of nice things about Jarrod and his family and about me and mine, even though none of what he says about my family is true. Jarrod and I ignore him and stare at each other. I get the impression that he's trying to ask me and tell me so many things through his eyes. But it doesn't matter, now. The time for discussions is over. Now, it's just about two words.

I take a deep breath. "I do," I say.

*

"I can't dance."

I'm the center of attention, again. This time we're outside with a breathtaking view of the ocean and the setting sun. Tables and chairs are set up for the three hundred guests, and a band is playing next to a dance floor. They announce that it's time for the first dance of Mr. and Mrs. Sinclair.

That's when I run away and hide in the maze.

*

It doesn't take me long to find the center of the maze. Perhaps two minutes. It's a simple algorithm, a binary system translated into rights and lefts. The center is quiet with a large stone bench to sit on. I kick off my heels, which have been pinching my feet, and curl my toes into the thick soft grass.

Heaven.

I take my first real deep breath of the day. I almost forgot the pleasure of breathing deeply. Things have been moving so fast that I've either been panting or holding my breath. But now I'm alone in the secluded maze.

The light is dim and I can barely hear the music from the band. Nobody is watching me, and I'm delighted for that. I take my veil off and toss it into the grass. I begin to unleash my hair, finding the many pins in it and removing them.

I shake out my hair and scratch my scalp. It feels wonderful to be free, at least on my head. My entire body, from head to toes, was bound in preparation for the wedding. I'm wearing Spanx, a push-up bra, and a choker around my neck.

With my head and feet free, I start to work on the rest of my prison. I remove my Spanx and my dress, leaving on just the slip. For the first time in a long time, I feel like myself and plop down on the bench.

There's a rustling in the bushes, and Jarrod breaks through them next to me. He's covered in leaves and branches, and he shakes them off his clothes.

"You're supposed to go around the bushes, not through them," I explain to him. "It's a maze. The trick is to find your way to the center."

Jarrod bends over and shakes his head like a wet dog, dropping leaves and twigs to the ground. "I know that," he says, sounding annoyed. "But I couldn't find my way to the center. I could hear you moving, and I knew which direction you heading, but I couldn't figure out the maze."

"It's really a very simple algorithm. A binary system, translated into lefts and rights."

"I don't find any algorithm to be simple. So I tore through the bushes. It's called cheating, Maria. Sometimes, it's easier."

"I've never cheated before."

"Of course you haven't," he says, quietly.

"I can't dance."

"I can teach you."

"Even if you teach me, I can't dance in front of three hundred strangers. I can't be the center of attention. I'm a scientist. I'm comfortable in a lab, preferably underground. I'm like a mole in a white coat."

Jarrod takes off his jacket and tie. He loosens his top button. He kneels down in front of me and puts his hands on my knees.

"Marie?"

We sit like that in silence for a long time. I don't trust my own voice to speak. I think I'll start crying, and I'll tell him this was all a terrible mistake. This is not the way to do things.

"We're living a complicated algorithm, Jarrod," I say, finally. "I can't figure it out. I don't know the right answer."

"Perhaps you just need time to understand it. I understand what you're feeling. It's normal. Of course, it's normal. We've just done a crazy thing. But you know what? I'm glad we did it."

"Of course you are. You get everything you want. You keep your company. You make your family happy. And you can do the big nasty whenever you want."

"I love doing the big nasty with you," he says. "But I don't know if you realize it or not, we're not doing the big nasty, anymore. We're way beyond that."

"We are?"

Jarrod takes my hand and caresses my palm, sending shivers up my arm. "My sweet scientist. My beautiful algorithm solver. Don't you know that I'm crazy about you?"

"No. Are you?"

Jarrod laughs. "Yes, I am. Can't you tell?"

"No."

"Then I guess I'm not doing it right. Being crazy about you, that is." He kisses my hand and holds it against his lips for a moment. "We can annul the marriage, if you want. Just give me the word."

"You would do that?"

"To make you happy I would do that."

Jarrod's cell phone rings, but he doesn't move to answer it. "Go ahead," I say. "Answer it. I don't mind."

"Are you sure? I only left it on for emergencies. It must be the office. Probably important."

"Answer it. It must be important."

Jarrod answers the phone and holds it close to his ear. He listens, intently. "Are you shitting me?" he demands into the phone. He stands up and paces around the bench. He runs his fingers through his hair, making it stand up straight. Occasionally, he comments into the phone, and it doesn't sound good.

There's a problem at his company, which could have cataclysmic effects. After about fifteen minutes, Jarrod clicks the phone off.

"Marie, I think I need to take you upstairs and then I have to run over to the company to put out the fires. Not that I think these fires can be put out. Dammit!"

"What are the fires?" I ask. I've never seen Jarrod like this. Normally he's calm, cool, and collected under all circumstances. But now, he's freaking out.

"It's complicated. I couldn't even explain it to you, if I wanted."

I get up from the bench and walk over to him. I wrap my arms around his neck and kiss him lightly on the lips. "You know, I don't even know the name of your company."

"Really? I never told you? It's Sinclair Information Systems."

"Of course. I should've guessed software, since it's Silicon Valley. Tell me your problem, Jarrod. Give me a chance to help you."

We lock eyes. I can tell he's debating with himself whether or not to confide in me. His company is his territory, and I'm hurt that he sees me as an intruder. But he blinks. He changes his mind.

"What the hell. You'll probably understand it better than I do," he says. "Our machines are down. We have a big problem with machine down-times. They're getting longer and more frequent. The engineers are stumped. It's a problem of numerical modeling and computation fluid dynamics. Does that ring a bell?"

I smile. "Yes, it does. Get me to your office. I'll show the engineers what to do."

*

I'm in my element. I'm happy. No, ecstatic. And I'm wearing jeans and a T-shirt. The only thing that could make me happier right now is if I had a bag of peanut M&Ms.

I've been working all night with Jarrod's engineers. They're a great group of guys, but they don't know a thing about cardan shaft misalignment.

"That's your problem. Straight and simple. My new measurements will solve it," I tell them as I crunch numbers on a computer. They huddle around me and take notes. I walk them through my computations. It's like Disneyland, but with numbers.

I understand why Jarrod is so protective of his company. It's a very special place. Even though it's high tech, the offices have a warm, family feeling to them. I wouldn't mind living here.

I get lost for hours in the work with the other engineers.

But I feel eyes on me, and I look up to see Jarrod watching me from the other side of the room. He sits in a chair, his elbow on the armrest and his fist resting on his cheek. But his attention is on me. He's seeing me like I'm an ape in the zoo or some other creature whose behavior needs to be studied.

I throw him a smile and go back to my work. Someone hands me a cup of coffee, and I take a sip. I refuse to take a break until I work out the last of the new measurements.

Finally, after the sun comes up and employees start to shuffle into work, I complete my computations and finalize them with the other engineers.

"You know that you've saved us, right?" one of the engineers tells me.

I look down at my ring. I wonder if he's talking about that or my math skills.

"You would've figured it out, eventually," I say, coming out on the side of my math skills.

But they continue to thank me. They offer me pizza and more coffee. I yawn. I'm really tired. I don't want to turn their offers down, but suddenly I'm too tired to keep my eyes open. Jarrod appears at my side and slips his arm around my waist to support me.

"You done good, Mrs. Sinclair," he whispers in my ear.

"Your company is beautiful," I say.

We drive off in his Mercedes. I open the window and let the cool breeze blow on my face. It feels delicious. I'm so tired that I'm actually looking forward to the blue room. But after driving for a few miles, I realize we're going in the wrong direction.

"We're not going to my grandparents' place," Jarrod informs me. "We're going to our place."

"Our place? We have a place?"

"Well, my place. Which is now our place."

My stomach flutters. For a moment, I forgot that I'm married. The marriage seems unreal, whereas the work seemed more than real.

"I'm not taking you to jail," he says. "If you don't like it, we can get a new place. But I think you'll like it."

"Does it come with M&Ms?" I ask. "I could go for some M&Ms."

"I think I can arrange that. By the way, I want to let you know I'm very impressed with your math skills."

"Thank you. I love math. Don't you think math is the most relaxing hobby?"

"I've never thought of math as a hobby," he says. "But watching you do math stirred me. In fact, it made me think of a number, fondly."

"Really? What number?"

Jarrod smiles. "Sixty-nine."

# CHAPTER 10

Jarrod's house is nothing like I imagined. I thought it would be a modern penthouse apartment of glass and stainless steel. Instead, he lives in a small cottage, circa 1920. There are two bedrooms and only one small bathroom. His furniture is homey and comfortable.

He's most proud of his guest room, which isn't a guest room at all. Instead, it's stuffed with antique personal computers. He shows me each one, as if they're his children. I'm itching to take them apart and study their insides. It's the engineer in me, but I don't think Jarrod would appreciate that.

"Hungry?" he asks.

"Starved."

Jarrod makes grilled cheese sandwiches on thick brioche

bread. We sit in his small kitchen and scarf them down. "These are delicious," I say. "I can't believe that someone wearing such an expensive suit would know how to make grilled cheese sandwiches."

"I'm surprised that such a talented scientist would be prejudiced and make judgments before testing her hypothesis."

I bite my lower lip. "You're right. I'm slipping. I've turned the corner into a prejudiced drunkard who picks up men in bars."

"Yes. I think that's what attracted me to you."

We don't do sixty-nine or any other number. We're tired and a little bit in shock. We lie facing each other in his Tempur-Pedic bed.

"I'm married," I say.

"What a coincidence. I'm married, too."

I can barely make out his face in the dark room. The only light is coming from the glow of his alarm clock next to the bed. Still, I can see how beautiful he is. I'm not an artistic person, but I appreciate how things are made. I'm an engineer. I recognize perfection when I see it. I'm reasonably sure his outward perfection goes down deep.

He's perfect inside and out. I'm sure of it.

The fact that he's looking back at me takes my breath away. And he smells so good.

"Why do you smell so good? What kind of cologne do you use?" I ask.

"I don't use cologne."

"Oh."

Jarrod touches me, tracing the borders of my face with his finger. "You were stunning to watch today," he says.

"You think? I didn't even recognize myself in that dress and makeup."

"I didn't mean at the wedding," he says. "Although you did look stunning at the wedding. But I'm talking about at the office. Watching you with the engineers, your brilliant mind figuring out a solution that has eluded the top people in the industry. Stunning. Sexy."

His finger glides along my lower lip. I open my mouth and take his finger in. I suck, gently. He moans. "Holy hell," he says, his voice low and gravelly.

I never knew that a finger could taste so good. I half wonder if he's coated it with something yummy, like chocolate or mashed potatoes. Whatever it is, I can't get enough.

If his finger tastes this good, I extrapolate that the rest of him must taste even better. I stop sucking his finger and scoot down his body until his shaft is poised at my mouth. The tip is wet, and I touch it with my finger. I push him onto his back and exchange my finger for my mouth.

He tastes delicious here, too. Smooth and silky. Hot and spicy. I lick him like an ice cream cone, while I cradle his balls in my hand. His breathing turns shallow and ragged, panting like he's running a marathon, even though I'm the one doing all the work.

I could do this forever, but I grow greedy and put all of him in my mouth. My head pumps, and my throat opens to take him in. I'm driven to make him come. I want to satisfy him. I've never been more driven to do anything more than that.

*

I sleep like the dead without dreams, but in the middle of the night, my eyes fly open. Jarrod isn't in the bed, but I see him sitting in an armchair in the room. He's staring at me, and I get the impression that he's been doing it for quite some time.

"Are you all right?" I ask.

He's silent for a moment, and then he sighs, deeply. "I think we need to talk."

"In the middle of the night?" I ask.

"Sorry about that. But I couldn't sleep, and I didn't want to waste one more day of your life."

"Waste a day of my life? What do you mean?"

"Watching you this evening was wonderful," he says, his voice soft and low. Serious. "You were like an artist. A great scientist completely in your element."

"I enjoyed it. I love problems to solve, and your engineers are fun to work with."

"I think we need to annul this marriage and stop this insanity," he says quickly, firing the words from his mouth like a machine gun.

I flinch, surprised and hurt by what he's saying. But he's serious. Dead serious.

He thinks we should stop this insanity. Insanity. It's an apt name for what we've been doing, but it still hurts my feelings that he thinks it's an apt name. Marriage with a stranger and giving up my dreams are insane, but I don't want him to give me up.

"In the morning, I'm going to drive you back to your studio so that you can get on with your life," he tells me, as if I'm an employee or servant that he can boss around. "I should never have made you do this. It was unconscionable of me."

"So, if I understand you correctly, Jarrod, you're going to decide for me what's best for me."

Jarrod stands up and paces around the room. "No. Yes. I don't know. But I refuse to let you sacrifice yourself so that I can follow my dreams."

He's right, of course. I shouldn't be sacrificing myself and my dreams so that another person can follow their dreams. But I'm smart enough to understand there's a way for two people to follow their dreams at the same time.

However, there's a bigger issue, something that Jarrod doesn't seem to understand. He still sees this situation as a marriage of convenience. But I've grown to see it more like a happy accident. I've developed feelings for him that he obviously doesn't reciprocate. At least, he doesn't reciprocate them to the same extent.

And that's why I have to agree with him.

"I don't want to wait until the morning," I say. My voice comes out croaky, filled with emotion. I will myself not to cry, but

I don't think I can last long without shedding tears. I feel an overwhelming desire to run away from Jarrod as fast as I can and not look back. If I look back, I'll turn to salt, or something much worse.

Jarrod stares at me, his mouth open. I've shocked him, but I don't know why. Isn't this what he wants?

I walk to the closet, careful to stay far away from him, in case I embarrass myself by hugging him or throwing my naked body on top of him. I gather my clothes into my small suitcase, while Jarrod stands over me, watching.

"You don't have to do this right now," he says. "You can wait until the morning."

"No, I need to do it this way."

"I don't want to hurt you. I don't want you to be mad at me."

I take my ring off my finger and hand it to him. "We don't always get what we want."

Jarrod closes my hand over the ring and pushes it back toward me. "I want you to keep this. It's yours. Keep it, sell it, do what you want with it, but I refuse to take it back. It's yours. I'll get my keys and drive you back to your place."

"No, please don't do that. Call me a cab or have somebody drive me, but I don't want you to drive me."

Jarrod argues with me for a minute, but I'm determined. I can't sit in the car with him right now. He calls his grandparents' chauffeur to drive me into town, and I wheel my suitcase out of the room. Before I leave, I drop the ring into a crystal bowl on a coffee table by the front door.

At least with this one gesture, I get to decide for myself what I do.

*

I step backward out of what's supposed to be my apartment and bump into the chauffeur. "I think you took me to the wrong address," I tell him.

"This isn't your place?" he asks.

I check the number on the door and the nameplate under the doorbell. They are correct. This should be my apartment. I peek my head back inside.

The size and shape of the apartment are mine, but nothing else is.

"I think someone broke in," I say.

# CHAPTER 11

The chauffeur snaps to attention, pushes me out of the way, and storms into my apartment, ready to take on any intruder or attacker. Since my apartment is so small, it takes him about fifteen seconds to scope out the place, even looking under the bed, in the closet, and behind the shower curtain.

"Nope," he says. "All clear. Nobody's home but us. Anyway, it's clean as a whistle. It doesn't look like anybody's tampered with it."

I step in and close the door behind me. "Nobody's tampered with it? What are you talking about? There's nothing here that hasn't been tampered with."

I point at my desk, which isn't my desk at all. Instead of a plank of wood on cinder blocks, there's a big honkin' antique desk and bookshelves, which climb to the ceiling, framing it. My papers and books are perfectly organized and tidied. I'm aghast. I feel violated.

"I've been violated!"

The chauffeur raises an eyebrow and sucks air through his teeth.

"No, not that way," I explain. "But my space has been invaded. Does this look like the space of a Ph.D. student?"

"I don't know, ma'am. I never finished high school. It looks like a designer studio apartment. Like you have unlimited money. Your bed is worth thirty thousand dollars. I've seen it in a catalog."

"Thirty thousand what?" I screech.

But he doesn't answer. He says goodbye and walks quickly out the door. I don't blame him. It's still the middle of the night, and he probably doesn't want to discuss interior design with a strange woman.

I stand in the middle of my apartment, unsure where to sit. Could somebody else have moved in while I've been away for the past week? How could that be possible? I still have the lease, and I would have been informed if they moved somebody else in.

The answer, I realize, is much simpler. My apartment, in all its poverty chic, must have disturbed the sensibilities of a certain billionaire, who I met and married recently. At some point during the last week, he must have snuck into my apartment and changed everything, or more likely, he ordered somebody else to do it.

I walk to the kitchenette to get a glass of water. It's now more like a kitchen than a kitchenette. It looks a lot like a fancy set from a show on the food network. Tears begin to stream down my face, and my nose runs.

"I have granite countertops!" I yell and breakdown in wrenching sobs.

*

Somewhere in the distance, I hear a knocking noise. Someone's pounding on a door, and I can't figure out why. I open one eye. The clock reads ten thirty in the morning. Even though I was upset, the bed is so comfortable that I've slept without moving. I haven't changed position all night.

The knocking gets louder, and I figure out that someone is actually knocking on my door. "Go away," I call. "My bed's too comfortable to get up. It's not my fault. Somebody bednapped my old uncomfortable bed. If I were sleeping in that bed, I'd get up right away. But I never want to get out of this bed, again."

"What are you talking about!" a man yells from the other side of the door. "It's the middle of the day. I don't give a hang how comfortable your bed is. My bed is pretty comfortable too, but you don't see me lounging around in it all day."

I recognize the voice. I jump up and make a beeline for the door. Throwing it open, I begin to apologize. Standing there is the head of the university's chemical engineering department. The one who had me thrown out on my ear.

"Dr. Farrington, I'm so sorry. I didn't know you were here. Why are you here? Come right in. Would you like some coffee?"

I grab Dr. Farrington's arm and tug him into the apartment. He stumbles forward, and I close the door behind him. He finds his balance and stares me down. He's tall, and I think he's forgotten how to smile somewhere along the line during his life. He's very good at scowling, though. It's definitely his signature look.

"What on earth are you wearing, girl?"

I look down. I'm wearing a silk nighty that falls just below my crotch. I cross my hands over my cleavage, which is putting on a show.

"My clothes were clothesnapped," I explain. "Somebody absconded with my sweatpants and T-shirts."

Dr. Farrington nods, as if clothes are clothesnapped all the time.

"It doesn't matter. I'm not going to be here for long. I just had some news for you. Your Ph.D. dissertation has been accepted."

"What?" I exclaim, throwing up my arms in celebration. I forget about my cleavage, letting most of my left boob pop out. "But you said I plagiarized my dissertation."

"That was before we knew that the dissertation from the week before was the plagiarized one. He plagiarized you. It was just a matter of timing. He came first, so we thought he was the original."

"How did you figure it out?"

"It was brought to our attention by a respected corporate investigative firm. They brought in forensic computer scientists, and looked at the two computers."

My eyes flash to my desk. My laptop is sitting there. Could someone have come in and taken it to study its hard drive? Of course they could have.

"So, you're now Dr. Marie Foster, Ph.D. You have two undergrad courses to teach starting Monday, and you're expected in the chemical engineering lab today to begin working on the research that you outlined in your dissertation. And none of this mammary gland business, Dr. Foster," he says waving his hand in the direction of my boobs. "Chemical engineers do not have breasts."

He's right. I've never seen a chemical engineer's breasts. Most of the time I forget I have breasts. "No problem, Dr. Farrington," I say. "I'll be there in an hour. Thank you so much. Thank you. Thank you."

Dr. Farrington walks to the door and opens it. "I never doubted you for a second," he says on his way out of my apartment.

*

I'm happy and sad at the same time. I'm both ecstatic and despondent. I have my life back. My dreams and my wishes have come true, and that makes me happy. But the other stuff that I never dreamed of and never wished for that came true before are no longer true now, and that makes me indescribably sad.

It's been a week since my name was cleared and I've been back at the university. I have two lab assistants, who are as enthusiastic about my research as I am. I work at least fourteen hours a day, but I don't feel the time pass by.

Still, sometimes I catch myself looking down at my hand, expecting to see Jarrod's ring there. But it's gone, just like he is. He hasn't called or contacted me, and sometimes I wonder if my crazy interlude with the hot billionaire was just a delusion or a dream.

Today isn't an official work day, but I go in at noon. I walk a few blocks toward the university, sticking my tongue out at the dry, ugly fountain in the town square as I pass it. Stupid fountain. The day of my dissertation hearing, I had tossed a coin in and made a wish that my dissertation was accepted. Instead, I was accused of cheating and thrown out.

That's the last time I ever do something superstitious.

Staying away from silly superstitions isn't the only thing I've learned in the past couple weeks. I've learned a lot. From the dangers of bars to the joys of oral sex, I think I'm a much wiser woman, now.

As I pass the bar on my way to work, I can't resist the urge to share my wisdom with another. I open the door to the bar and walk inside.

# CHAPTER 12

I take a seat on a bar stool. The same bartender is there, polishing glasses with a worn cloth. She's wearing a red minidress so tight that her butt looks like it's trying to escape. Ditto her gigantic breasts.

"What'll you have?" she demands.

"Hi, Layla. Don't worry. I'm not going to order my usual."

"What's your usual?"

"You know, what I had the last time I was here."

She shakes his head. "Nope. Your face doesn't ring a bell. So, what'll you have?"

"What do you mean, my face doesn't ring a bell? How could you have forgotten me? Your bar changed my life."

"If I had a nickel for every time somebody's said this bar has changed their life, I'd have five cents," she says.

I blink. "But that means you would have only heard it once," I say.

"Exactly. What'll you have?"

"Actually, I didn't come in to drink this time. Or to pick up strange men, for that matter. I changed my mind about changing my life and went back to my old life. So, I'm not drinking alcohol, but I've learned some things, and I want to share them with you."

"Listen lady, the rules of the bar are, if you don't drink, you can't share nada. So, what'll you have?"

"Iced tea?"

Layla grabs a glass and pours iced tea into it. "No problem," she says and hands me the glass.

"I can't believe that you don't remember who I am. I'm the one who drank the tequila shot."

"Oh! The woman who drank the tequila shot! Why didn't you say so before?"

"So you remember me?"

"Nope. Is that all? Because I have inventory to do."

Is that all? All of a sudden, I wonder if I really do have wisdom to share with a big-boobed bartender. Perhaps I don't have any answers. Perhaps she has all the answers, after all, and all I know is that I enjoy chemical engineering, and tequila makes me stupid.

"I don't understand about love," I say, voicing what I don't know instead of giving advice.

"Nobody understands about love. That's why I do a bang-up business. The more liquored up a person gets, the more they understand about love."

"But that's counterintuitive," I say. "If they're drunk, they can't think clearly."

"Exactly."

"I was married," I say. "Have you ever been married?"

"I'm married to my work, or at least I was married to my work." She shoots a glance at a man sitting in the corner. He looks a lot like Ryan Gosling, except his hair is longer, and he has a neck tattoo.

"Are you married to that guy?" I whisper. For some reason, I'm scared for him to hear me.

"Are you out of your mind," she screeches. "That jerk? That's the a-hole that's trying to take my bar out from under me."

Her voice cracks, and I spot a tear at the corner of her eye. I want to give her encouragement, tell her that happy endings exist, but I'm not altogether sure they do.

So, I lie.

"Have you tried making a wish at the fountain?" I ask her.

"The old, dried out fountain? Why would I do that?"

"People come from all over to toss coins in and make

wishes." That part's true. Stupid people. If only they knew.

"Do I look like I believe in that mumbo jumbo?" She looks down her nose at me and silently dares me to blink.

"No, of course, not," I say.

Despite her protests, however, I catch her glancing toward the door. She opens the cash register and takes out a quarter. "What the hell," she says. "It can't do any harm."

I'm not sure about that, but I don't dare argue with her.

I leave right behind her. I think about what Layla said about drunk love all the way to the university. I've only been drunk once, and it's true that being with Jarrod felt just like a shot of tequila. I can understand why people become addicted to love and alcohol. I've been jonesing for my hunky billionaire for over a week.

Just because he rejected me, doesn't mean that I'm any less drunk for him. Love. I can think it now. Say it now. It's no longer a word that holds negative power over me. Even though I hurt, I feel lucky to feel it.

Just like it was my first time drinking, it's my first time loving. It keeps me company throughout my days and nights, and even though I can't have Jarrod, anymore, at least my love for him keeps me company.

*

I'm crunching numbers on a white board. Sometimes it's better to see the problem in a big way like this and be able to take a step back to study it, instead of working it out on the small screen of a computer. Since it's a weekend, and the lab isn't really open, I'm the only one here.

The seclusion helps me advance in my work. It's great to be able to concentrate without the presence and noise of others. I'm just about to solve an equation on the board when I smell him.

He smells like he always has: expensive cologne, dollar bills, and all kinds of dirty, nasty sex.

# CHAPTER 13

I close my eyes, sure that I'm having a psychotic break or that I'm delusional. I've been working too hard and thinking too much about him, and now I've managed to conjure him, if only his delicious smell.

His scent is enough to destabilize me. In fact, I lose my balance altogether. I fall against the whiteboard, stubbing a marker with my chest and throwing the other markers across the room with my flailing hands.

I smell him first and then I hear him. His footsteps become louder as he runs to help me right myself.

Then, I see him.

I gasp because I'm surprised he's here and because he's just that beautiful. If I thought he was the love of my life before,

I'm pretty sure of it now because all I want to do is throw myself on him, wrap my legs around his waist, and never let go.

"Are you okay?" he asks. He's holding on to me, as if he expects me to fall down, which is totally wise of him because my legs are like rubber, and it's only a matter of seconds before I either pass out, have a heart attack, or, if he just moves his hands two inches up or down my body, I will have a massive orgasm.

"What are you doing here?" I ask. I'm surprised I can speak because I'm pretty sure I swallowed my tongue when he touched me. "Do you have annulment papers for me to sign?"

"No. I was just in the neighborhood."

"It's a nice neighborhood."

"It's okay, but I'm partial to one of its residents," he says.

I take a step back, gently pushing him away, and I try to catch my breath. I want to strip his clothes off and lick him from his head to his toes, but at the same time, I'm not particularly happy with him. He made a decision about my life without consulting me. He decided to throw me away, pretending that it was better for me. And now here he is, flirting with me, if I'm not mistaken.

"Are you flirting with me?" I ask.

"Yes. Is it working?"

"Yes and no. I'm torn between loving you and hating you."

Jarrod raises an eyebrow and smiles. Boy, he has a great smile. "Loving?"

"I didn't say loving. You heard me wrong." My forehead breaks out into a sweat, and I wipe it on the hem of my T-shirt.

Jarrod takes a step toward me, and I take a step back away from him. "My hearing is very good, Marie."

"Well, you know, men lose a good percentage of their hearing as they age."

"I'm only thirty-two."

"Thirty-two? I thought you were thirty."

"Nope. Thirty-two. Is that a deal breaker for you? Am I too old?"

I take two more steps backward and run into a chair. I'm off balance again, and I sit down on it with a thud. "Deal breaker? I thought our deals were already broken."

I'm proud of myself. I'm being strong and mature instead of a horny crybaby, which is what I really am inside, faced with Jarrod.

"Yes. I broke our deal. And you know what? I don't regret that. It was a shitty deal. We didn't deserve that kind of deal. It put our relationship on the wrong track. And I want more than that."

"Well, we wouldn't want you to get less than what you want," I say in my best bitchy voice.

"Touché."

He drags a chair over and sits down so we're sitting face to face.

"Not that I care," I say, trying not to look at him because he makes my blood rush through my veins, and I'm trying to stay tough and unfazed. "But what is it that you do want?"

"Isn't it obvious?"

"No, actually. It isn't. And I'm a trained scientist. A keen observer."

Jarrod drops to his knees in front of me and takes my hands. "Look at me," he commands. Reluctantly, I look down at him.

"I want you. I love you. I want to spend the rest of my life with you, loving you."

"You do? Are you sure?"

"I've never been surer of anything."

"What changed your mind?" I ask.

"Nothing. Don't you get it? That's why I canceled the deal. I don't want us to start our life together with a deal. I want us to start our life together the old-fashioned way. I want to start off with love and the desperate desire not to lose each other."

He caresses the palm of my hand with his thumb, and my body erupts in goose bumps. "That all sounds good," I breathe. "But maybe you should've informed me before."

"No doubt. But I got the impression that you didn't share my sentiments."

"Obviously, you're not a trained scientist. Not a good observer."

Jarrod raises an eyebrow. "Is that so? Did I read the situation wrong?"

"So, are you asking me to marry you?"

"We're already married."

"That's right. I forgot," I say. "So are you asking me to be married with you?"

"Yes. That's exactly what I'm asking you."

"Do you still have the ring?"

"No. I gave that back to my grandfather."

I try not to be disappointed, but I groan pretty loudly. I really liked that ring.

Jarrod rummages around in his pocket and pulls out a Cartier box. "But I did get you another ring, in case you wanted to forgive me and love me forever."

"Open it. Let's see."

He opens the small box, and I'm practically blinded by the ring. The stone is about the same size as the other one, but it shines twice is bright. Is that even possible?

"What do you say?" he asks.

"If it fits, sure. Why not?" But I'm giddy inside. My pulse is racing and my heart is pounding. I'm flooded with happiness that I've never experienced before.

It's not the ring that makes me happy, even though it's is

magnificent. It's Jarrod. Jarrod the magnificent who's in love with me as much as I'm in love with him.

Sitting in my lab in the university, trying on Jarrod's ring, I realize that this is what having all my dreams and wishes fulfilled feels like. I'm suddenly sorry for the rest of humanity, who surely can't feel what I'm feeling, because it's just too perfect.

The ring fits. I'm hypnotized by it and can't tear my eyes away from it. But then I smell Jarrod, again, and my focus shifts to him.

"About that number you were talking about," I begin.

"Number? What number?"

"I think it was sixty-nine."

*

Sixty-nine, it turns out, is a really good number. At first, I'm a little nervous to try it out, but Jarrod is very enthusiastic, and he promises to guide me through it.

He wastes no time. He hops up from the floor, grabs me by the hand, and pulls me to an open broom closet.

"See?" I say. "This is a broom closet. It looks nothing like my apartment. There's a big difference."

"Yes, I see perfectly."

But I don't believe him, because he's entirely focused on getting me naked in a hurry. He unbuttons my jeans and peels them off me, while at the same time, he kicks the door of the broom closet closed.

"We're going to do it in here?" I ask.

I'm naked, and somehow, Jarrod has taken off his clothes, too. His hands are everywhere… My breasts, my ass, and between my thighs. "Don't worry. Nobody will come in."

"I'm not worried about that," I pant, my voice coming out like a chihuahua in heat. "But there are a lot of toxic chemicals in here. And we're naked. What if we spill some?"

Jarrod pushes me up against the wall. His eyes are huge,

and he's looking at me like he's hungry and I'm a Big Mac. For the first time in my life, I desperately want to be a Big Mac.

"Don't worry about the chemicals. We'll eat only organic after," he says.

He crushes his mouth against my breast and swirls his tongue over my nipple. My insides heat up and turned to liquid. I dig my fingernails into his back, desperate for him to be closer.

"Eat me like a Big Mac," I plead.

He doesn't need more of an invitation than that. He trails kisses down my body until he's kneeling in front of me and pushing my legs apart with his head.

He does the thing that I love most in the world with his tongue, and I melt. I'm slightly worried that I'm going to collapse in a puddle of ecstasy onto his face and smother him to death, but I manage to stay upright while he skillfully devours me.

I've got the whole drunk love going on inside me. One tequila shot. Two tequila shots. As his tongue glides and circles and dives inside me where I long for him to be, I get drunker and drunker.

No way could I ever drive like this, I think like an idiot.

My intoxication evolves into some kind of higher level of consciousness, like Timothy Leary on a really rockin' day. I'm seeing stars, clouds, and I could swear I'm seeing a male version of the Rockettes, kicking their legs behind Jarrod in the tiny broom closet.

"I'm so close," I tell Jarrod, and I'm not lying. He's blowing me, but I'm about to blow like Krakatoa.

I'm inches away from the Big O. Centimeters. Millimeters. I'm… almost… there.

And then he stops.

At first, I think I've lost all feeling in my lower half. But I look down to see Jarrod looking up at me. "I think you're doing that wrong," I say. Doesn't he know he's not supposed to stop now? Certainly not when I'm so close!

"We need to change our position a little. This is only half of sixty-nine, Marie," he says.

"It's a thirty-four and a half?"

"Something like that."

"I really like thirty-four and a half."

"I could tell."

"I mean, I like it a lot," I insist. "Like more than anything."

"Don't worry," he says, tugging me down onto the floor with him. "The sixty-nine comes with a thirty-four and a half."

And it certainly does, and I certainly do. As our bodies lock together, each of us tasting the other—Loving. Possessing. Torturing—I come like a firecracker.

Boom!

Afterward, Jarrod cradles me in his arms next to the bottles of industrial-strength floor cleaner and the bleach.

"Does this mean you get your company back?" I ask. Despite it all, there's a still a little nugget of doubt in my mind that Jarrod is marrying me in order to keep his company.

"I bought out my grandfather a week ago. That's what took me so long to get back to you. There's lot of paperwork involved in a corporate buyout."

I'm not sure I understand what "corporate buyout" means, but I think it starts with an "L."

The End

Wish Upon A Stud Series #4
Just
SACKED
elise sax

# *Just* SACKED

(Wish Upon A Stud – Book 4)

elise sax

# CHAPTER 1

I shut the door behind me and let my eyes acclimate to the dark. Damn. He's still here. I try to avoid looking at him as I pass his table on my way to the back of the bar.

But he doesn't let me sneak past him. In fact, he grabs my arm.

I look down at his strong hand on my arm and then straight at him. Right into his emerald green eyes. Isn't it typical that the worst bastard on the planet is drop dead gorgeous? I wish he would do the drop dead part instead of just the gorgeous part. The fact that he looks exactly like Ryan Gosling goes to prove that there's no justice in this world.

"I've got a bat behind the bar," I tell him. "And I'll triple play your ass with it if you don't take your hand off me, immediately."

It takes him three seconds before he releases my arm. "I'm going to need to sanitize my arm, now," I complain. "Hey! Eyes up here, fink!"

He's staring at my chest. I'm used to this. Everyone does it, because I'm cursed with huge boobs. My bras cost more than my car payment. I have to get fitted by a bra guru down in Los Angeles. Not only do my breasts make my back hurt, but they've distracted every person I've spoken to since I was twelve years old.

"My name's not Fink. You know that." His eyes flick to my face but go right back to my chest. "It's Hank."

"Fink fits you better."

I turn on my four-inch heel and head back behind bar. My bar. My family's bar. But now my family is dead, and our bar is being foreclosed on, taken over by Mr. Hank Taylor, businessman and shark. And fink.

I serve my patrons two beers and a dirty martini. "You don't have to do that," Hank says, walking up to the bar.

"I have two more hours before you steal my business, and I plan on doing my job right up until you kick me out on my ass."

He leans over and puts his hands on the smooth mahogany. "I didn't steal it, Layla. I bought it fair and square from the bank."

I pick up my baseball bat and hold it high above my head. "Get your hands off my bar, or I'll knock your head into the next room."

His hands fly off, and he takes a step back. "Just trying to be nice," he says.

"You always were a giant ass-wipe," I mutter. Hank is a local. We went to school together until he dropped out in eighth grade. One year, he drilled holes in the girls' locker room wall and charged boys who wanted to take a peek.

"What was that?" The vein in his neck is pulsating, making his tattoo move.

"You heard me."

"Listen, you couldn't make the lease. It's business. Don't take it personal."

"Hey, it's only business for you, pal! It's personal for *me*!" I shout.

"Exactly," he says. "That's why you lost the bar, and I have it."

I literally see red. Hank Taylor's Ryan Gosling face is covered by a red film. So, is everything else. Obviously, I'm having an aneurysm. My brain has blown up, and it's coming out of my eyes.

"You probably should back up even further," I say. "You're still within an arm-swinging length, and I have a bat."

I don't know why I'm being charitable, why I'm warning him. There's nothing more that I want to do than to beat him into a pulp. But even though I'm seeing red, even though my brain has blown up, I still have a tiny bit of common sense left, and it's screaming at me not to wind up in prison. I mean, they don't have good bras in prison.

"What can I do so you don't hate me?" he asks.

"Go outside, look very carefully both ways up and down the street, and when a truck is driving by, jump in front of it."

Hank flinches, as if I've wounded him. His sensitivity surprises me. He resembles "the boy next door" up to a point. His longish hair and his neck tattoo are more representative of his true character… Shark. Fink.

"I could give you your job back," he suggests.

"I don't care that you fired me. I would never work for you."

"Where are you going to live?" he asks. I've lived over the bar my entire life. Now, he owns that as well. I'm homeless.

"In a shoe," I say. I don't want to have this conversation anymore. It's none of his business what I do with my life. He can't come in here and take everything I care about away from me and then pretend he gives a damn.

"How about this?" he says, slapping his hands together. "Let's make a wager. If you win, you get the bar back. If I win, you work for me and live over the bar."

"I like the truck idea better."

"I'm serious," he says.

"So am I. You don't see me laughing, do you?"

"How about a poker game?" he asks, ignoring my hostility. How does he do it? I'm giving him my very best hostility. "You win, you get the bar back. Doesn't that sound tempting to you, Layla?"

"I don't play poker."

"Scrabble?"

"Nope."

"Horseshoes?"

"You've got to be kidding."

"I give up," he says, throwing up his hands. "You have no talent."

"Actually, come to think of it, there is something I'm pretty good at," I say.

*

The bar is filled with bikers, wearing leather jackets, chains, and way too much facial hair. They're shouting nonstop, drowning out the sound system.

"Go! Go! Go!" they shout in unison, standing around the bar's center table where Hank and I are sitting.

There are two shot glasses and two bottles of whiskey on the table. One of the bottles is empty. Hank fills his shot glass from the other whiskey bottle. "Here's to swimmin' with bowlegged women," he says and throws back the shot. He closes his eyes for a moment, and I'm pretty sure he stops breathing. Then, just as I'm certain he's gone to meet his maker, he inhales sharply and opens his eyes. The bikers roar in approval.

"Not bad," I say. It's taking me a lot longer to drink him under the table than I predicted. I've out-drunk half the men in this town, but Hank is holding his own. The fink.

"You shed it," he says, his speech slurred. "You know what else isn't bad? Your dress. The way it hugs your body. Your ass looks like it's trying to escape."

He puts his fingers to his lips and kisses them in appreciation of my tight dress. The bikers hoot and holler in agreement with Hank's assessment. They start making nasty comments about my body. I wave my bat at them.

"Don't make me bust your chops!" I yell at the entire bar, and they shut up for a second before they erupt in more *Go! Go! Go!* chanting. They're rowdy but not really dangerous. I've been working the bar since I was five years old, so I'm not afraid of much. It's just a matter of setting boundaries.

It's my turn, and I fill my shot glass with the whiskey and swallow it down in one gulp. It goes down smooth. The whiskey stopped burning six shots ago. I have to admit, I'm feeling no pain. My veins are mostly filled with alcohol at this point. I'm no longer seeing red. Now, I'm seeing double.

"I like your jeans," I hear myself tell Hank over the cheers of the bikers. "Tight. Ripped. Just like your body."

Hank lifts one eyebrow and hiccups. "I thought you hated me."

The bar is stifling hot. I wipe my brow with the back of my hand. I'm kind of going in and out. "I do. That doesn't change the fact that you've got a bangin' bod."

"Talk about bangin' bods—" he starts.

But I have no idea how he finishes the sentence. Everything's a blur after that. Just a couple of snapshots of memory… Finishing the other bottle. Hank throwing a punch at a biker. And boobs.

*

I want to die. I want to never breathe again. Breathing hurts like a sonofabitch.

Dying would be a lot less pain.

I take a breath and wince. Yep, I wish I were dead. If I were dead, I wouldn't feel this way. Come to think of it, how is it possible that I can feel this miserable and still be alive?

Just more proof that life isn't fair.

It's not just my head. My whole body hurts. My throat, too. It's like something's died in my mouth, and it tastes indescribably bad. Not to mention I can't open my eyes.

I try to turn in bed, but every movement sends a knifelike pain shooting through my cerebral cortex. Then, someone moans, and even in my altered state, I know it's not me.

"What the hell?" a voice says next to me.

I manage to open one eye. "What are you doing in my bed?" I croak. Hank is lying next to me, and he's stark naked. His neck tattoo is just the beginning, I discover. He's inked all over his body. At least seven different, large tattoos. He looks like a UFC fighter. Crazy fit.

"This isn't your bed," he says. He sounds as bad off as I am.

But he's so right. We're lying on a small bed in a brightly lit room. It's not my bed, and it's not my room. The window's open and Mexican music is wafting through it.

"I have a feeling we're not in Kansas, anymore," I say. An old beat up television is on in the corner. A telenovela is playing in Spanish. There's a lot of Tijuana happening in the decorations of the room.

"Did you kidnap me and take me over the border?" I ask. Every word makes me cringe in pain. The reality of being in

Mexico hasn't quite hit me, yet, but my internal warning sensors are on and beeping loudly.

"Did I what? Did I… Huh?" he answers. He lifts up his right hand, and my left hand shoots up, too.

"Why did you handcuff us together?" he asks, looking at our chained wrists.

"Oh my God, we're handcuffed," I say.

"And who took off your clothes? Was it me?"

# CHAPTER 2

"There's no way I'm naked and handcuffed in Mexico," I say, despite the overwhelming evidence to the contrary.

"I can't believe you're naked, either," Hank says. "I thought it would take a lot longer to get your clothes off."

He turns his head, scans my body, and lets out a slow whistle.

"Really? Really? You're starting that now?" I shout and sucker punch him with my free hand, right in the gut. I make impact with a satisfying grunt. He bolts upright and clutches onto his stomach, pulling my hand so hard that I roll onto my side.

I try to right myself, but he's a lot stronger than I am, and he's got his chained hand glued to his middle. "What'd you do that for?" he growls.

"Because you're a douchebag. It's douchebag payback. Let me up."

He swings his legs over the side of the bed, stands, and yanks me with him. I scoot off the bed but stumble and fall onto my knees with my face smooshed up against his ding dong. I grab onto his hips and pull myself up.

"That didn't happen," I say, wagging my finger in his face.

"Oh, it so happened." He's smirking something awful. He's got a day's worth of growth on his face, and his hair is mussed up. Oddly enough, his breath isn't bad. I imagine mine smells a lot worse. Like a corpse or a men's bathroom at a football game.

"There's nothing funny about this situation," I say.

"Well, slightly funny."

"You won't think it's funny when I call the FBI on your ass for kidnapping me."

"Hey, don't look at me. I had nothing to do with this," he says, sounding convincing. "The last thing I remember, I was drinking you under the table."

"You're remembering that wrong. I drank you under the table. I won the bet, and the bar is mine."

"Ha!" he barks.

"Ha!" I bark back.

I have no memory of how we got here. I don't even know where here is. Besides being naked and handcuffed, I'm not injured, and I don't feel violated in any way. But I can't believe I lost to Hank Taylor. I've never lost a drinking contest. Never. The bar is mine, again. I'm sure of it.

Hank seems less concerned about our predicament than I am. He's focused entirely on my breasts, which are on full display, and it's obvious he likes what he sees. In fact, it's becoming increasingly obvious that he likes what he sees.

"Get that thing down," I say, taking a step backward.

He's growing by the second. Just how big can Hank's shlong get? Is he going for the world's record?

"I can't. I'm trying to think of other things, but I'm distracted."

"Make it stop. Think about dead puppies."

"You don't think I've tried that?" His eyes are focused completely on my boobs. I half-expect laser beams to come out of his eyeballs. I put one arm over my breasts, but it's like sticking a finger in a dike to stop it from leaking. It doesn't do much good.

"Get it down!"

"I can't help it. I'm a boob man."

I turn around and show him my back. "You're going to have to get that thing in line," I say. "What are you? Twelve? Get some control over it."

"Normally, I have a lot of control over it," he says, clearly affronted. "You have to admit, you're distracting."

I look around for something to cover me. There's no sign of my clothes, and the mattress is bare. Gross.

"Come on," I say, dragging him to the bathroom. But inside, there's only a washcloth and nothing else. "This can't be happening."

I grab the washcloth and cover one breast. Nope. Hank's still got the giant-sized boner.

"Get in the shower," I order.

"But I barely know you," he says, smirking.

"Just get in."

He steps in the shower by himself with his hand outstretched, since we're still cuffed together. I turn the cold water on him full blast and wait. And wait. And wait some more.

"I don't think this is having the desired effect," he says, staring at my boob.

"Cold showers are supposed to work," I moan.

"Usually, but not with a naked woman watching." He turns off the shower and plucks the washcloth from my hand. "To dry myself off," he explains, staring at me in the eye for once.

After he's done, he tosses the wet washcloth into the tub and steps out. "Let's figure this out. Maybe start with a key to unlock the cuffs."

He marches around the room, searching for a key from under the mattress and every scrap of furniture.

"Can't you just pick the lock?" I ask. "You must have experience with handcuffs."

Hank stops in his tracks and stands tall with his erection trying to touch his belly button. "Are you implying I've served time?" he asks, scowling. "Well, I haven't. I've managed to get this far without wearing these kinds of bracelets. But what about you? I can't imagine you haven't used your share of recreational handcuffs. Am I right, fifty shades of Layla?"

He arches his right eyebrow and cocks his head to the side.

"There are no fifty shades of Layla," I say. "No shade whatsoever, thank you very much."

I'm tempted to sucker punch him, again, when the room's door opens, and a little woman walks through. "Hola!" she says, happily and then freezes with her mouth open and her eyes wide, as if she's seen a ghost.

I cover my breasts with my free arm, but I don't need to bother. She's not even glancing at me. She's only got eyes for Hank's stiffy, which is quickly turning into a nice, normal flaccid penis.

"Hola," he says, waving.

# CHAPTER 3

"I think she had a stroke," I say. "You killed her with your boner."

Hank nods. "Armed and dangerous."

"She's not moving. Is that normal with a stroke?" I ask.

"I don't know. I've never had a stroke."

He walks us over to the little lady. She's about forty years old, and she's wearing a cotton dress and flats. Her hair is pulled back in a long ponytail. She's less than five feet tall, and she has tiny hands. Doll's hands. And she's not blinking.

Hank claps his hands together in front of her face, making my chained hand fly up. It works. The little woman blinks, gasps, and takes a step backward. She crosses herself. "Oh, dio mio," she cries.

"We're not crazy perverts," I say, trying to calm her. "Tell her we're not crazy perverts, Hank."

"We're not crazy perverts," he says. "We're just naked, and she has enormous jugs."

"Big help," I say.

He shrugs. "I don't think she's going to believe that we're not crazy perverts. I think we need to take another tack."

*

The other tack turns out to be money. Well, not actual money, but a promise of a large bankroll if she'll only find us some clothes to put on.

Hank gets a pair of jeans and a t-shirt, which he can't put on because of the handcuffs. Meanwhile, I'm wearing Daisy Dukes and a bikini top that looks like it's going to explode from stress.

She gives us both bright orange flip-flops that are too big on me and too small on Hank.

By the time we finish dressing—braless, and in Hank's case topless—we've begun to draw a lot of attention.

The little woman turns out to be Alma, the daughter of the owner of the motel we're staying at. She invites us downstairs for coffee, and we gladly take her up on the offer. Hospitality aside, I notice that Alma has slipped a butcher knife in her belt. She's not taking any chances with us, and I don't blame her.

Downstairs, we're surrounded by Alma and what we gather is her extended family….Five men and two women.

Neither Hank nor I speak much Spanish, but he's making progress with hand gestures. I just keep smiling, even though my head is pounding, and I'm handcuffed to a jerk in Mexico.

"Mexico?" Hank asks Alma, slicing his free hand through the air around him to signify his surroundings.

She nods. Her eyebrows knit together in one bushy line, and her hand touches the knife, belted to her waist. Her eyes never leave our handcuffs.

"Chihuahua," a man standing next to Alma tells Hank, loudly, slicing his weather-worn hand through the air, like Hank.

"Chihuahua," Hank repeats.

"The dog?" I ask.

"No, we're in Chihuahua, Mexico," Hank explains.

"Where's that?"

"A long way away from where we should be."

We finish our coffee. I have to pee like a racehorse, but there's no way in hell I'm peeing in front of Hank, and I don't see any way around that since we're handcuffed. I've been humiliated enough for one day. Enough for a lifetime.

I cross my legs. "Can we get the handcuffs off now?"

Hank does an elaborate thing with his hands, like he's performing some Fosse dance routine or something. But he manages to get his point across. One of the men leaves to get bolt cutters.

"You understood bolt cutters?" I ask Hank.

"I'm pretty good with languages. Telefono?" he asks.

The good thing about being stranded in another country with a rich man is that he has connections and can get us out of this mess.

"You'll see," he tells me with the phone in his hand. "One call to my business partner and this will all be just a bad dream."

"And I can get my bar back."

"Uh, no. It's my bar. I won the bet."

"No, you didn't."

"Yes I did." Hank puts his finger up for me to be quiet while his call goes through. "Harrison? You won't believe this." he says.

The conversation goes downhill from there. "No, *you* listen!" he shouts into the phone. "You can't do this!"

Hank listens, intently while his face is turning red and then purple. "I'll sue your ass!" he shouts, just as I think his head is going to explode. "You're going down for this! You can't do this to me! Hello? Hello?"

"What happened? What did he say?" I ask.

He sticks his finger up, again, and calls his partner back. "How about this for a message?" he barks into the phone. "You're going to prison for twenty years. You can't just steal everything I've worked for. I'm coming after you, pal!"

Hank is pretty scary when he's mad. He's already a bad boy with his ripped body, his collection of tattoos, his biker's wardrobe, and his shark attitude. But when he's angry, he's terrifying.

"You hung up on him?" I ask. "What did he say?"

"It went right to voicemail."

"I have a bad feeling about this."

"You think?" He runs his fingers through his hair and looks down at the table. He pushes some buttons on the phone and reaches his assistant. At least, he used to be his assistant.

"What the hell?" he says into the phone. "What do you mean, 'gone?' What do you mean, 'closed?' Well, stop them! Don't let them in the house! What do you mean?" He raises his voice and hops up, dragging me up with him. I can tell he's ready to punch something, and I hope it's not me.

"But I pay your salary, remember? I sign the checks! I'm the boss! Hello? Hello?"

"What happened? Did he hang up on you?" I ask. He pushes more buttons, but the calls all sound about the same from my end. From what I can tell, he no longer owns anything, and his bank accounts have been closed.

"Who else can you call?" I ask.

"That's a good idea. Who can you call?"

"What do you mean, me? You're rich. Don't you have a plane on standby?"

"Don't you know somebody who can send us cash for a flight home?" He looms over me, like a tall, desperate Ryan Gosling.

"If I had cash, I wouldn't have lost the bar. Does this mean you lost the bar?"

"I don't give a shit about your bar."

"Ah ha! So you admit it's still my bar! I knew I won the drinking contest."

"I have bigger problems than my bar," he says.

"Like where's the bolt cutters," I say.

It turns out Hank isn't that great with languages. He got the bolt cutter thing completely wrong. Instead of coming back with a means to get us out of our handcuffs, Alma's brother comes back with a Chihuahua state police officer with his gun pointed right at us and no sign that he wants us freed from our shackles.

"I have to pee," I say.

# CHAPTER 4

Hank puts his hand on my knee, and I let him. Trapped in the back of a police car, on my way to a Mexican jail, I could use some comfort right about now.

We tried to explain our situation to the police officer, miming the guzzling of booze and passing out. But we couldn't get our message across. Alma and her family looked at us, as if we were crazy and dangerous.

"I don't want to go to Mexican jail," I whisper to Hank in the back of the cop car. "I hear they don't have air conditioning, and you have to go to the bathroom in front of other people."

He pats my knee. "You're not going to jail," he says, but he doesn't sound convinced. He looks nervously out of the window. We're in the middle of nowhere. Just desert as far as the eye can see. Alma's motel was one of only a handful of structures along a dusty highway, and we haven't seen another sign of civilization since we left there fifteen minutes ago.

"What if a gang of really butch women pass me around as their sex slave?"

"Calm down. You're panicking and talking bullshit."

"Oh, yeah? I've seen *The Shawshank Redemption.* I know what goes on in the inside."

"Oh. Forgive me."

"Callate!" the cop yells from the front seat. It's the first time he's spoken to us. Before this, it's been mainly hand gestures and some growling. He's never shown much interest in our story. Instead, he listened to Alma's family and whatever they told him convinced him that we need to go straight to jail.

"He's talking to you," I tell Hank.

"No, that was directed right at you, beautiful."

Hank's fingers wrap around his door handle, and he pulls up. Nothing. We're locked in from the outside. He glances at me, searching my face to see, I gather, if I'm willing to do something crazy to get free.

I look through the window and watch the desert rush past us as the police car speeds down a cracked highway farther into the depths of nowhere. I nod at Hank. Whatever he's planning, I'm up for it.

But his plan—if he ever had one—will have to wait, because the car slows, and the police officer parks off the road next to a tall cactus plant. He turns the car off, gets out, and waits.

"Where's the jail?" I ask Hank.

"Not anywhere near here."

"I have a bad feeling about this."

"You think?"

The cop lights a cigarette and leans against the car door.

"What's he waiting for?" I ask.

"Not 'what.' Who," Hank says.

"Maybe the American authorities," I say, hopefully. "Maybe they're coming to pick us up and get us home."

Hank doesn't say anything, but his silence speaks volumes. American authorities don't meet with Mexican cops in the middle of the desert. American authorities have embassies and consulates, and none of them are located between a cactus and a patch of sagebrush.

"I don't like how this is going. I might be freaking out," I say. Hank's ignoring me, focused only on the cop outside, who's puffing his way through his cigarette like he doesn't have a care in the world.

Hank is taking up most of the backseat. He's rather large in a five-percent fat kind of way. He interlaces his fingers on his lap, pulling my handcuffed hand to rest on his thigh. It doesn't feel like a normal thigh. It's more like granite than flesh, but it fits with what's going on with his muscled upper torso, which is still on display.

"I hate you," I tell him. "I mean, I hate you even more than I hated you before, and I really hated you before. Really hated you."

"I grow on people."

"I just want to get back to my bar and hang a sign in the window: *This bar doesn't serve Hank Taylor.*"

Hank snorts. "*Your* bar. That's a laugh. It was your bar for three seconds after your father died, and maybe not for that long."

I raise my hand off his thigh and slam it down, but he deflects the blow and grabs my arm. "Punch me in the gut once, shame on you. Punch me in the gut twice, shame on me. I'm never letting that happen again," he says. "Besides, conserve your strength. You might need it."

He points outside to an oncoming black SUV that's driving like a bat out of hell and kicking up its own dust cloud. "The Americans?" I ask.

"What's the matter with you, Layla? I remember you as being smart in school."

I shut my eyes tight for a minute and then open them, again. Yep, I'm still handcuffed in the back of a Mexican cop car in the middle of the desert.

The SUV skids to a stop next to us, and the cop hops to it, opening my door. He waves his gun at me and yells something in Spanish.

"Don't wave that at me. If I had my bat, you wouldn't wave that at me."

"Don't antagonize the nice man with the gun," Hank says and scoots over, pushing me out of the car with his hip.

It's blistering hot outside. I shield my eyes from the sun with my free hand. I'm going to have a hell of a sunburn if I stay outside for very long. My bikini top doesn't cover a lot, and I keep having to hitch it up so I'm not completely flashing the world.

The cop takes my handcuffed hand, pulls a key out of his pocket, and unlocks our cuffs. "Thank you," I say. "See, Hank, nothing to worry about. He's on our side."

The SUV's door open and four men dressed in black step out. They're all wearing the same mirrored sunglasses and the same haircut. Something tells me they're not American and not here to save us.

It's easy to tell who's in charge. The other three stand back a couple of feet from him and don't move until he does. The leader approaches the cop, and they speak quickly in Spanish, sometimes shooting glances at Hank, in addition to the normal ogling of my breasts.

The guy in charge reaches into his pocket and pulls out a wad of cash. The cop drops his cigarette on the desert ground and grabs the money. Without counting it, he slips it into his pocket, and sits back in his car and drives away.

"I'm sure we can work something out," Hank tells the leader, but he ignores him completely, twirling his finger in the air like a helicopter, which I guess means that it's time for everyone to get back into the SUV.

Two guys grab Hank, and one guy grabs me, and they drag us toward the car. Hank struggles against them and manages to make contact with one of the guy's face with his fist, but it's his two fists against their four, and in a matter of seconds, we are shoved into the backseat.

"You're having a bad day," I say, looking at Hank's eye. It's already swelling up and turning purple. It's a relief to have him flawed and looking a little less like Ryan Gosling. It helps me focus, and I need to focus as much as possible now.

We're crammed together in the center of the back seat with the two goons on either side of us. "Don't worry," Hank whispers. "The last guy who gave me a shiner wound up in the hospital. We're not finished."

"I hate to tell you this, hero-man, I don't think they're scared of you. You're lucky you weren't shot or beheaded," I say to my would-be rescuer.

"She's right," the goon next to me says smiling. He unholsters his gun and waves it around. It's a really big gun.

I hate guns. I hate being threatened. I hate being kidnapped.

Without thinking, I knock the gun out of his hand and punch him right in his happy stick. While he's doubled over in pain, I leap up, wrap my arms around the driver's neck and pull back hard.

# CHAPTER 5

"I think my hand is broken," Hank says.

"Your hand's not broken," I say, giving it a squeeze to prove my point.

"Ow! That hurt!"

"It did not. You're such a baby."

Hank growls and bounces up and down on his chair.

"You can't break the chair. It's metal and bolted to the ground."

"I know that. I'm just expending energy in order not to kill you." He sounds like he's speaking through his teeth. Mad. I'm not too happy, either. Our wrists are bound together with zip ties behind our backs. Our legs are shackled to chairs, and we're in the middle of an otherwise empty hangar of some kind.

It's like a Tarantino movie without the soundtrack.

"This isn't my fault," I say.

"I didn't say it was. But my broken hand is definitely your fault."

"It's not broken. I can feel you making a fist. You couldn't do that if it was broken. Anyway, you shouldn't have tried to stop yourself with your hand."

"Excuse me? I was trying to stop myself from flying through the windshield."

"Maybe if you'd helped me, we wouldn't be in this mess."

"You mean in the mess, alive? Because from where I'm sitting, we're alive because of me and despite you, Layla."

He has a point. I was the one who incited the car accident. I was so happy to be strangling the driver that I didn't take into account that with him struggling against me, nobody was actually driving the car.

The kidnapper next to me recognized the danger before I did and took a break from holding onto to his balls in agony to shout "Crazy lady! Crazy lady!" and searched for the gun on the floor in order to shoot me, I assume.

The kidnappers' leader didn't have to search for his gun. It was readily available, and he pointed it right at me. Faced with certain death, I couldn't bring myself to stop strangling the driver—I'm stubborn that way—but Hank moved quickly.

He elbowed the goon to his right in the face and grabbed the leader's arm, making him shoot up through the roof of the car.

That's when we crashed into an enormous yucca plant that dented the SUV like an accordion and made all the airbags go off, more or less suffocating us and sending the leader to shoot off a whole round of bullets, some through the roof, some through the windshield, and one into the driver's leg.

"Naked and handcuffed. Dumped in a foreign country. Kidnapped. A black eye. A broken hand. Bound and imprisoned in the middle of butt-fuck nowhere. Have I forgotten anything?" Hank asks.

"Your hand isn't broken. Otherwise, you summed it up. Hold on while I try something."

I yank my hand against his, trying to extricate it from the zip tie. "Ow! What the hell? Stop!" Hank yells.

"Shut up. I'm almost there." I twist my hand against the tie, pushing and pulling against Hank. I wish I could see what I'm doing, but with my hands tied behind my back, it's hard to tell if I'm making any progress.

"My. Hand. Is. Broken," Hank breathes. I pull harder against the binds. "Heavy duty zip ties have a tensile strength of one-hundred-and-seventy-five pounds. You cannot break the damned zip ties, Layla. So please stop."

Because he says please and because I'm not getting anywhere, I stop. "My kingdom for a box cutter," I say.

"I can't tell you how happy I am that you don't have a box cutter. Take it easy. I'm here, too. Maybe I'll rescue you."

"Ha! That's a funny one. It's your fault all this happened. If you didn't try to take away my bar, I would be at home serving beer."

"I *did* take away your bar. And this isn't my fault. It was your idea to drink me into submission. I offered you a job and to keep your place above the bar. You wanted to suck down whiskey, instead."

"I don't take charity."

"A job isn't charity, Layla."

"I make my own way. I always have. You're not going to change that."

I can't see his facial expression, but he's quiet. I wonder if I've hurt his feelings, not that I'm going to say I'm sorry.

The quiet evolves into an awkward silence. I'm almost relieved when we're interrupted by three of our four kidnappers. I guess the fourth guy is taking the rest of the day off, considering he was shot a couple of hours ago.

The leader takes his sunglasses off and hangs them on the front of his shirt. He's attractive with big brown eyes, thick lips, and perfect skin. But he's pissed. I'm pretty certain he blames me for his car getting totaled and his henchman getting shot.

"You shot him. I had nothing to do with that," I say as he gets closer.

"What's happening? Who are you talking to?" Hank asks.

"The bad guys," I say.

"Leave her alone. She doesn't have a penny or any family. I'm the one with cash," Hank says.

The leader raises an eyebrow and walks around me to face Hank. One of the other kidnappers follows him, but the guy I punched in the groin stops in front of me. He's angrier than the leader, and he's scowling at me like he wants revenge, even as he sneaks looks at my breasts on full display in the bikini top.

"Set us free, and I'll get you whatever you want," Hank lies.

"Perhaps she is what I want," the leader says about me. "Maybe she's worth more to me than what you can provide."

I grow cold, and it's hard to breathe. I don't like where this is going.

"She's only worth something if you're into herpes," Hank says, trying to save me in an insulting way.

"Herpes. I don't give a shit if she has herpes. My clients aren't picky about hygiene."

"Uh—" I start, but I have no words.

"Believe me, I'm worth a lot more than she is," Hank continues. Since his business partner took him for everything he has, I'm slightly insulted by his assertion. However, there's no doubt he's being chivalrous. Instead of handing me over to them, he's trying to convince them that I'm not worth kidnapping or selling me into sexual slavery.

"He's got a lot of money," I say. "He's like Bill Gates, but dumb and uneducated."

"She's right," Hank says. "Just let me make a call, and I'll get it worked out for you."

"Give me the number, and *I'll* make the call," the lead kidnapper tells him.

"I really need to pee," I say.

"Me, too," Hank says. "How about letting us make a trip to the bathroom while you make the call."

I roll my eyes. I see right through Hank's idiot ploy, and it's not going to work. They're never going to just let us go free. If they don't care about herpes, they sure as hell don't care about pee.

"Tell me the number," the leader commands Hank, and stupid Hank gives him a number.

I figure I have a minute before they talk to Hank's partner and realize that he doesn't have two nickels to rub together, and I either have my head cut off or I'm sold to a guy without teeth who paints my nipples red and forces me to do all the sexual positions I normally refuse to do on principle.

The kidnapper walks past me, heading outside with the phone plastered to his ear. He puts his sunglasses on as he starts talking. He's too far away for me to make out the details, but the conversation is lasting a lot longer than I thought it would.

I avoid eye contact with the goon in front of me, but I know he's staring at me and thinking. It won't take a lot of convincing for him to rape or murder me. Or worse.

I twist my hands against my binds, making Hank wince, but he doesn't make a sound. After about five minutes, the leader walks back into the hangar with a big smile on his face. It's either good news or bad news. It's hard to tell with kidnappers.

"Good news, Mr. Taylor," he says. "Your business partner is happy to wire a million dollars."

"Does that mean I get to pee?" I ask. I have no idea what's going on. As far as I could tell, Hank wasn't lying about his business partner stealing all his money. So, who did the kidnapper call and why didn't Hank call him before when we were handcuffed at the motel?

"Yes, senorita, you may pee."

One of the goons hovers over me and takes out a knife. I hold my breath while he cuts the zip ties. My arms fall to my sides slowly, stiff and sore from being tied up for so long. The other guy unshackles my feet.

I stand up and stretch. I'm hoping there's a window in the bathroom so I can escape. It's the only plan I can come up with. I try to communicate with him with my eyes, making them dart toward the outside to signify our escape. But the idiot is ignoring me, totally.

What do I have to do? Semaphore? Smoke signals? Do I need to carry him out of here myself? I should just leave him with the kidnappers to fend for himself.

"Is the bathroom over that way?" I ask one of the kidnappers.

"Yes," he says, and keels over unconscious on the floor.

"What the—?" I say, but nobody's paying attention to me. The two remaining kidnappers are momentarily shocked to find their colleague flat on his face, but they quickly realize Hank is responsible.

Hank grabs the kidnapper's gun from his waistband and knocks him on the head with it while he's down on the ground. Then, he whips around and attacks the head guy. I guess he wasn't lying about his broken hand, because he's fighting one-handed. Clutching the gun, he runs after the leader, pushing him off balance.

The other kidnapper, who I had punched in the balls in the car, springs forward while going for his gun, in order to help his boss. "No!" I shout, kicking at his hand, but he's moving fast, and he's got a strong grip on his weapon.

I jump onto his back and wrap my limbs around him. "No! No! No!" I shout. He stumbles around like he's doing the robot dance in a club. I try to knock the gun out of his hand, but I can't reach it, and in his panic, he lets off round after round, emptying his gun into the wall.

He lunges for my head to dislodge me, but I jab my fingers into his eyes, making him spin around in agony, bucking me like he's a bull at a rodeo. He's a lot stronger than I am, and he pulls my hands off his eyes in a terrible fury.

"I can't hold on!" I yell to no one in particular, and I'm surprised when Hank appears with his arm raised and the gun still clutched in his hand, butt side out. He strikes quickly, landing the gun against the side of the kidnapper's face.

We topple over in a heap, me on top of the goon, but almost instantly, Hank has his arm wrapped around my middle and is lifting me high into the air. "Run!" he yells, settling me on my feet.

My flip-flops are long gone, flipped off my feet when the kidnapper was spinning me around. I don't care. I run like a bat out of hell, through the hangar, and out into the middle of the Chihuahua desert.

# CHAPTER 6

Hank is one step ahead of me, running while he holds my hand and pulls me along, sometimes looking backward to see if we're being chased. We aren't. He did a thorough job pistol-whipping our abductors, and I figure they're out for the count.

However, I'm not taking any chances, and I'm not slowing down, even though the desert floor is tearing the soles of my feet. Hank is faring slightly better. He's managed to keep his flip-flops securely on his feet, his toes curled tightly to keep them from falling off while he runs.

We go full out for about ten minutes before Hank stops. "Over there," he says, pointing toward a small outcropping of structures in the middle of the desert. "A town," he explains.

I shield my eyes from the sun with my hand so I can see better. It's not much of a town. A few shacks and several squat buildings. But I bet dollars to donuts that there's a toilet in the town and probably a cold glass of water.

"Let's go," I say taking a couple of steps, but my foot lands on a patch of prickly brush, and I hobble forward in pain. "Shitballs," I mutter and pick the splinters out of my foot.

Hank crouches down in front of me, his back toward me. "Hop on board."

"What do you mean?" I ask.

He slaps his shoulder. "Piggy back. I'll carry you the rest of the way."

"No, you're not."

"How long are you going to make me crouch here? Get on board."

"In your dreams, fink. I bet you want me to wrap my legs around you."

Hank stands up and turns around to face me. A bloody nose and a cut, swollen lip have joined his black eye in his face of pain. But he still has killer green eyes, and his battered face is still a dead ringer for Ryan Gosling. I'm hot and bothered, and it's not just because I'm standing in the desert in borrowed short-shorts and a too-small bikini top with splinters in my burned feet.

I take a step backward. "You're too close."

He arches an eyebrow. "Just so we're clear, Layla. Yes, I want you to wrap your legs around me. I want you to wrap your legs around me and cry out my name—Hank, not Fink—and I want to stick my face between your breasts, and I want to taste what I assume is your delicious pussy. Clear?"

"Clear," I croak.

"Good. But right now, we have about two miles to walk in order to get to civilization, and you can't do it barefoot, and neither can I. So, I'm going to carry your fine ass, and you're going to deal."

He turns around, crouches down, and slaps his shoulder with his good hand. I'm done fighting him, at least for now. I wrap my arms around his neck. He stands, and my legs circle his waist.

He groans. "You're heavier than I thought."

"This was your idea, not mine."

"It's okay," he says. "Your breasts are pressing against my back. I feel invigorated. I bet I could walk to California this way."

It takes about forty-five minutes to get to the town. Hank never falters or slows. He walks as if he's only carrying a backpack and not weighted down by a carbohydrate-loving twenty-three year old.

"I think I have third degree burns," I say as we reach the town. My shoulders and back are already blistered from the sun.

"Yeah, that sucks for you. I only have a broken hand." And a broken nose, if I'm not mistaken, and a black eye and other cuts and abrasions. He's sunburned, too, and he's going to have a funky tan line from me being draped over him.

"You didn't break your hand," I say, uncharitably. "But we should get you to a doctor, anyway."

He marches me into town, which looks like something from an old western movie with a two-lane highway running through its middle. It smells like fresh tortillas and barbecue. "I would kill to eat," I say.

"I could go for a beer and a Vicodin."

I shimmy off his back and walk into a small store to ask for directions to a doctor. "Good news," I tell Hank. "They have a doctor."

"A horse doctor or a real doctor?"

"In your case, a horse doctor would be a real doctor." I don't know why I'm being mean to him. After all, he saved my life, and he carried me on his back for miles through the desert. That's hero stuff, right? Still, I want my bar back, and the fink has my bar.

*

"One hundred pesos."

"That's a lot of money," I say. Actually, I don't know what the peso to dollar exchange rate is, but it sounds like a lot of money, especially since the doctor's office doesn't look like it's been cleaned in weeks, if it's ever been cleaned. Shouldn't we get a cleaning discount?

The office is the size of a standard walk-in closet, just enough room for the three of us and a stainless steel bed in the center. "I think this is the morgue," Hank says.

The doctor nods. "Morgue. Si."

"Morgue. Si," Hank repeats for my benefit, giving me his best puppy dog face. It's a pretty good face, even with the neck tattoo and the whole beaten-to-a-pulp thing happening. He's got me wanting to pet him and let him sleep on my bed.

"But you can fix his hand?"

"One hundred pesos."

"How about eighty?"

"Why are you negotiating, Layla?" Hank asks. "We don't have any money. Remember?"

I pull a wallet out of my pocket and count out eighty pesos. "Eighty," I say to the doctor and hand him the bills.

The doctor takes the money and starts to work, putting the x-ray machine into place over Hank's hand.

"What the hell?" Hank says, taking the wallet from me. "Where the hell did you get this?"

"I pinched it from the kidnapper."

"You what?"

"Old habit. But it came in handy, right?"

He looks through the wallet. "Not a lot in here."

"That's why I took the other guy's wallet, too," I say, holding the other wallet over my head.

Hank's mouth drops open.

I scowl, annoyed. "You're looking at me like I'm…"

"Al Capone. Enron. Jesse James. Ma Barker."

"Ouch. The Ma Barker reference hurt."

"I'm also wondering if you had something to do with our little trip to Mexico."

"That's on you," I say, pointing at him.

"Don't breathe," the doctor says, pushing the x-ray button.

The doctor sets Hank's hand and put it in a cast. His nose is broken, too, but it doesn't need to be set, and Hank doesn't want a bandage over his face. His cuts and scrapes are treated, and the doctor hands him a pill and a glass of water.

Hank glances at me. "What if it's ketamine?"

"It would probably be an improvement on your day."

"It's Tylenol," the doctor says. "I don't give ketamine for eighty pesos."

*

We score with the lead kidnapper's wallet. It's packed with pesos and dollars. "I'm in the wrong line of business," I note, paying for two track suits and two pairs of sneakers at the little store on the main street. "Kidnapping is where it's at."

"Or stealing from kidnappers."

My stomach rumbles, and once we're dressed, we sit down in a small restaurant. Hank is careful to sit at a corner table with his back to the wall. "In case we have visitors," he explains.

We order everything. While we wait for our main courses, I stuff five corn tortillas with salsa down my throat before I come up for air. Hank is keeping up with me, even though he's eating one-handed. I wonder what else he can do one-handed, and then I bite my lip to stop wondering.

Hank's tortilla is halfway to his mouth, but something in my face catches his attention. He drops the tortilla, and it lands with a splat onto his plate. "Layla," he says, his voice deep and dripping manly manliness. "I know the look you're giving me. I'm fond of that look."

"Oh, yeah? You've probably seen this look on millions of women's faces."

His lips curve up into a grin. "I'm like McDonalds. Billions served."

"Ew. And like McDonalds, not appetizing."

"The woman says *no no*, but her eyes say *yes yes*."

"So you speak eyes now, Hank?" But he obviously does because my whole body is saying *yes yes*. I'm positively screaming *yes yes*. I shouldn't be in the mood. I just had a near-death experience, I'm sunburned, and my feet hurt, but I'm so in the mood. Could it be danger turns me on? Or could it just be that riding a good-looking man through the desert that turns me on?

Hank searches my face for an answer, which is odd because normally he's fixed entirely on my chest. Since I'm finding it hard to look directly in his eyes, I look down at my plate, but there's nothing there. I've eaten everything.

Luckily, the waiter comes by with our orders in the nick of time. Enchiladas, chile rellenos, fajitas. It's a Mexican smorgasbord. I'll probably regret it later, but right now, I'm very enthusiastic.

"What's your plan?" I ask Hank with my mouth full.

"I'm going to get home, punch out Harrison, and get my company and money back. What's your plan?"

"I'm going to go with you to make sure I get my bar back."

Hank shakes his head. "Correction. *My* bar."

"*My* bar." I take a deep breath. "When we get back, we'll find witnesses, and I'm sure they'll come out on my side, and I'll get my bar back. Deal?" I ask.

"If you can find witnesses who say you won… Deal." He takes my hand and shakes it but doesn't let go. Instead, he studies it, letting his thumb inspect the palm and the inside of my wrist with slow circular motions.

Against my efforts, I squirm. I squirm a lot. "What do you think you're doing?"

"Seducing you."

"Oh, please. You're bruised, battered, and broken. Your parts probably don't work. You can't possibly be in the mood," I say, sort of breathless with my voice an octave higher than normal.

His head shoots up, and he looks me right in the eye. His pupils are dilated, as if he's just been to the ophthalmologist. The emerald green has turned smoky dark. There's no doubt he's in the mood. He invented the mood. He's the king of the mood. He's the mood czar.

"And I don't like you," I stammer, taking back my hand.

He raises an eyebrow. "That's okay," he says after a long moment. "I like you enough for both of us."

"Is it hot in here?"

"Smokin' hot."

I think about our situation, about his resemblance to Ryan Gosling. About him carrying me over the desert. About the possibility that he does really like me and isn't just trying to find a way to pass the time.

"I've never had sex with a man in a track suit before," I say.

"If you don't like it, I can have it off in five seconds. Ten seconds, tops."

He doesn't blink. He doesn't look away. So serious.

I like serious.

"Okay. Sure," I say. "What the hell. Let's find a room."

# CHAPTER 7

"Towels," I say, impressed. We've found a room in a nice house at the outskirts of town with a bathroom stocked with lots of fluffy white towels and sheets on the bed. Clean and pretty.

Finally relaxed, I take my first deep breath since I blacked out in my bar. Safe. But then a kernel of worry nips at my brain.

"What if the kidnappers find us? It probably wouldn't be hard," I say.

"They would have found us already, if they're looking. I think we're more trouble than we're worth."

It's a reasonable theory, and I'm tired enough to accept it. Hank surprises me by letting me take a shower, alone. I was sure he was going to jump my bones the second we got in the room, but he's being gentle with me. Or maybe he's just tired, too.

Either way, he's behaving out of character. He's nothing like the insensitive horndog that he usually is. But I'm so thankful he's turned over a new leaf. I need the time alone in the shower. The one deep breath was wonderful, but I need a few more, and I can't breathe easily around Hank. He's turned on some kind of hunter button inside himself and is looking at me like I'm today's dinner special.

It's more than his normal boob ogling. He's got stars in his eyes, and it's confusing me, making me short of breath and slightly overheated. Sometimes relationships are formed in the midst of danger. Could his interest in me be caused by our near death experiences together? Or perhaps the doctor's Tylenol was really ketamine?

"How many fingers am I holding up?" I ask him, holding up three fingers before I close the bathroom door behind me.

"Three."

Okay. So it's not ketamine, I figure, turning on the shower. I take off the track suit and peel off the bikini top, which I've been using as a bra. I didn't find a bra that fit in the small shop in the center of town, of course, and I miss the support.

I step into the shower. I've never felt anything so wonderful. The cool water soothes my sunburn and makes me feel human again. I close my eyes and stick my head under the nozzle.

Who would have thought getting fired would be such a difficult process? Usually, it's "You're fired" and a trip to the unemployment office. That's it. But everything in my life is hard, hard, hard.

I had to challenge my new boss to a drinking contest, black out, and find myself without a workable bra in Mexico. Not to mention the kidnapping. So typical.

I don't do anything the easy way. I've been working since I was five years old when my father taught me how to pull the beer tap. It was a week after my mother died, and it was time for him to go back to work at our bar.

Most dads would figure out they needed a babysitter, but not mine. He saw nothing wrong with raising a daughter in a bar.

One of his regulars finally pointed out to him that I needed to go to school, and that's why I was six months late to my first day of kindergarten.

Growing up in a bar isn't that bad. Sure, I never had a play date or sleepover, but I learned a lot about life, more than most people learn in twice as many years. There aren't a lot of eight years old who have given advice to battered women ("Leave him. Leave him, now.") while they served them cocktails or to closeted gay bikers ("Closets are for shoes. Are you a shoe?") while they served them a Corona.

But I did. That and much more. And it wasn't just the drama in the bar that matured me way before my time. More than any exposure to grown up issues, my lifelong attempts at making my father notice me have hardened me.

For my father, nothing was more important than the family business. If he didn't have to sleep and shower, he would never have left its four walls. The bar was everything, and if I wanted any relationship with him at all, I would have to become an integral part of it. So, that's what I did.

By the time he died six months ago, I had nearly twenty years of experience in the bar business, but I wasn't any closer to cracking the mystery of father-daughter relationships. He died of lung cancer and left me alone in the world with only the bar to keep me company.

And now that's going to be taken away, too, because my father had a world of debt I didn't know about before. Even if I tripled my clientele, I could never pay off what my father owed. So, no family for me and no bar for me.

Alone.

Alone sucks. Nobody to have my back. Nobody's shoulder to cry on. No rounded edges on a life covered in sharp corners.

Without anything soft, a person compensates by becoming hard. And I'm hard. Tough. I survive everything, including kidnappers. But for once, I wish that I wouldn't have to be so hard, that someone would be there for me to take some of the slack, to do some of the surviving so I just have to live.

It doesn't take a genius to figure out that Hank Taylor is not that person. He's just another in a long line of men I've been attracted to who would never be there for me, never support me when I need support.

And I need support. I need kindness, thoughtfulness. Love.

Hank Taylor can't provide any of that. He's a player and a fink. I mean, he has a neck tattoo. I think that proves my point.

*

I turn off the long shower and I dry my body. I run a comb through my hair and brush my teeth. I feel human for the first time in a long time. I put on the bikini top and the track suit again and open the door.

The scent of lavender and vanilla hits me as I walk out of the bathroom. The room is filled with flowers and lit candles. Hank is standing by the table in the corner, watching me. He smells good, too. Clean. His hair is wet, and I guess he found another shower somewhere.

"What the—" I say.

Hank waves his hands in front of him. "I didn't spend much of the kidnapper's money. I swear I didn't. I just wanted you to have something nice. You've had a shitty day."

"Oh," I say, my voice barely audible.

He steps toward me and takes me into his arms. "You deserve so much more, but I hope this gives you some comfort."

"But you have a neck tattoo," I say into his chest and begin to cry.

"Why are you crying?"

"I don't know, but it's pissing me off."

"Maybe it's allergies. You want me to get rid of the flowers?"

"No," I say, wiping my nose on his shirt. "I like the flowers. The candles, too."

"So, just an emotional time of the month?" he asks, clearly panicked.

"That's a jerk thing to say. You're such a jerk." But jerk or not, my hands crawl under his shirt, touching his taut belly and its crisscrossed muscles, and snaking around to his back and under his waistband.

"So the crying was foreplay?" he asks.

"You should probably shut up now."

"Okay, shutting up."

He doesn't lie. Instead of saying something else stupid, he cups the back of my head with his hands and leans over to capture my mouth with his. I sink against him, transported to that in-between consciousness that comes with arousal.

And boy, am I aroused.

Reality, fantasy. Fantasy, reality. I don't know which I'm in, but it doesn't matter because it feels good.

Hank is stellar at kissing. He could do it for a living and make a fortune. There's nothing tentative about him. He knows what he wants, and he's going for it. It's all about possession for him. He's in control, and for once I let myself be taken.

His lips, his tongue, and his strong hands own me, blurring the line between us. He sets the direction to take, and all I do is follow. My lips react to his. My tongue responds to his. His hands inspect my body, and my hands follow in kind.

He stops kissing me long enough to slip my shirt off of me, and then he kisses me again with ferocious need while he unties my bikini top and pushes down my pants. I can't get naked fast enough. I want to give him access to every inch of my body.

He lifts me in his arms and deposits me gently on the bed. I watch as he strips down quickly, and then he's back in bed on top of me, his mouth tasting the side of my neck, while his hands explore lower down.

I squirm beneath him, my knees rising, as his mouth journeys lower and lower, tasting my skin while his hands knead my flesh. "Yes," I moan to let him know he's doing everything just right.

Five stars to the man with the tongue.

If I had a blue ribbon, I would hand it over, I think, just as his tongue finds my sensitive nub and dances around it, making my body stretch, my arms reaching above my head to clutch onto the headboard.

He's tireless, which is good because I never want him to stop. This is now my favorite hobby—having Hank suck and lick me to oblivion is so much better than watching TV. Hell, it even beats chocolate.

My brain turns to mush as my body reaches the pinnacle of ecstasy. My heart races; my breathing stops. I'm so close.

And then I'm there. Right there. Right! There!

"Fuck!" I scream, apropos of everything. My body tightens, levitating me off the bed and then I fall back down into a boneless pile of mush, completely satisfied and half-dead.

My head flops to the side, and my mouth drops open. I can't open my eyes, can't find the energy to lift my eyelids. I've been used.

I feel Hank move from the foot of the bed to lie down next to me. I manage to crack open one of my eyes. He's staring at me, patiently waiting for me to catch my breath before we continue our horizontal mambo. He's also looking at me as if I'm changed, somehow, like a new woman has appeared in my place. Maybe she has.

"That was incredible," he says, as if he's reading my thoughts.

I nod. "Yes. I was so close to having an orgasm."

"Ha! Funny, Layla. That's a good one."

I put my hand on his arm. "It's okay, Hank. Not every man can get my eyes to roll back in my head. You made a valiant effort. Too bad it didn't work."

I turn around because I can't stop myself from cracking up, and I don't want him to see. It's terrible for me to lie to him like this, especially after he gave me the biggest orgasm of my life, but what's a little harmless torture between lovers?

Sure, Hank gave me a romantic evening and saved my life, but I still feel this strong desire to punish him for taking my father's business. And what better way to punish a man than this?

He leans over me, his head appearing upside down. "What?" he demands. "Are you joking? You blew up like an atomic bomb. I might have radiation poisoning from the fallout."

I touch his handsome face. "Nope. I'm sorry. But it's not important. A woman doesn't have to be satisfied every time. You can only do what you're able to do. Not every man is—well—you know."

"No. I don't know. What? What isn't every man? I am! I'm that man. I'm really that man!"

"Maybe we could play cards to pass the time. Do you like Crazy Eights?"

"What?"

"Or Old Maid. Old Maid seems on topic, considering the circumstances."

Hank gasps and falls back on the bed. I turn around. He looks wounded. I almost feel guilty, and I'm about to enlighten him about my trip to the moon, but he interrupts me with a burst of determination.

"Round two, beautiful," he says. "Get ready to blow your lid."

"*You* get ready to blow *my* lid," I correct him, but he already has his head between my legs, and my lid is already flying around the room.

*

"Nope," I lie, again after he gives me another orgasm. "Nothing. Don't worry about it. Some men are better at other things, like checkers or putting together furniture."

I bring him to the verge of a nervous breakdown, make him question his manhood, and rip his self-confidence out from the roots by the time he gives me my third orgasm of the evening.

But by now the joke is getting old, and I'm exhausted and thoroughly satisfied. So, I take pity on him and tell him he's dinged my dinger and plucked the brass ring.

"I knew I could do it," he says, collapsing on the bed. He's coated in a slippery layer of sweat. I get a towel and dry him off.

"You're a good man," I say, wiping his body clean.

He rubs his jaw. "I think I injured my jaw. And my tongue's sprained."

"All in a good day's work."

"Good?" he asks, looking up at me with his puppy dog face.

"Great," I say, patting him on his shoulder. "Would you like some water?"

He's halfway through a bottle of water when I decide to be really nice. Tired or not, he's still ready to party, and I'm feeling generous.

I wrap my hand around his arousal and begin to stroke him up and down.

"Wha-wha-what are you doing?"

"Why? Is this new for you?" I ask. "Okay, well, you see bees go from flower to flower and…"

"I know about the birds and the bees."

"Are you sure? Don't be embarrassed. I was a virgin all the way through middle school. I can talk you through this, if you want."

"You're a laugh riot," he says. He sits up and flips me over onto my back, pinning me to the bed. He lifts up one of my legs and positions himself over me. "Say yes, Layla."

"Yes….If you have a condom."

Hank has a condom. He must have bought it when he bought the candles and the flowers. Maybe they had a special: Buy flowers, get free condoms. In any case, he slips it on and slips inside of me.

He has a broken hand, a broken nose, a black eye, and enough scrapes, bumps, and bruises to make a stuntman blush. But he's the most able-bodied man that I've come across, and he knows what he's doing.

He rocks slowly. We fit together, perfectly, as if we were made for each other. I trail my fingers down his back and up, again. He really is beautiful. Perfectly formed arms, shoulders, chest. I'm so distracted by his body parts that I don't notice at first that he's watching me looking at him.

We lock eyes. The joking around from before evaporates in the heat that builds between us and is replaced by a seriousness I've never experienced. I read so much in his eyes. Passion. Desire. And there's also a question there, but I've no idea how to answer it.

I can only wrap my limbs around him and open my body even more. Welcoming him in this way, our eyes never breaking contact, I forget my loneliness. And I dare to hope that at least for now, I'm supported.

*

I sleep like a baby, safe and secure, wrapped in Hank's strong arms. I'm so exhausted that I don't dream, only sleep a much needed recuperative slumber. All of that changes about an hour before sunrise, though, when I wake in terror, fighting against an unseen attacker.

# CHAPTER 8

I try to scream, but the large hand is plastered on my mouth, and I can't pry it off. I start to kick and throw my body against him, frantic to get free.

"Shh!" he hisses. "It's Hank. You have to be quiet."

He's not comforting me with that bit of information. I want his hand off my mouth, immediately. I'm not exactly a Fifty Shades of Grey kind of girl. If someone is going to spank me, I'm going knock his head off. Or worse.

"You have to be quiet," he repeats in a whisper. "They're just outside. We got to haul ass before they find us."

He's starting to make sense. I peel his fingers off my mouth. "The kidnappers?" I whisper.

He nods. "I figure we have about one minute."

Hank hands me a dress. "What's this?"

"I bought it for you today. Put it on. We're leaving through the window."

I can hear men's footsteps in the hallway, coming our way. I slip the dress over my head and leap out of bed, putting on the sneakers as quickly as I can. Hank jumps out of the window and stands on the street with his hands, outstretched.

"Jump," he whispers into the night.

"What do you mean, jump?" I ask, sticking my head out of the window.

"Jump."

"But I have trust issues," I hiss.

"Jump!"

“Your arm’s broken.” He seems to think about that a moment, eyeing his cast, probably gauging its capacity to withstand the weight of a woman jumping from a second-storey window.

“Jump,” he says with a little less conviction in his voice.

There’s no way I’m jumping out of the window. No way. But the men in the hallway are getting closer, and my life is on the line. I stick one leg out of the window and sit on the sill. Then, I pivot my other leg out and flip onto my belly.

“What are you doing?” Hank hisses from below. “You can’t jump like that. What do you think you’re doing?”

“Stop backseat driving. I’ll be there in a second.” I scoot down until I’m hanging out of the window by my hands. “Where’s the ledge?” I ask, swinging my legs, searching for something to rest my feet on.

“What do you mean?” Hank asks, sounding a little testy.

“Normally, there’s a ledge,” I say, even though this is technically the first window I’ve climbed out of, so I’m not exactly an expert. I also don't have a lot of upper body strength. "I don't think I can hold on much longer," I whine.

In fact, my hands give way, and I finish the sentence as I plummet toward the ground. Luckily, Hank breaks my fall. To his credit, he tries to catch me, but I'm coming down feet first, and I land like a world-class kickboxer, first giving him a roundhouse kick to his ribs and then a sidekick to his back, making a terrifying sound right before I fall flat on his now prostrate body. It's a miracle… I don't have a scratch on me.

"Hurry. Let's get out of here," I say, pushing myself off of him.

Hank moans, but he's not moving.

"Come on," I urge him. "Get up."

He moans, again and flails his arms. "You're standing on my leg."

I move to the side. "Oh, sorry. It's a good thing I'm wearing rubber soles."

"Yes," he says, struggling to get up. "That was fortunate. It would've hurt if you weren't wearing rubber soles."

I grab his hand, and I start running. Hank hobbles after me. "Where are we going?" I pant.

"Away," he says.

"Run faster."

"I think my ribs are broken."

"So? That doesn't affect your legs. Keep moving."

"Layla, you're a great piece of ass, but—"

"Shh!" I push him down behind a pickup truck. "I hear them," I whisper.

I talk tough, but I'm not a violent woman. I don't own a gun and have never shot one. I'm not even a fan of action movies. But I wouldn't mind killing these kidnappers. They're down to two, as far as I can tell, roaming the town's main street looking for us.

"I wish I had my bat," I say more to myself than to Hank.

"We're going to steal this truck," he says, as if this will solve all our problems.

"No, we're not."

"We're getting out of Dodge."

"I don't steal. I know you steal—my bar for example—but I don't."

"*My* bar. Mine. We'll leave some money under a rock for the truck. It can't be worth much."

"Okay," I say. "It's not strictly kosher, but if we leave money, it's fine. Go ahead."

"Give me the wallet."

"You have it."

"I don't have it," he says. "Stop fooling around. Give me the wallet."

I pat my dress. "Look at me, Hank. I don't have pockets. I don't have the wallet."

"Why didn't you bring the wallet?" he hisses, wagging his finger under my nose. I push his hand down.

"Why didn't you bring the wallet?" I hiss back. "You had more time than I did. You were already up and dressed when you woke me up. You had plenty of time to think about the wallet. Now here we are in the middle of nowhere without any money, and I don't have a bra." I grab a fistful of the front of his shirt and pull him toward me. "I don't have a bra, Hank. I want a bra."

The sun is beginning to rise, and it's still pretty dark, but I can tell he's not blinking. I don't know if he's thinking, fuming, or having an aneurism.

"We're stealing the truck," he says, finally.

"No. I'm not a thief. The truck could be a family's only means of transportation. They might need it for their work. No way. I'm not stealing it."

I cross my arms in front of me. Hank breathes deeply out of his nose, like a bull ready to charge. I can tell he's about to act, and I won't have anything to say about it, but we're interrupted by a dark voice speaking in Spanish behind us.

# CHAPTER 9

Hank and I jump three feet in the air. I put my hands out in my best karate chop pose, ready to protect myself from the kidnappers, but it's not them. Instead, it's a small, elderly man holding a set of keys in his hand. He points to the truck and asks us a question. Obviously, it's his truck.

"See?" I say to Hank. "Karma is a bitch."

Hank ignores me. He points to the truck and the two of us. "North?" he asks the old man. "Can you take us north?"

The man nods, pointing to the sky. "Americanos?"

"Americanos," I say, gesturing toward Hank and me. The man eyes Hank suspiciously. Who wouldn't be suspicious of him? He looks like he's escaped from the trauma ward. Couple his injuries with his gang-style tattoos, and Hank looks like he's a big pack of trouble.

But the old man is looking at me, too. The dress Hank gave me is a flowery mini dress that cuts low on top. If Hank looks like bad trouble, I suppose I look like good trouble. The old man hedges his bets, and instructs us to climb into the back of his pickup.

We lie down low so we're not seen, and the truck roars to life and bounces down the street and hopefully to freedom.

The truck bed is filthy with dirt, straw, and bits of machine parts. But we don't dare sit up until we ride for an hour out of town. Hank has an eye on the sun. It's rising on our left, which confirms that we're driving north.

Every mile is a mile closer to home. Could I make it to sleep in my bed tonight? Do I even have a bed, anymore? Technically, it's Hank's bed, and I'm homeless. Technically, according to Hank, he's homeless, too, with his empire stolen by his business partner.

"Hey," I say. We're lying on our sides, staring at each other. I've studied his eyes under the different kinds of light, as the sun comes up. He has beautiful eyes. I could stare at them forever. "So, were you joking about your business partner stealing all of your money?"

He grins. "If I had any money, do you think we would be riding in the back of a truck through the desert with all of my bones broken?"

"All of your bones aren't broken."

"Most of them."

"A good percentage of them," I say, giving in. I haven't been exactly sympathetic about his injuries. He looks like he just lost the heavyweight championship fight against Godzilla.

"As soon as I get back to Esperanza, I'm going to break every bone in Harrison's body, I promise you that."

I believe him. He's pissed.

"So what was the million dollar phone call about, then?" I ask.

"I had the kidnapper call my safety net."

"Safety net?"

"Ronin."

"Ronin, like the Samurais?"

"Ronin, like a guy I can count on to be there when I'm kidnapped or when I have other things that need handling."

"Handling," I repeat, rolling the word around in my mouth. "That sounds scary."

"Ronin is scary."

"And Ronin has a million dollars?"

"I don't know how much he has. But he would never give me a million dollars, not unless I paid him two million first. He told the kidnappers what I needed him to say. He's good like that. I use him for other services, normally."

"Other services," I repeat.

"He'll expect payment for the phone call."

"Could he help us get out of Mexico?"

"He could help us when we get to the other side," he says.

"But he'll want money."

"I'll get the money after I break Harrison's bones."

It sounds like a pretty flimsy plan. I need him to get his company back so that he can give me my bar back. And just as soon as we find the bar's patrons, I can prove that I've won it back, fair and square.

It's a relief when we finally sit up. It's still uncomfortable, and I have to brace myself as we bounce around, but at least we can see where we are.

And we're nowhere.

The truck is following a cracked, two-lane highway through a vast, empty desert. There's no sign of life anywhere, except for the occasional snake or rabbit. It's not a place to be roaming around on foot, and suddenly I'm worried about our Good Samaritan's goodwill. Will it last until we're out of the desert? Is there an end to the desert?

"We'll be fine," Hank tells me, reading my mind.

"We don't have any water."

"We'll be fine."

I search his face, looking for some proof that he's telling the truth, but I can't read him. He's probably had a lot of lying experience in his life.

"We've had a wild ride the past couple of days," Hank says, smiling.

"A wild ride in hell."

He raises an eyebrow and grins. "There were some upsides."

I think back to my orgasm marathon. "There were some upsides," I agree.

Hank is smiling at me, his cracked lips turned up toward his bruised cheeks. He has two black eyes, now, I assume because of his broken nose, which is swollen. Despite his battered face, he's still strikingly handsome, and I've never seen him quite so happy as he is bouncing around the back of this truck, staring at me and thinking about our upsides.

"You look awfully happy," I say.

"I like you," he says, startling me.

"You do?"

"Yes, even though you're bad for my health."

"You're blaming me for that? None of that was my fault," I say, affronted, waving my hand at his multiple injuries.

"You jumped on me. I think half of my ribs are broken."

"You told me to jump."

Hank smiles even wider. "And I still like you."

I'm flustered. I look around for something to do, but I'm sitting in the back of a truck in the middle of the desert. I can't avoid Hank no matter how much I try.

"You like me because I'm not wearing a bra," I say, finally.

"Yeah, the no bra thing is great, but that's not why I like you."

"Why do you like me?" I croak.

"I'm happier when I'm with you. I like listening to you. You're fun."

"Shut up."

"You're addictive. I want more of you. I want to spend time with you."

"Because you're a horn dog," I say, scowling.

"You're right. I'm a horny bastard, and I like being naked with you. But I like you. I liked eating at the restaurant with you. I want to take you out."

"You mean on dates?"

"Yes. Without kidnappers chasing us. Dates where I don't break any bones."

I wonder if that's possible. So far, we're Danger Prone Daphne on acid when we're together. We go from one nightmare to another.

"You mean to the movies and to baseball games?"

"Do you like Hawaii? We could go to Hawaii," Hank says, as if he's just figured out the secret to cold fusion.

I've never been to Hawaii. I've never been on a plane. The Chihuahua desert is the furthest I've ever been away from home in Esperanza, California.

"Hawaii sounds nice," I say.

What am I saying? He's a fink. Why am I forgetting that fact?

"Good."

"But not until you give me my bar back."

"*My* bar," he says. "You mean you won't go out with me unless I give you a bar?"

"It's my bar."

"That's a very expensive date, Layla. More than Hawaii."

Our conversations always go back to the same thing. Can't he see that the bar is my life? Why doesn't he care about that? "We've been here before," I say.

"I recognize the tree," he says, making me laugh.

"Okay, no bar talk."

"Good. In fact, we don't have to talk at all. We probably have another hour to kill. You wanna make out?" He crawls across the truck bed, sits next to me, and wraps his arm around my shoulders. His face is inches from mine. Unbelievably, he still smells really good.

I answer his question with a kiss. His mouth tastes like sex and malted milk balls, for some reason, which is a good thing because I'm hungry. Our tongues touch, and it's all I can do not to hop on his lap and ride him like a rodeo champion. But I don't want the old man to kick us off his truck into the desert. So, I hold back my desire and satisfy myself with the best kiss, ever.

Without being in any kind of hurry, our kiss is long and languid, passionate and tender. It's different from the furious need we experienced last night. We've evolved to a more caring level. Kissing this way, I can almost believe that Hank really does like me. My fingers curl in his hair, and his good hand cups my breast, but it's all about the kiss. Our lips and our tongues dance together like the slow dance at the prom at the end of the night when the lights are off and everyone has a good buzz going from the spiked punch.

And then after we've kissed and kissed and kissed some more, the truck stops, and the old man steps out. I push away from Hank. "Where are we?" I ask.

The old man points beyond the front of the truck toward the horizon. "America," he says.

"That's the desert," I say.

"America. Go. Go," he says, pulling at my hand. But there's no way I'm getting out of the truck to wander aimlessly in the desert and die a horrible death, starved and desiccated.

Hank stands up and looks where the old man is pointing. "America?" he asks the man.

"Si, America. Go. Go."

"Don't believe him," I tell Hank, but he ignores me.

"Past the river?" he asks the man.

"Si. Go. Go."

Hank jumps out of the truck and helps me out. We thank the man and watch his truck drive back from where we came, its wheels kicking up dirt as it speeds down the highway and finally disappears in the distance. We're thrust into a quiet that scares me down to my toes.

"We're going to be fine," Hank tells me. "You'll be wearing a bra by suppertime."

"A bra," I breathe. It's been too long without good support. I feel like I have two five-pound bags of flour hanging off my chest. "Okay, I'll walk through the desert for a bra."

# CHAPTER 10

It's not a bad walk to the river. The morning heat is still bearable, and my shoes are comfortable. Hank is limping slightly, but he doesn't complain, once. As we get closer to the river, we notice groups of people dotting the shore.

"Is this a vacation spot?" I ask Hank.

"It's a jumping off spot."

"I'm done with jumping."

"Figure of speech," he says. "They're pursuing the American dream."

"Oh," I say, finally understanding that we're about to sneak into our own country with a lot of illegal immigrants. "This isn't going to be easy, is it?"

"It depends where we are. The Chihuahua desert stretches over three American states. We could be going into a quiet area or a highly enforced area."

"Holy shitballs. What if we're droned?"

"Considering our relationship so far, the drone would miss you entirely and hit me," he says.

"We have a relationship?"

*

We form a caravan of people, most of whom are carrying their possessions on their backs. Men, women, and children. They're all unsure why we're there— Americans sneaking into the States—but they're kind and share their water with us.

We follow the line of people through the shallowest part of the river, which is mostly a trickle over slick rocks. The further we walk, the quieter the people become. There's a palpable anxiety throughout the group, an oppressive concern about not knowing what's going to greet us on the other side of the river.

I'm praying for budget cuts, which will prevent the border patrol from patrolling this particular stretch of the border. Sure, I'm an American citizen, but I'm not sure that would prevent them from NSA'ing my ass for sneaking in without any identification papers.

We follow the group for hours, until the sun is high in the sky, making me squint against the bright light and making me crave a tall glass of iced tea.

All of a sudden, the group scatters. They run in every direction. "Are we caught?" I ask Hank.

He spins around, looking at the backs of the fleeing people. There's no sign of any kind of law enforcement. We're still in the desert, but in the distance, I can make out mountains.

"I think we're in New Mexico," Hank says.

New Mexico. It's a long way away from Northern California.

"That's a hell of a walk, Hank."

He seems to think about our predicament for a minute. For the first time, I feel bad for him. After all, he's worked since eighth grade to build his business, and it's been pulled out from under him during one unfortunate drunken night.

"This, my friend, is a cautionary tale about the evils of drinking," I say.

"You said it, beautiful. I'm going milk from here on out, or Dr. Pepper on special occasions."

He's still looking around, as if he's expecting a Batman kind of rescue. The others have disappeared into the wilderness, sure of where they're going. We should have followed them because we have no idea where we are. We could wander for days in the wrong direction, and we don't have any food or water. I'm getting frustrated at Hank's inaction. Does he expect us to stand around forever in the middle of nowhere?

"Come on," I say. "Let's pick a direction and go."

"Shh," he says. "Hear that?"

"I don't hear anything."

"Be quiet. You'll hear it."

I don't hear a thing, and I'm worried that Hank is having a mental breakdown, but then I hear it. *Whoosh. Whoosh. Whoosh.* I spin around. "Where is it?" I ask Hank.

"There," he says, pointing in the direction of the mountains.

The *whoosh whoosh* gets louder. I figure we only have a couple of minutes before we get droned to death. "Hank," I say, touching his arm.

"Yes?" He looks down at me, as if he's forgotten that I'm standing next to him.

"I just wanted to say, it hasn't been totally horrible being with you," I mumble, looking away because I can't take his eye contact. His beautiful eyes.

"Thanks, I guess."

"And I've been thinking about what you said about liking me."

"You have?"

"And maybe I like…"

The *whoosh whoosh* gets louder and cuts me off. A wind comes out of nowhere, blowing my dress up and my hair in my face.

"This is either good or bad," Hank yells over the noise.

I push my hair out of my eyes in time to see a black helicopter fly toward us. It lands a few feet away. I think about running, but I don't run very fast and certainly not without a bra. Even with a bra, nobody outruns a helicopter.

The blades keep circling while the helicopter's door opens, and a man dressed all in black jumps out and jogs toward us.

"Ronin sent me," he tells Hank. "Come this way."

*

We ride in silence for about ten minutes to a small airstrip in the desert, where a small plane is waiting for us. It's my first experience flying, and I love it. I can't get enough of looking out the window. We fly over stunning mountains and desert.

"This is like magic," I tell Hank, and he takes my hand in his. We're saved, at least until the mysterious Ronin figures out that Hank doesn't have any money to pay for his rescue.

After about an hour and a half, we land on another small airstrip, but this time it's paved and nearer to civilization. A black SUV is waiting for us with a Russian driver covered in tattoos and scars.

"Your brother?" I whisper to Hank.

"Ha. Ha."

We drive for about thirty minutes, and I'm surprised when the car parks at a sprawling truck stop. Hundreds of trucks are parked in a lot by the stop's main diner. A giant sign advertises a barbershop, hot showers, and five-dollar pancakes.

"Pancakes," I read. "I would kill for pancakes." And a shower. And clean clothes. I'm tired. "Where are we?"

"Closer," Hank says. "First we have to meet with Ronin. This is kind of his office."

He wraps his arm around my waist as we walk into the diner. It's packed with truckers, but all I can concentrate on is the smell of delicious truck stop food. Bacon. Pancakes. Coffee.

"I love America," I say.

It's easy to spot Ronin. He sits at a table with his long legs stretched out in front of him and crossed at the ankle. He's wearing jeans, a tight t-shirt, and a leather jacket. Heavy black boots stick out from his pant legs.

He has short brown hair and a short brown beard, which does little to take away from his handsome face. He watches us walk in, and he nods almost imperceptibly to Hank, who returns the nod.

Hank pulls a chair out for me to sit and then takes a seat himself. He signals for the waitress and quickly orders us a big breakfast, juice, and water.

"Do you need medical care?" Ronin asks Hank after the waitress leaves. His voice is low, and he speaks deliberately, as if each word is precious and meticulously thought out. I shiver. He oozes sexuality and danger. I want to smack him.

Hank places his hand on my leg under the table, as if he senses my discomfort.

"Thanks for the lift," Hank tells Ronin. "How did you find us?"

"I triangulated the call and figured where you would cross over. I was watching it for two days. I figured I owed it to you for the Wyoming thing."

"What Wyoming thing?" I ask.

"I forgot about Wyoming," Hank says.

"What Wyoming thing?" I ask.

“I haven’t forgotten,” Ronin says, pushing his sleeve up to reveal a long, ugly scar on his arm. “So, now we’re even.”

Hank fist bumps him, which I guess means thank you in guy speak. “I might have one more thing I need some help with,” he tells Ronin.

He shoots me a glance, as if this is my cue to give him some privacy, which really angers me. I’m not a child to be sent away when the grownups are talking. But I’m not all that interested in what they have to say, and besides, I figure I might as well go to the bathroom and give Hank a chance to get my bar back for me.

I’m the center of attention as I walk to the ladies room. I’m the only woman besides the waitresses, and my dress looks like a skimpy nightgown that barely covers what I have up top. I sigh, resigned to the unwanted attention from the men who are frozen in place, forks of food stopped midair between their plates and their mouths.

It’s a relief to finally make it inside the ladies room. It’s a huge space with at least fifty stalls, but I’m alone except for one other woman. She has long, curly blonde hair and is wearing a long red floral print dress and gold flats. She has a small black purse slung over one shoulder, and she's staring into a mirror, talking to herself.

"Fiona Jones," she says to her reflection. "Don't be wobbly. Buck up your courage. He's not that scary, and you have to do this. Daddy needs you."

She's not exactly a typical client for my bar, but I know her. Her family has a big ranch outside of town, and she makes baked goods and sells them around Esperanza. I love her apple crumble muffins, and her chocolate chip cookies are always a hit with my happy hour crowd.

"Fiona?" I ask. "What are you doing here?"

It takes her a moment to recognize me. She's jumpy. Nervous.

"Layla?" she asks, squinting. She looks me up and down, confused. Normally, I dress a lot like Beyonce, but I'm never falling out as much as I am right now. I look like I'm about to shoot a porn movie.

"I just got back from Mexico," I tell her, as if that explains it all. "How far are we away from Esperanza?"

"We're twenty miles east." Her voice hitches, and a tear rolls down her cheek. I jog over to her and touch her arm.

"Are you okay? Do you need help?"

It's odd, to say the least, the see Fiona Jones in a truck stop. She's twenty years old, but she acts like a prim and proper old lady from another era. I mean, she knits.

"I'm fine," she says, wiping her eyes. "I'm here to meet someone to get help for my family. I can't really talk about it."

"You're meeting someone *here*?" I ask, and then it hits me. Ronin. He's the guy who uses a truck stop as his office where he meets with clients who need special help.

I can't imagine what kind of help Fiona needs from Ronin. I'm pretty sure he specializes in broken legs and cracked skulls. Fiona specializes in mini cheesecakes.

"Listen," I say. "Be careful. The guy you're seeing doesn't play around."

"That's what I'm counting on," she says. "I even tossed a coin in a fountain to make sure this works."

"The fountain in Esperanza's square?"

"Silly, right?"

"Silly," I mumble, but I did the same thing with disastrous results. Instead of getting my bar back, I wound up handcuffed in Mexico. "But I'm sure it can't hurt."

"I have to do something. If not—" she says, her face overrun with anxiety and panic. Then, her eyes bug out, and her face turns green. "Oh, God," she moans and runs to a stall and closes herself in.

"Oh, God," she moans, again and begins to hack her guts up.

"Okay, then," I mutter. While she's spewing her breakfast, I survey the damage from my day in the desert in the mirror. I wash my hands and my face, and I comb my hair with wet fingers. I'm sunburned, and my hair is frizzy, but otherwise, I'm unscathed.

I'm anxious to get home and sleep for a full day—If Hank doesn't kick me out of my apartment—but I'm happy to get to eat a plate of pancakes and spend a little more time with Hank.

I look away from the mirror, surprised by my thoughts. Do I really want to spend more time with Hank? I realize I do. But I don't see how it can work between us. I had a business and a home, and he stole it all away. And I can't live off of his charity. That's just not how I roll.

But I think about the past couple of days with him. How he carried me through the desert, even though his hand was broken. How he tried to catch me as I fell from the second storey. How he looks at me. How he made love to me.

I take a deep breath to try to clear my head. Being a grownup sucks. I was perfectly content working in the bar and living above it. I didn't need my life turned around by a Ryan Gosling look-alike with a neck tattoo.

"Any better?" I call to Fiona. She's still locked in the stall, but she's been quiet for a while.

"I think so," she squeaks.

"Are you coming out? You want to have breakfast with me?"

"Don't say breakfast. I think I'll just stay here for a few minutes."

She moans, again, and I debate with myself whether to stay with her, but I think she wants her privacy, and besides, my stomach is growling for pancakes. "I'll be right out there if you need me. I'm with a guy who looks like he's been in a car wreck."

When I get back to the table, I can tell Hank and Ronin have been in deep conversation. Ronin is still sitting with his legs stretched in front of him, but he's on his phone giving commands. Meanwhile, Hank is knocking back a cup of coffee.

He stands when he sees me and pulls out my chair for me to sit. I'm not used to be taken care of. I like it, but I'm afraid to get used to it, because I'll be devastated to lose it.

Our food arrives as soon as I sit down, and I begin to eat like a bulldozer. I don't come up for air until I've gone through three giant pancakes, three strips of bacon, and a cup of coffee. Ronin finishes his phone call and tosses Hank a car key.

"Black Escalade out front," he tells Hank. He looks at his watch. "I have another appointment. So, if you'll excuse me."

I think he's going to get up and leave, but he's actually dismissing us. Hank stands and signals to me to get up. I look down longingly at my last uneaten pancake, but I decide to leave well enough alone. We have a car and I can be home in twenty minutes. Besides, I don't want to get Ronin mad.

"Thanks," I tell Ronin. Hank takes my hand, and I follow him out of the diner. He beeps the key, and a black Escalade comes to life a few cars down. We get in, and Hank begins to drive toward Esperanza.

The party's over, I think to myself, looking out of the window. Back to reality.

"I wonder where my leather jacket is," Hank says, staring at the road ahead, as he drives. "I really liked that jacket. I've had it for years."

"You're about to find out." I wonder if that's really true. Will we find out what happened to us two nights ago, how we went from drinking in my bar to naked and handcuffed in Mexico?

"I'm going to crack some skulls, but I don't want to do it dressed like this. I feel like a low-level Russian criminal."

"You need to dress for success to crack skulls?"

"I really liked my leather jacket," he says, adjusting his track suit. "Have you thought at all about Hawaii?"

I'm startled by the change of subject. He's still staring straight ahead, seemingly relaxed, but I notice his hand is gripped tightly on the steering wheel.

"Were you serious about Hawaii?"

"We could do Paris, if you don't like Hawaii."

"Paris? Are you serious?"

Hank glances at me, and the car swerves. He rights it just before we drive off the road. "Yes, Layla. I'm serious. What's the matter with me? Is it the track suit?"

"No. Well, the track suit is pretty ratty, but you're okay." I realize I've been holding my breath, but I can't get air. I pant and wheeze, trying to breathe, but my lungs refuse to work. Oh my God, I'm going to die in a car in a dirty dress with frizzy hair and no makeup. I'm not even wearing mascara.

I slap at the steering wheel and point to the side of the road. Hank reacts quickly, parking in the dirt rut by a tall tree. He turns the motor off and turns toward me. "Do you need a doctor? Are you having a stroke?"

I shake my head. I don't think I'm having a stroke, but I'm not sure. Do strokes make you feel happy and sad at the same time, as if the wheel of fortune has simultaneously landed on *jackpot* and *miss a turn*?

Hank's beautiful, battered face is so close to mine that I ache. Without thinking, my hand lifts off my lap and cups his cheek. At the contact, my lungs finally fill with air, and I can breathe.

"I can't. I can't," I say. A traitorous tear rolls down my face.

"You can't what? Am I making you cry?"

I nod. "I like you, too." I break down, blubbering.

Hank furrows his brow. "Oh. I'm sorry?"

"Don't you understand? I want to be with you. All the time. Forever. Like in the movies."

Hank swallows. "Are you proposing? Do I get a ring?"

"No! This can't work. Square peg! Round hole!" I yell, pointing from him to me.

"I seem to recall our peg-hole dynamics as being over the top awesome. This is a pretty big car. Do you want to test my square peg and your round hole in the backseat? Make sure they still fit? I'm all for beta testing."

"It is a big backseat," I say, thinking about it.

"I'm thinking doggie style."

"Doggie style's good."

"And the windows are tinted. That's a plus, unless you're into the whole exhibitionist thing. That's never been my bag, but I'll adapt for you." He arches an eyebrow and gives me a Cheshire cat grin. I blink and shake my head to try and clear it.

"No. No doggie style. I'm trying to communicate something to you."

"Missionary, then?"

"I do love missionary… No! No! Stop confusing me. You and I can't work out. You took my bar."

"*My* bar. But I'll give it back to you. Think of it as a very big ring."

My throat gets thick, and I'm having a terrible time swallowing. "I don't take charity," I say. "If I didn't win it back fair and square, I don't want it. I make my way in this life on my own."

"That's fine. I'm a modern man. I have no problem with my woman being independent."

"Your woman?"

"I like you."

Hank's doing the puppy dog face thing, again, and it's working. He has the most beautiful eyes I've ever seen. They have the power to make me melt into mush. I start to cry, again.

"Oh, geez. Don't do that, beautiful," Hank says, wiping my face with his sleeve. "You're breaking my heart. Maybe you won the drinking contest."

"Maybe I did, but if I didn't, we're stuck between a rock and a hard place. If you take my bar, I can't be with you. If you give me my bar, I can't be with you."

"Then let's set fire to the damned bar. Burn it to the ground. Then, nothing will get between us. I don't want to see you cry ever again."

His jaw is set. Determined and angry. For the first time, I see beneath the easygoing man who I've shared an adventure with. The kind of man who carried me through the desert has a strength beyond his years.

"We barely know each other," I say, softly.

"That can be fixed with time."

Hank kisses me, his warm lips feather soft on mine, relaying so much: compassion, desperation, possession. And love.

But he's wrong. We don't have time. We're only a couple of miles away from Esperanza, my bar, and the end of whatever Hank and I started.

# CHAPTER 11

There's no place like home. We park just outside my bar, and I'm giddy with excitement. I jump out of the car before Hank turns off the motor and run up to the front door. Hank runs after me, and we walk inside together.

"Holy shitballs," I say.

Hank rubs his eyes. "Holy shitballs."

The bar is decked out in streamers and balloons and hanging on the wall along the length of the bar is a *Welcome Back!* sign in neon pink. Cheers erupt from the biggest crowd I've ever seen in my bar. All my regulars are here, and a lot of people I've never seen before.

A well-heeled man in a custom made suit and a five-hundred-dollar haircut approaches us and slaps Hank on the back. "You made it back, pal. Drinks are on me."

"Harrison," Hank growls and sucker punches him in the face with a loud crack. Harrison goes down like a lead balloon, taking down two people with him. The bar grows completely quiet except for a loud gasp.

"You lousy crook. I'm going to kill you, and after you're dead I'm going to sue you for everything you've stolen from me and after that I'm going to put you in prison," Hank yells, standing over Harrison with his one good hand in his best boxer's pose.

"It was a joke!" Harrison says, crawling away from Hank's reach.

"A what?"

"I didn't steal anything. That was a joke. Everyone was in on it."

A mousy little woman helps Harrison up. "He said you would think it was funny," she says.

Hank's apoplectic. His head looks like it's going to explode. "Emma, you're my assistant. Why would you think I'd think it was funny?"

"Mr. Harrison said you always wanted an adventure like you had in Mexico," she says, standing in front of Harrison in order to protect him.

"Do you mean he's responsible for our trip to Mexico?" I ask her.

"I didn't mean for you to go, too," Harrison tells me. "How was I to know you were going to drink with him?"

My mouth's open in shock and nothing I do can shut it.

"What did you do? How did you do it?" Hank asks, clenching his fist.

"Anything's possible with a few C-notes. It was a joke!" Harrison says, taking a couple of steps backward.

I point at Hank. "Look at this man. He's roadkill. His face looks like mashed potatoes. He's Mickey Rourke, the later years. You did that to him. All for a joke. And we were kidnapped. And I was naked!"

The entire bar looks at my ample bosom. I step behind Hank.

"I'm going to break your neck," Hank tells Harrison, shaking his fist at him.

"Oh, my God," I say, just thinking about something. "You still have the bar. We can find out who won the drinking contest."

We ask everyone who witnessed the contest. At first, it looks like I drank Hank under the table, but then just as many people say Hank was the one who drank me under the table. It's a stalemate.

"What do we do in case of a tie?" I ask Hank.

"It means you win," he says, his puppy dog face back.

"Liar. You're just trying to give the bar to me. I told you this wouldn't work."

"You're a difficult woman."

The bar is a big party, the guests unaware of the drama taking place under their noses. My future rests in the balance. My future with the bar and my home, and also my future with Hank.

"We could do some kind of competition," Hank suggests. "Winner takes all."

"Oh, lord."

Luckily, Hank comes to his senses. Neither of us is ready to start again with a drinking contest or anything else. Still, we like the competition angle. It sounds fair.

"Competition by proxy," Hanks says, smiling.

"Deal," I say, shaking his hand.

*

"So, this is the inner sanctum," Hank says looking around my apartment over the bar. I hold his hand and walk him through the living room on the way to my bedroom.

"Very few lucky men have made it up here."

"I feel very lucky. This is better than the Powerball."

We step into my bedroom, and I strip his clothes off. "So, if it takes him more than forty hours to get home, the bar's mine."

"But if he gets back in less time, the bar's mine," Hank says, pulling my dress up over my head. He kisses the side of my neck and carries me to my bed.

"I feel a little guilty," I say, as he lies on top of me, fitting himself between my legs.

"I don't. The jerk had it coming to him. Anyway, what did he call it? A joke. Let's see how funny he thinks it is being the punchline."

It wasn't hard to get Harrison drunk, and getting him blotto was pretty easy after that. And he was right about the C-notes. Hank stole Harrison's wallet and handed over its contents to a couple of biker friends. That was a couple of hours ago. I figure he's sleeping it off in the middle of Mexico just as Hank is busy kissing the length and breadth of my body.

"I wonder if other people start their relationships this way," I say.

"You mean naked and handcuffed together?"

"I mean paying to have a man kidnapped and delivered to Mexico."

"We could have played Scrabble, but you didn't want to," he says, slipping inside me.

"Do you think he's okay?"

"I'll have someone check on him, make sure he doesn't get into too much trouble. Of course, he didn't do the same for us."

"All's well that end's well," I say, lifting my legs up so he can thrust himself deeper. I shiver with arousal.

"You're right. It's a great story we can tell our kids someday."

"Our kids? Wait a minute. What do you mean, 'our kids?'"

But he's not listening, and I've forgotten what I was saying. We make love all night and the day after. I keep the bar closed until we finally take a break forty-eight hours later. Just in time for Harrison to make it back.

The End

Wish Upon A Stud Series #5
Wicked
RIDE
elise sax

# *Wicked* RIDE

(Wish Upon A Stud – Book 5)

elise sax

# CHAPTER 1

"Fiona Jones, get your head out of the toilet."

My voice echoes in the empty bathroom, reverberating off the porcelain commode. I've been sitting on my knees, staring at the water forever. If I don't get up, I'm going to miss my appointment, and how will I ever find another killer to hire?

Killer.

My stomach clenches, and I get another rush of nausea. But I can't throw up, again. I'm tapped out. "You're such a coward," I tell myself. "Get up and get going."

It's not the first time that I've spoken to myself, but I'm not crazy. It's just nerves. Anybody would be a little nervous to be doing what I'm about to be doing. Not that I have a choice.

My family has tried every legal means possible to stop an evil man from stealing our land, robbing us of our livelihood, and now killing my father. Almost killing my father. And almost is too close.

Somehow, I have to make things right.

I finally work up the courage to stand up, and I let myself out of the bathroom stall. I check myself in the mirror. Not too bad. My curly hair isn't very frizzy. And you couldn't tell that I just finished throwing up my insides. I open my purse and take out a travel-size toothbrush and tube of toothpaste and brush my teeth.

Even though I'm about to hire a killer, I'm not going let my oral hygiene slide. One root canal three months ago has turned me into a maniacal toothbrusher. And don't get me started on dental floss and the all-mighty Water Pik. It's a religion based on fear, but I haven't had a cavity since I converted.

I take a piece of lint off of my long floral print dress and slip my purse over my shoulder.

"All right then," I say to myself. "You got this."

I open the bathroom door and step back into the truck stop's restaurant. This is my first visit to a truck stop. I bake for a living, selling my muffins, cakes, and cookies around the small town of Esperanza. But this is out of the town's limits. Way out.

I'm the only woman in the large restaurant, besides the overworked waitresses. Truckers from all over the country are seated at red booths with linoleum covered tables, eating pancakes, chicken fried steak, and other artery-clogging delicacies, taking a breather before they head back on the road.

The truck stop is a sprawling set up, comprised of much more than just the restaurant. There's a barbershop, bank, mini motel, and a gun store. I try to swallow. I'm completely out of my depth. Oversized men ogle me as I pass, looking for my killer.

All I know is that he has a regular table here, which he uses as his office. Vinny, the custodian at the University where I sell a lot of chocolate chip cookies, suggested I look up the killer when I told him about my problem.

But which one of these cap-wearing, goateed guys is the

one? I don't have a name. And I don't know what he looks like.

This is crazy. *I'm* crazy. Hiring a killer is crazy. What am I doing? I'm a pacifist. I was a vegetarian for three full months in high school. I don't kill people, no matter how evil, soul-sucking, thieving and murderous they are.

I kill spiders. That's about it.

I have a change of heart. Just as I'm about to turn around and forget the whole killer-for-hire thing, I spot him. He's sitting with another man at a corner booth. He's about fifty years old with a long beard and a scar down the left side of his face. He's fearsome, just like the killer that he is. He senses that I'm staring at him, and we lock eyes. There's no turning back now. No running away. I have to make this happen. I owe it to my father. To my whole family.

I approach the table, my gold flats click-clacking on the floor as I walk. My hand reaches for my purse, and I tap it, making sure it's still there. I'm carrying a lot of money. All the money I've earned during the summer.

"Are you him?" I ask the man. He's even scarier up close, unwashed and dressed in a flannel shirt. He looks me up and down from my shoes to the top of my head.

"I can be anybody you want," he says, his voice rough and gravelly, sending shivers up my spine in fear.

"Yes, I know. I've heard that about you. I've heard that you're a man who can get the job done."

The other man at the table laughs. "He can get the job done if you have a blue pill," he shouts.

The men at the surrounding tables laugh. I never expected that this was the way hiring a killer went, but I try to laugh with him, as if I'm cool and in on the joke.

Then, the laughter ends just as quickly as it began, and they stare with open fear at something above my head. "What is it?" I ask.

But I feel the presence behind me, and I turn around. A tall man--very tall, around six-foot-five--is hovering over me. He's wearing jeans, black boots, a tight T-shirt, and a leather jacket. He has short brown hair and big brown eyes, and he could be a model on any billboard in Times Square. Not that I've ever been to New York.

"I'm sorry," I say to the good-looking, tall man. "But I'm doing business here, and it's confidential. Top secret. So if you'll excuse us …"

He raises an eyebrow and cocks his head to the side. "You're talking business," he says, slowly as he's thought out each word carefully. As if he's reluctant to speak at all, but he's required to do so. "But you're talking business at the wrong table with the wrong man. Fiona?"

*Zing!* A lightning bolt hits me, knocking the stupid right out of my head. I look from the scary bearded man at the table to the tall good-looking man behind me, and it dawns on me that I've mixed them up. "Are you sure you're the one I'm supposed to talk to?" I whisper in his direction.

He sighs, blowing air on my face. His breath smells like

cinnamon and sugar. Two of my favorite things in the world. He takes my hand and pulls me away. I don't fight him. It seems like the most normal thing in the world for him to hold my hand. I haven't let a lot of men do that. There was my father, of course, and Jimmy in tenth grade, but otherwise I haven't had much male contact. As the oldest of three girls, I've spent a lifetime helping around the house, which is a ranch in our case. So not a lot of time for dating or holding hands.

But I sure like holding the killer's hand.

Killer. Oops. I forgot.

He ushers me to a table in the middle of the restaurant and pulls out a chair for me. I take a seat, and he tucks it back in and then he takes a seat on the other side of the table for himself. He immediately falls into a relaxed pose, stretching his long legs out in front of him and crossing them at the ankle. He adjusts his leather jacket so it lays flat on his flat stomach.

"What can I do for you, Fiona?" he asks. When he says my name I get a little flutter in my pelvis, like butterflies are trying to escape. It feels great.

"Say my name again," I croak and then clamp my lips together, embarrassed. My face gets hot, and I fan myself with my hand. I hope none of my other thoughts about him slip out.

He squints, as if he can't see me clearly. I shift my eyes to the side, because looking straight at him makes me squirm. I don't believe in auras, but he has a big fat manly aura. It's a deadly kind of big fat manly aura, shooting out manly aura bullets like an aura machine gun, hopped up on speed.

I want to duck and weave out of the way of his aura bullets, but it's too late. He's shot me full of holes, and now I need to be filled up again, and for some reason I'm looking at him to do the filling. Fiona, you need therapy, not a killer to fill your holes, I think to myself.

Whoa. My brain is going way off topic, and I have an important topic to discuss.

"I mean," I say, clearing my throat. "I have money for you. Lots and lots of money. I know you expect cash, and that's what I have. It took me a week's worth of trips to the ATM machine at the local 7-11, but I got it all."

I put my purse on the table and take out the bundle of money. "Well, not really all, but three-quarters, which is a lot," I explain. "I'll write you an IOU for the rest. I'm good for it. I make a bundle during pumpkin season. I do a pumpkin bread with cream cheese frosting that sells like hotcakes."

I hand over the money, putting it on the table in front of him. He looks at it and then to me and back at the cash. "Do you want the IOU now? I think I have a pen," I say, rummaging in my purse.

He scratches behind his ear and sits up straight in his chair. "Fiona," he says, his voice so deep, he practically rumbles. "Tell me what you'd like from me."

I lean forward and cup my hands around my mouth so nobody else can hear. "I want you to shoot the jerkface, lying bastard asshole cattle rustler who's bent on killing my father and stealing our land."

He nods. "Shoot," he repeats, dragging out the word.

"Oh, that's not the way you do it?" I ask, leaning even closer toward him. "You can use a knife, if you want. Stab the shit out of him. Can you do it so it doesn't hurt him too much? I don't believe in torture. Although he deserves it. In fact, if you want to break his legs first, that's okay."

"Knife."

"Poison?" I ask. "You tell me what you need. You're the expert."

He slips his hand between my elbows on the table and takes my purse. He scoops up the cash and stuffs it back in my bag and returns it to me. I reluctantly take it and lean back in my chair, defeated.

"I don't understand," I say.

"I don't kill people. At least not on purpose. At least not unless I need to. And sweetheart, I don't need to."

I'm stunned and not just because he called me sweetheart.

"But I was told that you help people."

He stands and puts his hand out to help me up. "You heard correctly. I help people."

"Maybe I have the wrong person. Maybe I was supposed to meet with the guy with the beard."

He squeezes my hand, getting my attention. "Please don't talk to the man with the beard or anybody within a ten-mile radius of this place. Do you understand?"

"Not really." I'm more than disappointed. I'm devastated. I've planned for this, saving my money and working up my courage.

He puts his arm around my waist and walks me out of the restaurant. "A woman like you shouldn't be in a place like this."

He's so right. I shouldn't be in a place like this, shouldn't be hiring a killer. Instead, I should be at home, baking lemon bars.

"What do you mean?" I demand, affronted. "I'll have you know I do a weekly shipment of caramel s'mores brownies to the

Esperanza Therapy Ranch for Troubled Boys. Some of those kids have a very checkered past."

He opens the front door for me, and I walk outside. The vast parking lot is a hive of activity. Huge trucks are coming and going, and truckers mill about, talking to each other.

"Go straight home," the killer orders, pointing toward the road. "It was nice meeting you, Fiona." He puts his hand out, and I shake it. He's got great hands. Big, like he is. His grip is firm and gentle at the same time. I like his hand.

"It was nice meeting you …"

"Ronin."

"Excuse me?"

"My name. Ronin."

"You let people know your name?" It's not very wise for a hired killer to go around announcing his identity.

He squints at me, again. "Yes," he says after a second.

"Ronin what? Or do you only have one name like Cher and Madonna?"

"One name. And nothing like Cher and Madonna. Are you okay to go home, now?"

"Sure," I lie. "I'm going straight home."

I watch Ronin walk back into the restaurant. The back half of him is almost as good as the front half of him. He has a lot of really good halves. But he's a jerk for not taking my money. How dare he reject me?

As soon as he's gone, I walk straight toward the truck stop's gun store.

*

"I need a really big one, but small enough to fit into my purse," I tell the gun shop employee. I've decided to take things into my own hands, proving once and for all that I've gone over the deep end. I show him my purse. It's small, but it has a large center pocket.

"You could go pretty big with that," he says, putting four large handguns on the counter for me to inspect. I pick up the largest one. "Heavy," I say, approvingly.

I aim it at a poster of *The Terminator* on the wall behind the salesman. "*Pew! Pew! Pew*!" I shout, pretending to shoot Arnold. "This is good," I say. "It probably makes really big holes."

"Honey, you could drive a truck through a hole that this gun will make on a person."

"Sounds effective." And easy. It's scary how easy it is to use. Can openers are more difficult to manage.

I *Pew! Pew! Pew!* a few more times, but am interrupted when a large hand comes down from behind me and grabs the gun, placing it gently on the counter. I turn around to see Ronin towering over me, again.

"You're a determined woman, Fiona." His hands are on his hips. Annoyed. For a moment, he really does look like a killer. Mean. In a sexy way. But he's not the only one who's annoyed. I'm pretty peeved, as well. If he would have done his job, I wouldn't be in a gun shop, pretending to shoot Arnold Schwarzenegger.

"I don't have a choice," I say, reasonably.

He stares me down for a moment, waiting—I suppose—for me to toss the gun away and change my murderous intentions. But he's right. I'm a determined woman.

"Fine. I changed my mind."

I search his face for a sign that he's joking. He's not. In fact, I'm not sure he's capable of humor. His face is hard like the rest of him. Big manly hardness.

My heart leaps, and I'm so pleased that he's going to help me that I hop up and down in place. I grab the gun and wave it under his nose.

"Do you need this?" I ask.

# CHAPTER 2

He doesn't want the gun. I figure he must have his own. He wraps his arm around my waist and ushers me out of the gun store. I'm getting used to his touch. It still makes me want to giggle uncontrollably and shout "Oh, mama!" but staying calm is getting easier.

"Where's your car?" he asks.

"I took the bus."

"Of course you did."

"We have one truck and one car on the ranch, and I try to leave them for my family as much as possible. I only drive when I have shipments to make or if I'm going to a movie after dark."

"Where are we going?"

"Half Crescent Ranch. Northeast Esperanza," I say. My heart races with the idea that we're going straight to my arch-enemy's ranch. My father and his friends have tried unsuccessfully to get on the property. Ed Sullivan, the owner of Half Crescent, has gobbled up neighboring ranches through cattle rustling, stealing water rights, and other terrorist maneuvers. One rancher after another has given up the fight to survive and has sold out to Sullivan at a greatly reduced price. My father is one of the few who has held on and has kept fighting, but not without consequences. Near bankruptcy and a heart attack have raised the ante. It's now up to me to protect my family.

Sometimes the best defense is the best offense.

Ronin nods and walks quickly across the parking lot. He's so tall, with such long legs, that it's hard for me to catch up. I'm practically jogging next to him. Men avoid his gaze as we pass. I don't know if it's his reputation or just the fact that he's a big strong guy in a leather jacket and boots that makes people scared. But I'm thrilled that he's scary. The scarier the better, as far as I'm concerned. I just want to get this whole thing over with, and I think Ronin's the guy to make it happen.

We walk past big rigs until we get to an empty, quiet part of the parking lot. "Where's your car?" I ask.

"Right here."

"Where?" I don't see anything. Just empty parking spots and a fancy motorcycle.

He walks toward the bike and hands me a helmet. "I've never been on a motorcycle," I say. Without a word, he takes back the helmet and places it on my head, clicking the strap together under my chin.

He lifts his leg over the motorcycle and sits on the leather seat. I decide not to point out that it's illegal for him to ride a motorcycle without a helmet. I'm not sure if he's being chivalrous giving me his only helmet, or if he doesn't want to mess up his hair. He has beautiful hair.

Ronin slaps the spot on the seat behind him, inviting me to get on board. I sling the purse strap across my body and straddle the motorcycle.

"This isn't too bad," I say, swinging my legs back and forth. It's very comfortable. I don't know anything about motorcycles, but I can tell it's a very expensive model. Ronin turns around and stares at me like I'm doing something wrong. "What's the matter?"

He gets off and stands over me, still staring. "Your dress."

I look down. My dress is draped over the motorcycle like a flowery tablecloth, covering the back tire and the backside of the motorcycle down to the asphalt parking lot ground.

"We can't go like that. Your dress is a deadly weapon like that," he says.

"Sorry." I adjust the dress, but it's long and gets snarled in the back tire. I tug, but it snarls worse.

"I've got this," I tell him, as he stands over me, watching me struggle against the material stuffed in the workings of his fancy hot rod.

"I think it's coming free," I groan, yanking and pulling, twisting and turning in my seat to get leverage.

Ronin covers his face with his hand. "You can't ride like that, even if you get it free. It's dangerous."

He grabs a handful of my dress and rips it. In a matter of seconds, he rips it all the way around until instead of wearing a long dress, I'm rocking a micro-mini. Ronin frees the fabric from the motorcycle and throws it away in a nearby trashcan.

"You ripped my dress," I say, shocked.

Like always, Ronin doesn't reply. He swings his leg over the motorcycle and kick starts it to life.

"You ripped my dress," I repeat, raising my voice above the sound of the motor.

"Hold on tight." He leans back, reaches behind me, and pulls me close to him so that his body is wedged between my legs. He takes my hand and puts it around his waist, and I follow with my other hand, holding tight to his rock hard stomach.

"This doesn't seem very safe," I say.

"Hold on tighter." I scoot up a little more until there's no space between us. I rest my chin on his back and hug his waist tighter, feeling the muscles of his abdomen push back against my arms.

"Holy hell," I mutter, and he puts the motorcycle into gear. I'm wrapped around him like paper on the best Christmas present ever. This has got to be at least second base. Maybe third. I'm warm all over, despite being half-naked and blown by the wind, as he accelerates out of the parking lot. Ronin is a lot of man, and I fight against a strong urge to wiggle against his backside and travel my hands up and down his body. Especially down his body.

I shake my head in the heavy helmet, trying to clear my thoughts, which are foreign to me and completely out of character. I'm a virgin. I mean, I'm a virgin physically and mentally. Most of my thoughts are taken up with baking, my family, and reality TV.

I've had very few take-me-now thoughts… except when I watch Hugh Jackman movies. But Ronin leaves Hugh in his dust.

Hugh Jackman plays Wolverine. Ronin *is* Wolverine.

Except Ronin's younger and doesn't have sideburns.

So, I'm horny. I admit it. I want to roll around with the killer. I want him to smear my naked body with honey and lick it off. Slowly.

The motorcycle isn't helping matters, either. It's *vroom-vroom*-vrooming me in a very pleasant way. My insides are humming. I'm straddling a vibrator while I have a fine piece of ass between my legs.

Oh, lordy.

It's about twenty five miles to Ed Sullivan's ranch, the jerk, no account thief who I want to kill. Ronin drives like a bat out of hell, passing car after car, truck after truck on the road. He zips in out, making the bike dip and lean, which takes my breath away.

And all the time, the motor is humming between my legs. No wonder he likes to ride a motorcycle. It's pornographic travel. It's erotica for the commuter. It's multi-tasking at its finest…

sexual gratification while you get to where you're going. Ahem, as it were.

There's no question that I'm getting stimulated. About five miles into our trip, I figure I'm one pothole in the road away from my eyes rolling back in my head. I might even sing the National Anthem or something equally embarrassing. I'm pretty sure I'll be able to hit all the high notes, though.

In order to calm myself down, I try to think of something else. Something not quite as stimulating. I envision congress, rotten meat, and dog poop, but it doesn't help. The close proximity to Ronin and the vibration underneath me, has got me right to the edge of ecstasy.

"Whoa mama!" I yell out.

"Are you okay?" Ronin asked.

I don't answer. I clutch onto him even tighter, as my body begins to tremble and shake. I'm crossing the bridge toward satisfaction, and I'm powerless to stop it. My thighs clench tightly on the bike, and I moan. Then, it's over. My first sexual experience with Ronin, and he's totally unaware it happened.

"Are you okay back there?" Ronin shouts above the noise of the road. "Do you want me to pull over to the side?"

"No, I'm good." Good? I've never been better. I wonder if my father would be upset if I sell the truck for one of these fancy motorcycles with big engines. I wonder if Ronin would travel with me wherever I go, or at least let's say, three times a week.

We continue a while and turn off onto a single lane road. We're back in Esperanza. I've lived here my whole life, and I know every nook and cranny. Half Crescent Ranch is no different. I've been there a million times, taking shortcuts through the property and swimming in a large pond there. Not that the owner ever approved. Ed Sullivan has always been mean. But not like this. Now he's dangerous.

It's a beautiful time of the year. A rare cool day at the end of the summer. I'm anxious for the fall to begin, because that's my busiest time of the year. As the leaves begin to change colors, people get a taste for sweet baked goods. I also make a mean hot apple cider. Not only is the business better, but I like wearing the clothes, the jackets and boots. And I love walking in the cold night air, sometimes around the ranch or at the lake that's nearby.

Tall trees border the narrow road. Beautiful country here. Peaceful. "Turn right at the next dirt road," I tell Ronin.

We get to it after a minute. Half Crescent Ranch is just ahead. We can't see it, yet, but it's just past a few turns in the windy road. I'm giddy with anticipation, the excitement that justice will finally be done. But my hopes at a quick confrontation are dashed when Ronin pulls over to the side of the road and turns off the motorcycle.

He gets off the bike and helps me off as well. He stares at me, as if he can read the answer of some unspoken question on my face.

"What's going on? We're not at the ranch house yet. It's a little bit further," I say.

"So you still want to do this? You still want to kill an actual person?"

"I thought I made that clear. Where's the confusion for you?"

He runs his hand over his face and looks down at his boots. "Why do you want to kill this guy? Do you want to go to prison? Is that on your bucket list or something?"

I don't have a bucket list, but if I did, prison wouldn't be on it. I can only sleep on a Tempur-Pedic mattress, and I don't think I'd like communal showers unless it's with the cast of *Magic Mike.*

"I told you," I say, my patience wearing thin. "He's a no good lying, thieving asshole who's trying to kill my father and take our ranch."

"Sounds like a job for the sheriff or at least a lawyer."

I cross my arms in front of me. "And the mayor and PETA. And they were all worthless. A big fat zero."

"Really? Even PETA? Normally they're pretty scary."

"They all said that Sullivan hasn't done anything illegal,

and they wouldn't go beyond questioning him. That's when he got restraining orders on my whole family."

"Sounds like they have a firmer grasp on reality," Ronin says.

"Are you saying this is all in my head?"

"I have doubts about your head, lady. You're not hiring me to DJ a bar mitzvah, you know."

He has a point. I'm in over my head. Certifiable. I left my moral compass at the door. And yet what else am I going to do? Did Patton hesitate? Did Macarthur balk?

I punch Ronin's arm as hard as I can. "Listen. I'm paying you good American money. Greenbacks and lots of them. Just because I bake pies for a living doesn't mean I'm not smart. I was a straight A student all the way through eleventh grade. Twelfth grade was slightly harder, because I had a small television addiction that threw me off track, but normally I'm very intelligent. Street smart."

Ronin rubs his arm. "Street smart?"

"So we're going to get back on your motorcycle, and we're going to drive a half mile down the road until we get to that jerk's house," I say, wagging my finger at him. "Then you're going to shoot him or stab him or poison him or beat him to death or whatever it takes, but we're going to get this done, and we're going to get this done today because I have a lot of baking to do, Mister. I have an entire kindergarten class that's waiting for their crumble muffins for tomorrow's PTA breakfast. Do we understand each other?"

"Ms. Jones, I haven't understood you since the first moment I saw you. Nothing in this world surprises me, but I can't make heads or tails out of you."

"Thank you."

"That wasn't exactly a compliment."

"It sounded like one to me."

But Ronin is ignoring me. He's looking at something

behind me, and he's not happy about it. Before I can turn around to see what he's looking at, Ronin grabs me by the arm and yanks me behind him. Then I see what's got him worried.

The lying thieving jerk who wants to kill my father and steal our ranch is standing right next to us with his shotgun cocked and ready to blow our heads off.

# CHAPTER 3

I rub my eyes to make sure that I'm not seeing things. Nope. He's still standing a few feet away with a gun pointed right at us. He's a tall, thin, mean old man, wearing jeans and a plaid shirt. He has gray steely eyes, which are open in a permanent squint, as if he's trying to figure out how screw over everyone around him.

I hate him.

I try to push Ronin out of my way so I can confront Sullivan, but Ronin keeps me behind him with one strong arm.

"May I help you, sir?" Ronin asks him in his best Boy Scout voice.

"One move, and I'll shoot your head clean off," he says. He's like a gristled old man version of the Wicked Witch of the

West.

I want to melt him.

I keep trying to push Ronin out of my way, but he's got a good grip on me, and he's very strong.

"We were just driving by, sir. Thought we would say hello."

"I don't know you, but I know that bitch behind you is big trouble. You're on my land, and I have every right in the world to shoot you dead."

"You shut up, you mean old man!" I scream, peeking out from behind Ronin. "Karma's a bitch! And you can call me Karma. Ronin's going to shove it up your ass. He's killed tons of mean old bastards and he'll kill you!"

"It's going to be like that, is it?" Ed Sullivan sneers and hacks a lugie, which lands on the ground with a disgusting splat. He lifts his rifle up to his face, fixing us in his sights.

"Sir, please. This is all a big misunderstanding," Ronin

says, calmly.

"A misunderstanding? I speak English just fine, and she was speaking English."

"Loco English," Ronin mutters. I elbow him in his back and try to escape his grasp. He grunts but doesn't loosen his grip on me. "We're just going to get on the bike and ride away, and I promise you that you'll never see us again."

"He's lying!" I shout. I finally manage to wiggle away from Ronin. Wagging my finger at Ed Sullivan, I charge him, but Ronin stops me mid-charge, picking me up with one arm around my waist and pulling me against his side, as if he's carrying a coat.

"Let me at him!" I shout, kicking and swinging my arms, like an Olympic swimmer.

"Just passing by, huh?" the old man growls, aiming the shotgun directly at me. "No court in the world would convict me if I shoot you two right here. You're trespassing."

"There might be one or two courts who would convict

you," Ronin says. "This is California."

Sullivan pauses, I guess thinking about Ronin's reasoning, but he doesn't lower his gun. "Her whole family is worthless trash. A thorn in my side. But you ain't going to last much longer, karma bitch. I'm going to mow down your whole family. Grind you to dust. You hear me? Each and every one of you no account losers is going to wind up dead and buried or on your way out of town on a potato truck."

"A potato truck?" I shriek. "This isn't potato country. A lettuce truck maybe, but not a potato truck. Don't you know anything?"

My normal, happy self, which had turned to a vengeful, murderous self, has changed again, this time to a crazy, idiot self.

I'm devolving.

And I'm more or less hanging upside down. So, I'm devolving and humiliated. But the humiliation is short-lived. All of a sudden, Ronin lets go of me, dropping me to the ground. I land with a thud, taken by surprise and unable to break my fall.

Ronin is quick. He launches himself at Sullivan, like a bull. I half-expect steam to come out of his nose. But it happens quick. He gets to Ed in a couple of strides and grabs the barrel of the shotgun in one strong hand, lifting it upward, just as the thieving jerkface lets off a round.

The shot explodes with a huge noise, and I clap my hands over my ears. Ronin rips the gun out of Sullivan's hands and removes its shell. The thieving jerk goes after Ronin, but Ronin holds him back with one hand.

"I don't like being shot at," Ronin tells him, calmly.

Sullivan unsheathes a knife from his waistband and threatens Ronin by swatting the air in a wide arc. "How about being stabbed? You like that?" he yells.

With blinding speed, Ronin unarms him with one hand, pockets the knife, and does a ninja move on Ed's hand, forcing him to his knees. "Take it easy," Ronin says. "I'm not going to hurt you. But I don't want you to hurt me, either. Can we make a deal to just calm down? Truce?"

"What do you mean truce?" I ask, getting to my feet. "You have him where you want him!"

Ronin shoots me a terrifying look that makes me clamp my mouth closed and makes my forehead break out in a sweat. "I'm just saying it would be convenient," I squeak.

Ed Sullivan lobs another lugie, this time hitting Ronin's left boot. "I'm not making any deals with you!" he shouts. "The minute you leave, I'm going to track you down and make you suffer. I'm going to destroy everyone you love, everything you've worked for, and then I'm going to tear you down piece by piece until you wish you were dead."

Ronin turns toward me. "You were right. He's mean," he says.

I stand up and dust myself off. "I told you so. And he's on his best behavior. Usually he's worse."

"I was trying to play nice," Ronin tells Sullivan, still holding his hand in some kind of kung fu grip. "But you decided to go the hard route."

Ronin drops Sullivan's hand and marches toward me. "On the bike," he growls. He grabs me by my collar, pulling me the last few steps to the motorcycle. I hop on, and so does Ronin. This time, I'm not shy about scooting up all the way and wrapping my arms around his middle.

He starts the motorcycle and slowly makes a U-turn, still holding the shotgun in one hand. As soon as we're facing the right direction, he speeds off past Sullivan, who's shaking his fist at us like an old man in a cartoon who shouts at kids to get off his lawn. When we get a few feet past him, Ronin throws the shotgun away, hitting a tree.

I hold on for dear life, as we speed onto the main road. "I have no idea where I'm going," he yells, but he doesn't slow down.

"Two miles down," I yell against the wind. "The Flat Iron Ranch."

It dawns on me that I'm bringing a killer home. Well, he's not much of a killer. Killers don't normally throw away a perfectly good gun or pocket a knife without using them. Orgasm or no orgasm, I picked a real dud of a hired assassin.

I hope he doesn't think he's getting any money for his pitiful performance. Not even gas money. If I were honest with myself, I'd say I'm relieved he didn't actually murder Sullivan, but he could have at least scared him more. Broken his resolve to take our land. Scared him off, made him want to finally leave us alone. Ronin failed on every level. Instead of scaring him, he only made him mad.

We turn onto the dirt road that leads to our ranch. We pass through a wood gate with a picture of a flat iron on it. I never understood the name, but the land has been in our family for over a century, and it's always been the Flat Iron Ranch.

We race down the dirt road until I see our house. It started off as a typical ranch house a hundred years ago, but succeeding generations have added their touches to it. An extra floor here. Another wing there. The result is a large, sprawling compound, which I love. I never want to live anywhere else.

Ronin parks his motorcycle near the front door. I climb

off and hand him his helmet. "Well, I can't say it was nice meeting you," I say. "Nothing personal, but you're the worst killer in the world. If they give killers licenses, yours should be revoked."

Ronin furrows his brow and studies my face, as if he expects something to fly out of my mouth. "Fiona, I'm going to explain this to you one more time in case somewhere in your brain there's a modicum of intelligence and a little less loony bin. I'm not a killer. Not a hired killer in any case. I do do favors for people. I get people out of jams. And yes, I've had quite a bit of military training. But I'm not an assassin for hire, and I don't go around killing people who beautiful girls don't like. No matter how beautiful they are."

Beautiful? I giggle and flip my hair. Ronin is extremely attractive. I've never been in such close proximity to such a good-looking man before. And it's not just his looks. He emits something that revs my endorphins, no matter how pissed off I am.

"You're a liar. I can understand that the thieving jerkface scared you, but there's no need to lie. Let's just call it a day.

Pretend we never met. You go your way, and I'll go mine."

I open the door and slam it closed behind me. I throw my purse on the table just inside and march to the kitchen, where my parents are.

"I've had a terrible day," I announce.

My father looks up from making himself a sandwich. "Who the hell did you bring home?" he asks.

"What do you mean?" I turn around. Ronin is standing larger-than-life in the kitchen. His leather clad upper torso seems to go on forever… stretching from Mom's "Bless this mess" sign on one wall to Dad's collection of nineteenth century farming tools on another. Our kitchen has never looked quite so sexy.

"What are you doing here?" I ask.

He puts his hands on his hips, banging one elbow on the "Bless this mess" sign. "I'm not done with you."

# CHAPTER 4

Ronin is a very good-looking bull in our dilapidated china shop. His head almost touches the kitchen's ceiling. And he's massive. Wide. His chest goes on forever, and the sleeves of his leather jacket are bursting from the pressure of his muscled arms.

He's bigger in the house than he was outside or in the truck stop. Either that, or I'm just now really noticing him. It's so odd to see him in my kitchen that I'm paralyzed with surprise. Totally forgotten is the fact that he's a hired killer and a failed one.

He's completely out of place. Our house is decorated in "eclectic worn". Thirty year old couches next to homemade, wood end tables, Tiffany lamps, and ceramic crafted ashtrays. Not that anybody smokes. They're usually used for pistachio shells or gum wrappers.

"You invited a motorcycle gang member to the house, Fiona?" my mother asks, giving him the once-over.

My mother Valentina is a beauty. She's one of those freak women who's gorgeous at fifty-five with no makeup. And she never wears makeup. Her long, thick red hair is usually pulled back in a single braid, and she makes all of her own clothes. Since she's a terrible seamstress, she usually winds up making a muumuu, which she belts at the waist with a huge assortment of belts, more often than not a utility belt.

She's a dynamo with a tool, and she handles most of the repairs on the ranch. Whether it's a fence or the diesel generator, if it's broken on our ranch, you'll probably find a beautiful middle-aged woman in a muumuu and utility belt fixing it.

"He's not a gangster. He's a cop," my father says, adjusting his underwear. Dad doesn't believe in wearing pants in the house. The minute he walks inside, he strips down to his tighty whities and a T-shirt.

Ronin stares at him a moment, and then his focus shifts to

the house. The kitchen, the breakfast nook, the family room. I can't imagine what he's thinking.

"I'm not a gangster or a cop," he says, quietly.

"I know a cop when I see one. I used to eat breakfast every Tuesday with three Esperanza cops. I know cops. I bet you're an over-easy, man, too," my father says, hopping on his heels, excited like he's discovered penicillin.

"Scrambled," Ronin corrects him, his voice low in his throat. My mother sighs and clutches at her chest. I take a step back, in an attempt to get out of range of Ronin's cloud of whatever he's emitting. Whatever it is, it's got my mouth dry and my eyelids sticky. I'm wondering if he's packing a biological weapon.

I'm pretty sure he is.

"So who are you?" my mom croaks.

"He's with me," I say, finding my voice. "He's—"

"Fiona's friend," Ronin interrupts me.

My mother takes a few steps closer to Ronin and inspects him, as if she's searching for the fine print. "What kind of friend?"

"I wouldn't exactly say friend. He's a… well…" I don't know what to say. My family has been actively trying to stop Sullivan, but I'm not sure how they would react to me hiring a killer. It could go either way. I mean, the guy deserves it, but I suppose if they wanted him dead, they could have always burned down his house with all the gasoline we have lying around the ranch.

Burning down his house. Why didn't I think of that before? That would be a lot cheaper than hiring a killer.

"A what? What is he?" my mother asks, poking him in the belly.

"A friend," Ronin says. "A special friend."

He walks around my mother and takes three steps toward me. There's a look of determination on his face that I haven't seen before, and if I'm not mistaken, he's smirking. "What? Huh? Um…" I trip backward until I bump into a cabinet, bruising my ass. Ronin doesn't stop until we're nose to nose—or actually nose to belly button.

"A special friend," he repeats, tracing a line down the side of my face with his finger.

"Oh," I breathe. His light touch is even more effective than his motorcycle's vibrations. I've never been this excited in the kitchen. Not even when I made homemade candy for the first time.

It occurs to me in a distant, under-the-influence kind of way that we're the center of attention, that my parents are focused entirely on us. And why wouldn't they be focused on us? Their virgin daughter is getting felt up by a biker god in their antiquated kitchen.

"Valentina, I think our baby girl is affianced," my father says. "Maybe I should put on pants for this."

My father hasn't put on pants in the house since Grandma died. The thought sobers me up enough to become aware of my surroundings beyond Ronin. I sidestep him just in time to see my sisters walk in.

Olivia and Viola are Irish twins with long red hair like my mother. Olivia is a devotee of cowboy chic, and Viola goes more for the Dolly Parton look. Both of them work the ranch with my father, handling the cattle.

"We're back!" Olivia announces. "It was our biggest shopping trip ever, and we only spent three dollars!"

Olivia and Viola stop dead at the kitchen entrance when they get an eyeful of Ronin. "Why's a cop here?" Viola asks.

"He's Fiona's special friend," Mom says.

"Special friend?" Viola and Olivia ask in unison.

Mom nods. "Dad was thinking of putting on pants."

Viola and Olivia gasp. I'm getting more than tired of being the center of attention.

"Did you bring me my diet meal?" my dad demands, forgetting about the pants.

Viola hands him a large McDonalds bag. "Right here."

Dad grabs it from her and swings the bag in front of Ronin's face. "McDonalds diet. I've lost thirty-five pounds in three months. And nobody gets tired of a Big Mac. God's food."

Ronin nods and glances at me.

"He had a heart attack, and his doctor said he has to lose weight," I explain.

"Where have you been hiding your special friend?" Viola asks me.

"I thought I had gotten rid of him, but he's like mold."

Viola's widens her eyes until she looks like a character in Japanese anime. "Your special friend is a stalker?"

"I'm not a stalker," Ronin rumbles, making the females in the house take a step toward him.

"Do you want me to kick him out?" Dad asks. "Give me a minute to finish my fries and put on my pants. Valentina, where's my pants?"

"I'm not a stalker," Ronin repeats.

"I had a stalker once," Olivia says, taking a seat on a barstool near Ronin. "He didn't look like you, though. Much shorter with a really big nose. Long like Pinocchio. And his name was Leslie. Is your name Leslie?"

"His name's Ronin, and he's not a stalker."

Dad sits at the kitchen table and spreads out his fast food. "Are you a samurai?"

"Uh, no," Ronin says.

"Ronin what? Are you Bulgarian? You look Bulgarian," my mother says.

"Just Ronin. And I don't think I'm Bulgarian."

"One name like Cher or Madonna?" Viola asks him.

"Nothing like Cher or Madonna," he says.

"Like a cop?" Olivia asks.

"I told you so!" Dad yells through a mouthful of fries.

"I'm not a cop."

"Oh my God, I'm late with the muffins." I make a beeline for the pantry and take out the flour and sugar.

I measure out the ingredients on the counter. I fall into a familiar rhythm, almost a fugue state. This is my zone. My form of meditation. I started baking when I was four years old, even before I learned to tie my shoes. I taught myself to bake with old cookbooks and boxes of recipes I found in the attic. I think some of the recipes date back to the invention of the pen, probably left by my great-grandmother or maybe her mother.

When I discovered the magic of yeast, I made so many cinnamon buns that I gained forty pounds in two months. I decided right then and there at the tender age of twelve to start my own business and help my family financially, but instead of making myself fat, I've fattened up half the population of Esperanza. Sometimes I partner up with Raine Harper, who's a caterer in town. She cooks, and I bake.

"Are you strong, Ronin? You look strong," Olivia notes. "Care to help me with the groceries? I did a six-carter this time. Huge haul!"

"Sure. Come on, friend." I'm just about to turn the mixer on when Ronin grabs my hand and pulls me out of the kitchen.

My sisters follow us outside, obviously thinking that we're going to help them with the groceries.

"Let go! I have muffins to make!" I shout, pulling against him. But Olivia is right; Ronin is strong. He's got a fistful of what's left of my dress, and he's not letting go. I swing my arms wildly, trying to hit him with my wood spoon and kick, but he stays out of reach. I only mange to flick muffin batter on his leather jacket. I'm not exactly Buffy the Vampire Slayer. I'm more like Betty Crocker on a slow day.

"Damned mesomorphs!" I yell.

"I've got sixty-two bottles of laundry detergent," Olivia announces happily, opening the truck's tailgate. "So glad we have an extra pair of hands to lug it upstairs."

"What the—" Ronin starts, seeing Olivia's stash.

"She's an extreme couponer," I explain, finally pulling away from him in his moment of confusion.

"An extreme what?"

"Couponer," Olivia announces. "I got three hundred tubes of toothpaste, and guess how much it cost me?"

Ronin stares at her. "You have to guess," I tell him. "She won't move on until you guess."

Ronin pushes up his sleeve and pinches his arm. "Yep, I'm awake," he says. "I don't know. Two hundred dollars?" he guesses.

"Nope! Guess again," Olivia says, hopping on her heels, delighted that he guessed high. She's been an extreme couponer for two years, and I don't see an end in sight. She used to be a compulsive gambler, but free antiperspirant gives her a much bigger high than any poker game in Vegas.

"Three hundred dollars?"

Olivia explodes with laughter. "You'll never guess! You'll never guess! You're way off."

Ronin hangs his head and puts his hands on his hips. "Give it to him, Olivia," I say. "He's about to blow. Not that that means much. He's a lot of bark, if you know what I mean."

"A dollar fifty!" Olivia announces, triumphantly.

Ronin's head snaps up. Impressed. It's the rush of a bargain. Nobody's immune. "Three hundred tubes of toothpaste for a buck fifty?" he asks.

"I'm never paying for groceries again," Olivia says, smiling. "This one insists on buying fresh, though," she says, pointing at me.

I wag my finger at her. "I don't tell you how to handle steer, and you don't tell me how to handle baked goods."

"What steer? We've been rustled down to nothing."

"Cattle rustling?" Ronin asks. "Like in the Wild West?"

Viola grabs a couple bottles of laundry detergent. "Are we doing this or what? Why is everyone just standing around? Fiona, did you do something to your dress?"

Olivia skips over to the truck and picks up a couple bags of groceries, but Ronin grabs my hand and pulls me in the other direction. He clamps his hands on my shoulders and faces me, leaning down to get right in my face.

"I've decided to help you."

"You have?" I ask. "You're going to kill Ed Sullivan? Should we go back to the truck stop and buy the gun?"

"No. No guns. But I think he needs some comeuppance."

"You're going to beat him to death? It's too bad you didn't think about that earlier. Just think how you could have beaten him to death with his own shotgun!"

"No, Fiona. No death. No killing. There are other ways to get justice."

His eyes are dark and bore through me. I wonder if he's

playing chicken with his eyes. Well, if he is, he wins, because I can't keep his gaze. It makes my throat close and my uterus spasm. I stare at his nose, instead. It's perfectly proportioned and as straight as a razor, but it doesn't make my airways close.

"There's kerosene in the barn," I say. "It would be pretty easy to set him on fire."

"I'm trying real hard to go with my gut that you're a nice girl in a bad situation instead of the other thing."

"What other thing?"

"That you're a psycho."

I punch his chest, and he doesn't flinch. "Psychos are crazy, Ronin."

"I know."

# CHAPTER 5

"This isn't my normal way to make deliveries," I shout above the roar of Ronin's motorcycle. He doesn't reply, as usual. It's like talking to a mime. I'm half-convinced I've had a psychotic break and have developed an imaginary friend. But I'm not exactly a creative person, and if I created an imaginary friend, he wouldn't be a gorgeous, muscled monster with a kickass bike. I'm just not that clever. I mean, creating Ronin… that's genius.

"Do you have to pay taxes per word?" I shout. "Is that why you don't speak? I can loan you some money if you want to communicate."

Nothing. Nada.

I'm sixty-percent certain I've been abducted. I'm not totally sure, but there's a pretty good chance I'm going to wind up sold to a biker gang in Sausalito or a suicide cult in Albuquerque. The only thing that's got me doubting that I'm Patty Hearst in discount shoes is that I've got a backpack full of muffins. Kidnapping victims seldom get to bring homemade baked goods with them.

But it was a hell of a fight to bring the muffins. Ronin said that time was ticking away, and we needed to get going.

"Going where? Ticking away to where?" I asked, gesturing with my wood spoon.

He didn't answer, of course. To his credit, he helped Olivia and Viola with their half-ton of cheap non-perishables, organizing them neatly in Olivia's stash in three rooms of the house. While he was busy with that, I quickly prepared the crumble muffins.

But then Ronin was back and urging me to leave. I held him off for a little while. "I have to finish the muffins. You don't want to let down the PTA. They're vicious. They'll cut you."

It was a fight, a disagreement between us that lasted until

the muffins finished baking and cooling afterward. And then he allowed me enough time to bag them up and put them in a backpack but not enough time to change my clothes.

I still look like a castaway who forgot to shave her legs this week.

Wherever we're going, we're going by way of Josephine Farrell's house. President of the PTA, Josephine is not a person to trifle with, and she's not going to be pleased that I'm lugging tomorrow morning's treats in a backpack.

I always come through for my clients, unless I have a contagious disease. So hired killer or no, since I don't have a fever, the PTA is going to get its muffins.

"You didn't make the turn," I shout. Ronin ignores me as usual. Instead, he pushes the motorcycle faster down the road. "Josephine lives back there," I say, tugging at his back. "Turn around."

"No time," he shouts back, finally. "Josephine will have to wait."

"What do you mean? Turn it around!"

"No time. Sit back and hold on tight."

Now I'm eighty-percent sure I'm being abducted. I tug at his back, again, but he ignores me. I look down at the road's yellow dotted line as we speed past, even faster now that we're on the highway.

I contemplate my escape. How to jump off a moving motorcycle without getting skinned alive on the blacktop? Is it even possible? Perhaps if I tuck my legs under me, I could sort of roll off the bike and land safely. It sounds like a better plan than letting a killer-for-hire kidnap me.

Decided, I adjust my body to better swing my leg over, all the while gripping on to Ronin's jacket for dear life. "What are you doing? You're going to fall," he shouts at me.

"I have to deliver the muffins," I explain, scooting backward, slightly.

"What the hell?"

It's a tug of war with me the prize, and he wins. Never slowing the motorcycle and deftly fending off my one-handed slaps, he manages to pull me close and pins my hands in front of him.

"I wish you could have been half this aggressive with the jerkface lying bastard," I mutter. But he doesn't hear me, or he ignores me as usual, and he doesn't stop the motorcycle until we're an hour out of town, up in the mountains, at a security shack with two guards dressed in black combat uniforms and mirrored sunglasses.

Ronin says a couple of words to them, and they nod. It's obvious that he's in charge. The guards don't give me a second look, which makes me wonder how common abducted girls in ripped dresses are around here.

Ronin drives slowly up the path and through what looks like a military compound of barracks.

"Are you a marine?" I ask him.

"Army. Retired."

"You're kind of young to be retired."

There are no army bases near Esperanza, and I wonder if he's brought me to some secret government location. Like the Gitmo of the west. Maybe he's abducting me to torture me and get secrets out of me.

But the only secrets I have are about the yeast in cinnamon buns and how not to bake cookies too long. I'd gladly divulge those secrets without any torture.

The compound consists of three long rows of squat, trailer-like buildings and one square one at the end. Men in fatigues and regular street clothes walk in and out of the buildings. They nod at Ronin as we drive past, but they don't salute.

Ronin drives to the small square building at the edge of the complex and parks the motorcycle in front. He hops off, and helps me off, as well.

"Is this it?" I ask.

"This is it."

"The end of the road." I sneak a glance around, trying to find an escape route, but there's nothing but mountains around the compound, and it's doubtful with all the security that I could get out.

I could use the motorcycle, if I had the key. And if I knew how to drive a motorcycle.

Ronin looks down at his boots. "Yes. Literally the end of the road. Come on inside. I have work to do."

I stomp my gold flat on the ground and cross my arms. "I'm not going in there with you. Look, you can't just go around kidnapping women. You were too good to kill an ogre like Sullivan, but it's fine to kidnap me and drag me out to some prison farm? Nuh uh. Nope. I don't think so. Take me home."

Ronin raises an eyebrow until it almost disappears into his hairline. "Fiona Jones, you're the nuttiest woman I've ever met. Fruit loops. Did you forget to take your meds today?"

"What does that mean?"

"Come on," Ronin says, sighing. He opens the front door for me. I sneak a peek inside. It's standard linoleum and white walls with no frills desks and topographical maps on the walls. No torture devices, as much as I could see. "Go on. I'll feed you."

At the thought of food, I remember the PTA and grow angry again. "I need to deliver the muffins."

Ronin leans in close, and I smell his cinnamon sugar breath. "I promise to take good care of your muffins and I promise that they'll be delivered before the PTA meeting tomorrow."

"It's not a meeting. It's an event."

"The event," he says, correcting himself.

"So, you're not abducting me?"

"We're here to figure out how to handle your neighbor, Mr. Sullivan."

I slap his arm. "Is that why we're here? Why didn't you tell me before? Great! Let's start brainstorming. Do you have drones?"

*

But we don't figure out how to handle my neighbor. We don't strategize or come up with a plan. In fact, *we* don't do anything. The minute we enter, men come rushing at us, hanging on Ronin's every word. He barks orders at them, one after the other, and somehow, one of those orders is to get me away from him.

Two young men, dressed in black fatigue pants, black boots, and black turtlenecks usher me out of the room with a polite but firm "right this way, ma'am," and before I can think to refuse or at least ask Ronin what's going on, I find myself wedged between them, as we walk down the hallway and out the back door to another building and a room filled with supplies.

"What size are you, ma'am?" one of the men asks me. He's tall—about six foot four—but not as tall or as scary as Ronin. He has blond hair, and his colleague has black hair.

"It's not polite to ask a woman her size," I say. I'm a size ten. I tried for years to get to a size eight, but it was way too much trouble, and I wasn't allowed to eat baked goods, which is a deal-breaker, as far as I'm concerned.

The blond scans my body and grabs some clothes and a pair of boots from off the shelves and hands them to me. "You can change in there," he says, pointing toward a door. The clothes and boots are just like theirs. Commando.

Black isn't really my color, but I decide not to argue. Besides, I'm tired of wearing a torn dress, and being a commando with steel-toed boots sounds cool to me.

The clothes fit perfectly, and I feel tough and in control in them, much better than in a floral dress and gold flats. I check myself out in a small mirror on the wall of my changing room. I look the part. All I need is a beret and mirrored sunglasses, and I could be the star of any World War Two movie. I make my hands into a gun and do the James Bond pose, shooting myself in the mirror and then blowing at the tips of my fingers.

"So cool," I tell myself in the mirror. I should dress like this all the time. My toes have plenty of room in the boots, and the laced tops support my ankles. They would be perfect for the long hours of standing I have to do for my job.

"Do you think I can keep the boots?" I ask the two soldiers, when I leave the changing room. "And can I get sunglasses like yours?"

They exchange looks with each other. "I don't know, ma'am," the dark-haired one says. "I got these at Target."

"Oh." It was disappointing and it kind of broke the whole commando spell. They must have caught on to my disillusionment because the blond quickly jumps in about the rest of the gear.

"All special ops," he says, and the other one nods in agreement. I cock my head to the side, pretty sure that the whole ensemble was really bought on sale at Target.

"Show her the night vision gear," the dark-haired one tells the other.

They scramble, retrieving clothes, gear, and weapons to show me. It's a parade of warfare. Show-n-tell with a military theme. While they show off their supplies, they tell me a little about Ronin's operation. They're a kind of mercenary outfit. Technicians. Consultants. They don't give me too many details about Ronin, though, just that he's the boss and can do no wrong.

"This is the coolest thing ever," I say, slipping the night vision goggles on my face. I'm decked out in a Kevlar vest, the goggles, and a machine gun. "Take a picture of me," I urge them. "I wish I had Instagram. Get my left side. It's my best side. Should I scowl or smile?"

The dark-haired soldier pulls out an iPhone from his pocket and gets me into frame. I decide to smile, and he takes the photo. After he forwards it to my email, we play around with other poses. My favorite is my Rambo pose, squatting on the counter with a belt of bullets around my neck and clutching two machine guns in my hands.

I yell out a war cry, and he takes the picture. We all crack up, which makes me inadvertently grasp one of the guns too hard and shoot off a few rounds into the ceiling.

Guns are loud. Machine guns are really loud. And they have a kick. I've never shot a gun until now, and the shock of it keeps my finger securely clamped on the trigger, and I watch as the gun spits out bullets in a wide arc above me. It's just a matter of seconds before it's going to spin around and kill my companions.

Luckily, they're professionals and manage to at once tackle me and rip the gun out of my hand. With the gun securely out of my reach, we land in a heap on the ground. The blond is lying across my legs, and my upper body is lying on top of the dark-haired one. The gunshots don't go unnoticed. A half dozen commandos rush into the room, ready to take on whatever terrorist has invaded their compound. Ronin is the first one through the door, a pistol raised in his hand, and a look of murderous determination on his face, which changes to complete disbelief when he sees me lying on the floor.

*

"I'm not speaking to you," I say, grabbing a pork chop off a platter and slapping it down on my plate. Ronin and I are sitting at a small table in a bedroom in the compound. "This is quite a spread."

"I thought you weren't talking to me," he says, spooning mashed potatoes onto his plate.

"I was talking about food. It's different." It's a lot of food, and I'm ravenous. I'm a good eater, but Ronin blows me out of the water, eating enough to choke a horse. "I don't see why we couldn't have eaten with the others in the cafeteria."

"It's called a mess, and no way am I letting you close to my men again. You're a danger."

"They like me."

"They're just grateful you didn't shoot them, and they're grateful I didn't fire them."

I wag my fork at him. "You yelled at them enough." But he didn't yell at me. Instead, he was nonplussed. He had no words. He helped me up and carefully removed the bullets and weapons from me.

I noticed that his mouth turned up in the tiniest of smiles

right before he let his soldiers have it for giving a guest hardcore military-grade weaponry. Then, after he finished barking orders at everyone, playing with his computer, and making a series of phone calls, he ushered me into this room for dinner.

"They work for me. If they don't do a good job, I yell at them," he explains, shoveling more food into his mouth. His appetite spurs mine, and we're eating quickly, as if we're contestants in an eating contest.

Then, suddenly, the food is gone, and Ronin and I are left with our forks in our hands, staring first at our empty plates and then at each other.

His brown eyes grow big and dark, and a heavy curtain of tension falls between us. "Lordy," I say, taking a big gulp of air. But the air is filled with hormones that I have no experience with, and I cough.

Ronin has stopped blinking and so have I. I'm not exactly sure what's going on, but my pelvis seems to be fairly certain. It's pulsating, like it's Saturday night at the club. And maybe it is.

Maybe it's party time. Maybe it's finally time for Fiona to let her freak flag fly.

But I'm not totally sure what a freak flag is, let alone how to fly it.

Ronin's eyes tell me that he is very familiar with freak, and he's an expert flier. "I may kiss you, Fiona Harper," he says. His voice is deep and smooth like velvet.

Yum.

"Kiss me?"

"Yes. God help me."

Ronin places his fork gently on his plate and takes my hand in his. An electric current zings its way through my body, like a high speed train. "Are you going use your tongue?" I ask.

"Excuse me?"

"Your tongue when you kiss me. Are you going to use it?"

Ronin has been massaging my palm with his thumb, but he

stops. "Uh, well, I was planning on it. Yes. Why do you ask?"

"I've never kissed with tongue," I explain. "I've never really kissed at all."

"I have a feeling you'll be a quick learner."

"You think so?"

He doesn't answer. Instead, he stands, pulling me up by my hand. He steps around the table and pulls me against him, wrapping his arms around me. I can feel all of him pressed up against me, and he feels wonderful.

"You're hugging me," I giggle, breathlessly. It's much better than Nora Roberts ever described. A drop dead gorgeous man in perfect condition pressing his body against mine. His desire oozing out of his pores and changing the atomic makeup of the air.

It's so good, and it makes my body react in a new, delicious way that I never imagined before.

But he doesn't stop there. His head dips down, and he captures my lips with his. They're warm and soft, surrounded by rough stubble. I close my eyes and lean into him. I'm in an altered state, my identity changed in an instant from Fiona Jones to another being altogether. Something sexual and sure.

Pleasure will do that. Chemistry. More powerful than any drug. Better than science fiction or magic.

Ronin opens his mouth slightly and slips his tongue into my mouth. He was right. I'm a quick learner. My tongue greets his, and our kiss deepens. My arms wrap around his waist.

I never want to stop kissing Ronin. I wonder if all kisses are this good, or if he's particularly talented. Luckily, Ronin doesn't seem to be in any hurry to stop, either, and we continue until my lips are chapped and my breath depleted.

We pull away at the same time, but we continue to hold each other. I rest my head against his chest, listening to his heart pound. Mine's going at a pretty good clip, too.

"Kissing is much better than I thought," I say. "Is sex as good as that?"

"No," he says. "I mean, usually sex is much better than kissing. But that was over the top kissing."

I step back out of his embrace. His face is red, and his lips are swollen. "I thought so," I say. "It wasn't normal lips to lips, even with the added tongue."

"No, it wasn't."

I scratch my head. "I wonder why."

Ronin raises an eyebrow, which could mean that he knows why or doesn't. In any case, he's careful not to touch me again because he doesn't want to "fly into the Bermuda Triangle," he explains. He points me toward the bed and orders me to sleep. I argue with him briefly about going home and getting to work against Ed Sullivan, but he assures me that we'll implement a plan in the morning.

The bed is small and narrow with a thin blanket and tiny pillow. Still, in my exhaustion, it looks wonderful. "Well, if we're going to implement the plan in the morning," I say, getting into the bed. I turn on my side and immediately begin to drift off. The last thing I see before I fall asleep is Ronin sitting on a straight-backed chair, his legs outstretched and his arms crossed in front of him. He watches me with a look of consternation on his face and something else: Determination.

*

I don't dream. Normally, my sleep is filled with dreams, but not tonight. Perhaps my unconscious feels helpless to create anything more dreamy than my first real kiss. I don't even possess the ability to replay it in my mind.

So I sleep deep with my mind resting in darkness. But ranchers' daughters are used to getting up early, and they wake up to small noises, in case something needs to be handled. That's why I woke from my deep sleep when Ronin clicked the door closed behind him, as he snuck out without me.

# CHAPTER 6

I grab my boots and open the door as quietly as I can. Crouching down, I see Ronin's feet at the end of the hall, as he turns the corner toward the front door. I pad out in my socks, trotting after him.

Cracking open the front door, I see Ronin get into a small black van. I drop to all fours and crawl out to the van and open its back doors just enough to squeeze through as the engine starts up. I hop in and carefully close the doors as the van takes off through the compound.

I put my boots on and try not to make noise as I bounce around the back of the van. There are no windows, so I can't see out, but we drive along a bumpy road for a while and then it turns smooth. We're on the main highway, I assume.

The inside of the van is stocked with military gear. All black and high-tech. There's a lot of money behind Ronin's outfit, whatever it is. I don't think he's a hired killer, but a hired soldier is close.

I have no idea where Ronin is going, but I'm pissed off that his priorities are with some other job and not mine. I don't want to let my family down. If we don't do something, Sullivan is going to gobble up our ranch and then what will become of my family?

They only know ranching. It's who they are, their identity. I feel responsible to help them, to save them, and I'll do whatever it takes to do that. Without me, what will they do?

We drive for a long time, and I doze on and off, but finally Ronin stops the van. I hear him drive it up onto the side of the road and park. I take two breaths and then as quietly as I can, open the back door. I crouch down and run for the trees and hide behind one.

From my vantage point, I see Ronin open the car door and

get out. He looks left and right, adjusts his belt, and walks into the tree line a little ways away from me.

I can't believe that I've outsmarted the big mercenary commando guy. I feel like a real hot shit. Perhaps I should take up soldiering. I wonder if it pays more than muffins.

I'm all about stealth while I follow him. He has no idea that I'm there. It's pretty dark, but I know where we are. We were just here this morning. We're on the road on Ed Sullivan's property. Ronin has snuck back here without telling me, ready to take on my evil neighbor. I take back everything I was thinking about Ronin. His priorities are in the right place, and by the right place I mean, with me.

We walk for about five minutes, and we're almost to the main house and out of the safety of the trees, when Ronin stops in his tracks. I stop, too. Without turning around, Ronin says, "What the hell do you think you're doing?"

At first, I think he's talking to someone else. But as far as I can tell, there isn't anyone else. We're the only ones out in the woods in the middle of the night. Nevertheless, I freeze in place and don't say a word.

"Well? What the hell are you doing, Fiona Jones?"

I look around stupidly for a place to hide. I think about running away, but I'm in the right, and there's no reason to run. Ronin should have taken me with him, if he's going to kill my neighbor. After all, it was my idea.

"What am I doing here? What are *you* doing here?" I demand with my hands on my hips in my best elementary school teacher impression.

Ronin turns around to face me. "I'm doing my job. You're getting in my way. Go back to the van and wait for me." He says the last part with an imperious tone, as if he's used to being obeyed but has the sneaking suspicion that he won't be on this occasion. Boy, is he perceptive.

"Nuh uh," I say, shaking my head. "You can't kill him without me here."

"I'm not going to kill him, crazy lady. I don't just kill people because they're mean or annoying. If I did that, the whole world would be dead, including you. In fact, you would be the first one to go. You would be dead and buried in a heartbeat, that is, if anyone cared enough to bury you."

"Is that the way you talk to a woman after you stick your tongue in her mouth?"

Ronin throws his hands up in the air. "No! None of this makes any sense. Don't you get that? I shouldn't be kissing you. I shouldn't be on this man's property. But there you go. I'm helping you out. For some reason I'm attracted to you. And for some reason I give a damn if you get shot by this guy. So, go back to the van and wait for me. Besides, why would you want to be with me while I kill a man? Is that some kind of sick fantasy of yours?"

I kick at the ground and look away. There's an awkward silence while I pretend I'm not there. "I see," Ronin says, catching on to my frame of mind. "You don't want me to kill him."

"Yes I do!"

"No, you don't. You want this problem to go away, and that's what you thought needed to happen, but you don't want him dead. You would have stopped me. You wanted to make sure I didn't do it." He looks up at the sky and takes a deep breath. "Well, that's a relief. At least you're not a psychopath."

"Psychopath? I'm not the one with my own army."

"Go back to the van."

"Nope. I'm going with you. I can help."

"You don't even know why I'm here."

He has a point. I have no idea why he's here. "I do too know why you're here. And you need my help."

Ronin takes two steps forward and leans in. Even in the dark, I can see the disapproving, disbelieving expression on his face.

"Okay. I have no idea why you're here. But I got this far. I can help you."

"I'm doing reconnaissance work."

I nod. "And if I knew what that was, I could help you."

He grabs hold of the front of my shirt and pulls me, as he continues walking toward the house. "Just stay quiet and out of the way," he hisses.

We walk to the edge of the trees and stop. "What are we waiting for?" I ask.

Ronin slaps his hand over my mouth. "Shh!"

He stares out into the darkness. It's completely quiet. It's clear that nobody's around. After a minute, he grabs my shirt again and pulls me behind him. We don't approach the house, as I thought we would. Instead, we walk around the perimeter of the property.

The ranch looks very different than how I remembered it. There's no sign that it's a ranching operation, anymore. No animals. Instead of the normal machinery and vehicles one would see at a ranch, there are big industrial machines that have no place here.

"This isn't right," I whisper to Ronin.

"I know. But it's what I expected."

He pulls out a tiny camera and takes some shots of the machinery. Then, we continue to scout the rest of the property. There's machinery everywhere, and the ground is dug up.

"This is the pond that I used to sneak over to swim in," I explain to Ronin, as we stand on the ridge over it. "But it's not the same."

I don't know if he's listening to me. He's busy taking lots of pictures. "Ronin, I think I know what this is. I know what Ed Sullivan is doing."

"We better get going," Ronin says. "They're not going to like us being here. They're going to want to make us disappear."

We walked down the hill from the pond, but it's too late. Two trucks are racing toward us from the direction of the house with their bright lights lighting us up. "I'm thinking this isn't good," I say.

He grabs my hand, and we run at a breakneck pace. I'm a baker, and the only exercise I normally get is beating egg whites. But Ronin could win a gold medal in track. I stumble as we run, trying to keep up with him. But he doesn't leave me behind. He helps me up over and over and we continue to run.

No matter how fast we go, whoever's in the trucks has seen us, and there's no way we can outrun them. Within a couple minutes, they block our path. An arm pokes out of the truck's open window and shoots a bullet into the air, effectively stopping us in our tracks.

"You can shoot them or ninja their ass, right?" I ask Ronin.

"Just don't say a word. Okay?"

I don't see how me not talking is going to help matters, and I wonder why Ronin isn't shooting up the place so we can escape. Besides his miraculous tongue, Ronin has been a dud all the way around.

"You couldn't leave well enough alone, you stupid girl."

I'd recognize the voice anywhere. It's the jerkface, lying bastard asshole cattle rustler, who wants to destroy my family and take their land. Ed Sullivan steps out of his truck with a shotgun in his hand. He's not alone this time. He's brought along five goons. They're all dressed badly, with bed heads and unshaved faces.

They don't look friendly.

"I know what you're doing here," I shout at him. "It's totally illegal. And I'm going to call the cops."

Ronin slaps his forehead and looks down at the ground.

"That's a shame, little girl," Sullivan growls. "If you were just dumb like your family, I could have let you go."

I shoot a look at Ronin, and he nods. "Yeah. I told you to not say a word," he says.

"Oh," I say.

While Sullivan has the shotgun aimed at us, the other five

guys approach us, like coyotes going in for the kill. I bite a fingernail and try to figure out an escape route. What would James Bond do?

But it turns out that James Bond is next to me. As they approach, he takes out two men with his ninja moves. I cheer him on.

"Get 'em! Hit them where it hurts!"

"Run!" Ronin orders me. I take off running, but it's too late. Two of the men grab me and hold me down.

"You better stop, or I'll shoot her. I swear I will," Sullivan growls.

Ronin stops fighting, immediately, and Sullivan knocks him across the head with his gun. Ronin falls to the ground, unconscious.

I'm sure he's dead.

*

He isn't dead. I can see the rise and fall of his chest as he breathes. After they knocked him out, they hogtied him and threw us into a truck. Then, they locked us in a small utility building on the edge of the property.

Even though the building is no bigger than a shed, it has steel walls and a barred door. Inside are shelves of materials and bottles of chemicals, but as far as I can tell, no weapons to help me get out of my bindings. Ronin is lying on his belly on the floor with his limbs hogtied behind him. I'm slightly more comfortable, sitting with my hands and feet bound in front of me.

We've been this way for about twenty minutes. I've tried to wake up Ronin several times, but he's out cold. "You're supposed to save me," I hiss at him. "You've been a complete dud. Don't think I'm going to pay you one cent. You were supposed to kill *him*. He's not supposed to kill *you*."

Ronin groans, and his eyes flutter. "You're alive," I tell him.

"Thank you for the bulletin," he groans, again. "I can't

believe he coldcocked me."

"With the butt of his shotgun. You must have the hardest head on the planet. You're not even bleeding."

"I'm probably bleeding on the inside. That's the only bright side of this. I'll be dead in an hour."

"Are you joking or are you serious?" I ask.

He tugs at his bindings, moving his limbs, slightly. They've tied him very tight, and he can barely move an inch. But that doesn't seem to dissuade him. He moves parts of his body incrementally, like a break dancer in slow motion.

"You're not going to get out of that," I say.

"Your confidence in me is heartwarming, Fiona."

"Well, besides your skills at kissing, I don't think you have any other talents."

As the last word leaves my mouth, his left hand escapes from his bindings and then it's only a matter of seconds before he's out. He stands and looks down at me. "You were saying?"

"Okay. That was kind of cool."

He quickly frees me, and I rub my sore wrists. "Now what? You can get us out of here, right?" I ask him.

He ignores me as usual and inspects the door and the rest of the room.

"He's fracking, you know," I tell Ronin.

"Yes. I figured that out."

"Fracking is illegal around here. That's why he gobbled up the other ranches. He doesn't want anyone to know about it."

"Yes," Ronin repeats. "I figured that out."

"He might have polluted this whole area. He needs to be stopped. He could go to jail for it, or at least get a big fine."

Ronin continues to look for a way out. "Yes. I understand all of that. It'll be easy to stop his operation, if we get out of here alive."

"I have to get out of here. I have muffins to worry about."

"I haven't forgotten about your muffins."

"I have a business to run, you know. I can't let people down." My voice rises, and I realize that I'm beginning to panic. It's not just fear of the PTA that's got my anxiety up, but it's the reality that I may be dead in a few minutes that's freaking me out.

"I have a business to run, too. So, I understand." He finishes looking around, and stands next to me. "Do you want the good news or the bad news?"

"Can we skip the bad news altogether?"

"I don't think so."

"Okay. Give me that first." I close my eyes and flinch, my preferred way of getting bad news.

"The bad news is I can't get us out of here."

I bolt forward and grab two fistfuls of his shirt. "That's really bad news. I don't want to hear that kind of bad news."

I push him forward and he takes a few steps back until we're pushed against the shelves.

"There's good news too, remember?" he reminds me.

My hands drop, as I feel a wave of relief wash over me. "Oh, that's right. What's the good news?"

"We're not dead yet."

I slap the side of his head. "That's it? That's your good news? That's false advertising, buddy. False advertising." I pound his chest with each word. He grabs my hand and then lifts me up in his arms pulling me close to him.

"Are you done?"

"No."

"That's what I thought."

He sits down on the floor with me on his lap. His puts his arms around me, not so much in a hug but more to restrain me. Even imprisoned with the threat of death hanging over him, he still smells of cinnamon and sugar. And if I'm not mistaken, he's giving me a look of desire with his sexy eyes.

"Oh," I breathe.

Sufficiently calmed down, he takes one hand and caresses my head.

"What are you doing?" I ask him.

"Petting you."

"Like a dog?"

"No. Nothing like a dog."

"It feels good. You can keep doing it."

"Thank you."

The room grows warmer, and the threat of being murdered recedes into the background. I never thought that being petted could calm me so much, but maybe Ronin is as talented with petting as he is with kissing. Speaking of kissing…

"The longer we stay alive, the better our chances are to stay alive and escape," he explains, his voice soft and strong.

"Oh."

"Don't give up hope, yet."

"Will you tell me when I should give up hope?

"Sure," he says. His hand moves to my face. With one finger he caresses my forehead down to my cheek and then my lips. The room is definitely getting warmer, and so am I. In fact, I'm on fire.

"Maybe we should have a signal when you want to tell me."

"What kind of signal?"

"Well, I'm not an expert in these things," I say. "But may be you could kiss me. That could be the signal."

"That's a good idea. Maybe we should practice it, so we'll be ready when the time comes."

Without further discussion, he cradles my face in his hands and bends down, capturing my mouth with a ferocious need. This time, I'm an active participant, giving as much as I'm taking.

I get the rush of pleasure, but it's even more intensified. Perhaps because of the danger that we're in or perhaps it's just because Ronin is now more familiar. My body is reacting to his kiss, like a drug addict reacts to his next fix.

Since I don't know how many more kisses with Ronin will be in my future, there's a desperate need in the kiss. Pleasure, desire, and need. They combine in a Fourth of July, fireworks spectacular type of a kiss.

And Ronin has more tricks up his sleeve. As we continue to kiss, his hand dips down and cups my breast, and his thumb gently caresses my nipple through the material of my shirt. The electric current of pleasure rips through my body in an almost unbearable level.

The thought passes through my mind that I've missed out on this wonderful experience for so many years, and then the thought is quickly replaced with a worry that I'll never have this wonderful experience again.

Sure, I could probably scrape up another man in town to kiss me and perhaps even marry me, but it wouldn't be Ronin and something tells me that nobody else can compare.

Ronin puts one arm behind my head and moves so that I'm lying on the floor, my head on his arm, and his body on top of me. He holds most of his weight on his one forearm, but I love the feel of his long hard body on me.

Can this get any better?

My legs have a mind of their own. My knees lift up, allowing me to cradle Ronin's body between my legs. He moans, which has the surprising effect of increasing my arousal. I squirm underneath him and clench my legs around him.

And then Ronin surprises me.

He stops.

I open my eyes to find him staring intently at me. "What is

it?" I ask. "Did I do something wrong?"

"No, you're doing everything perfectly."

"Okay, so keep kissing me. And do that thing with your hand again. I really liked that."

"Fiona, I'm a man of great control, but we're going to have to stop or not stop. Do you understand what I'm talking about?" he asks. I purse my lips and try to kiss him, but his head is out of reach.

"No. I don't, but if I had to choose between stopping and not stopping, I think I'm going for the not stopping," I say.

"Normally, that would make me very happy, but I if I'm not mistaken, you've never done this before, and I'm not about to take your virginity on a concrete floor when the bad guys might walk in at any second. Besides, I don't have a condom."

"So, you're a hired killer who worries about safe sex?" I ask.

"I'm not a hired killer. I'm a former Army Ranger who

helps people. I'm a good guy."

I chew on the inside of my cheek. "A good guy with an STD?"

"No. A good guy who doesn't want to get you pregnant. Not yet, anyway."

At the "not yet" comment, I stop breathing. I forget to inhale until Ronin gets off me and helps me up. No matter how much I want to trip the horizontal light fantastic with him, I'm touched that he would like to make my first time more romantic than doing it on a concrete floor in a makeshift prison.

His timing is impeccable, too. As soon as we're standing, Ed Sullivan and two of his henchmen enter the room. Ronin pulls me behind him, but I peek out to see the action. They're surprised that we've escaped our binds, but not too surprised and not too concerned. They gesture with their guns for us to leave, and we walk outside.

"It isn't too late to turn yourself in," I tell Sullivan.

"You're a slow learner, Miss Jones," my criminal neighbor says.

"Mrs. Jenkins said I was her best student in third grade," I say.

They push us to walk faster, and I realize that we're heading for the pond, which once was clean and cool and offered me a lot of enjoyment on summer's days, but now was acting as a runoff pond for his fracking business. The water was probably now more lethal than a long weekend at Chernobyl.

"I have a bad feeling about this," I say.

"You think?" Ed Sullivan says.

"She has a point, you know," Ronin says. He's calm and cool as a cucumber. He doesn't seem to be at all worried about dying. "If you stop now, you just pay an environmental fine. Continue on, you add kidnapping and murder into the mix. Do you really want that?"

I notice that he's addressing his words not to Ed Sullivan,

but to his lowlife workers. It's a wise strategy. I can imagine that they're not being paid enough to risk a lifetime in prison or the death penalty.

But the ploy doesn't work. They don't even pause in walking us up to the ridge of the pond. "This is the way my life is going to end?" I ask. "I'm a virgin who's never traveled anywhere or done anything? That's just not fair. I've never even gotten a parking ticket. I've never howled at the moon."

"Calm down, Fiona," Ronin says. But I can't calm down. I'm on a roll. I might be having some kind of seizure or aneurysm.

"I've never run with the bulls in Pamplona or gotten a bikini wax," I continue. "I've never gone on a no-carb diet or gone to Sea World. Sure, I know about Blackfish and that it's cruel to keep orcas in a tank, but Sea World sells frozen bananas dipped in chocolate, and if you combine that with childlike entertainment, well, where else can you find it? I knew I should've had sex in the shed. Now I'll never have sex. I'll be a sexless corpse. I'll be dead with a highly underused vagina. Underused vagina! Underused vagina! Nobody's used my vagina!"

"I'll use your vagina," one of the goons offers, taking a step toward me.

"Nobody's going to use her vagina," Sullivan says. "I should have shot them when they first came on my property."

"I won't take long," the goon continues. "We've got hours before the sun comes up."

"I don't want you to use my vagina," I say. "I want him to use my vagina." All heads turn toward Ronin, and Ronin shrugs. "This is turning out to be a shitty day," I add.

"Stand them side-by-side," Sullivan instructs his men. I hold Ronin's hand, preparing myself to be shot in the back of the head and to be thrown into the toxic sludge. What a way to die. I wonder if my family will think I ran away or was abducted by Ronin. It doesn't matter now. I will have lungs full of slurry in a minute.

"I think my aneurysm is back," I tell Ronin. "I'm hearing things. A whirring noise."

“It’s not an aneurysm. It’s a helicopter.”

“What the hell?” Sullivan says, looking up. One look at the black attack helicopter makes his men run off. It looks like I might live to see Sea World.

“How did that happen?” I ask Ronin.

“Subdermal tracker,” he says showing me his arm. “They tracked me.”

“Like a dog?”

“Nothing like a dog.”

*

It’s just like D-Day, except without Tom Hanks. Men throw ropes down from the helicopter and shimmy down, ready to take on everyone. Within a matter of minutes, the entire Esperanza Sheriff’s Department is here and Ed Sullivan and his men are taken off to jail.

Somebody hands me a sandwich and a bottle of apple

juice, and I take a bite. Ronin is busy shouting orders and updating the Sheriffs. But he takes his time to see how I'm doing.

"Do you want the good news or the bad news?" I ask him when he finally gets back to my side.

"Is there ever good news with you?"

"The good news is that we're still alive," I say. "The bad news is I have thirteen minutes to get my muffins to the school, and I don't even know where my muffins are."

It's the worst thing I can say, because Ronin hands me over to one of his men to get my muffins and to get me on my way. I don't even have the chance to say goodbye or thank you to Ronin, and I wonder if my great adventure is over forever, and if I'll never smell his cinnamon and sugar breath again.

# CHAPTER 7

I've become the talk of the town since I helped take down Ed Sullivan's illegal fracking operation. They're even talking about having a parade in my honor and the mayor wants me to speak in front of the town's famous fountain, where I made a wish to kill Sullivan.

Not that I told anybody I wanted him dead except Ronin. Probably people would frown on my murderous intentions.

With nobody worried about losing the ranch or having our livelihoods ruined, my family is calm and happy. Olivia has been extreme couponing a lot, and my business has been getting nonstop orders.

But icing cinnamon buns no longer gives me the joy that it once did. And I'm not even a little excited about making the cookies for the Boy Scouts' end of the month meeting. Instead, my thoughts often go to Ronin and the adventure we had.

Even more than the adventure, my thoughts are filled with the man, himself. How handsome he was and kind to me, when he wasn't insulting me.

"I guess I can go to Sea World now, though," I say to myself in the kitchen.

"What did you say, dear?" my mother asks me.

I wake up out of my thoughts. "Nothing. Just thinking out loud."

She takes my hand and walks me into the living room and sits me down on the couch next to her. "You've been thinking a lot, lately," she says. "You've been through a terrible ordeal."

I'm confused that she would be calling Ronin an ordeal, but then I realize that she's talking about almost being murdered.

"Yes. It was a terrible ordeal."

"But now you're safe and back with us, and life has never been better," she says.

"Yes. Never better."

*

I wrap the cookies onto two platters and take them out to the truck to deliver them to the Boy Scouts. "Let me help you with that," I hear as I approach the truck.

I jump in surprise. Ronin is there on his motorcycle, staring at me in all his leather-jacketed glory. He looks even better than before, perhaps because I know what he feels like on top of me, and I know what his tongue feels like inside my mouth.

"I didn't hear you drive up," I say.

"Stealth, baby."

He gets off his motorcycle and takes one of the platters from me and puts it in the truck. "Why are you here?" I ask. I haven't heard from him in the week since we last saw each other. I've figured that he went off to fight insurgents in a developing country or was sleeping with some woman who was smart enough to bring her own condoms.

"I can't stop thinking about you, Fiona," he says. "And not just because you're a walking disaster zone. I can't stop thinking about you because I want to be with you, because…"

"Because you want to kiss me again," I supply.

"Yes. Kiss you again and be with you. I want to be with you...Probably for the rest of my life."

I try to swallow, but my throat won't comply. "That sounds nice."

He smiles, and my insides do a flip-flop. He steps toward me and takes me into his arms.

"But," I say. "I live in a ranch house with my family, and you're a, well, I don't know what you are, but it's not a ranch hand."

His smile drops. "No, I'm not a ranch hand. I'm not a homebody. I'm all over the place. But with all the adventures I've had in my life, I've never had a greater adventure than being with you."

He's saying all the right things, except that it's not enough for me to leave my family. I can't leave them. How could I? They're my life. They're my everything. I can't just abandon them.

I don't say any of this to Ronin, but he probably reads it from the expression on my face.

Impossible. He and I are impossible.

I put my head on his chest and let him hug me one last time. Tears stream down my face, but I'm resolute. There are more important things in this world then being happy.

*

Ronin's motorcycle roars off into the distance, and I get in the truck and start it. It's a five-minute drive to the Boy Scout meeting, and when I arrive, the cookies are still warm, much to the delight of the boys.

Because I'm the town hero now, I'm invited to give them a

talk about the great fracking adventure. They're all riveted and delighted, but my mind is elsewhere.

"Were you scared?" A boy asks me after I finish.

"No," I say.

"Why not?"

I think about the answer. It's staring me in the face, and I don't know why I didn't think of it before. I don't answer him and I wave goodbye, hopping into the truck and rushing back to the ranch. I run inside and up the stairs to change my clothes. When I get back downstairs, I kiss my parents goodbye.

"Why are you dressed like Rambo?" My father asks me.

"Because she's starting her life," my mother explains.

She drives me out of town and up into the mountains, dropping me off at a small security shack.

"Tell him I'm here and I'm not leaving," I tell the soldiers on duty. They get on their phones, and a couple minutes later the sound of Ronin's motorcycle comes closer. My heart beats loudly in my chest, and I'm as excited as a kid who's next in line for the roller coaster.

"Will you take me to Sea World?" I ask him when he arrives.

"I'll take you to Washington State, and we'll swim with the orcas. Free and happy."

"Just as long as I'm with you."

He takes me in his arms and gives me the third kiss of my life. My insides melt, and I'm sure there's no place I would rather be.

"I brought you a present," I tell him after we finally stop kissing. I dig in my pocket and take out a long string of foil-covered condoms. "I thought this would come in handy," I say.

"Let's try them out, now," he says.

I hop on the back of his motorcycle, and we ride toward our greatest adventure.

The End

# About the Author

Elise Sax worked as a journalist for fifteen years, mostly in Paris, France. She took a detour from journalism and became a private investigator before writing her first novel. She lives in Southern California with her two sons.

She loves to hear from her readers. Don't hesitate to contact her at elisesax@gmail.com, and sign up for her newsletter at http://elisesax.com/mailing-list.php to get notifications of new releases and sales.

Elisesax.com

https://www.facebook.com/ei.sax.9

@theelisesax

Made in United States
North Haven, CT
03 October 2022

24926322R00333